SHANNON SAGA

Angels Flight

Andrea Star

SHANNON SAGA

Angels Flight

TRACIE PETERSON
and
JAMES SCOTT BELL

BETHANYHOUSE
MINNEAPOLIS, MINNESOTA 55438

Published by Bethany House Publishers
A Ministry of Bethany Fellowship International
11400 Hampshire Avenue South
Bloomington, Minnesota 55438
www.bethanyhouse.com

Printed in the United States of America by
Bethany Press International, Bloomington, Minnesota 55438

Library of Congress Cataloging-in-Publication Data

Peterson, Tracie.
    Angels flight / by Tracie Peterson and James Scott Bell.
        p. cm. — (Shannon saga ; 2)
    ISBN 0-7642-2419-0
    1. Los Angeles (Calif.)—Fiction. 2. Women lawyers—Fiction. 3. Racism—
Fiction. I. Bell, James Scott. II. Title.
    PS3566.E7717 A84 2001
    813'.54—dc21
                                                                    2001002563

TRACIE PETERSON is an award-winning speaker and writer who has authored over thirty-five books, both historical and contemporary fiction. Her latest series, YUKON QUEST, is set in gold-rush Alaska. Tracie and her family make their home in Kansas.

Visit Tracie's Web site at *www.traciepeterson.com*

JAMES SCOTT BELL is a Los Angeles native and former trial lawyer who now writes full time. He is the author of several legal thrillers; his novel *Final Witness* won the 2000 Christy Award as the top suspense novel of the year. He and his family still reside in the City of Angels.

Jim's Web site is *www.jamesscottbell.com*

Books By James Scott Bell

Circumstantial Evidence
Final Witness
Blind Justice
The Nephilim Seed

Books By
Tracie Peterson & James Scott Bell

SHANNON SAGA

City of Angels
Angels Flight

Books By Tracie Peterson

Controlling Interests
Entangled
Framed
The Long-Awaited Child
A Slender Thread
Tidings of Peace

WESTWARD CHRONICLES

A Shelter of Hope
Hidden in a Whisper
A Veiled Reflection

RIBBONS OF STEEL*

Distant Dreams
A Hope Beyond
A Promise for Tomorrow

RIBBONS WEST*

Westward the Dream
Separate Roads
Ties That Bind

YUKON QUEST

Treasures of the North
Ashes and Ice

*with Judith Pella

Laws are not made for particular cases, but for men.

—SAMUEL JOHNSON

Part One

Chapter 1

Los Angeles
March 1904

"SO AFRAID."

The Chinese woman, who called herself Wong Shi, was trying not to cry. She was young, pretty, tiny. Kit Shannon thought she looked like finely crafted porcelain, with skin glowing under a veil of white powder.

They were sitting in the single room that was the law office of Kathleen Shannon, attorney-at-law, overlooking Broadway. Wong Shi had come to Kit's office unannounced. That was fine with Kit, who had not had a paying client in over two weeks. Six months after her admission to the bar, she was still struggling to pay the rent. Even though Aunt Freddy had offered her considerable wealth to help, Kit felt she had to do this on her own. She believed that if it was still God's will that she practice law in Los Angeles, the means would appear.

"What are you afraid of, Wong Shi?" Kit asked.

The woman tugged at her plain gown. Her small, bound feet darted in and out from underneath her hem like scared mice. Her eyes were black opals, and her dark hair was long and shiny. Kit guessed she was near her own age—twenty-four—though she looked like a mere girl.

"They say they send me back," Wong Shi said.

"To China?"

"Yes, yes." Her English, though heavy with an accent, was good. She clearly had an education.

"Who says this?" Kit asked.

"Immy . . . Immy . . ."

"Immigration?"

"Yes, yes."

Kit was aware that free Chinese were not viewed with favor in America. As coolie labor, barely above the level of slaves, certain interests valued them as a supply of cheap workers. But they were not valued for much more. Especially in Los Angeles, where strict lines were drawn around the area people were starting to call Chinatown.

"Did they give you a reason?" asked Kit. She was not an expert on immigration law but recalled that the newspapers—the *Times* and the Hearst-owned *Examiner*—had reported a spate of hostile activity aimed at immigrants these days. Now the federal government was getting involved.

Wong Shi started to cry. Her delicate hand went before her face, as if she were ashamed.

Kit got up from her chair and went to Wong Shi, putting an arm around her shoulder. "It's all right," she said softly. She drew a kerchief from the pocket of her skirt and handed it to Wong Shi. "You just tell me everything you can."

With a sniff, Wong Shi dabbed at her eyes with the kerchief. "I am come to America to marry," she said. "Chung Yu send for me."

"When?"

"Year ago."

"Did you marry?"

"No." Wong Shi looked at the floor. "Chung Yu gone."

Kit returned to her chair behind an oak desk. After getting a pencil and paper, she instructed Wong Shi to tell her story.

It was a typical one for a young woman alone in the city. Kit had heard variations on it from the prostitutes who had come to her after the Ted Fox murder trial. There she had vindicated Ted's good name by finding the real killer of a young girl of the streets, Millie Ryan. Kit's reputation as a friend of the down-and-out had spread through the lower regions of Los Angeles.

Wong Shi had been told by Chung Yu, her childhood sweetheart, to leave home and family for America. He promised her an elaborate wedding and a home in the paradise of Southern California. Life here would be better than in her village, which was still feudal. Though Wong Shi had come from a family of some affluence and had been educated in a missionary school, her prospects in a culture barely out of the Middle Ages were dim.

In America, Chung Yu promised, they would find wealth and opportunity. Wong Shi was only faintly aware that Chung Yu was a highbinder of the Hop Sings, a *tong*—the warring arm of a large Chinese family. Though controlled from China, tongs were active in San Francisco, New York, and now Los Angeles.

But when she arrived in San Pedro harbor, after a three-month trip over land and sea, Chung Yu was not there. Had he forgotten? Or worse, changed his mind?

With nowhere to turn, Wong Shi was nearly nabbed by a local cop as a vagrant. But an older Chinese man appeared to vouch for her. His name was Li Fong, and he explained this was his work— to help Chinese fresh off the boats avoid the authorities.

Li Fong took Wong Shi to Chinatown, to a small room in the back of a laundry run by a woman named Lu Choy. Here Wong Shi found refuge until she could locate Chung Yu.

Wong Shi's voice lowered as she told Kit what happened next. It was as if she feared someone might overhear her. "One night there was a commotion outside my room at Lu Choy's. A man—very big—come in. He say only he was of the Bing Kongs."

Kit shook her head.

"Bing Kongs are tong, like Hop Sings. Hate Hop Sings. Blood shed."

"Go on," said Kit.

"Man say Chung Yu was 'dead man.' He say if Chung Yu come back, I tell Bing Kongs. If I no tell, I die with him."

Wong Shi paused, blinking her eyes. Kit waited patiently for her to continue. Wong Shi explained that soon after the threatening visit, she got the word that Chung Yu had fled the city. He left her no note or other word. All her hopes were gone.

So were Wong Shi's prospects. Lu Choy, full of the spirit of free enterprise that made her laundry a success, offered Wong Shi a proposal. Wong Shi had shown her skills in the art of Chinese massage. Wong Shi had the ability to make knotted muscles sing. Such a skill could bring in a modest income.

It did. Wong Shi's reputation spread beyond the rough borders of the Chinese ghetto into greater Los Angeles. Indeed, some of the wealthier and more powerful male citizens frequented the back of Lu Choy's laundry.

One of these men was a frequent visitor. Soon he was demanding more than a massage. When Wong Shi refused, even after being offered more money than she had ever seen, the man told her he would seek revenge.

A week later she was taken by two men to the Office of Immigration. She was told that if she did not book passage back to

China, she would be arrested and thrown in jail.

"On what charge?" Kit asked.

"They no tell me," Wong Shi said. "But they say I am prostitute." Wong Shi began to cry.

Kit went to her again. "All right," she said softly. "I'll go see what I can find out for you."

Through teary eyes, Wong Shi looked at Kit, then grabbed her hand and kissed it. "They tell me you would help," she said.

"Who?"

"The girls who come to laundry," Wong Shi said.

The ones who had known Millie Ryan.

"You go on home now," Kit said.

"But I must pay," Wong Shi said.

Kit knew that whatever Wong Shi paid would be slight. "We can handle that after I see if I can help, all right?"

"I pay with chickens?"

"No, no chickens!" Kit said with a laugh. "We'll talk about payment after."

The small Chinese woman smiled then. Her face fairly glowed with gratitude. She must have bowed ten times before she left the office.

It was quite a courtesy, Kit mused. But courtesy did not pay bills. And Kit needed something that could do just that. She turned to the letter on her desk. It had been hand delivered by a servant of Mr. Alfred Mungerley.

And Mr. Alfred Mungerley, people said, was made of money.

Chapter 2

"MONEY, MISS SHANNON," Alfred Mungerley said, "is the key to everything. It's a golden key and can unlock a great future for you."

Kit Shannon nodded politely, though she disagreed. Mr. Mungerley had asked her to his home for some reason, and she would hear him out. Aunt Freddy would be shocked if she did not listen to this wealthy neighbor with courtesy and respect.

They were seated in the drawing room of Mungerley's mansion, a third again as large as her great-aunt Freddy's, which was just a stone's throw away in Angeleno Heights. After entering the huge reception hall, Kit had been shown by a butler past a series of alcoves and rooms to a magnificent court with six Pompeiian columns. The columns circled a fountain below and a stained-glass ceiling above. It was here Alfred Mungerley had greeted her.

The drawing room in which they held their meeting was designed in elegant Spanish Renaissance tradition. Indeed, everything in Alfred Mungerley's possession seemed dipped in affluence. He was in his mid-fifties, trim, and—according to Aunt Freddy—wealthier than Croesus. He smoked a fine cigar; after a full six months as a lawyer in Los Angeles, traversing law offices and courtrooms and other bastions of the male-dominated profession, Kit could smell the difference between a moneyed cigar and the nickel variety. Alfred Mungerley was obviously a man used to the finer things in life.

"And it is quite clear," Mungerley continued, "that you have the brains to earn a great deal of money in your chosen profession. What you did to Heath Sloate!" Mungerley snorted with glee. "So many of us wanted to see him get his comeuppance. Little did we know a girl would be his Waterloo. Excuse me . . . a young lady."

"That's all right, Mr. Mungerley," Kit said. "I just hope to be thought of as a competent attorney."

"But you are, Miss Shannon. More! You are the toast of Los Angeles."

Old toast, perhaps. The newspaper circus that had attended the murder trial of Ted Fox and the exposing of Heath Sloate was long past. The flow of paying clients Kit might have expected was never more than a trickle. Kit had heard whisperings—usually expressed loudly for her benefit—that the world was simply not ready for a female trial lawyer, no matter how clever. And certainly not one who had just turned twenty-four years of age.

"Thank you, Mr. Mungerley," said Kit. "Perhaps someday I will live up to your opinion of me."

Mungerley chuckled. "Not if your aunt has anything to say about it, eh?"

True. Half a year after Kit's debut in court, Aunt Freddy still could not get used to the idea that her niece was a lawyer. Kit loved her aunt dearly, but she was growing weary of Aunt Freddy's insistence that she assume her "womanly role" and settle down to raise children. While Kit did want that for herself, she was not going to rush to the altar. She had come to Los Angeles to practice law, to work at seeing justice done for even the most miserable of citizens. They were entitled to the dignity of the Constitution as much as . . . well, people like Freddy and the Mungerleys.

"I am very fond of your aunt, you know," said Mungerley. "Freddy and I have been friends ever since I built my modest dwelling."

Kit looked again at the exquisite architecture of the room.

"So I know she is looking out for you. But I am aware she has a less than enthusiastic appreciation of your ambitions."

Kit shifted self-consciously in her seat and smoothed her gray serge skirt. It was hardly the kind of attire one would normally wear to be entertained by a man as influential as Alfred Mungerley, but there had been no time to go home and change. She toyed with the black braiding of the matching jacket, knowing that Aunt Freddy would be positively appalled to find her so shoddily clothed while visiting. "I know it's hard for her," Kit said. "She comes from a different time and place, and her ways are settled. But I am praying that soon she will come to embrace me fully."

"Praying," Mungerley said. "That's a good thing. Never hurts to have God on your side, eh?"

"Never," Kit agreed. And she believed it with all her heart. She never would have been able to stand up to Heath Sloate, one of the most powerful men in Los Angeles, without her faith that she was in God's will.

Mungerley said, "And I understand she has certain reservations about Mr. Ted Fox."

The mention of her friend's name startled Kit. Even though Ted worked for Mungerley at the bank, she hadn't expected he would become a topic of conversation. She did not want to talk about her romantic perplexities. Despite having been wooed by some of the most eligible men of the city—including the impossibly handsome young actor, John Barrymore—Kit kept finding herself thinking of Ted Fox.

His was the face that played most in her mind's eye, though she tried to prevent it. There remained the matter of his lack of faith, a frustrating resistance to God.

"Well," Mungerley continued, "Ted is a fine young man. A great future lies ahead of him. He's weathered that nasty murder trial business, thanks to your efforts. I can't think of a better match."

Thankfully, a domestic entered with a tray of coffee. She was young, perhaps Kit's age, and quite pretty. Her golden hair was pulled tightly under the maid's bonnet, and her milk white skin was flawless. She might have been the product of some high-society family herself, but for the eyes. There was a hardness about them that hinted at a tougher background. Kit, having grown up an orphan in Boston and New York, knew about such a past.

The maid poured two cups of coffee, curtsied, and left.

"To the point, then," said Mungerley. "I think I have a way for you to make good sums of money doing legal work and, at the same time, show Freddy how valuable you really are. Interested?"

Kit had certainly never expected this turn of events. Intrigued, she leaned forward. "Yes, sir."

Mungerley took a puff of his cigar, the smoke almost obscuring his face with wispy tendrils. "I have a close friend in the land business, and, as you know, that is a very valuable business to be in. Nothing is so valuable as land over the long term. And when our city gets its water source, Miss Shannon, there will be a demand for land that will make a buffalo stampede look like a ladies' tea."

Kit nodded. From the moment she arrived in the City of Angels, she had sensed the drive for land. Los Angeles was a city set in the middle of a sun-washed but undeveloped frontier. Those who bought up that frontier might someday come into large profit.

Mungerley continued. "My friend, a Mr. Taylor, is a man of broad vision for Los Angeles. He is an ambitious man and is in need of just the right lawyer to assist him along the way." Mungerley leaned forward. "Such a lawyer could profit substantially by hitching her wagon to him at the beginning."

The sound of it both interested Kit and caused hesitation. She did need money if she was going to survive as an attorney. With her own office now she had rent to pay. Yet she had not gone into law to make herself wealthy. She had pledged never to do any work merely for material profit.

As Kit pondered the suggestion, Mungerley said, "Will you see him?"

"I will meet with him, of course," Kit said.

"And take him up on his offer?"

"I will need to hear the details first."

Mungerley smiled. "Good show. Freddy says you are a young woman of principle. I like that. We need more of that around here. Just take one small bit of advice from a man with experience."

"Sir?"

"Never discount the power of money."

The biblical warning about the love of money being the root of all evil came to Kit's mind, but she said nothing. Mr. Mungerley, though wealthy, was a decent man, and she would never insinuate anything about his motives.

"All right, then," Mungerley said. "I'll let Taylor know you're coming to see him. Miss Shannon, this could be the start of big things for you. Very big things!"

"Thank you, Mr. Mungerley."

"Not at all, not at all." He puffed contemplatively as Kit took a sip of coffee. Then he said, "Now I must mention one more thing, my dear."

Kit looked up at the somber tone of his words.

"I am a man who makes his living anticipating problems and then finding ways to avoid them. It's a special skill I have, and I use it well. Right now I see a problem, and I would like your help in solving it."

"Whatever I can do to help," Kit said, puzzled at what it could possibly be.

"That's the ticket. As I said, I am quite fond of your aunt, and I know that this would trouble her greatly. That's why I am coming to you. I hope she will never have to know."

"Know what, sir?"

"You have a young gardener there, a Mex."

"Yes, Juan," Kit said. He was the younger brother of Kit's maid and friend, Corazón. Aunt Freddy had hired him several months ago on Kit's recommendation.

"You saw the serving girl who came in a few minutes ago?" Mungerley said.

"Of course."

"Very pretty, wasn't she?"

Kit nodded. "Very."

"Well, it seems that this gardener of yours has been making, shall we say, eyes at Gloria when he sees her. That is what she tells me at least."

"Juan?"

"Yes."

"But I'm sure—"

"No need to try and defend him. I'm not here to make accusations. What I am here to do is intervene in what could well become an ugly situation." Mungerley stood then, as if his next words carried particular import. "Los Angeles, Miss Shannon, is a delicate balance of the old and the new. There are other divides, of course. Rich and poor. Laborers and employers. Natives and Europeans."

Kit put her coffee cup down as Mungerley paced the room.

"Some things do not mix," he said. "And were not meant to mix. If your young gardener were to make some inappropriate advance—even a longer look than is in keeping with his station—it might very well explode in your aunt's face. And I don't think Freddy's heart could take something like that."

Yes, Kit thought. Her heart was a question these days. And nothing got it beating faster than scandal.

"So, Miss Shannon, all I propose is that you take your influence—I understand you are quite close to the lad's sister—and talk to him. Tell him in no uncertain terms to keep away from Gloria. That it would be best if he did not even look at her should she pass his way. Am I making myself clear?"

Kit held her anger in check. There was no sense in engaging Mungerley in a debate on the equality that was supposed to be part of a democratic system. Especially when no one else in high society seemed inclined to yield to such thinking. Perhaps another time. "Quite clear, sir," she said.

"Then you'll do it?"

It would not be a pleasant task, but for Aunt Freddy's sake and, truth be told, for Juan's sake, as well, Kit said, "Yes, sir. I will talk to him."

"That's the ticket!" said Alfred Mungerley. "Miss Shannon, one of the most important lessons in life is to know when to take direction from those with more experience. You have shown that willingness. I am supremely confident that you are going to go quite far, my dear. Quite far indeed."

Chapter 3

KIT'S HEART FELT like a large stone as she returned to Aunt Freddy's home. She knew it was in part because of the unpleasant task that lay before her—talking to young Juan. It did not feel right, but she had committed to doing it.

But there was another reason, and it was that she knew she would soon be moving out. Aunt Freddy had insisted that Kit live with her again after Kit had spent several weeks living in one of Earl Rogers' offices. Her former employer had graciously offered it to her so she could continue to assist him in Ted's defense.

Aunt Freddy's offer proved too good to turn down. Having a bath and good bed, and most of all having her dear friend Corazón near her, sealed the deal.

But now it was clear that Kit needed to be out on her own. Aunt Freddy was simply not giving up on her desire to see Kit stop practicing law and marry anyone except Ted Fox. The importunings had become daily drumbeats of opposition. It had to stop.

This change would create a greater degree of uncertainty in Kit's life. Kit had stopped accepting money from Aunt Freddy, barely managing to pay the office rent by herself. If she were to move out, that would mean a lodging expense added to her monthly bills.

But if God truly wanted her to practice law here, He would provide for her. Maybe this Mr. Taylor was part of God's answer. Still, there was nagging suspicion that rose up to trouble Kit. Her legal training had taught her to look beyond the surface, for appearances were often deceiving. On the surface, Mr. Mungerley had presented a most appealing proposition, but upon digging deeper, Kit couldn't help but wonder why Mungerley had come to her, a woman. If this situation was as good as he suggested, then why not give it to one of his cronies—one of the "good ol' boys" who frequented the courts of Los Angeles?

Corazón met Kit in the entrance hall. The sight of her lifted Kit's spirits. She was so much more than a servant to Kit. She was almost a sister, though Aunt Freddy would have been scandalized at any such notion.

"You would like a bath, yes?" Corazón asked.

Kit sighed. A bath sounded wonderful. But not now. "Corazón, is your brother in his quarters?" Juan lived in a small bungalow on the back portion of Aunt Freddy's estate.

"*Sí*, I think." A look of concern came to Corazón's face. "There is something wrong?"

Kit put a hand on the maid's arm. "Don't worry. I just need to talk to him. Will you come and translate?"

"Madam is waiting to see you."

"Let's not tell her I'm home just yet." Kit knew that no talk with Aunt Freddy was ever short. "Let's go see your brother first."

The two walked softly down the long central corridor of the Fairbank mansion, through the kitchen, empty at this hour, and out through a back door. The long cobblestone walkway gave Kit time to clear her mind and focus on what she would say. The situation called for diplomacy and tact, a delicate balance that could be threatened by the topic.

The golden glow of candlelight poured out from the window of Juan's bungalow. Kit could hear the soft strumming of a guitar. She hated to interrupt what appeared to be a pleasant evening of quiet respite. But she had to. Corazón knocked on the door.

Juan opened the door, guitar in hand. *"Hermanita!"* he said, beaming a smile at Corazón. His smile dropped, however, when he spied Kit standing close behind. No doubt he thought it odd indeed that a mistress of the house should be coming to his quarters at this hour of the night.

Corazón's rapid-fire Spanish seemed to put him at ease. She even laughed lightly and motioned to the guitar as she and Kit entered. Kit thought she understood enough Spanish to interpret Corazón's praise of Juan's playing. Juan looked briefly to Kit before crossing the room to put the guitar away. Kit noted his guarded manner and wished she'd come for a less threatening reason.

Turning away, lest he find her watching him, Kit surveyed the gardener's quarters. The room was small but well kept, with two wooden chairs and a table on one side, and a bed with a colorful *serape* on top of it on the other.

Juan rested the guitar in the far corner, and then offered the two chairs to his guests. *"Por favor,"* he said, motioning to the chairs.

Kit followed Corazón in and took a seat. She smiled at Juan, hoping to put him at ease. He was a handsome man, just twenty, strong and healthy. Working in the sun obviously agreed with him.

"Good evening, Juan," Kit said.

Juan nodded in return.

"Juan, I have been to see Mr. Mungerley down the road," Kit said.

Corazón translated that into Spanish. Juan looked puzzled.

"He asked that I convey a message to you."

Through Corazón, Juan asked, "What is the message?"

"Do you know his domestic, called Gloria?"

When he understood the question, Juan's look turned suspicious. "What of her?" he asked through his sister.

"Mr. Mungerley says that you have been, well, looking at her in a way that is not right."

Juan vigorously shook his head. "That is a lie!"

"Then you don't look at her?"

"I see her, yes,"—Corazón interpreted—"but she is the one who looks at me!"

Juan's eyes flashed with anger. It was quick anger, Kit thought. Volatile. Perhaps even dangerous.

"Now, Juan, I only want to be sure that you do not get into trouble."

"It is that girl who is trouble. She talks to me. I do not understand, but she makes faces and touches her own body. She smiles at me. I shake my head, but she will not stop! I do not like her!"

It seemed to Kit that there was something deeper in Juan's expression of denial. But this was not the time or place to go into that. "Juan, if you keep away from her, all should be well. Can you do that?"

He paused before answering through his sister. Finally, he said, "I will try. But she seems to know when I am outside, and where to find me." He looked around his room, as if her presence might be there now.

"That's all, then," Kit said. "If you are careful, there should be no problems."

Juan did not seem convinced. Corazón spoke to him some

more, Kit catching a few of the words. She seemed to be telling her brother not to worry. But he looked worried as they left.

On the way back to the main house, Kit asked, "Do you think Juan understood?"

"I think," Corazón said. "I hope . . ."

"Hope what, Corazón?"

"I hope that he will not do something, how you say, bad."

"Bad?"

"My brother, he has a bad temper. He is sometimes getting into fights. Miss Kathleen. . . ?"

"Yes?"

"Will you pray for my brother?"

Kit put her arm around Corazón. "Of course I will. And you can pray for me right now."

"Why?"

"Because I'm going to talk to my aunt."

Aunt Freddy was in her usual evening spot in the drawing room, near the fire, a crocheted throw around her shoulders, sipping tea. The tea, Kit was sure, had Aunt Freddy's usual slug of evening bourbon in it.

"There you are!" Aunt Freddy said as Kit entered. "The hours you keep!"

Kit kissed her aunt on the cheek, noticing how tired she looked. At seventy-one, and carrying too much weight, her aunt was slowing down physically.

"I was on a professional call," Kit said. She did not want to mention Mungerley for fear it would lead to his concerns about Juan. Kit had to fight to convince Aunt Freddy to hire Juan in the first place. Though he did an excellent job, Kit knew her great-aunt would not hesitate to let him go to avoid a scandal, especially one as potentially explosive as this one.

"My dear, my dear!" Aunt Freddy said as Kit sat on the sofa.

"A woman like you shouldn't be on professional calls at this hour! You should be home, putting your children to bed, and preparing for your next party."

Same old argument, Kit thought. "Aunt Freddy, you have been so good to me. I know we've had our differences about my law practice. But now that I have my own office, I feel it's best if I move somewhere closer."

In the firelight, Aunt Freddy's face reflected surprise. "Do you mean moving out of this house?"

"Yes, I do."

"But where shall you live? Who will look after you?"

"Remember, I lived in the back of Mr. Rogers' office for a time."

"Scandal! That is why I took you back in. I couldn't have my own niece in such a condition!"

"I'll get a room that is in a nice location and be very content."

Aunt Freddy let out a huff. "Down there with the commoners!"

Kit laughed. "We're not in the Middle Ages, Aunt Freddy. This is the land of equal opportunity."

"Nonsense! There will always be classes. It's the way of the world. I heard Mr. Joseph Pomeroy Widney speak of it in a lecture."

Freddy loved to attend lectures at her club. The only problem was she usually accepted everything the speaker said as gospel.

Aunt Freddy continued. "The Anglo people, you see, were meant to thrive in climates like Southern California. Los Angeles is the City of the Sun, and here the Anglos have a natural superiority."

"I am afraid I have to disagree with this fellow," Kit said.

"But he is a doctor. And he gives lectures!"

"Well," said Kit, "perhaps I should give a lecture."

Aunt Freddy's eyes opened wide. "Don't you dare!"

"Why not? Surely you have women lecturers. I saw that Carrie Nation was lecturing on temperance at Chutes Theater."

"She carries an ax!"

"All the more reason to listen to her, then."

"You're playing with your old aunt now," Freddy said, softening.

"Only because I love you so much," Kit said.

"Then why must you move away?"

"It won't be far. We will see each other often. Perhaps I'll join your club. Would you like that?"

"As a lawyer?"

"How about as your niece?"

Freddy smiled at last. "I don't think the club will ever be the same."

Kit rose, went to her aunt, and kissed her gently on the cheek. "I will try to be on my best behavior," Kit assured her, but she wondered just how she might react if she heard someone spouting such views. Her deceased father—beloved Papa—was a man of such integrity; he could never be silent in the face of evil talk. Yes, it sometimes got him into trouble, but he never backed down when it was an issue of God's truth against the world's.

And Kit, after six months as a lawyer in Los Angeles, knew one thing for certain—she was her father's girl.

Chapter 4

TO KIT, the Norwood Building on Broadway was audaciously Angeleno. Its five stories of Romanesque design seemed to radiate restlessness, as if inside all the raw energy of the young century was waiting to be unleashed on everything old and traditional. Kit felt a coolness as she entered the building, a slight air of animosity seemingly from the interior itself. She shook this off as nervousness and reminded herself she was here for a business call.

As Mr. Mungerley had noted, Dayton Taylor's office was on the third floor. It was one of the large ones, as it had a reception area with a private secretary. She was a woman in her fifties, Kit judged, with graying hair done up severely, seeming to stretch her face into the taut, antagonistic expression with which she greeted Kit.

"Are you here for the position?" the woman said the moment Kit walked through the door.

"Position?"

"Cleaning. You certainly didn't have to come all dressed up.

You'll get that fancy dress dirty." The woman rose and walked toward her.

Kit looked down briefly at her rose-colored walking suit. It was one of her simpler professional suits. Meeting the woman's stern gaze, she shook her head.

"Excuse me," Kit said, "I'm not—"

"There is no need to put on airs for my benefit."

"I am here—"

"Because it will make no difference to me."

"—to see Mr. Taylor."

The secretary stopped short, looked at Kit up and down. She seemed shocked. "What is your business with Mr. Taylor?"

"He has asked to see me. My name is Kathleen Shannon."

The woman slowly shook her head. She went back to her desk and flipped the pages of an appointment book. "There is no mention here of an appointment. Perhaps you have made a mistake."

"Perhaps you should check with Mr. Taylor."

The woman's face grew antagonistic. "I am not used to being addressed that way by young women who storm into this office."

A soft answer turneth away wrath, Kit thought. "I am sorry if it seemed that way. I am here at Mr. Taylor's request."

Suddenly the light of recognition entered the secretary's eyes. "Shannon. You're that lawyer."

Kit was taken aback by the secretary's animosity.

"I don't approve of women trying to act like men," the secretary said. "Do you feel no shame?"

Suddenly the inner door opened and a portly man with short, slick black hair and a pencil mustache appeared. The buttons of his vest strained mightily against his body. "What is the commotion?" he said.

The secretary immediately composed herself. "This woman claims to be—"

"Miss Shannon?" the man finished.

"At your service," Kit said.

"I am Dayton Taylor," said the man, smiling yellowish teeth at her. "Please come in."

Kit felt the disapproving stare of the secretary as she followed Taylor into his office.

The morning sun shone brilliantly through the large window, the bustle of Broadway visible below. The cigar odor in the office was in stark contrast to that Kit had noted at Mungerley's. Mr. Taylor apparently liked the cheap variety. Her stomach turned slightly as she took the chair offered her by Taylor.

"Alfred says wonderful things about you," Taylor said. He sat behind an oak desk and looked at Kit. She judged him to be in his middle forties, his girth giving him an older look. She could not figure out why she felt slightly uncomfortable with his gaze. Perhaps this was just a case of jittery nerves at meeting what could become an important client, as Mr. Mungerley had indicated.

"I am flattered, sir," Kit said.

"Wonderful things, indeed. And I followed your exploits in the Fox case, as did most of Los Angeles. Well done."

"Thank you."

"It takes a keen intelligence to pull off something like that."

Kit nodded this time. It seemed Taylor was spending a lot of time on compliments. She had the odd sense that she was about to be sold something. But what?

"Keen intelligence is what I need," Taylor continued. "Do you know anything about me?"

"No, sir."

"Then I'll tell you. I am a gold prospector." He leaned back in his chair, seemingly awaiting Kit's response. She didn't know how to respond. The California gold rush of the middle 1800s was long over. There were still prospectors left, but they were generally hardened types living in shacks in the mountains—and a long way from prosperous.

"You have a mine?" Kit said.

Taylor smiled and tapped his head. "My mine is up here. The gold I am talking about is not that stuff buried in the ground. It is the ground itself."

Kit slowly shook her head.

"Real estate, Miss Shannon. I am talking about real estate. This is the new gold for those who have the vision."

That did make a certain amount of sense. Los Angeles had seen a land boom in the '80s soon after the Southern Pacific finished its tracks to the city. But there had also been a bust in 1888. It seemed Taylor was one of those who anticipated a return to the boom years. But this was pure speculation. Unless Taylor knew something others did not.

"I have that vision, Miss Shannon, and before we go any further, I want you to take this." He reached into his vest pocket and came out with a shiny silver dollar. He placed it on the smooth surface of his desk and slid it to Kit's side.

Puzzled, she picked up the coin and looked at it.

"That is my initial payment," Taylor said.

"You do not have to pay me yet, Mr. Taylor."

"Oh, but I do. And I have. What I am going to say to you now is confidential. You are, at least for the next few minutes, my lawyer. Understood?"

Kit nodded. This Taylor was clearly adept at protecting himself.

"Miss Shannon, have you heard of the Owens Valley?"

"No, sir."

"Then let me ask you this. What is the one natural resource that is holding our fair city back from becoming one of the leading metropolises in the country?"

Kit considered his question for a moment. "Water," she said.

"Precisely. We do not have an adequate water source to support a large population. But there is adequate water northeast of here, in the Owens Valley. Rich farmland, lush and thriving. Now the only question is how to get it down here."

"An aqueduct?"

"You impress me again with your intelligence, Miss Shannon. Yes, an aqueduct. A technical achievement of momentous proportions. Even now, as we speak, certain interests in this city are laying the groundwork for just such a project."

Kit furrowed her brow. "But wouldn't that mean the farmland you speak about would become dry?"

Taylor did not answer immediately. Instead, he patted his stomach with his hands. "The farmers will be paid," he finally said. The way he said it was curious, like a poker player not yet ready to reveal his hand.

But the general outlines of his plans began to become clear to Kit. She said, "And when that water does flow here, it will be followed by people, and land will become all the more valuable."

"Miss Shannon, I am speechless," Taylor said with a laugh. "Alfred was absolutely right about you. So I shall tell you exactly what it is I have in mind. There is a small stretch of land that was incorporated last year. They call it Holly Wood. Have you heard of it?"

"I have heard the name."

"It was actually the vision of a couple named Wilcox, who bought one hundred sixty acres of orchard and began turning it into a bucolic township. I see more of the same beyond Holly Wood and well into the San Fernando Valley. In short, Miss Shannon, I want to begin buying that land, which I expect will make me and my professional associates"—he leaned toward her—"including lawyers, wealthy beyond our wildest dreams."

His eyes were full of dreams of gold.

For a moment Kit felt the dream herself. This was America,

after all. Wealth was something within the reach of those bold enough to go after it. And with money, she would be free to practice law on her own terms. She would not be beholden to Aunt Freddy or anyone else. But then the old biblical caution about money and its temptations came to mind.

"What is it that you see me doing?" she asked.

"I will naturally need legal help in all of this," Taylor said.

"But why me? Surely there are more experienced attorneys in the area of real estate."

"There are indeed. But they are too meddlesome and seek too many concessions. I need someone who will be simple, loyal, and competent."

And not ask questions, Kit thought. "What would be the nature of this work?"

"The land I am speaking of is mainly undeveloped land, interrupted occasionally with orange groves, fig and apricot orchards, small farms. Much of this land is owned by an odd assortment. Mexican and Injun farms, scratching out a meager existence. Chink vegetable farmers. Very few whites. And why is that? Because the land is parched and limited."

Kit sat upright. "Until the water comes."

"Until the water comes," Taylor repeated. "But that won't be for several years. In the meantime, I buy."

"And I would oversee the legal transactions."

"Discreetly. It is not in my interest that anyone should know what I'm doing."

"Even the sellers?"

Taylor's eyes narrowed slightly. "Least of all the sellers."

"Because if they knew how valuable their land might become, their price might be quite a bit higher."

Taylor put his hands out in an affirmative gesture. "That is why you will not tell them you are a lawyer, only a representative. Being a woman, you will put the sellers at ease. It won't take much to get their signatures on a piece of paper."

"That would be deception."

"No, that is merely withholding information. You see, Miss Shannon, the only thing more valuable than land around here is information. With it, you can control the world. Now, wouldn't you like to be in that position?"

Kit shifted uncomfortably in her chair. If there had been any moment she had felt tempted to work with Mr. Dayton Taylor, it was long past. "I'm sorry, Mr. Taylor."

He seemed completely taken aback. "Am I to understand you are turning me down?"

"I am afraid so."

"Do you mind telling me why?"

"I would prefer to keep my reasons to myself."

Suddenly Taylor slammed his hand on his desk. It produced a sound like a gunshot. "No!" he bellowed. "I am not a man who is accustomed to being refused. I demand that you explain yourself!"

His sudden change of attitude startled Kit for a moment. But she did not look away from his gaze. "All right," she said. "I am not prepared to be a part of a scheme to defraud small landowners out of their homes. These people should have representation them-selves."

Taylor shook his head. "You obviously don't understand the way things are done. Young lady, fortunes are made because some people are smart enough to strike and strike hard. It's the law of nature and capitalism."

Kit stood up. "It is not my law," she said.

"You wait one minute," Taylor said, standing himself. "What I have told you will remain confidential. You are bound."

"I am bound not to reveal what has been said here, yes," Kit said. "But I am not bound to stand by if I know people are being cheated."

Taylor's face became dangerously red. He took a moment to search for words. "There are a number of us who did not appreciate what you did to Heath Sloate."

What *she* did to Heath Sloate? He had done it to himself. He would soon be going on trial for his complicity in framing Ted Fox for murder. She was only the instrument used to expose him.

"Oh yes," Taylor said at Kit's hesitation. "He has a number of powerful friends still. You won't find us so easy to trifle with."

Kit stood her ground. "I do not trifle with anyone, sir."

"See that you don't," said Taylor. "If I ever hear that you have breathed a word of our conversation, or if I see your name associated with any obstacle to my plans, believe me—I will crush you."

Oh, she believed he would try, all right. This was another man cut from the same material as Heath Sloate. He wore his suit of malignant artifice more comfortably than his ill-fitting suit of clothes. She would be dealing with this type over and over again in the years ahead. Only God could give her the strength to withstand it. And it would be a strength no one could overcome.

Kit placed the silver dollar she had been holding on Taylor's desk. "As your former attorney," she said, "I advise you to obey the law."

She turned quickly and walked out of his office.

Chapter 5

THE CALIFORNIA CLUB was the exclusive enclave of some of the most powerful men in Los Angeles. Set on the eastern edge of Bunker Hill, it offered a breathtaking view of the city below and ocean beyond. It was here, amidst the deep browns of leather and maple, the lush carpeting and hushed tones, that fortunes were made. And broken.

Ted Fox felt out of place. He had come tonight as the guest of his employer, Alfred Mungerley, who expressed his intention to offer Ted's name to the club's membership committee. Ted, decked out in stiff evening wear, would much rather have been in his greasy coveralls, out on the bluffs, working on the three-cylinder engine that he hoped would power his flying machine.

Yet he was practical enough to know that he would need backing, and that meant meeting the right people. And Alfred Mungerley seemed to have taken him under his wing. He figured there was no harm in allowing that to happen.

After the older man guided Ted through a roomful of introductions, the two settled into a pair of comfortable chairs near the fireplace. Mungerley ordered a whiskey from a waiter, then lit one of his ever-present cigars and tossed the match into the flames.

"So what do you think, young Fox?" Mungerley said.

"Quite impressive," Ted answered, his blue eyes reflecting the flickering fire.

"Young man, it is much more than that! This is where the future is located for those smart enough to grab it."

"Well, sir, my hands are ready."

"That's the ticket. I knew I picked a good one when I singled you out. Now, tell me more about this idea of yours."

Ted smiled and felt as if a king were just waiting to grant his request. "Well, it's the air, Mr. Mungerley. Man's conquest of the air."

Mungerley nodded as he puffed. "Ah, you mean those Wright brothers?"

Ted nodded eagerly. Last December, in a little stretch of beach in North Carolina, Wilbur and Orville Wright had accomplished what many considered impossible: powered, sustained, controlled flight. Their aeroplane flew one hundred twenty feet this way.

"That's just the beginning, sir," Ted said. "I believe powered flight will revolutionize the world we live in. Think of it. We won't be bound to roads and carriages. Trips that take a day now will take an hour! Man will someday be able to circle the world!"

"Pish tosh!" Mungerley said. "That's fantasy. That's Jules Verne, not Thomas Edison."

"With all due respect, sir, we've only begun to scratch the surface. I have this idea for a monoplane which—"

"Mono what?"

"A monoplane, sir. One wing on either side of a cockpit."

"Cockpit?"

"Seat for the pilot."

"Pish tosh."

"The Wrights use a biplane design. It's highly efficient, but I think it limits the speed with which—"

"Speed! All you young people today can think about is speed!"

"The world is moving fast, sir."

"Bah!" said Mungerley with a wave of his hand. "Give me slow and steady and smart. You want my advice, boy?"

"Certainly."

"You marry that Shannon girl."

The sudden change of subject jolted Ted. Not merely the change, but the subject. "Sir?" he said.

The waiter returned with Mungerley's drink. He took a long sip and said, "Ah! That's the ticket. You know, Mrs. Mungerley doesn't approve, but she won't be back for two days." Mungerley snorted a laugh. "So I think I'll have another after this one!"

Clearing his throat, Ted said, "You were saying?"

"Oh yes, Miss Shannon. I saw her yesterday on a legal matter. You must admit she is beautiful."

"Yes."

"And very clever."

"That too."

"You have been keeping company with her, haven't you?"

"On occasion."

"Well, with all this talk about speed, you seem to be dragging your heels when it comes to love!" Mungerley let out a satisfied laugh.

"No, sir, it's just that . . ."

"Come on, we're alone here."

"Well, she keeps her own counsel, so to speak. She is a very religious woman."

"Nothing wrong with religion. I am a churchgoing man myself."

"No, sir, nothing wrong. But I have the feeling no man is going to find first place in her heart."

Mungerley said, "Pish tosh. Now you listen to me. When I was your age and saw a young belle, I went after her like a buffalo goes after . . . what do buffalo go after anyway?"

"Grass."

"Yes, well, I would create a one-man *stampede*. I would woo her until she fell before the onslaught of my affections. You should do the same."

Before Ted could answer a gruff voice said, "Mungerley!"

Ted turned to see a stout man in ill-fitting evening attire charging toward them.

"Taylor," Mungerley said, "come join us. May I present Mr. Ted Fox?"

The man Taylor barely nodded toward Ted. To Mungerley he said, "What were you thinking, man, when you sent me that harridan?"

Mungerley's face tightened. "Harridan?"

"Yes! That Miss Shannon! What an impudent, stupid woman!"

A ripple of anger coursed through Ted Fox. Who was this man, and what had he to do with Kit?

Alfred Mungerley, as if sensing Ted's discomfort, said, "Now, Dayton, you're obviously overwrought. Perhaps we should talk about it at a later—"

"I want her dealt with," Taylor interrupted.

"How?"

"I want her name dragged through the mud. She can't get away talking to me like that. The strumpet!"

Ted stood up. His hands were clenched. "Mr. Taylor, I'll thank you not to talk about Miss Shannon in that way."

The round man turned toward Ted and glared. "Just who are you?"

"A friend of Miss Shannon's," Ted said.

"Humph," snorted Taylor. "I don't care who you are. I'm telling you, she's a disgrace to womanhood. Pretending to do a man's job—"

Taylor's voice was caught short as Ted grabbed the man by his lapels. He pulled Taylor's reddening face close to his own. "I said not to talk about the lady that way."

A startled Alfred Mungerley shot quickly to his feet. "Gentlemen!"

Ted hardly heard him. His pulse was pounding in his ears. "And if I hear that you have spread a bad word about her, you'll be hearing from me."

Taylor's eyes bulged wide. Mungerley placed his hand between the men and pushed.

"Do I make myself clear?" Ted said.

"Do something!" Taylor said to Mungerley.

"Let go!" said Mungerley.

Ted released Taylor, who stumbled backward while letting out a stream of air. "He can't . . ." he sputtered. "I'll . . . he . . ." Still flustered, Taylor glared at Ted, turned, and exited the room as quickly as his chunky legs could carry him.

"That was not called for!" Alfred Mungerley said.

"Oh yes, it was," said Ted.

"I was thinking of putting you up for membership here! But you can't go around roughing up the members!"

"With all respect, sir, I am not going to sit by and let him talk that way about Kit."

"Perhaps she deserved it."

"Kit's not like that. Taylor must have—"

Mungerley raised his hand. "Now, don't go making accusations against Dayton Taylor. Not within these walls."

"These walls are getting awfully close." Ted started to loosen his tie.

"See here, now," Mungerley said, putting a hand on Ted's shoulder. "Cool off a bit. Go see your young lady and find out what happened. Maybe she needs a word to the wise. You know, she is fighting an epic battle. A woman in the courtroom? It's unheard of. She doesn't need to make enemies."

Ted knew that to be true. Kit had managed to earn the enmity of many of the police when she exposed the former chief, Orel Hoover, in a conspiracy to subvert justice in the Fox case. Even though it was his own son who committed the prostitute murders, many on the force remained loyal to him.

"Yes," said Ted. "I'll talk to her."

"Good, good," Mungerley said. "I'm sure this will all be water under the bridge."

If the bridge doesn't burn down first, Ted thought.

Chapter 6

"HELP ME. . . ."

The cop on the beat, "Big" Ed Hanratty, wasn't sure he had heard a voice. There was a slight wind tonight, blowing down Hill Street from the north. It whipped through the ghostly outline of Angels Flight, which was closed up for the night. The funicular system that ran two narrow cars up and down from the wealthy section of Bunker Hill stopped operating at nine o'clock.

Now it was nearly midnight, and there was no one about. Officer Hanratty liked it that way. Even the flophouses at the bottom of the hill were quiet tonight. The city seemed in a peaceful sleep.

"Help . . ."

This time Hanratty knew it was neither the creaking of the Flight tracks, nor the whistling of the wind. Someone—a woman—was in trouble.

It seemed to come from above, up at the top. Bunker Hill.

Hanratty paused a moment. He would have to take the stairs

to find out what was wrong. They loomed before him like a sheer rock face on the side of a mountain. When he was a younger man, that wouldn't have mattered in the slightest. But at fifty years old, with a stomach now larger than his barrel chest, it was a different matter.

"Please . . ."

Without another moment's hesitation, Hanratty started up the stairs. As he did, his imagination conjured up visions of mayhem at the top of the stairs. He'd been patrolling these streets—his beat was the "lower depths" as opposed to the fancy section—long enough to know that the explanation was undoubtedly going to be found in alcohol or money. Most of the crimes these days were among the poor, and a great number of them were induced by the free flow of beer and whiskey that watered this town. The temperance movement had barely made a dent here.

Halfway up, Hanratty paused to catch his breath. As he did, he pondered that he was halfway between two worlds. Above him was wealth, privilege. The grand Victorian mansions of Bunker Hill looked down on the city like royal enclaves. Below was the world of the strugglers, the transient, the poor. For a penny they could ride Angels Flight up to Bunker Hill. But they could never stay.

"Help!"

The cry was more insistent, yet weaker somehow. Definitely a woman, and something was terribly wrong. Hanratty could see the outline of the Olive Street observation tower atop Angels Flight, looking down at him like a huge eye.

"I'm on my way!" Hanratty shouted and pushed himself upward once more. "Can ya hear me?"

No answer.

As Hanratty got closer to the top the wind grew stronger. The smell of laurel mixed with the scent of mown grass wafted down from the hill. It was, Hanratty thought, the smell of wealth.

At the top of the stairs the moonlight was bright enough to illumine the reception porch of Angels Flight and the small booth where the fare was collected. But Hanratty could make out no human figure.

"Miss?" he questioned. "Can ya hear me, miss?"

Behind him, a groan. Only a few feet away, against the railing that set off the face of the hill from the walkway. Hanratty dropped to one knee and saw that it was a young woman, barely breathing.

Her face was against the wrought-iron fencing. Hanratty pulled her gently toward him, rolling her over on her back.

Her face was streaked with blood. Her hair was matted and coarse. Her eyes were closed.

"Can ya hear me?" Hanratty said.

The woman moaned, did not open her eyes. She was, Hanratty saw, quite pretty, which made her injuries seem all the more outrageous. Someone had beaten her. And in that moment, Hanratty decided that someone was going to pay.

"All right, then," he said. "We will take care of ya. Ed Hanratty will see to it."

Chapter 7

KIT HAD TO COOL her heels for twenty minutes before the federal lawyer met with her. The Federal Building on the corner of Main and Fifth was a squat, spare, unfriendly looking building. And the people inside, Kit decided, were a perfect match for it. No one smiled; no one said a word to her as she sat in a hard chair in the law library of the United States government.

During the wait, Kit took the time to pray about her client, Wong Shi. As had become her custom, Kit prayed that the truth would be made known and that justice would be served. That was the best she could ever hope for, for her clients.

She spent the remainder of her time poring over the rules of evidence in the California code. This was another of her customs—using spare time to study up on the rules. One of the things Earl Rogers had taught her was that a trial lawyer had to know the evidence rules backward and forward. These rules governed what could and could not be considered by a jury. You never knew during the course of a trial or hearing when an issue of evidence might arise that could make or break a case. The only things you could know were the rules and how to argue them.

The door to the library opened and the federal attorney entered.

He introduced himself as Roderick Bellows. He was in his forties and wore a high starched collar with his suit, which was dark brown and perfectly creased. His hair was slick and parted in the middle—like Earl Rogers', Kit thought—but unlike Rogers', Bellows' hair framed a humorless expression that stayed with him throughout the meeting.

"I understand you are here in the matter of the Chinese woman, Wong Shi?" Bellows said, getting directly to the point. He threw a file folder on the table and sat down opposite Kit.

"I am," Kit said. She tried not to appear nervous, but she had never handled any matter on a federal level before. This was a different type of jurisdiction—more severe, less discretionary. But, she reminded herself, the man at the table was still only a man, and perhaps would listen to reason.

"I am surprised she even hired counsel," Bellows said.

"Why are you surprised?"

"Well . . ." He left the thought unexpressed, but it was clear what he was thinking: *She's just a poor Chinese.* "I am even more intrigued about why you agreed to represent her."

"She came to me for help," Kit said.

Bellows shook his head. "I read about you and the Fox case. I guess everybody around here has. Fascinating."

Kit waited for him to explain.

"You, a woman of obvious charm and breeding, wanting to dig down in the dirt with us. I just can't—"

"Mr. Bellows," Kit interrupted. She had heard so many variations on what he was saying that she didn't care to hear another.

"I am here to discuss Wong Shi. It is a legal matter, and I would appreciate keeping our conversation on that level."

With a look of consternation Bellows said, "Of course." He opened the file. "It is a federal offense for anyone to bring or cause to be landed in any state a person born in the empire of China, or the empire of Japan, or the islands adjacent thereto, for the purpose of prostitution. Are you aware of this?"

"I looked up the statute, yes."

"The woman Wong Shi was placed here for that purpose. It's very clear. She may voluntarily go back to China or face arrest and deportation. It's really up to you."

His tone of voice was clearly intended to convey that Wong Shi's fate was sealed. But Kit had spent the last several days preparing for the next few minutes.

"May I point out," Kit said, "that the statute refers to *someone else* bringing in the foreign-born person, not the person herself."

Bellows nodded. "True. But this is only the foundation for reaching an immigration decision. This woman came here to engage in prostitution."

"How do you know this?"

"We have a complaining witness."

"His name?"

Shaking his head, Bellows said, "That is confidential. I'm sure you understand."

"No, I am afraid I do not understand. Under the Sixth Amendment to the Constitution every person accused of a crime has the right to be confronted by the witnesses—"

"Miss Shanley—"

"Shannon."

"I know the Constitution. And I'm sure you know that it only applies to citizens of the United States."

"And I'm sure you know that non-citizens who are prosecuted

under the terms of a state or federal statute are granted, *ab initio*, the rights of citizens under the Constitution."

Suddenly Bellows looked flabbergasted. It was clear he had not anticipated she would be this prepared. He cleared his throat. "I . . . I do not think you are completely correct on that matter. . . ."

"Oh, but I am. The Supreme Court so ruled in 1868. I have the name of the case if you want it."

"Even so, what is your point?"

"My point is simply this: Unless you provide me the name of the witness and a copy of any statement he has made, I will file for a writ of habeas corpus in federal court and let a judge tell you to do it."

A full, consternated gasp issued out of the mouth of the federal lawyer. "You can't be serious."

"Why not, Mr. Bellows?"

He seemed to be grasping for an answer. When none came, Kit stood and said, "I shall hear from you, then?"

Roderick Bellows stood up and faced her. "Why on earth are you doing this? She is just a Chinese."

Kit felt her cheeks redden. "She is my client, sir."

Bellows said, "Don't mistake the federal courts for your Wild West state courts, Miss Shannon. You'll find we can make life very difficult for those who meddle."

"I don't intend to meddle," Kit said. "I intend to let the law do that."

———

Kit was still muttering to herself when she got back to her office. She almost let out a scream when she opened her door and had flowers thrust toward her face.

"I've been waiting for you," Ted Fox said. He smiled.

It was a windy day, and Kit wondered what she must look like. She pushed a strand of hair behind her ear and straightened her hat. Taking the flowers from Ted, she inhaled their aroma. She closed her eyes at the lovely smell.

"Thank you," she said. "To what do I owe the pleasure?"

His grin was boyish and charming. "Pure pleasure, Kit Shannon. Would you like to see something amazing?"

"Are you going to levitate?"

"Ha! Give me a kiss and perhaps I will."

"Then I am afraid your feet must remain on the floor."

"Coquette! Come with me, then."

"Where?"

"You will have to trust me."

Kit smiled. "May I at least keep my eyes open?"

"For this you will definitely want your eyes open."

His company had come at a perfect time. It had been over a week since she'd last seen him, and she needed a break from her office and the conundrum of the federal law. "Lead on," she said.

They strolled, arm in arm, down a busy Broadway. The Broadway Department Store had a display of new fashions in its window—a row of collarless dresses, which were coming back into fashion. A sign in the window advised, *Say Good-bye to Tight Ribbons and Linen Collars!*

"You would look grand in one of those," Ted remarked.

"Do you think?" Kit said.

"I think you would look grand in anything. I'm especially partial to that lemon-colored arrangement you wore to dinner a couple of weeks ago."

"How very unusual that you should have taken note," Kit replied casually. But secretly she was delighted by his comment.

"I take note of a great many things," he said, giving her a wink. "Especially when they come in such lovely packages."

Oh, he was gifted with the gab today. But Kit loved it. After the exchange with that awful Bellows, Ted's charm was a sweet balm to her. They walked on another block until they came to a portico with a large green-striped awning over it.

"Here we are," said Ted.

"Where?"

"The Nickelodeon."

Kit laughed. "You like the moving pictures?"

"Wait until you see," Ted said. "We are going to witness a train robbery."

He led her inside. To Kit's surprise, nearly all of the wooden chairs in the small theater were filled. Ted found them a pair in the middle.

The front wall was covered with a red curtain. To the side was a small piano. A stout woman sat on the piano bench, waiting.

"What is this?" Kit asked.

"Shh," said Ted. "Just wait."

A man walked to the front of the theater and pulled open the curtains covering the front wall, revealing a white screen. Two other men began dimming the lamps on either side of the theater, until the room was completely dark.

A whirring sound from the rear, and then light on the front wall. And images. A title appeared: *The Great Train Robbery*.

The pianist began to play.

Then a train, moving. In one of the cars, a man at a safe. Suddenly, men with guns burst in and shot him! Kit, along with most of the audience, gasped.

The flickering images moved fast, the story of the robbery continuing for ten minutes, until the bandits were surrounded by a posse in a forest. A shootout began. A woman in the audience shouted, "Oh my!"

Then, suddenly, the face of a man with a mustache and cowboy hat filled the entire screen. He was looking straight at Kit.

The man pointed a gun at her face.

People in the theater screamed.

The gun fired!

And then the lights came on. Kit Shannon caught her breath.

"Did you like it?" Ted asked.

"I've never seen anything like it."

"Moving pictures have come a long way, haven't they?"

A voice behind them said, "Kit!"

Turning, Kit saw the reporter Tom Phelps. He had become a friend after Ted's trial—and it was good to have a friend on the Hearst newspaper, the *Examiner*.

"Hello, Tom," Kit said. "You covering the Nickelodeon beat now?"

"You might say." He shook hands with Ted Fox. "I think there is a future in these things."

"Moving pictures?" said Kit.

"As you can see, the theater was packed. I believe Mr. Edison would like to see an entire industry come from his machine."

"Never happen," Ted said. "You can't get rich charging people a nickel."

"If there's enough people, you can," Phelps mused. To Kit he said, "Have you heard about Sloate?"

"Only that his trial is set for next month," Kit said. Sloate was to be tried for several felonies arising from his machinations during Ted's trial.

"He's hired a new attorney," Phelps said.

"Who?"

"Clarence Darrow."

Kit's chin dropped. Darrow! He was the most famous trial lawyer in the country. The Chicago attorney was reportedly a magician in a courtroom, able to sway a jury with the tone of his voice and the power of his intellect. He was also an outspoken atheist, who often debated Christian clergy. Now he was coming to Los Angeles. The thought that Heath Sloate might be acquitted through Darrow's efforts sickened her.

Phelps said, "You worried?"

"Maybe a little," Kit said.

"There is something more I need to tell you."

Kit looked at the reporter. He seemed reticent. "What is it?" she asked.

"I'm covering the trial," Phelps said. "And I've heard some things. Sloate still has powerful friends in this city."

The warning from Dayton Taylor echoed in Kit's mind.

"And he has spread the word that he wants revenge. On you."

Kit felt a chill. Would she, and this city, never be free of this man?

"Don't underestimate him, Kit," Phelps warned.

"I won't," Kit said, even as she wondered what she could possibly do.

"Are you being called as a witness at the trial?" Phelps asked.

"No. Elinor Wynn is turning state's evidence. She is really all they need."

"I agree," said Phelps. He touched the brim of his skimmer and added, "Well, I must be off. Call me if I can help, Kit." He exited the theater.

Ted put his hand on Kit's arm. "Are you all right?"

Nodding, Kit said, "I will be."

"Then we have one more stop to make," Ted said.

"Where?"

"Angels Flight."

It took them ten minutes to walk there. At the corner of Third and Hill, they boarded one of the two white cars, the one named "Olivet." The other car was called "Sinai." Colonel J. W. Eddy, who built the railway system in 1901, knew his biblical mountaintops.

They sat on one of the slatted wooden benches as the ride began. As Olivet coursed upward, Sinai came down, the two perfectly balanced cars passing in the middle. In two minutes they were at the top, Ted paying two pennies to the attendant in the wheelhouse. From there it was a short walk to the open-air patio of the Hill Crest Inn that served a four o'clock tea.

The view was clear all the way to the ocean. As they sat, Kit marveled again at the sun-drenched paradise Los Angeles had turned out to be. Growing up in a stifling orphanage in Boston, and then spending the next several years in a stuffy rooming house on New York's Lower East Side, Kit appreciated the wide expanses and clean air.

Kit also marveled at the extravagant Queen Anne and Eastlake mansions of prominent families like the Crockers and the Bradburys, which dominated the summit of Bunker Hill. It was as if the ride on Angels Flight had taken her from the drab and ordinary world of most Angelenos to the heady Olympus of the wealthy and favored few.

"Now, then, Kit," Ted said, "I have something I want to discuss with you."

"What is it?"

"Our future."

Kit had expected Ted would bring up the subject. He had been dancing around it for months. She loved his company. The question she had, though, was did she *love* him? *Could* she love him, with the issue of his faith still unresolved?

"What do you see there, Mr. Fox?"

"I see you and I see me and I see a big aeroplane."

Kit laughed. "And what insane person is on that aeroplane?"

"Your husband."

The word both thrilled her and gave her pause. She could picture no other man as her husband.

"In case I was not being clear, Kit, that was a proposal of marriage."

"This is so sudden," Kit said, trying to buy time.

"Are you surprised?"

She lost herself in his blue eyes for a moment, then recovered and said, "No, Ted."

"Then let me ask you a question. What do you see in the future?"

After a moment's pause Kit said, "I see a husband who loves God as much as I do."

Ted sat back in his chair. "I know how important your faith is to you, Kit. I respect that."

"I know."

"And it is not that I disbelieve. We've talked about that."

"Yes."

"Perhaps, over time, I might come to a greater faith."

Kit looked at her hands. She noticed she had entwined her fingers and was squeezing them hard. "Ted, when I was a little girl there was a family that lived near us. The wife was a church member and active in the community. Her husband did not go to church. I remember seeing the woman from time to time, and she always looked under a burden. I once asked Papa about it, and he said, 'She is bearing her cross.' I know now what he meant."

"But, Kit"—Ted took her hand—"I love you. I have loved you ever since that night I saw you in the hall at your aunt's. I want to be your husband, to take care of you. In this whole matter of religion I will be receptive. I will try. Can't that be enough for now?"

Before she could answer, a waiter in a white apron came to the table. "Good afternoon, folks," he said. "We will be serving tea in just a bit. We're a little behind because of the trouble."

"Trouble?" Ted said.

"The girl who was found up here last night. Terrible."

The waiter looked like he was dying to share the news. So when Ted asked about it, he was more than happy to oblige. "A girl, a young woman really, was found by a cop, terribly beaten. Can you imagine that? Here! But the good news is they caught the fellow who did it. A lousy Mex! Works as a gardener for one of them big houses."

Kit's heart jumped in her chest. "Did you say gardener?"

"I did," said the waiter. "You just can't hire them Mexicans anymore."

"What was his name?"

"The Mex?"

"Yes!"

"Gee, I don't know. Their names all sound the same to me." He laughed.

"What is it, Kit?" Ted said.

Kit asked the waiter, "The name of the girl who was attacked. Do you know that?"

The waiter shook his head. "She was white, though. That's for sure. And I think she was a maid."

The world seemed to close in around Kit as she stood up. "I have to go, Ted."

"But why?"

"Trouble."

Chapter 8

KIT TOOK A CAB to Aunt Freddy's. The horse that drew it, though, seemed to be the slowest animal in the city. The sun was low in the sky when Kit finally walked through the door. Jerrold, Aunt Freddy's butler, saw her come in.

"They are in the study, Miss Shannon," he said, his gray eyebrows drooping sadly.

"Who?"

"Oh, everybody. It's dreadful, miss."

Kit practically flew into the room. In the big chair by the fireplace sat Aunt Freddy, dabbing at her eyes with a handkerchief. Alfred Mungerley stood at her side, gently patting her shoulder. At the far end of the room, in a corner, Corazón was sobbing into her hands.

In the middle of the room, in a stiff, dark green suit, stood Detective Captain Michael McGinty. Kit had dealt with him during

Ted's murder case. He had the stub of a cigar planted in the corner of his mouth.

"Oh, Kit!" Aunt Freddy wailed. "It is so terrible!"

At that, Corazón looked up from her chair and cried loudly, "Kit!" With her accent it sounded like *Keet*!

Without hesitation Kit went to Corazón and put an arm around her shoulder.

"Don't you talk to her!" Freddy said.

"Aunt Freddy," Kit demanded, "tell me what is going on."

McGinty pulled the cigar from his mouth and said, "Now everybody pipe down. I am in charge here."

"Detective McGinty," Kit said, "why are you here?"

"Routine questioning, Miss Shannon."

"They arrest my brother," Corazón said.

"That's right," said McGinty. "Mr. Mungerley's servant, Gloria Graham, was attacked last night."

"Savagely," Alfred Mungerley added. "In a manner I shall not mention here."

"And," said McGinty, "she made an identification. We arrested Juan Chavez early this afternoon."

Corazón cried, "Is no true!"

"Oh, dear!" Freddy said.

"There, there," Mungerley said. "No one blames you, Freddy." He looked at Kit. "I tried to warn you about him." There was a tinge of anger in his voice.

Kit felt Corazón trembling. Could it possibly be true that Juan did this? Perhaps he did it out of anger because he had been accused by Gloria of "looking" at her. If it were so, it would be a disaster for everyone in this house.

"What I want to know," McGinty said, "is when was the last time anybody here saw Chavez. Let's start with you, Mrs. Fairbank."

Aunt Freddy sighed heavily. "I thought he was trouble the moment I brought him here."

"When did you see him last?" McGinty asked.

"Oh, I don't know. I don't keep track of such things, I—"

"Try."

"Oh, dear. Let me see." She patted her cheeks with the handkerchief. "I believe I saw him in the garden yesterday. Yes, yesterday it was."

"About what time?"

"It was in the morning or afternoon."

"Can you tell me which one it was?"

"Oh, I don't know!" She blew her nose.

McGinty rubbed his face. "How about you, Mr. Mungerley?"

Mungerley shook his head. "I've never seen that boy. I only know what Gloria has told me about him. She came to me in tears. She was quite frightened of him, I can tell you that."

"All right," McGinty said, turning to Corazón. "How about you, miss?"

Corazón shook even more. She looked at Kit, as if pleading with her.

"Detective McGinty," Kit said. "Corazón is obviously distraught. Can this wait?"

"Why?" said McGinty. "So she can come up with a story?"

Kit stood up straight. "What do you mean by that?"

"Well, the kid's her brother, and she's a . . ."

"A what?" Kit snapped. "A Mexican?"

McGinty put up his hands. "I didn't say that."

"You didn't have to," Kit said.

"Kit!" Aunt Freddy shouted. "You stop this right now!"

Corazón grabbed at Kit's arm. "Help him," she whispered. "Help my brother."

"What was that?" McGinty asked. "What did she just say?"

Kit patted Corazón on the shoulder, then walked to the middle of the room where she could address McGinty directly. "Where is Juan Chavez now?"

Squinting, McGinty said, "That's no business of yours, if you don't mind."

"But I do," Kit said. "I want to see him."

Aunt Freddy squealed, "No!"

Shaking his head, McGinty said, "You better not."

"His sister has asked me to," Kit said. "Now where is he?"

The room grew suddenly, heavily silent. For a long moment it seemed no one knew what to say next. Even Kit. What had she just jumped into?

It was Alfred Mungerley who broke the silence. "Miss Shannon," he said softly, but with a firmness that bespoke authority, "your aunt is upset. This has been a very unpleasant day for all of us. Don't you think, in view of family considerations, you should let someone else get involved in this matter?"

Kit paused, thinking perhaps he was right. But then she looked at Corazón, almost doubled over with fright. A hundred different thoughts raced through Kit's mind. If Juan was guilty, if the evidence was conclusive against him, *could* she represent him? She had vowed to represent only those she believed innocent.

But this was Corazón's brother. She couldn't turn her back on him at this moment. Yet if she undertook to represent him and later became convinced that he was indeed guilty, she was bound to continue her representation.

And then there was Aunt Freddy. Kit loved her aunt and knew that this was already an emotional trauma for her. If her own niece should become the defense attorney, what would that do to her?

Lord, Kit thought suddenly, *what should I do?*

She recalled a memory of her father, when he had come back home after ministering to a poor family on the other side of her hometown. The father of the family was dying. He was a nobody in the eyes of society. And a drunkard. But her father said that he had shared the gospel with him, and that he had called out to Jesus just before he died. He told eight-year-old Kit that if the Bible taught anything, it was that we were here to reach out to "the least of these."

And that was what Juan and, in truth, Corazón were in this city. Mexican laborers. They had no one to care about them.

"I must at least talk to him, Aunt Freddy," Kit said.

"Oh!" Aunt Freddy blurted, then cried into her handkerchief.

Alfred Mungerley shook his head disapprovingly at Kit. Mc-Ginty said, "Not a wise decision, Miss Shannon."

Kit swallowed and turned to McGinty. "Where is he?" she said.

———

McGinty took Kit in his carriage to police headquarters. As they rode down from Angeleno Heights toward the central district, McGinty said, "I admire you, Miss Shannon."

Kit looked at him, a bit stunned. McGinty was a veteran of the police force, and she had not made friends on the force when she rooted out former chief Orel Hoover.

"I mean," McGinty said, forming the words around his cigar, "you have guts. You did in the Fox case, and you do now. But a word to the wise."

Kit waited.

"This ain't a good thing to get involved in. I understand you wanting to help your friend and all, but this ain't going to be a pretty sight. You got a Mex raping a white girl. It'll be all we can do to keep him from being lynched."

It was the first time Kit had heard the word *rape* in connection with Juan. It froze her. McGinty was right. This city was divided among class and race. As long as everyone "kept their place," all was well. Try to cross the line, though, and the opposition would be fast and firm. Commit a crime, especially one like this, and it would be like the forces of hell unleashed.

"So this is not something for you to get into," McGinty said. "You could easily become a hated person in this city."

She had never thought of it that way before, but it was true. Defending someone like Juan Chavez would result in her taking the brunt of the city's rage. But should that even be a consideration? Didn't Jesus say you would be blessed when men hate you for His sake? And isn't that why she was a lawyer? For His sake, and His passion for justice for the oppressed?

Of course, there was Aunt Freddy to consider. This was a family matter. Juan was part of the household, and all this would surely tax her aunt to the extreme. And what of Corazón? This was tearing her apart.

In the back of her mind, too, was the unpleasant thought that Juan might be guilty. Gloria had given the most condemning testimony there is—an eyewitness identification by the victim.

"Another thing," McGinty said, guiding the carriage onto Main Street. "He could be sent away for a long time. Twenty years, maybe. But if he pleads guilty, a judge might go easier on him. It'll be tough, you know, him being a Mex. But he could get the minimum, which is five years in the pen."

There were so many considerations. Kit felt them all jumble in her mind. What would be best for Juan? For everyone?

They arrived at the central police headquarters. McGinty had told her that Juan was in one of the holding cells there and would remain there until Monday morning. Then he would be arraigned and transferred to the county jail.

Inside, the policemen on duty seemed to be in an agitated state. Kit had been here a few times on various cases, but tonight she sensed a difference. There was a hatred in the air. And she knew that hatred was directed at Juan Chavez.

She felt pairs of eyes glancing at her from all around, and she could almost hear their thoughts.

Here she is again, that Shannon woman.

Gonna try to make us look like fools.

We can take care of her if we have to. . . .

McGinty said, "Before I let you see him, I want you to talk to Officer Hanratty." He led Kit to his desk in the middle of the room. He made a motion to a man on the other side, and he approached them.

He was huge, and his malicious glare and large, curling mustache only made him seem larger.

"This is Miss Kit Shannon," McGinty said.

"I know who she is," Hanratty snapped. "And I know why she's here. To help that lousy Mex."

"All right," McGinty said, "I just want you to give her the facts."

"She interested?" Hanratty said.

"You may address me directly," Kit said to Hanratty.

He looked down at her. He seemed like Goliath. "Why should I?"

Because McGinty told you to, Kit thought. But McGinty stood by silently, as if seeing if she could pass this test. Kit took a breath and said, "You will have to tell me sooner or later," she said. "I am an officer of the court. You are an officer of the law. Why make this tougher than it has to be?"

That seemed to get through to the large cop. "I found the victim beaten and half dead. I hailed a night-owl hack and got her over to Sisters Hospital. She almost died."

"Was that the conclusion of a doctor?" Kit said.

"Whaddaya mean by that?"

"I mean is that a medical opinion or your opinion?"

"What difference does it make?"

"None, maybe," Kit said. "But I want to be precise."

Hanratty cast an annoyed look at McGinty, "Do I have to put up with this?"

McGinty nodded. "Go on with your story, Ed."

With a huff, Hanratty continued. "I came in and made a report, then I went back to the hospital."

"What time was that?" Kit asked.

"About ten o'clock."

"Did you see Gloria?"

Hanratty looked surprised, as if Kit shouldn't have known the name of the victim. "Yeah, I saw her. Talked to her. She gave me the identification, and then we went out and grabbed him."

"Wait a moment, please," Kit said. "Do you mean she just blurted out the identification, or did you question her?"

"Now what difference does—"

"Officer Hanratty," Kit said, "this time it makes a great deal of difference." She saw McGinty looking at Hanratty, as if he were interested in the answer, too.

"Well, I . . ." Hanratty hesitated as if trying to remember. "I walked into the room, and I told Miss Graham who I was."

"What was her condition?"

"She was all bandaged up, but she could talk. And the first thing she said to me was 'Juan Chavez did this.' "

"The first thing?"

"The very first thing. So I questioned her some more, and that was all I needed."

Kit looked at the floor. "As you know, Officer Hanratty, there are sometimes reasons a person may be wrong about who perpetrated a crime."

"She ain't wrong," Hanratty said.

"How can you be sure of that?"

"Because the Mex confessed."

The news hit Kit like a fist. It must have shown all over her face because Hanratty said smugly, "That's right."

McGinty bit the end off a fresh cigar and spit the tip into a spittoon. "You want to see him now?"

The holding cells were down a cold stairwell and through a thick door. A jailer nodded at McGinty. He did not acknowledge Kit, but silently unlocked the door.

There were six cells, two rows of three. They were just like cages. In fact, there was straw on the floor as one might see at an animal exhibit in the zoo.

At the second cell on the right, McGinty stopped and nodded. Kit saw, in the far corner, a figure curled up on the floor. He had his head between his knees, his arms wrapped around his legs.

"Juan?" Kit said.

The figure slowly lifted his head.

Kit's breath left her with a start.

Juan's face was a beaten, bloody mess. His eyes were swollen nearly shut. But he saw her. And when he did, he burst into tears.

Chapter 9

THE *LOS ANGELES DAILY TIMES* was the leading newspaper in the city. It was ruled as a virtual fiefdom by General Harrison Gray Otis. A Civil War veteran who also took the field as a brigadier general during the Spanish-American War, Otis was a staunch conservative. Bitterly anti-union, he considered his newspaper almost a military operation. In fact, he referred to his staff as "the phalanx."

The opposite profile belonged to the newspaper mogul William Randolph Hearst and his attempt to compete with the *Times*. His *Los Angeles Examiner* was launched in 1903 with the backing of the massive Hearst fortune and his penchant for "yellow journalism." Also, Hearst was a populist, firmly on the side of the workingman.

As if these papers represented both sides of a divided personality, Frederica Stamper Fairbank could not bear to prefer one over the other. She shared the political views of General Otis more than she did the garish Mr. Hearst. Yet it was the Hearst paper she turned to most frequently. If you wanted gossip, you went to the *Examiner*. It had funny papers, too. Freddy could not resist catching the adventures of Mrs. Katzenjammer and Happy Hooligan.

Her butler, Jerrold, got the papers each morning for her hot off the presses. In fact, his fingers were usually stained with ink for the rest of the day. This Saturday morning as Aunt Freddy sat down in her morning room for coffee and a look at the news, she found herself trembling. She was afraid she might see her niece on the front page!

Oh, what had Kit done? Last night had been absolutely horrible. Kit had come home in a fury, railing about the police beating a confession out of her gardener.

Well, what of it? If he confessed, he was guilty. And if he was guilty, a beating was too good for him!

But then Kit had announced her decision to represent him as his lawyer!

The front page of the *Examiner* was filled with the story. A photograph of Gloria Graham was set at a slight angle over a photo of Angels Flight. Next to that was a photo of an officer named Hanratty, who had found the girl.

And then there was the story, which Freddy read with a rapidly beating heart. She saw her own name in the middle of the story, listed as the employer of the man who had been arrested.

The only good news was that there was no mention of Kit. Maybe, in the light of day, with a good night's sleep behind her, Kit would see that it was a hopeless cause.

But when Kit came through the door, dressed to go out, Freddy could see that her face was as firm in its resolve as it was last night.

"Good morning," Kit said. "May I join you?"

"Oh, dear!"

"What is it?"

"You haven't changed your mind?"

"No, Aunt Freddy," Kit said, taking a chair. She poured herself a cup of coffee from the serving pot.

"Just look at what will happen!" Aunt Freddy held up the front page of the *Examiner* so Kit could see it in all its sordid detail. "If you take this case it will be *your* picture on the front pages!"

Kit took the newspaper and looked closely at it. "Yes," she muttered.

Aunt Freddy's spirits rose. "You agree, then?"

"Yes, I do, Aunt Freddy. The newspapers. They will be crucial to this case."

"Oh my dear—"

"So I'd best get down and talk to Tom Phelps."

Aunt Freddy blinked. "Who?"

Kit took a quick sip of coffee and stood up. "A reporter for the *Examiner*. I'll need his help if I am to defend Juan."

Aunt Freddy dropped her cup of coffee on her lap.

"Look out there!" Kit said, rushing to her and grabbing a linen napkin on the way. She dabbed at the wetness on Aunt Freddy's dress.

Aunt Freddy seemed not to notice. She just stared at Kit. "I . . . I . . ."

"Oh, let's not talk about it now, Aunt Freddy." Kit kissed her on the head. "I'll see you at the Women's Club at two. I promised to join you, remember?"

"Oh, dear!"

———

Kit took the stairs to the second floor of the *Examiner* building. The city room took up most of that floor. It was filled with a haze of smoke and the sounds of a busy newspaper—voices shouting for copy boys, scuffling chairs and feet, and here and there the clattering sound of typing machines. While some of the reporters sat at desks scribbling with fountain pens, others—the younger ones, Kit thought—had typewriters right on their desks.

It was Saturday morning, so the paper was getting ready for the Sunday edition—larger and with more lurid features to try and entice readers from the more staid and conservative *Times.* A voice in Kit's head asked, *Are you sure you want to do this?*

Then she saw Tom Phelps striding across the city room, staring at a sheaf of papers in his hand. He was in his shirt sleeves, his tie loosened.

"Tom!" Kit called out over the din.

Phelps looked up, as did several other reporters in the vicinity. A few whistles rang out for Kit's benefit. She felt herself blush.

"All right, you mugs," Phelps said. "Get back to work!" He came to Kit and offered his hand. "This is a surprise!"

"May I have a few minutes, Tom?"

"You can have all day if you want it, Kit."

"Just a few minutes. Where can we talk?"

"My desk. Come on."

He escorted her across the hardwood floor, strewn with crumpled papers and a few cigar and cigarette butts. Kit stepped lightly.

Tom Phelps's desktop was a variation of the floor. Paper was everywhere, crumpled and otherwise, and an ashtray held what must have been a week's worth of cigar butts. And right in the middle was a contraption labeled *Remington Standard Typewriter No. 3.*

An older gentleman, with a gray mustache and eyeglasses perched on the end of his nose, was making an adjustment to the typewriter with a tool. He looked up.

"Ernie," Phelps said, "I'd like you to meet Kit Shannon."

The man nodded to her, his gray eyes twinkling behind the glasses. "Pleased to meet you," he said.

"Ernie is the typewriter man around here," Phelps explained.

"Worked for Remington itself before the paper hired him. He can fix anything."

" 'Cept a horse race," Ernie said.

"Need my desk for a bit," Phelps said.

"I'm finished," Ernie said. "But don't you go pounding them keys like you were a blacksmith or something. This is a delicate machine. She likes to be coaxed."

His smile was engaging, causing Kit to smile, too. Ernie nodded at her and strode off.

Phelps pulled a wooden chair up to his desk and motioned for Kit to sit. "Now, what brings you here to my world?"

"Tom, I'm going to need your help."

The reporter leaned his chair back, hands behind his head. "I'm listening."

"I know you are on the side of the common man."

"That's the Hearst religion."

"Well, my religion teaches me that all men are of equal worth in the sight of God."

"Mr. Hearst would agree with that. It gets him votes."

"My question is, do you believe that?"

Squinting, Tom Phelps said, "And aren't you full of the Irish blarney this morning? Why are you questioning me, Kit Shannon?"

Kit did not avert his gaze. "I am in earnest, Tom. I am going to defend Juan Chavez."

Phelps sat back up in his chair, the legs landing on the wooden floor with a loud *thwack*. "You?"

"Me."

He shook his head. "This is going to be a powder keg."

"Why? Because Juan is a Mexican and the victim is white?"

"That's the reality of it."

"I want to change the reality."

Phelps eyed her warily. "Which is why you came to me."

Kit nodded.

"This is a newspaper, Kit. I'm a reporter. I can't . . ."

"Come now, Tom. You are a reporter on a Hearst newspaper. This is not the seat of objectivity."

Laughing, Phelps said, "You've got me there. But this! If I appear to favor Chavez in any way . . ."

"All I'm asking for is fairness. Give him the presumption of innocence the law gives him. Tell his side of the story. You know the *Times* is going be against him. Tom, I'm asking you to be what you know you are—a reporter. One who reports the facts, no matter where they lead."

"Do you know the facts?"

"I know one fact for certain. Juan Chavez was beaten until he confessed."

Tom Phelps stroked his chin. But he did not look shocked, as Kit had expected. "That's interesting," he said, "but doesn't mean much."

"How can you say that?"

"Because cops beat confessions out of people all the time."

Kit felt her chest tighten. "And you accept that?"

"I report, Kit. That's what I do. And I'm telling you, if they have a confession from Juan Chavez, that's it. End of case. Even if he got roughed up a bit."

Shaking her head, Kit said, "I can't accept that."

"It's the way it is."

"Does that mean—"

"It means there's nothing I can do for you, Kit. I wish I could, but not on this one. It's too volatile. We'd lose readers if we sided with Chavez."

Kit stood up. "I suppose I was mistaken to come here."

"Say, Kit, you don't—"

"I thought you might be one reporter in town who might write the truth, the whole truth, and nothing but."

"So help me God?"

"Yes," Kit said. "God help you." She walked out without another word.

Chapter 10

THE WOMEN'S CLUB of Los Angeles met in the expansive garden of Mrs. Eulalie Pike, a sixty-year-old socialite whose husband, Otto, had brought her and his Eastern millions to San Francisco in the mid-'70s. Finding the social scene fairly well established and calcified in the City by the Bay, Eulalie had been the one to suggest a move south to Los Angeles. There, she opined, she might be able to someday "rule the roost."

Otto Pike had at first been against it. What could he possibly have to do in an arid land of *pensiones* and *ranchos*, where things were more Spanish than Anglo? He had nixed the idea and would have remained steadfast, but for a bit of information that came his way in a friendly poker game.

He learned that the Southern Pacific had decided to make Los Angeles its terminus, to be completed around 1881. He did not hesitate. The Pikes moved in the spring of '78, and Otto Pike began buying up land in the vicinity of the train depot. That bit of speculative foresight multiplied Otto Pike's already considerable fortune.

For Eulalie, he built a huge mansion of Victorian design on Adams Street, with five acres of orange and magnolia trees surrounding it. The property was so prodigious, it seemed much like a city park one might find in Boston or Philadelphia. It was not a wonder to anyone that it was here Eulalie, one of the founders of the Women's Club, held court like a Renaissance monarch.

And it was here that Kit, distracted by Juan's condition and the seeming indifference of Tom Phelps, met Aunt Freddy for the afternoon program.

"Now, we won't go out of our way to talk about what you do when you are not socializing," Aunt Freddy cautioned.

"Let's tell them I am one of those French dancers," Kit snapped. "You know, the kind with the feathers?"

"Kit Shannon! You behave yourself!"

Kit wished she were back in her office, poring over a law book or her Bible. In fact, she wished she were anywhere but in this hotbed of gossip and social preening. She had to admit, however, that it was a lovely spot. Flaming geraniums and snow-white calla lilies formed hedges all around, and morning glories wantonly climbed to the top of the evergreen trees, hanging from the branches in graceful festoons.

Kit had attended several high teas and even a couple of formal luncheons since coming to Los Angeles, but nothing had quite prepared her for this. She likened it to being presented at a royal court, though all she knew of such matters was taken from books and magazines.

Grand dames glided across the manicured lawn, each dressed impeccably in their afternoon fashions. Each one seemed more elaborate than the next. Kit's own gown of pale-rose-and-gold-striped silk had been picked by Aunt Freddy. It seemed important to her aunt, so Kit had let her summon a local seamstress to the house to make all the adjustments. At least Aunt Freddy seemed pleased. *"A soft and appropriate vision of womanly youth!"* Aunt Freddy had said, beholding the final product.

Kit had thought the gown a great exaggeration of propriety for an afternoon luncheon, but now seeing the other women, she knew, if anything, she might be a bit underdressed.

"Don't drag your parasol, Kathleen," Freddy admonished. "Ah, Mrs. Canton, may I present my great-niece, Kathleen Shannon." Freddy launched so quickly into the introduction that Kit hardly had time to worry over the parasol or anything else.

"Charmed to meet you," the matronly woman, clad in plum-colored taffeta, stated rather formally. She looked down her nose at Kit through a long-handled eyepiece, which she lowered and lifted almost with every breath.

"Is this the young woman we've heard so much about?" Mrs. Canton continued.

"Oh, Agnes, do forgive me," Freddy said quickly. "I see Marion Deters has come, and I would be decidedly remiss if I failed to see her."

Mrs. Canton nodded knowingly and said nothing more of Kit. Kit was grateful for the getaway, but she knew it was hopeless to believe she might make it through the entire luncheon without someone making an issue of her scandalous career.

As Freddy masterfully controlled her friends and their questions, Kit smiled and nodded. She also studied the lawn setting. A small stage and podium had been arranged at the far end, with a cluster of damask-covered tables gathered around in a horseshoe fashion.

Most luncheons began at one, but very formal gatherings such as this were often given to later hours. Freddy had told her that Mrs. Pike was responsible for the finest and most elegant of affairs and that it was a real privilege to partake in her soirées.

Kit thought it would have been much more preferable to spend the afternoon anywhere else.

"You must be Frederica Fairbank's niece," a young woman not much older than Kit declared. "I positively adore your aunt."

Kit smiled at the dark-haired woman. "Then we are in agreement, and yes, I am Kathleen Shannon."

"Wonderful! I'm Delia Bryce. My mother and your aunt are good friends. Why, I practically grew up crawling under the tables of the Fairbank estate." The plain-faced girl chattered on incessantly. Freddy conversed with the girl's mother, to whom Kit had been introduced only moments before the invasion of Delia Bryce.

"I positively adore Mrs. Pike's social gatherings," Delia continued. "You never know what you might see. Why, did you notice that Mrs. Everhart has come today and she's with child!"

"No, I—"

"Not that I mind," Delia interrupted Kit's attempt to reply. "But there is a certain amount of decorum that was established long before either Mrs. Everhart or myself came into this gathering. Mother is positively scandalized by the matter. And what about Cornelia Jordan?" She looked to Kit as if expecting some great response.

"Yes, well . . ." Kit hesitated, uncertain as to who the woman was, much less what she should think about her.

"Exactly!" Delia declared. "If she thinks we're likely to overlook such a matter—well, she simply has another think coming."

Freddy turned at this point and motioned Kit to follow her. "We will dine with Mrs. Bryce and her daughter."

Kit nodded, dreading the ordeal. Delia looped her arm through Kit's. "We shall be good friends, I'm sure. Mother says I have a certain presentation about me that naturally draws people to me. I must say, at times it is a burden." She lowered her voice and stopped momentarily, forcing Kit to meet her gaze as she repeated the word, "Burden." Nodding as if Kit should understand everything from that simple statement, Delia disengaged herself to choose a chair.

"You will sit here," she commanded Kit, motioning to the seat beside her. "I have decided to make you my special project."

Kit tried hard not to roll her gaze heavenward. *Dear Lord,* she prayed, *give me patience.*

Kit took her place at the elegantly set table, finding herself sandwiched between Mrs. Bryce and Delia. Across from her, Aunt Freddy sat her plump form down and began removing her gloves.

"I must say, Eulalie does an admirable job with the tables," Mrs. Bryce commented.

"Unlike Mrs. Silvers, whose flowers were so full and high you couldn't even visit for fear of taking a mouthful of gardenias," Delia threw out.

"Oh my, yes," her mother said. "Eulalie would never make such a dreadful mistake."

Kit diverted herself by mentally contemplating legal terminology, court cases, and state statutes—anything that allowed her to focus on something other than the high-pitched chattering of Delia Bryce.

Luncheon was served on fine china with a lobster crepe as the starting entrée. This course blended over to a beautiful, artistic presentation of rack of lamb with tiny dilled potatoes and sprigs of mint.

At least the food is good, Kit thought, completely fascinated that in spite of making a portion of her meal disappear, Delia Bryce had not stopped talking.

"Mother, we must have a party for Kathleen. I want the entire world to know what a dear friend she has become," Delia announced.

All gazes were fixed on Kit who stammered, "That isn't . . . well . . . what I mean to say . . ."

"No need to thank me, darling Kathleen," Delia continued. "Mother and I know exactly how you feel."

Kit nearly sighed as she finished off the last of her potatoes.

The salad course came next—a wonderful fruit arrangement atop lazily draped leaves of romaine. And last, a dessert of apple charlotte russe, which everyone, including Delia, declared to be a culinary masterpiece.

Iced tea flowed freely, and Kit was grateful, as the afternoon had warmed considerably. It was either that or else Delia's ballooning sleeves of silk organdy and lace were insulating Kit from the light breeze. Kit could only pray the ordeal would soon conclude. As the last of the luncheon was cleared away, the tinkling of a bell drew her attention.

Under a flowered trellis at the wooden podium stood Eulalie Pike in a flowing gown of mauve crepe de chine. "Ladies, ladies," she cheeped. "We are about to begin the lecture. Please turn your attention toward the front."

Aunt Freddy leaned forward, pulling on her gloves. "Now we are primed for some culture, dear."

Kit, for her part, cautioned herself to be polite and attentive. She quietly replaced her own gloves and folded her hands in her lap. This was for Aunt Freddy. The fence between them needed mending.

"Our speaker this afternoon," said Eulalie Pike, "is Dr. Edward Lazarus. . . ."

Lazarus? Kit thought. *Where have I heard that name before?*

"As you all know, Dr. Lazarus is minister of the Hill Street Methodist Church."

Kit remembered now. She had gone to that church once and heard Lazarus preaching about how the Bible was merely a collection of human writings, full of errors. Kit, her Irish tongue ablaze, had not been able to contain herself. She had taken Lazarus to task on the steps of the church, and he, in turn, had taken offense at her temerity.

Now she would have to be his captive audience? *Oh, please,* she thought, *make this go quickly!*

After polite, gloved applause, Lazarus took his place at the podium and smiled. "Thank you, Mrs. Pike, for that very lovely introduction," he began. "It is indeed a great pleasure for me to address you this afternoon on a topic of which, I am sure, all of you cultured ladies are aware. It is my welcome task today to enlighten you further on this issue, which carries important social significance."

Kit saw heads nodding all around. If there was anything the Women's Club of Los Angeles appreciated, it was social significance.

"I speak today of the search for religious truth. At my alma mater, Boston University, where I received my doctoral degree in divinity, trouble has been brewing. . . ."

Boston, Kit thought. He must have been there the same time she had been in St. Catherine's Orphanage.

"I call this trouble the battle between progressives and those who cling to the past. Almost," Lazarus added, "between adults and those who refuse to grow up."

In her wicker chair, Kit began to squirm uncomfortably. She sensed where he was going, and it was not a pleasant place.

"This battle has come to Los Angeles, as some of you are aware. A magazine published by some of the troublemaking students at Boston University is being sent all over the country. It accuses certain members of the faculty, and even myself in a recent issue, of heresy! As if the objective search for truth can ever be heretical!"

Some of the women patted their hands together in approval.

Kit doubted they knew exactly what they were clapping for.

"And now they have formed what they are calling the Bible League of the Methodist Episcopal Church and have formulated what they say is the correct doctrine concerning the Bible!" His voice was rising with indignation.

Kit felt her hands gripping the sides of her chair. *Steady,* she told herself. *Don't cause any discomfort to Aunt Freddy! Steady . . .*

She kept thinking of her father. If he were here, he would not stand by silently as a man—let alone a cleric!—denigrated the Word of God! Her father's preaching had always been centered on his love for the Bible and his unshakable belief that it was a divine book with real power. *Sharper than any two-edged sword, piercing even to the dividing asunder of soul and spirit . . .*

"But what they espouse is childishness! Against scholars who are schooled in the modern forms of interpretation, they insist on clinging to the view that the Bible is somehow a magic talisman dangled from heaven by God. No! The Bible is a wonderful collection of stories from an ancient people. But it is a human book. And if we are to feel its full power, we must understand that its humanity, with all of its flaws and mistakes, is part of the story."

A muffled sound issued from Kit's throat. Aunt Freddy turned, a scolding look on her face. She put a finger to her mouth and uttered, "Shh!" Even Delia shook her head as if to reprimand Kit.

Kit pursed her lips hard, as if a torrent of words were being held back by a dam. *Steady . . .*

"There is great liberation in this, you know," Lazarus said, stepping to the side of the podium. "It is as if we have emerged from a thousand years of fog, to see with enlightened eyes. All great movements in history have been met with the sort of reactionary feeling we are witnessing today. But the forward movement of progress cannot be stopped by such as these! The truth will always prevail!"

Kit looked around at the faces of the women, all of them seemingly enthralled by the handsome, honey-toned minister. *If he is telling us this,* the faces seemed to say, *then it must be true.* She felt herself wanting to stand.

Don't do it, she said to herself.

Aunt Freddy, as if sensing Kit's agitation, turned with another look of rebuke. *What are you doing?* she seemed to say. *Do you want to cause a scandal?*

Kit forced a smile, but the result only made Aunt Freddy look more concerned.

"The Bible, we must all admit, is not going to solve our problems for us—as if we can wave it around and invoke its words like chants. We must grow up and face the problems of this world with the brains that we have been given, with the knowledge that has come to us through enlightenment, and use the Bible as a wonderful book of reflections and principles that we can, on occasion, seek for our edification."

"No!"

Kit was as shocked to hear her own voice and looked sheepishly at the scowling faces that surrounded her.

The dam had burst, and Kit stood up, even as Aunt Freddy squeaked, "Oh dear!"

Delia stared at Kit in wide-eyed wonder, scarcely seeming to know whether to comment or merely watch as the drama unfolded.

Voices began to chatter like angry hens.

Eulalie Pike's voice rose above all the other clucks. "Young woman! How dare you interrupt Dr. Lazarus!"

Seeming only momentarily nonplused, Lazarus said, "Mrs. Pike, I am sure this young woman is merely venting an understandable emotion. I understand. Part of the . . ." He stopped. "Do I know you?"

"We have met," Kit said.

"Sit down!" Aunt Freddy ordered, but Kit was already walking past their table toward the front. Other voices echoed Aunt Freddy's demand.

"Ah yes," said Lazarus, his face darkening. "Now I remember. Miss, will you allow me to continue?"

"Yes, yes," voices said. "Sit down!"

Kit looked quickly at Aunt Freddy. She seemed ready to faint. Well, Kit was here—in the middle of the storm. She addressed the women. "I apologize to you and to the speaker for my outburst. By all means, let Dr. Lazarus continue. But I will not stay and listen to this poppycock any longer."

A collective gasp rose from the assemblage, as if a gas were being released from a giant balloon.

"Young woman!" Lazarus snapped. "You are obviously not prepared to listen to the truth!"

"I am, but not as a captive audience. If you would like to debate this issue, however, I challenge you to do that."

Lazarus looked surprised. "You wish to debate *me* on the issue of biblical scholarship?"

What am I doing? Kit asked herself, but there was no backing down now. "Yes," Kit said.

That seemed to please the minister. "If you insist, but I must warn you I shall not be gentle with you simply because you are a woman."

Kit opened and closed her fists. "You may reach me at the law office of Kathleen Shannon on First Street." She turned and walked out of the lovely garden, which was now deathly quiet.

Chapter 11

TED FOX GRUMBLED as he tightened the wing brace on the model plane. It was not out of frustration with the model itself, for that was coming along nicely. The problem was that he kept thinking about Kit Shannon.

"What're ya mumbling fer?" Gus asked. In his greasy overalls, the skinny Gus Willingham looked like a connecting rod in a gas-powered engine. In fact, the gas engine for the full-scale model aeroplane was his baby. Gus hailed from Detroit, where he had worked on automobiles.

They were in the "barn" Ted had constructed on the bluff over-looking Santa Monica beach. His mother had bought this piece of land—all sand and dirt and not much else—from that swindler Heath Sloate. It had passed to Ted when she died in December and had turned out to be good for one thing: as a place for his work-shop.

"Ah, I just want the thing to fly," Ted said in answer to his assistant.

Gus spit on the floor. "That ain't it. It's that girl."

"Gus, do you mind?"

"The girl?"

"Spitting on the floor."

"No, don't mind at all." He spit again. "What I do mind is all the time ya spend moonin' after her when she's turned you down."

"She hasn't turned me down. Officially."

"Unofficially, then. And yer better off. You need to keep yer mind on the flyin'."

Ted stepped back from the model and took a long look. It had a twenty-foot wingspan, the wings themselves made of willow ribs and silk. The two propellers were also made of silk stretched across a wooden frame. It had a rudder and a forward facing "elevator," and an engine housing at the front. That was the key.

Up until the last few years, powered flight was only a dream because the power had to come from steam engines. But steam engines required boilers, which made the engines much too heavy to use on delicate flying machines. Some inventors had tried to come up with lighter weight steam engines, but they in turn did not generate enough power to make anything fly.

Ted had designed, and Gus had helped to build, a gas-powered engine that was compact yet powerful. Whether it could power a plane was a question yet to be answered.

But Ted's questions about Kit Shannon kept running through his mind. Gus was right. He'd better keep his thoughts on his business, because someday he would be sitting in the cockpit of an aeroplane trying to do what men only dreamed of before—fly like the birds.

Why had she turned him down? Why? Ted threw his wrench on the ground. It came within an inch of Gus's toe.

"Hey!" Gus said.

"Come on," Ted said. "Let's see if this thing can get off the ground."

Gus opened the big doors and let in the brilliant afternoon sunshine. He and Ted then carried the grooved, wooden launching track outside and set it on the ground. There was only a slight wind, coming from the west.

Once the track was in place and braced, Ted and Gus each took hold of one wing and brought the model to the track, setting the launching wheels in the groove.

"It's beautiful," Ted said.

"That it is," Gus agreed.

"Then what are we waiting for?"

As Ted held the model in place by holding a wing, Gus went to the engine and fired it up. With a bang and a puff of smoke, the gas engine began churning, and the twin propellers started to spin.

This was it. Gus ran back to the other wing and waited.

"Not yet," Ted said. He felt the vibration of the engine in the sinews of the wing. But did he feel pull? "Steady... steady... now!"

As one, Gus and Ted pushed the tiny plane down the track, four feet above the ground, until it reached the end.

They let it go.

With breath held in check, Ted watched his dream take off. It stayed airborne and steady for about ten feet, then suddenly the nose dipped and the plane crashed into some scrub bushes.

"No!" Gus cried.

The pair ran to the downed model. The engine still chugged, but, like a dying man's last gasps, it made no difference. Both propellers were cracked, and the elevator was almost completely detached.

The two men stood silent over the ruin for a moment before Ted said, "It flew, didn't it?"

Gus scratched his head. "Couldn't tell fer sure. Did she glide, or did the power take her?"

That was the question, and Ted could not answer it. But inside he felt a heaviness that told him he was a long way from proving a gas-powered plane could fly.

He heard the crunch of footsteps behind him and whirled around.

"Kit!"

She stood as if she were appearing from thin air, but a carriage in the distance explained how she had gotten there.

"It looked wonderful," she said. "Did it survive?"

Ted shrugged. "We'll have to assess the damage."

Gus grunted at Ted's side. He did not look pleased to have a guest here. "Gus," Ted said, "this is Kit Shannon."

"I figured," Gus said, then he turned his back and trudged to the barn.

"He's a little surly," Ted said. "What are you doing here?"

"I owe you an apology for rushing off yesterday."

Ted looked into her green eyes, dazzling in the afternoon sun. She had always been beautiful to him, but never more than at this moment. "Was there trouble?"

Kit nodded. "The brother of my dearest friend was arrested. I am taking the case."

"Another case?"

"Not just another, I'm afraid. This one is going to be ugly."

"Why?"

"Because the city will hate my client. And probably me."

Suddenly Ted had his hands on Kit's shoulders. "Why do you do this, Kit?"

"I must," she said simply.

"It doesn't change the way I feel about you," Ted said. "Nor the fact that I want you to marry me."

The sound of ocean waves came between them, carried on a stiff breeze. Ted sensed a sudden coolness in the air.

Kit looked down. "I can't," she said.

Ted took his hands away. "Why?"

Raising her head to look at him, Kit said, "I heard a man speak today. A minister. What he said I could not bear. I'm afraid I made a bit of a scene in front of my aunt and the most important women in Los Angeles."

"What does that have to do with me? With us?"

"Only this. I cannot compromise in my beliefs. If I did, I know it would lead to unhappiness. For both of us."

"Why don't you put it simply, Kit? You don't love me." He stared into her eyes. "Is that it? Because if it is, tell me."

Kit looked away from him, silent.

"I want you to tell me," he said.

"Please don't make this harder on me than it already is."

"You do love me!"

"Don't, Ted!" she said quickly, and then turned and began to run to her carriage. Ted took a step toward her but stopped. If there was one thing he knew about Kit Shannon, it was that when her mind was made up only heaven could move it, and even then it would be a struggle.

Kit turned the carriage around and was off down the road.

Gus appeared at Ted's elbow. "Good riddance," he said.

Ted grabbed his collar, "How would you like a mouth full of broken teeth?"

―――――

At home Kit packed quickly. It was a task accomplished through a haze of tears. How she hated to hurt Ted. And Aunt

Freddy. And Corazón, too, because she was moving out.

Was she just a curse to everyone she held dear?

Where was Corazón anyway? There had been no sign of her when Kit had arrived home. Perhaps she was at the farmers' market. She sometimes went there on Saturdays for Aunt Freddy.

She heard the big front door slam. Aunt Freddy was home. Kit's heart already feared and mourned the loss of their closeness. Not that she wouldn't see her aunt on occasion—that was, if Freddy would allow it after what had happened. But Kit longed to make their relationship a good one. She had hoped, prayed really, that they might be close. Now all hope of that seemed to dangle by the tiniest of threads.

Well, time to get this over with, Kit thought. She suspected her great aunt would be seeking relief from the day's events with a nip from the brandy bottle in the library. The austere, dark-paneled walls seemed the perfect setting for their meeting. Kit struggled to think of just the right words to say, for the last thing she wanted to do was cause further pain to her aunt.

"Hello, Aunt Freddy," Kit said quietly as she entered.

Freddy, her hand already raising a glass to her lips, paused. "Oh, why do you do these things?" Without waiting for an answer, Freddy took the shot of brandy fully into her throat.

"I am sorry I caused you concern today," Kit said.

"Mortification!" Freddy corrected.

"Try to understand me, Aunt Freddy."

"I cannot understand," she said, pouring another glass.

Kit went to her and put her hand on her aunt's arm. "Don't drink," she said. "It's not good for your health."

The old woman paused for a moment, then put the glass down on the mahogany table. She then sat heavily in a chair. "Oh, Kit. I had such dreams for you. Even after you insisted on being a lawyer.

I thought at least you might find your place in society. But after today . . ."

Kit sat on a footstool and took Aunt Freddy's hands in her own. "I know how important all of that is to you. But you have to understand that it isn't to me. I don't care to have the approval of all the right people."

Aunt Freddy's eyes flashed wide. "How can you say such a thing! If you are not approved of by the right people—why, you are finished!"

"I am concerned only with the approval of God, Aunt Freddy."

"God!"

"Yes, and what happened today was because of that. I felt I had to speak up for God."

"And just who are you to speak for God?"

The question brought her up short. Who indeed? Only one who loved the Lord and the Word, as her father had. Was that enough?

"I want you to know that I love you, Aunt Freddy." She looked at her aunt, and when Frederica began to cry, Kit felt tears of her own. "It is just better for us to have our own worlds right now. But I hope I will always be welcome here."

Aunt Freddy sniffed. "Of course, my dear." She held out her arms, and Kit fell into them. They embraced for a long time.

"May I come and see Corazón anytime I wish?" Kit said. She felt Aunt Freddy stiffen. "What is it?" she asked.

"I should have told you, I suppose," Aunt Freddy said.

"Tell me what?"

"I had to let her go."

The shock hit Kit like a wave. "But, Aunt Freddy—"

"It was for the best, child. With that awful business with her brother, I couldn't very well have her stay here."

"But where will she go? Where is she now?"

"I have no idea."

Kit stood up, shaken. "I must go to her," she said. "I'll have Julio take my things to the hotel."

"Oh, dear," Aunt Freddy said. "Everything has become such a mess, hasn't it?"

Chapter 12

CHIEF DEPUTY DISTRICT ATTORNEY Judd
Ashe was relatively young for his high office. Most of the senior
deputies were longtime veterans of the courtrooms. Ashe, at thirty-
seven, had risen through the ranks of prosecutors first by establish-
ing himself in San Diego, then by being called to Los Angeles personally by District Attorney John Davenport. Davenport wanted
Ashe for one main purpose—to win the cases the office needed to
win.

Ashe had proven more than equal to the task. He had won all
of his cases with only one exception, a robbery case where the defendant had hired Earl Rogers. That loss was a stinging one, and
Ashe was aching for the day when he would face off against Rogers
again.

This morning, though, Davenport had called him into his office to reach a joint decision on where his courtroom prowess
would best be served.

Davenport, a dapper man in his early fifties, considered himself a master politician. He liked the machinations of his office as much as the day-to-day battles of the courtroom. He also enjoyed selecting the right lawyers in the office for particular cases. Like a chess master, he loved to move pieces and formulate strategy.

"I'm nervous, Judd," he said, "I don't mind telling you. We have two cases that are like powder kegs, and the newspapers are holding the matches."

Ashe nodded. "Now that Darrow is coming in to defend Sloate, we know that will be front-page news."

"Precisely. You ever seen him?"

"No."

"I have. And he is everything they say he is. The only other lawyer nearly that good is Rogers."

"A name I hate."

"Me too, Judd. But back to the case. Are you ready to do battle with the likes of Darrow?"

Ashe did not hesitate. "Of course," he said. He viewed Darrow as merely another giant to be felled in what would be his own legal legend.

"But that is not all we have to be concerned with. I'm even more worried about this rape case."

"That's a solid conviction. We have a confession, don't we?"

"That's part of what concerns me. The cop was heavy-handed. That may not play well to a jury."

Ashe shook his head. "That won't matter. He's Mexican. The jury will assume he probably deserved it."

Davenport put his fingertips together and thought for a moment. "Perhaps. But if something should go wrong, this city will be in an uproar. We could have riots in the streets, from Sonoratown to Bunker Hill. And I can only imagine what Otis will do to us in the *Times*. He will be crying for blood. Ours."

"There is always a chance of that."

"Only if this case goes to trial. That's where you come in, Judd."

"How?"

"You can try to force a plea of guilty before trial. Use all your powers of persuasion and the evidence we have to convince the defendant's counsel that it will behoove all of us to get this thing settled quickly."

"And do we know who the defendant's counsel is?"

Davenport hesitated before answering. "Kit Shannon."

That brought a broad smile to Ashe's lips. "Imagine that."

"Don't underestimate her, Judd. Heath Sloate did that and look at him now."

No, he would not underestimate her. But Judd Ashe knew there was no way on God's earth he could not convince a woman posing as a lawyer that she was out of her element, especially in a case as one-sided as this.

There was one other aspect to this that came to Ashe's mind. If, for some reason, Shannon would not listen to reason, there would be a very public trial. Shannon was associated in the minds of the citizens with Earl Rogers. He was her former employer and still her friend. A public defeat would put not only her but, in a way, Rogers himself in their places. It would show them that the District Attorney's Office was back in control of the criminal justice system in Los Angeles.

"So what is your preference, Judd?" Davenport asked. "Do you want to put your full attention into preparing for Darrow? Or do you want to concentrate on the rape case?"

Ashe did not hesitate in his answer. "The latter."

"May I ask why?"

"Certainly. Darrow would be a great challenge, but Shannon

will be around for a long time. Let's break her now, while she's still green."

————

Kit Shannon placed her father's Bible on the counsel table. The federal courtroom was larger than what she thought it might be, but it was still a courtroom. And she had pledged to always have the Bible with her in courts of law.

Since she had read Blackstone's *Commentaries* at St. Catherine's, Kit knew that Anglo-Saxon law was derived from the principles of God's written revelation. She wanted the original lawbook with her at all times.

Roderick Bellows seemed singularly unimpressed with this display. He hardly gave Kit a glance as they took their positions to argue before the federal judge.

The regal judge, one Laidlaw Matlock, sat at his post like some potentate. Federal judges were appointed by the executive branch and held their seats unless death, incompetence, or impeachment intervened. Judge Matlock looked very much alive and competent.

But was he impartial? Kit could not read him. He had bushy gray eyebrows over serious, dark eyes. The courtroom—empty for this hearing, save for the two attorneys, the judge, his clerk, and a stenographer—seemed like a forbidding cave, with danger all around.

"In this matter of Wong Shi," said the judge, staring at the two attorneys, "we are here on a writ filed by the defense. That would be you, Miss Shannon?"

"Yes, Your Honor," Kit said.

He regarded her for a moment. "You are a member of the bar?"

Kit swallowed. "Yes, Your Honor."

"Remarkable," the judge muttered. Then he looked at the opposing lawyer. "Good morning to you, Mr. Bellows," the judge said.

"Judge Matlock," Bellows said, nodding.

They knew each other! This was a serious disadvantage. Knowing a judge personally was almost as good as having a winning argument.

"Miss Shannon," said the judge, "you are asking this court to issue an injunction against the government's proposed action for deportation of this Miss Wong Shi. In other words, to stop the United States government in one of its official duties. That's a very serious thing."

"Yes, Your Honor," Kit said. Agreeing with him at this point seemed like a very good idea.

"A writ of this kind is only issued under extraordinary circumstances."

"This is an extraordinary circumstance," Kit said. "It is about where my client will live her life."

The judge nodded, pursed his lips, and turned to Bellows. "What is the government's response?"

"Your Honor," the attorney began, "as you know, our office has been given the duty to oversee problems of immigration in this city, especially when those problems enter the area of vice. We are given wide discretion to make such decisions. We have made a decision in this case, Your Honor. The subject, Wong Shi, was brought here for the purpose of engaging in prostitution and has been so engaged since she came here. She must be deported. It is as simple as that."

Judge Matlock blinked, then looked at Kit. "Miss Shannon?"

"Your Honor," Kit began, "we deny the allegation made by the government. Wong Shi is not a prostitute. She is a poor working girl trying to get along in her new home."

"We have evidence that she *is* a prostitute," Bellows said.

"Evidence we are not being allowed to confront," Kit said. "That is our fundamental right under the Constitution."

"Which only protects United States citizens," Bellows said.

Kit could not believe it. He was making the same argument to the court as he had to her, even after she had shown him it was wrong! Was this what the federal government meant by justice?

"All right, all right," the judge said. "Let me see if I have the essence of this. Miss Shannon is arguing that the Constitutional right to confront and cross-examine applies. Mr. Bellows is arguing that it does not. If it does not, that's the end of it. The government may proceed against Wong Shi. Now, have I got that right?"

It seemed to Kit that Roderick Bellows had a smug look on this face when he answered, "That is exactly right, Your Honor."

Kit could only agree. That really was the center of her argument. If it failed, Wong Shi would be returning to China.

For the longest minute Kit had ever experienced the judge was deep in thought. Finally he looked at Roderick Bellows and said, "It seems to me the right to confront the witnesses against you is basic."

Looking surprised, Bellows quickly said, "Not in this type of a case."

"Why does the type of case matter?" asked the judge.

Bellows looked as if the wind had been knocked out of him.

"Miss Shannon," the judge said, "is that a Bible on your table?"

"Yes, Your Honor," Kit said, surprised.

"Would you be so kind as to bring it to me?"

Kit complied, wondering what this could possibly mean. The judge opened the Bible and began leafing through the pages. "Well-worn and well-marked," he muttered.

"It was my father's," Kit said.

"Truly?"

"He was a preacher."

"Well, that's grand."

From behind, Roderick Bellows' desperate voice said, "Your Honor! If I may ask what is—"

"I'm getting to it, Mr. Bellows," said the judge. "Here it is. The book of Proverbs, chapter twenty-four, verse twenty-eight. 'Be not a witness against thy neighbour without cause; and deceive not with thy lips.'" He looked up at Bellows. "If that principle is good enough for the Lord God, it's good enough for the United States of America."

In stunned silence, Bellows looked at the judge.

"Now," said Judge Matlock, "I am inclined to grant the injunction Miss Shannon is requesting. If you would like to present this court with evidence to support your position, you may do so on Thursday morning."

"But, Your Honor—" Bellows said.

"And if the evidence is not forthcoming, your actions against Wong Shi will cease. This matter is put over until Thursday at ten o'clock."

"But—"

The judge banged his gavel, cutting off any further words from Roderick Bellows. Then, with a smile, he handed Kit's Bible back to her. "You be prepared, too, Miss Shannon," he said.

She nodded and took the Bible, and silently thanked God that His Word had not returned void.

Chapter 13

BACK AT HER OFFICE, Kit began compiling a list of witnesses to be interviewed for Juan's case. She was interrupted by a knock at the door.

It was Earl Rogers. Kit was happy to see her former boss. They had not spoken in weeks, and she had some questions for him.

He came in, dressed sharply as always. His vested suit was white, and his deep blue tie was held in place with a diamond pin. Kit marveled again that the best trial lawyer in the world was just down the hall from her and considered her a peer.

He carried a newspaper in one hand. "You have been a busy little bee, haven't you?"

Kit looked at him quizzically. "What do you mean?"

Rogers held the newspaper up and read: " 'The monthly meeting of the Los Angeles Women's Club took an unexpected and rude turn on Saturday, upsetting many of society's most notable female members.' "

"Oh no." Kit put her head in her hands.

"You know," said Rogers, "the society columnist for the *Examiner* is really quite good."

"Don't joke, Earl. Just give me the rest of the obituary."

"Obituary?"

"Mine."

Rogers cleared his throat and continued. " 'Miss Kathleen Shannon, the attorney, was the guest of her great-aunt, Mrs. Frederica Fairbank of Angeleno Heights. The afternoon's speaker was Dr. Edward Lazarus of the Hill Street Methodist Church. Unfortunately, Miss Shannon proved her qualifications as a mouthpiece when she failed to keep her own politely closed.' "

Kit groaned. She could picture Aunt Freddy reading this right now, clutching her heart.

" 'Not content to enjoy the elegant luncheon, hosted by Mrs. Eulalie Pike at her Adams Street residence, Miss Shannon proceeded to challenge Dr. Lazarus to a debate on the subject of his lecture. Apparently, Miss Shannon has mistaken the study of law for the study of theology, the latter subject being the province of Dr. Lazarus, who holds a doctorate degree from Boston University.' "

"How much more is there?"

"Almost over," Rogers said. He read again: " 'If such a debate should occur, our advice to the sponsor is to hire a referee to keep Miss Shannon in her corner when it is not her turn.' "

He looked up. Kit felt hot and cold waves washing over her at the same time. She had been castigated before, but had never been held up to public ridicule. It was a new experience, and she wanted to find the nearest rock to crawl under.

"At least they spelled your name right," Rogers said. He sat on the corner of her desk. "I thought you should hear it from me first, because there is something you must not do."

"What might that be?"

"You must not let this interfere with your work. You are going to be called worse things than this while defending Juan Chavez."

She knew that to be true, but it did not diminish the immediate hurt and humiliation.

"I myself have collected a variety of epithets in my time," Rogers said. "And I expect many more in the course of my life. Don't ever let them get to you. You remember what it says in the Bible, don't you?"

Kit smiled slightly. Rogers' father, like her own, had been a minister. Even though Rogers did not retain the faith of his father, he honored his memory always. Kit held out the hope he would return to God someday. She prayed for him regularly.

"Tell me," she said.

" 'Blessed are ye, when men shall revile you, and persecute you, and shall say all manner of evil against you falsely, for my sake. Rejoice, and be exceeding glad: for great is your reward in heaven: for so persecuted they the prophets which were before you.' "

He had quoted from memory and, so far as Kit could tell, perfectly. Immediately a peaceful warmth came over her, as if a comforting and protective blanket had been placed around her shoulders.

"Thank you, Earl," she said.

"You know your name is going to be all over the papers once Chavez goes to trial."

Kit nodded.

"I have one question for you. Did you get paid up front?"

That was Earl Rogers' first rule for criminal defense. But of course Juan Chavez had no money to speak of, and she had not thought to ask for any. Sheepishly, she shook her head.

"What am I going to do with you?" Rogers said. "You'll never get rich defending people for nothing."

"I know," Kit said. "That's what everyone keeps telling me. But this is a special case. It's the brother of my best friend."

Rogers shook his head. "Ah, Kit, you may be too good for this world. Meantime, keep your wits about you. I have a feeling the District Attorney is going to pull out all his guns against you. If you feel the heat, come talk to me."

"I will. Thank you." She felt her gratitude deeply. God had placed this man in her life for a purpose.

Before leaving the office Rogers said, "Oh, and I thought you'd like to know."

Kit waited.

"I'm off the sauce. Haven't had a drop in a month."

"That's great news!" Kit replied. Rogers' bouts with the bottle were already legendary among the legal professionals of the city.

He nodded, and then he was out the door. But he had left the newspaper on Kit's desk. She picked it up again and read the society column. It seemed even worse the second time.

———————

Kit took the Temple Street trolley to Beaudry Avenue, then walked a block to Sisters Hospital. It was a quaint, peaceful-looking brick building surrounded by green and flowering grounds. Five years ago this was "out in the country." Now it was encircled by residences and graded streets.

Inside Kit was met at the front desk by a white-clad nurse. She was a large woman, expressionless as the brick exterior.

"My name is Kathleen Shannon," Kit said. "I am an attorney. I need some information."

The nurse cocked her head. "Did you say attorney?"

"Yes."

"But . . ."

Kit waited for her to say "you're a woman," but the nurse did not complete the thought.

"What information do you need?" the nurse asked.

"Who was on duty last Thursday evening when the patient Gloria Graham was brought in?"

The nurse paused, seemingly unsure what to do.

"The information is important, I assure you," said Kit.

A voice said, "What information?"

Kit turned to see a man walking toward her. He was tall, wore a white smock, and possessed an air of authority.

"Dr. Kenton," said the nurse, "this woman claims to be an attorney, and she wants—"

"She doesn't claim to be," the doctor said. "She is. Don't you read the newspapers?"

Kit felt a slight blush coming on. She hoped he wasn't referring to this morning's newspaper! If he was, he gave no indication. He turned to her and extended his hand warmly. "I am Dr. Jeffrey Kenton."

"Kathleen Shannon," she said.

"A pleasure. Welcome to Sisters Hospital. What is it you wanted to know?"

"A patient, Gloria Graham, was brought in last Thursday evening. I want to know who was on duty."

"Are you defending the attacker?"

"The alleged attacker," Kit corrected.

Dr. Kenton shook his head. "I don't envy you your task."

"May I have the information?" Kit did not want this to turn into an argument, but she was prepared to stand her ground if need be.

Amazingly, Dr. Kenton smiled. He was handsome in a cowboy sort of way, with rugged good looks that would have seemed at home on a horse on some open range. "Of course," he said. "I know that it is part of the legal process and that you will get the information eventually. I will help in any way I can. I attended to Miss Graham when she was admitted to the hospital. She needed immediate medical attention. We have a staff of forty here, and I was assisted by several nurses."

"Were you with the patient throughout the night and into the morning?"

"Not continually. Even doctors have to sleep." He smiled again with an easy charm that was not offensive.

"Did you talk to the policeman who brought her in, Officer Hanratty?"

For a quick moment Dr. Kenton looked surprised. "You have done good work already."

It sounded like a compliment, and Kit accepted it with a welcome heart. In view of what had been written about her in the paper, it was pleasant to hear something nice about her for a change. Dr. Kenton was becoming more interesting to her by the second.

"To answer your question," Dr. Kenton said, "yes, I spoke with Officer Hanratty."

"Can you tell me what he said?"

"He told me what Miss Graham's condition was when he found her."

"Anything else?"

"No, that was all I asked about. I had to attend to her immediately."

"Were you with her when Officer Hanratty questioned Miss Graham?"

Once more, Dr. Kenton looked amazed. "I was, yes. Did you question Officer Hanratty?"

"Not exactly." Kit shook her head. "He gave me the story himself, in no uncertain terms."

"That sounds like Big Ed Hanratty."

"You said you heard him question Miss Graham?"

"Of course. I wouldn't have allowed him to do so without me there."

Kit felt the next question sticking in her throat but managed to coax it out. "Did you hear Miss Graham identify her attacker?"

Slowly, and it seemed to Kit reluctantly, Dr. Kenton replied, "I heard her say, quite clearly, that it was Juan Chavez."

"I see." This was devastating news. Officer Hanratty, in her mind, was under a cloud of suspicion for the way he had beaten the confession out of Juan. That called into question his report that Gloria had identified Juan as her assailant. But now there was another witness to the statement, and he was an unbiased and respectable doctor.

"I'm sorry," Dr. Kenton said. He seemed to understand exactly what she was feeling.

"May I ask just one more question?"

"Of course."

"Did anyone else see Miss Graham while she was here?"

Dr. Kenton shook his head. "No."

"But you weren't here at the hospital, or with her, all the time."

"That's true," he said, "but as the attending physician, I would know. I make it my business to know everything about my patients."

Which is why he must be good at his profession, Kit thought. And also why he would make a strong witness for the prosecution.

"I can see this is not good news for you," Dr. Kenton ventured. "I'm sorry."

Kit nodded. "The law deals in facts, Dr. Kenton. We can't change them to suit our purposes."

"It is the same in medicine. I try to remember that all facts are ultimately the will of God."

"Yes," Kit said. "I believe that, too."

The doctor seemed pleased. "Do you? That's great!" He paused and smiled again, and Kit basked under its warmth. Then he said, "I know we have just met, but would it be too forward of me to ask for permission to call on you?"

Chapter 14

THE WESTMINSTER HOTEL for Women, at the bottom of Bunker Hill near Fourth Street, had been a fixture in Los Angeles since 1880. It was the pet project of Mrs. Daeida Wilcox, who believed the single women of the city needed a fortress of protection from the cattlemen and gamblers who were such an important part of the early economy. Under her watchful eye, the hotel prospered. It housed up to fifty young ladies at any given time. Its newest guest was Kit Shannon.

Kit's room on the fourth floor looked out on Third Street. From her window she could see the lower platform of Angels Flight. A million questions flooded Kit's mind. What had really happened there? What events had led to Gloria's beating and rape? Why had Gloria been out that night unescorted? If Juan were the one initiating the interest in Gloria, then why had he appeared so angry—so adamant that the interest was all on her part?

"He might just be saying that to remove suspicion from his

own inappropriate behavior," Kit reasoned aloud. "But then again, he might be telling the truth." And whether he was guilty or innocent of having an interest in Miss Graham, it certainly didn't mean that he was guilty of the rape. No, Kit was convinced he was telling her the truth where that matter was concerned.

A knock on her door brought her attention back to the moment. "Who is it?" she called, not at all expecting visitors.

"It is Corazón," her former maid replied.

Kit pulled open the door and smiled. "Corazón, I'm so happy to see you! I was afraid my note might not have reached you, and that you would not realize that I'd left Aunt Freddy's house."

"Oh, sí," Corazón said, her expression betraying her worry. "I get your note and come right away. I am, I think, feeling bad for you."

Kit ushered Corazón into the room and closed the door. "But why? You needn't feel bad for me because of this—" Kit waved her arm. "I had already determined that moving would be in my best interest, as well as Aunt Freddy's. If you believe that the situation with your brother has caused Aunt Freddy to drive me from her home, then rest assured, it isn't true."

Corazón seemed to relax a bit. "I feel glad that you say this. I no want to lose you as my friend."

Kit shook her head and smiled. "You could never lose me as a friend. You're the only real girl friend I have in all of Los Angeles."

"You will not have friends because of my brother." Corazón's statement was delivered without emotion, yet Kit knew the weight of the words tore at her friend's heart.

Putting an arm around Corazón's shoulders, Kit drew her to the small table and chairs that made up the sitting room of her suite. She pressed Corazón into a chair, then sat opposite her.

"You must understand, Corazón, I would lack friends and social standing whether I took your brother's case or not. I won't lie and say this situation won't get ugly, maybe even violent, but it isn't Juan's fault that I am without a collection of friends. I knew I wouldn't be seen as a popular woman when I sought to practice law. There are just some places women are not to venture, according to society, and the courtroom is one of those places.

"Do you suppose men who practice in those courtrooms want their own womenfolk catching word of my ventures? Can you imagine the chaos and conflict it might cause if the larger percentage of the female population rose up to educate themselves and work at something other than tending the home and their families?"

"But you say you want a family someday," Corazón replied.

"And I do," Kit answered enthusiastically. "I most assuredly want a husband and children—a home of my own. But I also know that God has called me to this mission, for this time and place. But even so, I am a threat to the neat and concise little world that the men of Los Angeles have built for themselves. I have, if you will, broken the rules of proper society by overstepping my bounds."

"But if you no step over, then Juan, he have no one to speak for him."

"I would like to believe that some more experienced lawyer would have come forward, but I am of the same mind as you. I don't think anyone would have cared. They would have made a pretense of due process, but it certainly wouldn't have been to Juan's benefit."

"I fear for him, Kit. I am much afraid no one will listen. We are Mexican, and to those who have my brother . . . that is nothing." Tears formed in her eyes as her voice caught.

"Well, you and Juan are something to me," Kit said. "I will do everything in my power to see that justice is served."

"You believe him . . . sí?"

Kit struggled with how to answer. On one hand, she felt confident of Corazón's belief in her brother's character, but on the other hand, she was his sister, and how else could she respond? Seeing the desperation in Corazón's eyes, Kit tried to speak honestly. "I am trying to see that justice is served and that your brother has a fair trial. I am trying to learn all the facts and see to it that Juan isn't condemned on a forced confession. I wish I could tell you something more encouraging, but we both know this won't be easy."

Corazón wiped her tears. "So much changes. You live here now. I do no work for Mrs. Fairbank."

"What will you do for a job?" Kit questioned.

"I do not know. I know how to clean and how to fix hair and be a help to ladies, but I no get job if I not give—how you say?—paper from Mrs. Fairbank."

"References?"

"Sí, references. I can no ask for this from Mrs. Fairbank."

"Well, I can vouch for you." Kit suddenly perked up. "Wait a moment. I saw a sign downstairs calling for domestic help. Would you be interested in working here?"

Corazón's moist eyes sparkled. "Oh, sí! We would then be close, I think."

"Then I shall speak to the management and see that you are considered for the position. I'll give a personal reference, and if they need more, I'll squeeze it out of Aunt Freddy." She smiled and reached out to touch Corazón's hand. "We are in this together."

This time, Corazón's tears seemed to be of gratitude. "I am of much thanks to you, Kit."

Kit nodded and patted Corazón's hand.

"Is Mr. Fox much angry that you do this for Juan?" Corazón asked.

Kit sat back, startled. "Why do you ask about Ted?"

"I know he love you much, but I worry this might make him to be unhappy with you."

"No, Ted isn't angry. In fact, he asked me to marry him."

"Truly? This is a good thing, no?"

"Yes and no," Kit said. "I was honored by his words, but his heart is far from God. He has no interest in the things that are most important to me. I don't think I realized how very difficult this could make things until Mrs. Pike's luncheon. I can't stand by and see God's Word misused, nor can I defend an attitude that would blatantly mock God." She sighed. "No, I do not see how I can marry Ted unless he feels the same love for God that I do."

It was Corazón's turn to reach out to Kit. She squeezed Kit's hand. "God has a plan, no?"

"Yes, I've no doubt about that. But sometimes it's hard to understand that plan. For instance, today I met a very nice gentleman—a doctor. He's the doctor, in fact, who cared for Gloria. He spoke to me with great respect and kindness. He's a Christian, and he's asked me to receive him as a caller."

"*Es verdad?* The men, they come to you like the flies to the horses, I think."

Kit laughed. "I hadn't thought of it that way."

"What will be your answer to this doctor?"

"I don't know," Kit said. "Perhaps I'll whinny."

Kit stepped out into the warm evening. She wanted to a take a walk with God.

Strolling outdoors and praying, thinking, felt good to her. She had started the practice months before, both as a way to get to know the city and to spend time with her Lord.

She needed that time tonight. Tomorrow would be the crucial preliminary hearing in the rape case against Juan Chavez. Kit knew that it would be a crowded event, covered in all the newspapers.

As she walked down Fourth Street toward Broadway, Kit noticed the streets were quieter than usual. Few pedestrians appeared. It was almost as if the citizens had shut themselves up in their lodgings, awaiting some good reason to come out. The preliminary hearing would be such a reason.

Dear God, give me wisdom tomorrow. Help me to see what I must.

Was Juan guilty as charged? He passionately denied it. Corazón denied it. Kit's heart denied it, too, but her head was telling her something different.

Kit took notice of the buildings that were becoming more familiar to her. The Trust Building on the corner of Fourth and Broadway was massive and imposing. It held both the Berlitz School of Language and the Fante School of Shorthand. Some of the girls at the Westminster took classes there.

Next to that was the Angelus Building, with its gaudy advertisements painted on the side. Even in the dim starlight Kit could make out the large eyeball with *Miss Mary Grafton, Occultist* underneath. Los Angeles was a city of spiritual quackery.

At Spring Street, Kit turned left. Ahead of her loomed the offices of the *Los Angeles Examiner*. She knew, without being able to see, what was painted on that wall. *Read by all classes of people, from capital to labor. News without prejudice. Fair, free, and fearless.*

Was it fair what the society reporter had written about her? Kit wondered bitterly. And was it fair that Tom Phelps would turn a blind eye to what the police did to her client?

Lord, you have called me here! I can't fight these battles alone. Send people to help me, Father, who are as committed to you as I long to be.

She thought of Ted then. He was not committed to faith of any kind, except in himself. Yet that faith was strong, so strong it had come between them. She had been right to call off any thoughts of marriage. It could not be, though she loved him. Only two hearts that were one in Christ should covenant in marriage. If only Ted were—

Kit heard a sound behind her, like the clicking of boots. Instinctively she turned. And saw nothing.

Had something fallen? There was nothing apparent. The street was empty. But she had an immediate feeling that she was not alone.

She walked a little more briskly now and realized she was heading for her office. It was a haven of sorts for her, and she thought she might go there to pray in quiet.

The clicking again. Kit whirled.

Again, nothing.

Her throat tightened. Even though this was the "nice" section of town, she couldn't help remembering that not too long ago a killer stalked vulnerable women on the streets of this city. If it happened once, perhaps it could happen again.

Click.

It was coming from around the corner, echoing off the buildings.

Clack.

It grew louder, closer. Instinctively Kit took a step backward. For some reason she felt this sound was coming at her, that someone *knew* she was alone.

She felt the cold exterior of the *Examiner* building. And then she saw it. A horse, *clip-clopping* on the street. But who was the horseman?

Kit peered at the figure atop it and saw he had a large rounded hat. A policeman!

Her relief was instantaneous, and she scolded herself for being so silly. She realized her hand was on her throat.

"Are you all right, miss?" the policeman said. "I saw you walking alone."

"Quite all right, officer. Thank you."

"On your way home, are you?"

"I was out for a stroll."

"Well, then, you might want to just keep walking." His tone was sharp, and then Kit realized why. A young, unescorted woman on the street! That was not a normal sight unless the woman was engaged in the world's oldest profession.

A jolt of anger hit Kit, but she was controlled as she said, "I am on my way to my office."

"Office?" The policeman sounded dubious. "What sort of office?"

"Law."

She could not see his face in the darkness, but she sensed it had grown dark itself.

"Is your name Shannon?" the officer said.

"It is."

"Well, I'll be," he said, not hiding the mockery in his voice. "Then I'll leave you with a word of advice. Don't walk alone at night. It might not be healthy." With that, he turned the horse around and rode off.

Kit did not hesitate in accelerating her own pace. She walked the final two blocks to her office in quick order.

With her master key she unlocked the front door of the building, then took the stairs to her office and let herself in. Even in the darkness she felt a sense of relief. She felt her way to her desk and retrieved a match, then lit the desk lamp. She took a moment to catch her breath, then noticed an envelope on the floor.

Someone must have slipped it under her door. She picked it up and saw that the envelope was blank. She opened it, took out the folded page, and returned to her desk to read it.

It was typewritten:

```
You will not proceed further in the case of
the man Chavez. You are a meddler. I take
care of meddlers. I will take care of you
unless you back away. Believe me.
```

Kit could hardly breathe. Questions pummeled her.

Who?

And how?

In a locked building?

How long ago?

Why?

She heard a scraping noise outside her door. She looked up. It stopped.

Someone was there. She didn't dare make a sound. The silence hung heavy in the air.

Then a knock. Someone at her door!

She remembered Earl Rogers telling her she ought to get a gun. Since she would be dealing with the criminal element in the city, times just like this should be expected. She had not taken his advice. She didn't like guns. But now she wished she had one. The warning note, someone outside the door . . . it was all danger.

Another knock. Kit doused her lamp. She could not escape out her window. She was on the second floor.

Then a familiar voice said, "Kit?"

It was Bill Jory, Rogers' investigator.

Sweet relief washed over her. Bumping a chair on the way, she ran to the door and flung it open.

"Oh, Bill!" She enfolded him in a big hug.

"Nice to see you, too, Kit," he said with a laugh. "I saw the light under the door and—"

"See me home, will you, Bill?"

"Home?"

"Please, just see me home."

———————

Kit was pleased to find Corazón waiting for her in the lobby. She needed the comfort of her friend just now. And Corazón had the best antidote for the ills of the day.

"Please to read me from the Bible?" Corazón said.

They had done so several times before. It helped Corazón with her English lessons. At the same time, it fed her hunger to know the Bible. Teaching Scripture helped Kit, as well. It felt as if she were carrying on a family tradition. She had learned the Word of God from both her father and her mother. It was good to pass along her knowledge.

They went to Kit's room and sat on the bed together. Kit took her father's Bible from her briefcase and opened it on her lap. "What shall we read?"

"About Jesus." Corazón's pronunciation rendered the name *Hay-soos.*

"Ah," Kit said. "A very good choice." She thought a moment about what gospel she might read from. Leafing through the pages gently, she paused now and then to read some of her father's notes.

She came to the fourth chapter of John. "Here," she said. She remembered this chapter well. She had heard her father preach it at least three times. It was one of his favorites.

Kit began to read. " 'Then cometh he to a city of Samaria, which is called Sychar, near to the parcel of ground that Jacob gave to his son Joseph.' "

Corazón frowned. "I try to understand."

"You will," said Kit. " 'Now Jacob's well was there. Jesus therefore, being wearied with his journey, sat thus on the well: and it was about the sixth hour.' "

"Ah," said Corazón. "He is tired?"

"Yes," said Kit. "Even our Lord got tired sometimes. 'There cometh a woman of Samaria to draw water: Jesus saith unto her, Give me to drink. (For his disciples were gone away unto the city to buy meat.) Then saith the woman of Samaria unto him, How is it that thou, being a Jew, askest drink of me, which am a woman of Samaria? For the Jews have no dealings with the Samaritans.' "

"Explain, please," said Corazón.

"Yes," said Kit. The words of her father's sermons came to her as clear as if he were speaking to them in the room. "You see, in those days the Samaritans were hated by the Jews. They were considered dogs. No, worse than dogs."

Corazón's eyes were thoughtful. Kit realized then what she should have realized from the start. Corazón was a Samaritan. So was Juan. In the eyes of most of the powerful, the Mexicans were dogs. Or worse.

"What did the Lord say to the woman?" Corazón asked.

Kit looked at the Bible again. " 'Jesus answered and said unto her, If thou knewest the gift of God, and who it is that saith to thee, Give me to drink; thou wouldest have asked of him, and he would have given thee living water.' "

"Alive water?" said Corazón.

"Listen: 'The woman saith unto him, Sir, thou hast nothing to draw with, and the well is deep: from whence then hast thou that living water? Art thou greater than our father Jacob, which gave us the well, and drank thereof himself, and his children, and his cattle? Jesus answered and said unto her, Whosoever drinketh of this water shall thirst again: But whosoever drinketh of the water that I shall give him shall never thirst; but the water that I shall give him shall be in him a well of water springing up into everlasting life.' "

"Eternal?" said Corazón.

"Yes," said Kit. "Forever. For always."

"Ah. Is beautiful."

Kit put her arm around Corazón, and they remained locked in an embrace for a while. Then Corazón said, "What is to become of Juan?"

"We shall do all we can."

"Will God make him free?"

It was a question purely from the heart, as a child might ask a parent. Kit remembered when she was very young and befriended a scraggly dog. He was a mongrel, and no one claimed him. Kit did not know where he lived. But she would sneak him food and pet him.

One day she went out from her home into a nearby field and found the dog dead. She never knew if it had died or been killed. It did not matter to her. In tears she asked her mother if God could bring the dog back. If she prayed hard enough, would God do this?

She did not understand her mother's answer then. There were some things God would just not do. Not because He could not, but because it would not be best for us. Kit could not think of any reason it would not be best to bring the dog back to life.

Corazón's voice had that same, girlish desperation Kit had once known. God could do anything. Surely He would make Juan free. Corazón wanted Kit to assure her.

"God will do justice," Kit said firmly. "Our God will do justice. Juan will be set free. I know it." She was surprised at how firmly she said it.

"May I stay with you this night?" Corazón said. "I am not wanting to be alone."

"Of course," Kit said, pulling her closer. "We'll be like school-girls."

"Sí, like the schoolgirls." Corazón laughed. "Read to me more from the Bible, sí? And then we pray for Juan."

"Yes," said Kit. "We pray for Juan."

Chapter 15

TED FOX LOOKED at the document but saw nothing but clustering characters, like gnats swarming. *Snap out of it, man!* he told himself. *There are other women in the world!*

But not like Kit Shannon, a voice answered.

He was about to argue with himself once again when Alfred Mungerley entered his office. "Good morning, Fox," he said.

"Good morning, sir," Ted replied. He was surprised. The president of the bank did not often make personal calls.

"How are you getting on with Mr. Taylor?"

He was referring to the document on his desk. All Ted knew so far was that it bore the name Taylor.

"I'm just getting to it, sir," Ted said.

"Time enough for that." Mungerley sat and pulled out a cigar, lighted it, and said, "You know there's a commotion over at the courthouse this morning."

"Commotion?"

"Your Miss Shannon and her new client."

Ted folded his arms. "The trial starts today?"

"Only the first hearing, from what I understand. It's a nasty business, I don't mind telling you."

Nodding, Ted waited for the man to reach his point.

"I thought you two would have been engaged by now," Mungerley said.

Ted cleared his throat. "She has refused me."

Alfred Mungerley let out a stream of cigar smoke. "That can't be."

"It is."

"Turned you down? How could she?"

"She's a woman of deep faith. I have to respect her for that."

Mungerley uttered a grunt. "That may be. But I was hoping you would help me with a little item concerning Miss Shannon."

"What is that, sir?"

"I care about her aunt a great deal. This whole business about my girl and her gardener, and now with her own niece defending him—poor Freddy is not taking it well. Do you think you might be able to convince Miss Shannon to drop the case?"

"I don't think so, sir," Ted said. "Not if I know Kit Shannon. Once she's made a commitment to a client, there's no changing her mind."

"You sound like a man who is still in love."

Ted was speechless in agreement. Yes, he was in love—and he did not want to be! Not with that tempestuous Irish . . . lawyer!

"You are still on speaking terms with her?" Mungerley said.

"I think I am."

"Good. You can do me a great favor by keeping an eye on her. Let me know from time to time how she's getting along. Perhaps I can soften the blow for Freddy. Be a peacemaker of sorts."

"That's good of you, sir, but—"

"Mark my words," Alfred Mungerley said as he stood up. "She'll wake up and come around to you yet. Don't give up, boy. That's not the American spirit!"

———

Kit heard the angry shouts when she was a block away from the courthouse.

"Lynch him!"

"String up the Mex!"

"Hangin's too good for 'im!"

Corazón gripped Kit's arm in fear. Kit patted her friend's hand as they hurried toward the courthouse steps. An inflamed mob milled about the street, with police officers trying to keep them in some sort of order.

This was terrible. It was only the preliminary hearing and already the ugly face of vengeance was shouting for Juan's blood. Kit helped Corazón up the stairs.

Suddenly a bull-like policeman put a hand on Kit's shoulder, stopping her. "Where you going?"

"I'm an attorney," Kit said.

The cop glared at her. For a moment she wondered if this was the same policeman from last night. He looked at Corazón. "Where does she think she's goin'?"

"She's with me," said Kit.

"Not a good day for a Mex to be out."

"Stand aside!" Kit ordered.

"I know you," the cop said, but he removed his hand and let her pass.

The interior of the courthouse was teeming with people. Kit saw Corazón's eyes watering. "Don't worry," she said to her friend. "Just do as I say."

Corazón nodded and squeezed Kit's arm.

The courtroom of Judge Samuel Hollins Pardue was full. Kit recognized several members of the press, including Tom Phelps, who looked at her as she came in and then averted his eyes. Kit told Corazón to wait in the back and walked to the railing.

She was greeted there by Judd Ashe.

"Good morning, Miss Shannon," he said, holding open the swinging gate for her. His politeness seemed forced. Kit knew Ashe by sight, but they had not spoken until this moment.

Kit thanked him and placed her briefcase underneath the table for the defense. Ashe followed her there.

"I thought perhaps we might talk before the hearing," Ashe said. "An awful lot of time and trouble can be spared the people of California if your client would plead guilty and take a sentence of five years."

The man got right to the point. "I am inclined to move forward with the preliminary hearing," Kit answered.

"I won't be putting on my strongest evidence," Ashe warned.

"Be that as it may."

"Believe me when I tell you that the evidence of guilt is over-whelming."

Kit did not want to believe him, but she could find no reason not to. Still, the injustice of what Hanratty did to Juan burned within her. She had to do something about it, but what?

Ashe said, "Did you happen to see the crowd outside?"

With a slight shiver Kit said, "Of course."

"Then you understand how dangerous a situation this is. If this goes forward to trial and the evidence comes in and is splashed all over the newspapers, we could have a bloodbath on our hands."

True, Kit thought. *Sadly, terribly true.*

"Now all we have to do to avoid that is have your client admit what he did. You know we have a full confession anyway. Why prolong the agony?"

Something in Ashe's voice struck her like cold steel. He wasn't requesting, he was demanding, a guilty plea. He had some reason beyond the desire to avoid a trial. Even beyond, she sensed, his expressed concern for the city. Whatever it was, it was a vulnerability. Could that be an indication that the case against Juan was not, in fact, as strong as everyone supposed?

She remembered the warning note she had received last night. Another consideration. If Juan pleaded guilty it would be over. She would have no reason to fear.

Immediately another thought came to her, clear as if her own father were whispering it to her. *God hath not given us the spirit of fear.*

"My client has the right to a preliminary hearing," Kit said. "We will proceed."

Ashe shook his head. "I will crush you, Miss Shannon."

A sudden, unrestrained stream of passion coursed through Kit, and she could not hold back her words. "That would bring no honor to you, Mr. Ashe. It would bring shame on you and your office."

"I am sure I don't know what you are talking about."

"More's the pity, sir. The canons of ethics call upon the prosecutor's office to seek justice, not to win cases or crush opposing lawyers. You represent the people of California, Mr. Ashe, but more than that, you are supposed to represent the highest ideals of law and justice."

"I do not need a lecture on ethics from you, Miss Shannon."

"I beg to differ," she said sharply. Ashe's face flushed slightly, and his jaw muscles twitched. He made no further comment. He turned his back and returned to his counsel table.

A brown-uniformed deputy sheriff came through a side door, leading a shackled Juan Chavez into the courtroom. Immediately a murmur arose from the assembled people. It had an angry sound to it. Juan's eyes, still darkened from the beating, looked like those of a terrified animal.

The deputy practically threw Juan into a chair.

"Unshackle him!" Kit demanded.

The deputy, a squat man with a bulbous nose, looked incredulous. "I don't take my orders from you," he snapped.

"This man is in a court of law, not a jail cell."

"I don't care if he's in hell," the deputy said. He walked away.

A roaring heat erupted inside Kit. For some reason she turned and directed her stare at Tom Phelps, sitting in the first row. This time he did not look away. Kit would not allow it. She told him with her eyes that this was the type of justice his silence was allowing to continue.

Judge Pardue entered the courtroom as his clerk ordered everyone to stand and announced that court was in session. Kit studied the judge's face. It was rather thin and without hair, giving the judge a youthful look. But his eyes were keenly intelligent and his manner sharp. "The People of the State of California against Juan Chavez," he said without pause. "Is the prosecutor ready?"

"Yes, Your Honor," Ashe said.

"Defense?"

"Yes, Your Honor," said Kit.

"Proceed."

"Your Honor?" Kit said, standing.

Judge Pardue looked surprised at the interruption. "What is it, counsel?"

"I have two requests, Your Honor, before we begin. First, I would ask that the shackles be removed from my client. He is here as an accused with the presumption of innocence. He should not be treated like a convicted criminal."

"Does the prosecutor object?"

Ashe stood now and seemed to be formulating an answer as he

did. "We . . . think the prisoner may be dangerous."

Kit shot him a look. "On what evidence?"

"Your Honor," Ashe said, ignoring Kit. "It is quite well known that the temperament of these people is quite volatile. There is no reason this court should take a chance."

"That is an outrageous assertion!" Kit said. "Mr. Chavez is a man, not a temperament! He deserves to be treated as anyone would be in court."

"All right, now," Judge Pardue said. He seemed to study Juan for a moment. Then he looked to the deputy sheriff who had brought him in, standing against the side wall. "Deputy," he said, "take the shackles off him."

Both the deputy and Ashe looked stunned. The deputy didn't move.

"Well, do it," said the judge. "This man does not look like he is going to cause you any trouble you cannot handle."

When the deputy finally came to Juan, the judge said to Kit, "But I will not hesitate to order him bound again if he causes any trouble. Is that clear?"

"Yes, Your Honor," said Kit.

"You had another request?"

"Your Honor, my client speaks only a little English. I would ask the court's permission to have an interpreter present with me at counsel table."

Ashe said, "He doesn't need to understand everything that goes on," he said. "Only you do, Your Honor."

"Miss Shannon, you want this court to halt the proceedings in order to find an interpreter?"

"If I may refer the court to section 1884 of the Code of Civil Procedure, which holds the evidence rules for criminal trials as well, it states that 'when a witness does not understand and speak the English language, an interpreter must be sworn to interpret for him.' The word is 'must,' Your Honor."

The judge looked at Kit. "I am familiar with the code," he said dryly.

"There need be no delay," Kit replied. "I have an interpreter ready right now." She turned and motioned to Corazón. She came to the rail quickly. "This is the sister of my client," Kit said. "She speaks both languages. I would ask the court to allow her to interpret."

"We must object," Ashe said.

"On what ground?" Kit said.

"We know nothing about her, Your Honor. She may be a congenital liar."

Kit whirled on him. "Is it part of your temperament to degrade everyone with different colored skin?"

The comment seemed to stun Ashe, as if he were struck with a fist. Kit heard voices in the background and saw the press men vigorously scribbling notes.

"Miss Shannon," Judge Pardue said, "you will direct your comments to me and not the prosecutor. Is that understood?"

"I apologize, Your Honor. But if I may refer the prosecutor to section 1884 once again, it states that 'any person' who is a resident of the county may be summoned and sworn as an interpreter. It does not exclude relatives."

Judd Ashe was silent. The judge sighed and said, "All right. I see no reason why we can't swear in this woman like we would any other witness. Bring her forward."

Kit opened the gate for Corazón, who was shaking. Kit patted her arm. The clerk came forward with a Bible and administered the oath to Corazón. With visible relief, she sat next to her brother.

"Call your first witness," the judge ordered.

Chapter 16

"BIG" ED HANRATTY took the stand and was sworn in.

"Officer Hanratty," Judd Ashe said, "you are a policeman with the force here in Los Angeles?"

"Yes," said the cop, who was dressed today in a suit that ill fit him.

"What is your beat?"

"I walk Hill and Broadway, from First to Fifth."

"And were you on duty the night of March twenty-four of this year?"

"I was, yes, sir."

"What time was that?"

"I came on duty at nine at night."

"And did you have occasion to walk by Angels Flight that night, at around midnight?"

Kit said, "I object, Your Honor. Mr. Ashe is leading the witness, not letting him answer for himself."

Judge Pardue said, "This is just a preliminary hearing, Miss Shannon."

But the rules of evidence still applied, Kit knew. Why was the judge taking such a cavalier approach? Didn't anyone care about fairness here?

"My objection remains," said Kit. "I would like the officer to state his own testimony, not get it fed from the prosecutor."

Judd Ashe did not look pleased. But he waved his hand in the air and said, "Your Honor, this is not worth arguing about. I will change the form of my question."

"Go ahead," said Pardue.

"Tell me, Officer Hanratty, in your own words, what happened around midnight on the night of March twenty-four."

"I was walking my beat, as I told ya, and I was on Hill Street near Third, right by Angels Flight, when I heard a noise. It sounded like a woman's voice. And it sounded like she was in distress."

"Where did the sound come from?"

"From up on top of Bunker Hill."

"At the top of Angels Flight?"

"Yes, sir."

"What did you do next?"

"I took the stairs. As I got up toward the top, I heard the sound again. It was a shout for help. I kept going, and when I got there I found Miss Graham."

"What was her condition?"

"Very bad. She had blood on her face. She was almost unconscious. She had been beaten."

"Objection," Kit said. "Incompetent, irrelevant, and immaterial. This witness is not a medical doctor. He could not know how she was injured."

Judge Pardue nodded, and as he did Kit thought she detected

the smallest inkling of respect for her. It was not much, but she took some hope in it.

"I'll sustain the objection," said Pardue.

Judd Ashe almost stumbled backward in surprise. Quickly, he said, "We will not need that part of the testimony, Your Honor. We have something more devastating."

Looking a little impatient, Judge Pardue said, "Well, then why don't you present that right now and save us all time?"

Ashe nodded once and went to his table. He picked up a piece of paper and handed it to the witness.

"Officer Hanratty," said Ashe, "do you recognize that piece of paper?"

"Yes, I do," Hanratty answered. "It is my report on the interrogation of the defendant, Juan Chavez."

Something clicked in Kit's mind.

Ashe said, "Now, when you interrogated—"

"Excuse me, Your Honor," Kit said as she stood up. Ashe whirled on her, and the judge looked impatient.

"What is it, Miss Shannon?" said Judge Pardue.

She hoped she knew the answer. As she spoke, she pulled the evidence rules from her briefcase and riffled through the pages. "Your Honor, the prosecutor is giving the witness his own notes to refresh his recollection."

"Yes," said the judge. "Can we get on with it?"

Kit felt a surge of relief as she found the section. "If I may refer the court to the evidence rule in section 2047 of the code. It states that when a witness seeks to refresh his recollection from notes, 'the writing must be produced, and may be seen by the adverse party, who may, if he so chooses, cross-examine the witness upon it.' Your Honor, I wish to see those notes and cross-examine Officer Hanratty."

The stillness in the courtroom was as thick as a morning fog.

For a long moment it seemed like no one even moved lest a fragile silence be broken.

Judge Pardue looked at Kit. "Bring that to me."

She handed him the evidence code. The judge read the section slowly, thoughtfully. At her right hand Kit felt Judd Ashe tensing.

Finally the judge looked up. "That's what it says, Mr. Ashe. Allow Miss Shannon to look at the notes and question this witness."

"But, Your Honor!" Ashe said.

"Read it for yourself," said Judge Pardue, holding the book out to him. Ashe looked at the evidence code as if it were a dead animal, huffed, and shoved the notes toward Kit.

She took them, not knowing what she would find there. She prayed that it would be something.

The notes were two pages in a hand that was bold and, thankfully, easy to read. It detailed briefly the circumstances surrounding Juan's arrest and questioning, and his alleged confession.

"I will now cross-examine, Your Honor," said Kit.

"Proceed."

"Officer Hanratty, are these notes your own handwriting?" She showed the pages to him but would not let him take them.

Dismayed, Hanratty said, "Yes, those are my notes. Can I see 'em now?"

"Not yet. You wrote these notes to reflect the truth, the whole truth, isn't that right?"

"Of course." The big cop was starting to look hot under the collar. Clearly he had not been expecting to be grilled by Kit Shannon so early in the proceedings.

"So everything that is important to this investigation would be in this report, is that not true?"

"Yes, that is true."

Kit turned from the witness momentarily to consider what to

ask next. There were several avenues she could take. She wondered what would Earl Rogers would do. *"Cross-examination,"* he was fond of saying, *"is the greatest engine for truth ever discovered for use in a court of law."* Somehow, she had to get the judge to see what she knew about the big cop and Juan Chavez.

To the witness Kit said, "Officer Hanratty, you did not have an interpreter in the room when you questioned my client, did you?"

"I . . . I speak a little Mexican. Ya have to in this city."

"A little? Is that what you said?"

"Enough," Hanratty said sternly.

"Officer Hanratty, as far as my client is concerned, how can you know exactly what is enough?"

Corazón's whispered translation was audible to the courtroom as the policeman fumbled for an answer.

"Let's just say," Hanratty replied, "I know he understood what was going on."

"Did he tell you he understood?"

"Well, he looked like he did."

"You mean he looked frightened."

"He sure did."

Kit had not anticipated that Hanratty would so readily admit this. But now that he had, she pounced.

"If an innocent man is thrown into a cold room with a policeman known as 'Big Ed,' wouldn't you expect him to be frightened?"

The policeman's look betrayed his answer. He had not seen the trap coming. Everyone in the courtroom, Kit knew, could see how large the cop was—especially in his tight suit—and how small Juan looked in his simple jailhouse-issue clothes.

"It's not my job to make people feel comfortable," Ed Hanratty said.

Kit could hardly believe her ears. She only hoped the judge was hearing it the way she was.

"So you admit my client was frightened in your presence?"

"Nobody gets the better of Ed Hanratty."

Kit looked at the notes. Now came the most important series of questions of all. She took in a deep breath and said, "You write in here that my client, Juan Chavez, confessed to the attack on Gloria Graham."

"That's right." Hanratty suddenly looked more self-assured.

"What were his exact words?"

Hanratty scowled. "He said he did it."

"Officer Hanratty, I am asking you what his exact words were."

"Objection!" Ashe said. "Miss Shannon is badgering the witness!"

A sudden ripple of laughter swept through the courtroom. Ashe turned, his face becoming a pink scowl. Even Kit knew how absurd that must have sounded to the newspapermen. Little Kit Shannon badgering Big Ed Hanratty! She almost smiled herself.

Judge Pardue said, "Overruled."

"Answer the question," said Kit.

"When I asked him if he attacked Gloria Graham, he said, 'Sí.' "

"Can you show us in your report where you note that he said the word *sí*?"

Kit placed the pages on the railing of the witness box. Hanratty took up the pages and seemed desperate to find a notation that would save him.

"I didn't say that exactly," Hanratty said quietly. "I said he confessed. That's what I said, and it is right here." He held up one of the pages triumphantly.

"Those are your words in the report, then," Kit said adamantly.

"So? I was there."

"Unfortunately," Kit said, "we were not. All we have are your notes. Now, Officer Hanratty, do you recall that I came to see Juan Chavez while he was in your custody?"

"Yes, I remember that."

"You beat Juan Chavez severely, did you not?"

Hanratty stiffened but did not back down. "I had to," he said.

"Did you use your fists?"

"Yes, because—"

"Did you use anything else? A nightstick?"

"I didn't need anything else," he said, almost proudly.

Now Kit moved quickly. "So, Officer Hanratty, you dragged my client, Juan Chavez, into the police station, where he sat frightened and alone, without someone to interpret your questions or give answers, and you beat him until his face was bloodied and bruised, and then you claim he confessed. Is that right, Officer Hanratty?"

The big cop sniffed. "No, Miss Shannon. I had to hit him because he was like an animal. After he confessed, he attacked me! I had to beat him down."

As Kit pondered this sudden, new information, she heard a commotion behind her. Juan was standing by his chair, his face in agony. "No!" he shouted. "No, no, no!"

Judge Pardue banged his gavel. "Tell your client to sit down and be quiet."

Kit nodded to Corazón, who gently pushed her brother back in his chair. Kit glared at Hanratty with a burning sense of injustice. "Where does it say anything in your notes about Juan Chavez attacking you, Officer Hanratty?"

The cop shrugged. "I didn't see as I had to put it in there. I'm telling ya now."

It was time to address the court. "Your Honor," Kit began, "the rules for the admissions of confessions in court has come down to us from English common law, where it was stated that any confession forced into the mind by the flattery of hope or the torture of fear is inadmissible. Juan Chavez was tortured not only by fear, but by the fists of this man"—she pointed at Hanratty—"who literally beat a confession out of him if, and I emphasize this, we can believe him. The court is the sole judge of his credibility, which I hereby call into question. Your Honor, this confession is not voluntary or reliable. I would ask the court to suppress it as evidence in this case."

Judge Pardue looked over to Judd Ashe. "Your response?"

Ashe rose and walked to the center of the courtroom. His face conveyed desperate concern. "Your Honor, this is a preliminary hearing. We are not here to prove every aspect of our case. Only to give you enough information so you can order the defendant to trial. Miss Shannon has no proof for her allegation that Officer Hanratty beat a confession out of the defendant. It is all innuendo and speculation! Officer Hanratty has testified to the facts. He is a police officer. He swore to tell the truth. And he has, Your Honor."

The courtroom grew still as Judge Pardue sat back in his chair and looked, studiously, at the ceiling fan. Kit knew, as she guessed everyone in the room knew, that this was where the case might be decided. If the judge were to suppress the confession, the strongest evidence against Juan would not ever come before a jury. But if he ruled it admissible, through the notes of Officer Hanratty, it would be an almost insurmountable obstacle to overcome; the jury would be made up of twelve white citizens who were not likely to give the benefit of any doubt to Juan Chavez.

What would the judge do? Kit could almost hear that question ringing in the minds of everyone in the courtroom.

After what seemed like an eternity of waiting, Judge Samuel Hollins Pardue brought his gaze back to the attorneys. "It is true, as Miss Shannon asserts, that a confession of a crime must be freely given in order to be used as evidence against a defendant. This proceeding, however, is only to adduce probable cause against the defendant, not a finding of guilt. That is for a jury to decide. And that is where I am going to leave it. I am denying the defense motion to suppress this confession. The defense may, of course, seek to have the trial judge suppress it. Defense counsel may also argue the facts to the jury and let the jury decide. For my part, I am satisfied that there is enough information here to bind Juan Chavez over for trial."

He banged the gavel. It sounded like the harsh slam of a prison door. And then another sound arose, a desolate sobbing.

Corazón was weeping on her brother's shoulder.

Chapter 17

AUNT FREDDY'S HANDS trembled as she read the morning *Examiner*, her worst fears realized. The morning newspapers were an essential element to Aunt Freddy's routine. No one who wished to preserve—or better—her social standing in Los Angeles could afford to skip the society pages. And now Kit's name and likeness were all over the front page!

With a tiny yelp escaping her throat, Freddy peered at the huge drawing of Kit's face in the middle of the page. The artist had done his work well. Kit's penetrating eyes and even the flame of her hair seemed perfectly captured in black-and-white. And all around her, like ghostly heads floating about some medium's chamber, were the smaller faces of the men with whom Kit was somehow involved.

A large banner headline flew above Kit's portrait: THE WOMAN WHO HAS TAKEN A CITY BY STORM.

Storm! Freddy thought. *More like a hurricane leaving social destruction in its terrible wake!*

Freddy recognized the men who hovered around Kit, and she noted each name as she read the small paragraph that accompanied the renditions:

> *Dr. Edward Lazarus. One of our fair city's most respected ministers, his views on religion were publicly challenged by Miss Shannon. He, in turn, has challenged her to a debate.*
>
> *Heath Sloate. This once prominent member of the legal and social community of Los Angeles was bested by Miss Shannon in a murder trial. He now faces his own trial on several charges.*
>
> *Earl Rogers. The noted defense lawyer is Miss Shannon's sponsor and inspiration. Is it any wonder she uses courtroom tricks to sway the jury?*
>
> *Ted Fox. Scion of a prominent family, banker, adventurer. He was successfully defended by Miss Shannon in the Prostitute Murder case.*
>
> *Juan Chavez. Accused in the horrific attack on Gloria Graham, he is also being defended by Miss Shannon. Will the truth ever be known?*

The last item took Freddy's breath away. She felt faint. But the pressing need to know all of the horrid details kept her reading. A story written by Tom Phelps ran down the entire right column of the newspaper.

> *Kathleen "Kit" Shannon has become the eye of many storms since her arrival in Los Angeles last year. She is among the first women to be admitted to the bar in California and the first to try cases in court.*
>
> *Her aptitude as a trial advocate was amply demonstrated in her defense of Ted Fox on the charge of murder. Her opponent in that case, Heath W. Sloate, was no legal light. Not only did Miss Shannon prevail in that instance, she also brought Mr. Sloate into the courtroom as a defendant. His trial is now pending. He has retained the services of Clarence Darrow of Chicago.*

Of interest to many is what it is that drives Miss Shannon to defend criminals, even those as poor as Juan Chavez, defending the charge of rape.

The answer may be found in her devotion to God. Miss Shannon believes that she has been called to her profession. Indeed, she relies upon the Bible to guide her in her work almost as much as books of law.

This may explain Miss Shannon's zeal in confronting Dr. Edward Lazarus of the First Methodist Church on Saturday last. Dr. Lazarus represents the progressive school of Biblical studies, while Miss Shannon adheres to a traditional faith in the inspiration of the Scriptures. A public debate is being arranged, and it will, no doubt, prove most interesting and entertaining.

Less entertaining are the details of the crime allegedly committed by the man Miss Shannon is defending. Gloria Graham, a pretty, young domestic in the employ of Mr. Alfred Mungerley, was viciously attacked and violated last Thursday night. All evidence points to the guilt of the defendant, Juan Chavez, an itinerant laborer last in the employ of Mrs. Frederica Fairbank of Angeleno Heights.

Freddy stopped reading in order to still her heart. Oh, that her name should be included in the sordid details! She closed her eyes and hoped her heart would remain steady.

———

Ted Fox jumped off the trolley and furiously walked a block along First Street. It was a sunny day and the city's pedestrians were out in full force. The noontime crowd was out and about for luncheons and shopping. Ted noticed none of it, however. Each step he took was another reminder that Kit Shannon was making his life a mess.

He could not stop thinking about her! He almost had by yesterday, but then this morning he made the mistake of purchasing the *Los Angeles Examiner*.

It was Kit Shannon all over, and his own likeness, too!

He decided then he was not going to let her off the hook. She had told him that she would not consider marriage. Well, he did not have to take her at her word. Mr. Mungerley was right. She would come around and succumb to the American spirit—the spirit of Ted Fox.

That spirit included stopping at the florist on the corner of Broadway and First. He purchased a colorful bouquet and bounded across the street.

He paused in front of 238 W. First. On the second-floor window, on the Broadway side, he saw the lettering: KATHLEEN SHANNON, ATTORNEY-AT-LAW.

As he pulled his vest taut and his suit coat straight, the front doors of the building opened, and Kit Shannon walked out.

She was not alone.

Opening the door for her and emerging onto the steps was a tall dark-haired man of obvious breeding and charm. He took Kit's arm as they descended the steps together.

It was too late for Ted to move. Suddenly he was face-to-face with the couple.

Kit's face turned a deep shade of red. Ted couldn't bear to think what his own facial expression was. He stupidly held the flowers in front of him, like a beggar with a cup.

"Why, Ted," said Kit, barely above a whisper.

"Miss Shannon," Ted replied curtly. He looked at the stranger who was still holding her arm.

Quickly, Kit said, "Oh, may I introduce you to Dr. Jeffrey Kenton? Dr. Kenton, this is Mr. Ted Fox."

The doctor smiled and extended his hand. Ted switched the flowers to his left hand and shook.

Kit looked at the bouquet.

Ted looked at Kit looking at the bouquet. And then he noticed the doctor's quizzical expression.

"I just love flowers," Ted said to Dr. Kenton. "Don't you?"

Kenton's face grew more perplexed, but he said, "Why, certainly."

Ted touched the brim of his hat. "Well, it was jim-dandy bumping into you, Miss Shannon."

"Ted—"

"And a great pleasure to make your acquaintance, Doctor."

"Ted—"

"I wish you a wonderful afternoon of refreshment and . . . whatever else may come your way."

Ted turned and walked back toward Broadway. He did not hear Kit utter another word. Once around the corner he pounded down Broadway like a thundering herd. He didn't know if he felt anger or jealousy or disappointment or all of the above. The only thing he knew was that he was through with Kit Shannon.

He threw the flowers in the gutter and walked on.

———————

"Mr. Fox seemed rather surprised to see you," Jeffrey Kenton said.

Kit said nothing. They were sitting at a table in the restaurant of the Nadeau Hotel. "I do believe he had come to call on you," he added.

That much was obvious—as obvious as the hurt look on Ted's face when he walked away. Kit looked at the condensation forming on her water glass.

"If it is not too forward of me," said Dr. Kenton, "may I inquire into your relationship with Mr. Fox?"

"A professional and somewhat friendly one," Kit replied.

"Nothing more." As she said it, she felt her heart slip a little. But it was the truth, and she needed to face up to it.

"I hope you do not take offense, Miss Shannon. We doctors can't help prying into the facts."

"Like a lawyer," said Kit with a smile. She might have taken some slight offense from someone else, but not Dr. Jeffrey Kenton. She felt at ease in his presence.

"I am very glad you accepted my invitation," Dr. Kenton said. "I have been wanting to talk to you ever since you came by the hospital. Then, when I saw this morning's newspaper—"

"Oh, that newspaper!"

"It was a rather flattering portrait, Miss Shannon."

"But I don't want publicity," Kit said. "I want to do my work."

"This may bring you more work, Miss Shannon."

"It is an ill feeling knowing the eyes of an entire city are upon you."

"I cannot say that it is an unpleasant experience for my eyes." He smiled.

A waiter appeared at that moment with a basket of warm bread and a dish of *pâté de foie gras*. "Our specialty of the day," he said rather formally.

Dr. Kenton looked to Kit. "Something cold to offset the warmth of the day. How does that sound to you?"

"Marvelous," Kit replied, noting the sparkle in his eyes. He seemed so openly delighted to be sharing her company.

"The salmon is served on a bed of fresh romaine lettuce, with melon slices and strawberries," the waiter added.

"I think that sounds good for both of us," Kenton said nodding in approval. "And perhaps some iced tea."

When the waiter had gone, Dr. Kenton looked to Kit questioningly. "May I return thanks for our meal?"

"Oh, please do."

They bowed their heads, and Dr. Kenton said a blessing. As he did, Kit felt her heart warm. "Thank you," Kit said after the prayer. "That was nice."

"I was raised on a farm, and I learned that good things do come from God. My father taught me always to return thanks before eating a meal."

"Your father sounds like a fine man."

"He was. A lay pastor in a small church in Liberty, Indiana."

"My father was a preacher, too," Kit said. "He taught me to love God and drink deeply from the Bible."

Kenton nodded. "Your faith will help you in the practice of law, as it has helped me in the practice of medicine."

"How did you become a doctor?"

"It began with the care of the animals on the farm," Dr. Kenton said thoughtfully. "I was always fascinated with the cycle of life and death, birth and disease. I wanted to know why. As I grew up, I wanted to know why with people, too. I eventually went to Baltimore, Johns Hopkins, to study medicine."

"How did you end up in Los Angeles?" Kit asked.

"My fiancée's family was here."

Kit felt a slight jolt inside her but said nothing.

"She died," Kenton said.

"I am so sorry."

"It was several years ago." He paused, as if deep in remembrance but fighting not to let it darken the conversation.

"Dr. Kenton—"

"I would like it very much if you would call me Jeffrey."

"All right. I must tell you that you may be called as a witness for the prosecution."

"I know that," Kenton said. "I have told you the same thing I told them."

"Thank you. If I cross-examine you, I will not make it unpleasant."

Smiling, Kenton said, "For that, Miss Shannon, I am deeply relieved."

"Call me Kit."

Kenton nodded. His warmth and kindness were enveloping Kit, and she knew it. Might he be a gift from God? A man who not only shared her faith, but who was a professional man, someone who could understand what she was going through?

"Jeffrey, I just need to be very clear about two things, and then we will not speak of it again."

"Fair enough."

"Are you absolutely sure no one saw Gloria Graham in the hospital, outside of you, the medical personnel, and Officer Hanratty?"

"Absolutely sure."

"And are you absolutely sure that she gave the name Juan Chavez to Hanratty?"

"I heard it myself, as clear as a bell."

His answers were like spikes driven into her spirit. Even if she managed to get Juan's confession thrown out of court, this identification would seal his doom. The horns of a wicked dilemma impaled her further. She had pledged only to defend those she was convinced were innocent, but Juan clearly appeared guilty. On the other hand, this was the brother of her dearest friend, and Corazón was adamant that he was *not* guilty. How was she going to handle this?

Kit looked to the side and saw Earl Rogers approaching. A large man in a rumpled suit was with him.

"Hello, Kit!" Rogers said jauntily. "Fancy meeting you here."

"Earl Rogers," said Kit, "this is Dr. Jeffrey Kenton."

"Pleased to meet you." Rogers shook his hand and then looked at Kit. "And this is someone I want you to meet. May I present Mr. Clarence Darrow."

The rumpled man extended his hand to her. It was large and rough, like a laborer's. Darrow had deep creases in his face and unruly brown hair. He was, it seemed, the antithesis of the dapper Rogers. What they shared, however, was a mutual respect. They were twin giants of the courtroom.

"I am charmed, Miss Shannon," said Darrow in a deep, resonant voice that sang of the Midwest. "I very much wanted to meet you."

"Me?" Kit said with surprise.

"I am a frequent debater," Darrow said, "on subjects that interest me. One of them is religion, especially the topic of our English Bible. I understand that is a favorite topic of yours."

"Don't get her started," Rogers said. "She is not one of your rhubarb pushovers."

"We must discuss it sometime," said Darrow. "Perhaps publicly."

"I . . ."

"Come now, Miss Shannon, it would be fun."

Kit, aware that the other two men were saying nothing and apparently finding this good sport, said, "I am afraid I'm all booked up for such fun."

"You mean the debate referenced in the paper?" Darrow said. "I would like to join in. Perhaps you could find a second and we'll rent out the Morosco Theater. How would that be, Earl?"

Rogers said, "You would pack the place."

Kit was getting light-headed. "But—"

"Done!" Darrow bellowed. "Now let's eat. A pleasure meeting both of you."

And suddenly he was gone, a gleeful-looking Earl Rogers in his wake.

"My," said Kenton, "think of it. You on the stage against Clarence Darrow, defending the Bible!"

Kit put her hand on her forehead. "Yes, but that is *Clarence Darrow.*"

Jeffrey Kenton took Kit's hand. "Ah, but that's what the Israelites said about Goliath."

She did not feel very much like David, however. She felt, rather, like a lamb about to be slaughtered.

Then she realized she felt something else. A warmth that came from Jeffrey Kenton's hand ran up her arm through her entire body. It was a feeling she liked.

"You have the dinner with Dr. Kenton?" Corazón asked Kit later that evening.

Corazón had come upstairs after her shift at the hotel was complete. Kit was pleased that the manager had agreed to hire Corazón and give her a back room downstairs in which to live. It was almost as good as when they both lived with Aunt Freddy. Almost.

"Yes, it was very nice. He's a good man—a godly man." Kit began pulling the pins out of her hair and turned with a smile. "It makes all the difference in the world to share time with someone who feels about God as you do."

"Sí, they understand you."

"Yes," Kit agreed, letting the tangle of curls fall past her shoulders. "Like-minded is a good word. Maybe even like-hearted."

"Your heart is happy with Dr. Kenton, I think."

"The time I spent with him was very pleasant, indeed. I've agreed to take a picnic with him on Sunday after church."

Despite having worked all day, Corazón motioned for Kit to sit while she took up Kit's hairbrush and began brushing through the tangles. "I am glad you have fun. You need to spend more time not working so hard."

"But I love my work. I feel God's presence all around me when I strive to make rough places plain and crooked paths straight."

Corazón said nothing, and Kit realized she probably had stumped the girl with this Biblical analogy. She was too tired to strike into a conversation explaining herself and so instead spoke of the matter that had troubled her heart since earlier in the day.

"I'm afraid I hurt Mr. Fox's feelings," Kit said.

"How did you do this?"

"He arrived at my office just as Jeffrey and I were leaving. He had flowers." Kit could still see the hurt and anger in Ted's eyes. "I think he had come to see me and apologize, but there was nothing he could say. We can never be more than friends—at least not with his heart turned from God."

"He love you much."

"Yes, I know he does."

"I think you love him much, too," Corazón added, pausing in her brushing to look at Kit's face in the mirror.

Do I? Kit wondered.

Chapter 18

KIT'S HEAD WAS SWIMMING on her way to the federal courthouse. She had to concentrate on the Wong Shi case, but so much was happening all at once.

She had a load of investigating yet to do in Juan's case. That would occupy most of her time in the coming days and weeks. But the threatening note was still an unsolved mystery. Who had sent it? It could have been almost anyone in the city of Los Angeles, so high were the passions surrounding the case. Would the sender carry through on his threat?

And the *Examiner* had turned her into some circus sideshow. Her every public move was watched. In fact, sitting on the Main Street trolley, she felt dozens of surreptitious looks cast her way. Was this only her imagination? Or was she going to be on permanent exhibit?

Then there was this matter of debating with Lazarus and, perhaps, Clarence Darrow! How had that happened? From one spontaneous exchange she was now being thrust into, of all places, the Morosco Theater! Could she turn her back on the challenge?

To top everything off, Dr. Jeffrey Kenton had come into her life just as Ted Fox had walked out. Her heart still held a place for Ted, but her mind battled to close it up. Now Jeffrey had come into her life and with the one thing she craved most in a man—a strong, vibrant Christian faith. Surely God's hand was in this, wasn't it?

She tried to clear her mind as she alighted the trolley and walked to the courthouse. As she approached the steps she saw Wong Shi, surrounded by what seemed like members of her family. But she had no family in Los Angeles. Who were these people?

"My friends," Wong Shi explained. "Come to hold hand."

Kit smiled and nodded. "That's fine."

"You save me now?" Wong Shi asked.

Kit's throat tightened. She barely managed to say, "Let's go inside."

Roderick Bellows addressed Judge Matlock. "Your Honor, the government is ready to present its chief witness against the woman known as Wong Shi."

"You may proceed," Matlock said. He looked at Kit with sympathetic eyes, but Kit knew he was going to base his decision on what the witness had to say.

Who was this man who was walking toward the witness stand? He looked to be around sixty, small and grayish, with a puckered and severe expression on his face and a wisp of wizard's beard on his chin. He was sworn and gave his name as G. Austin Daugherty.

Kit looked at Wong Shi, sitting in the gallery. Kit asked with her eyes if Wong Shi recognized this man. Wong Shi's eyes were wide with fear.

Why? Kit couldn't ask now. Bellows was beginning his questioning.

"Mr. Daugherty," Bellows said, "what is your title?"

"I am the director of the League of Public Decency of Southern California."

"And how long have you held this position?"

"Nigh on seven years, sir." Daugherty answered with short, clipped words, as if he were taking bites out of the questions. Kit scribbled notes.

"What are the general duties of the League?"

"To bring decency and codes of civic conduct to our community. To root out seeds of corruption and disgorge them."

"And we are all appreciative of that, sir," Bellows added. Kit thought of objecting but did not. She sensed fairness in Judge Matlock. He would overlook embellishments.

"Now, then," said Bellows, "are you familiar with the petitioner in this case, one Wong Shi?"

Daugherty's face darkened. "I am."

"And how are you familiar with her?"

"I heard about what she was doing down there in Chinatown, which is, as you know, a den of all sorts of sin."

"I must object to that," Kit said. "Such a sweeping statement is a slur on all of the good people who live and work in the Chinese section of the city."

"I will disregard the statement," Judge Matlock said. "Mr. Daugherty, stick to the facts."

"Yes, sir," Daugherty said. "As I say, I heard a report about this woman and went to investigate. I found her. She spoke English quite well, and I began to talk with her."

"What was your purpose?"

"To save her from the error of her ways."

"What specifically was that?"

"Prostitution."

"Were you able to convince her?"

"Alas, no. When she did not feel obliged to take my advice, I registered an official complaint with your office."

"Thank you," Bellows said as he turned to Kit. "Your witness."

Kit stood and walked slowly toward the witness stand, questions forming in her mind. Something was missing here. What was it? She looked at the judge. What was he thinking? It would be quite simple for him to deny this petition and allow the government to do what it was so efficient at, deporting undesirable aliens.

That's when it hit her. The missing piece was Wong Shi herself. She was not another nameless, faceless blot. She was a human being. The judge had to see that.

Kit motioned for Wong Shi to come forward. She hesitated at first, the fear evident on her powdered face. Then, slowly, she stood and shuffled toward Kit.

"Your Honor," said Kit, "this is my client, Wong Shi. I would like her to sit at my counsel table while I question the witness."

Judge Matlock nodded. "Proceed."

Kit took Wong Shi's hand and guided her to a chair at the table. She patted her hand before returning to the witness.

"Mr. Daugherty," she said, "you say this child is a prostitute?"

Without any hesitation—or any look toward Wong Shi—Daugherty said, "She most certainly is!"

His attitude lit a flare inside Kit. "I advise you, sir, to be very careful what you say."

"I do not need advice on that," the witness responded. "I shall say the truth!"

"Then listen to my question," Kit shot back. "Do you know for a fact that Wong Shi is a prostitute?"

"I do indeed."

"If you know for a fact, then you must know it of your own personal knowledge."

"Of course I do. I would not say so otherwise."

"Mr. Daugherty, are you a married man?"

Daugherty opened his mouth, but words did not issue forth. Suddenly his cheeks reddened, forming angry blotches. "Don't you try to cast insinuations! I never did any such thing!"

"I only asked—"

"I know what you are trying to do!"

"I am seeking the truth, Mr. Daugherty! You said you knew Wong Shi was a prostitute of your own personal knowledge. I ask you, how can that be unless you employed her yourself?"

"Objection!" Bellows shouted.

"No, Mr. Bellows," said the judge. "I think the question should be answered."

Now Daugherty's face, in various places, showed purple. This was not a man used to having his own decency called into question. But twisting the truth was indecent. Kit bore in on him. "How do you know of your own personal knowledge?"

"Everybody in Chinatown knows."

"You said you had personal knowledge—"

"Her reputation is notorious."

"That, sir, is hearsay."

"It is not! It is the truth! Everybody knows it."

"Everybody knew the world was flat at one time," Kit said. "Now tell this court, under oath, the name of one man you know who can testify here for us that he consorted illegally with Wong Shi, thus making her a professional prostitute in defiance of the laws of the United States."

Dead silence. The very air seemed to be listening.

"I . . . don't recall," Daugherty said.

"One name!" Kit demanded.

"I can't remember."

"Your Honor!" Kit turned to Matlock. "This testimony is incompetent and irrelevant. This man has no personal knowledge of the charge. One can only speculate about the motives of this man and the government, but speculation is not evidence. Nor is hearsay. If I may quote Professor Greenleaf: 'In disputed issues one cannot depend on the mere assertion of anybody, however plausible, without scrutiny into its basis.' Your Honor, the assertions of the witness are without basis, and I ask the court to grant the petition."

Roderick Bellows looked pallid as he stood up. "Your Honor . . . the government wishes to rely upon this evidence, not to convict Wong Shi of a crime, but only to do what is in the best interests of the country. We must be given that opportunity."

Judge Matlock did not hesitate in his answer. "The government does what is in the best interests of the country when it follows the rule of law. The petition is granted, and the government is enjoined from taking any action against Wong Shi."

With a short bang of the gavel Matlock rose and stepped off the bench. Bellows' mouth dropped open, but it was too late to say anything else.

Wong Shi looked confused. Kit took her hand and said, "It is over. You can stay."

A smile—something Kit had never seen on the face of the young woman—broke across Wong Shi's face. A single tear meandered down her white cheek.

Wong Shi stood up and said, "To you I owe my life."

"You owe me nothing," Kit said

"But I must pay!"

"Go back to Chinatown, and be happy."

They were interrupted by Roderick Bellows. "I congratulate you, Miss Shannon," he said, "but let me assure you this won't happen again. I may have underestimated you this time. I shan't make the same mistake."

"It is the law you must never underestimate, Mr. Bellows."

Then Kit took Wong Shi by the arm and walked toward the courtroom door.

Chapter 19

GUS SHOOK HIS HEAD and said, "Yer nutty!"

"No," said Ted Fox. "Just in a hurry."

"You can't hurry this!"

Ted rubbed oil into the wooden propeller so hard it produced a series of incensed groans from the prop. "We have to hurry! The Wrights showed it could work with double wings. Somebody has to do it with one. That's us."

Gus, his greasy coveralls sagging on his thin frame, said, "We ain't done it small. What makes you think we can do it big?"

"Power." Ted nodded toward the three-cylinder Anzani engine on the far end of the table. It was a French design, originally used to boost power in "V" motorcycle engines. Ted was sure it would lift a monoplane.

"We got to test her first!" Gus insisted.

"That's what I'm going to do, isn't it?"

"Yer gonna end up face down in the sand!"

"I will make it work!"

"Not if you keep rubbin' the prop like that! There won't be no wood left!"

Ted threw down the rag and walked to the door of the barn. The sea air felt heavy and oppressive on his face.

"What's eatin' at you?" Gus said, coming alongside.

"Gus, what do you think about women?"

"I don't think about 'em at all. No profit in it."

"I think you're right."

"You have to fight 'em. That's why man was put on this earth."

"How do you fight them, Gus?"

"With my hat."

"Hat?"

"I grab it and run."

"And what do you think of doctors?"

Gus shrugged his shoulders. "Don't want to see 'em if I can help it."

"I don't trust them. They sneak around, looking for something to cut out of you."

"Well, yer in fine fettle today, my friend."

Ted kept looking out at the bluff, to the sea. "I'm through with women, Gus! And doctors! Through! Let's build this plane. Let's make history."

"I still think yer nutty," Gus said.

Kit stood at the top of Angels Flight and scanned the scene. Gloria Graham had been found near the fence. The pad was visible to at least three large homes. At random, Kit walked to the one east of Angels Flight.

The door was not answered by a butler, as one might expect on Bunker Hill, but by an old, frail-looking woman in a cloth robe.

She might have been a crone from some Grimm fairy tale.

"Yes?" said the woman in a creaking voice.

"Ma'am, my name is Kathleen Shannon."

"Are you from the Owl?"

"I beg your pardon?"

"Owl Drug Store! I called for tooth soap and violet breath tablets. Where are they?"

"No, ma'am, I'm not—"

"Then who are you? What do you want?"

"Are you the lady of the house?"

The crone looked Kit up and down. "If I'm not, who is? Come, come, why are you here?"

"I am a lawyer looking into the matter—"

"You're a woman!"

"Yes, I think so."

"A woman lawyer? Nonsense!"

"I assure you. I promise I won't take much of your time."

"I have nothing *but* time. All right. Come in."

The old woman swung the door open, and Kit was overpowered by the heavy scent of mothballs and old leaves. Kit had never smelled anything quite like this. It was like being in a decaying forest preserved for a museum. The only thing that seemed to be alive, apart from the woman, was a canary in a wicker cage that watched, silently, as Kit came in.

"You're an awfully pretty girl to be a lawyer," said the woman as she led Kit into a library. "Sit down," she ordered.

Kit complied. No servants appeared, as one would expect in a house like this. Kit wondered if this woman lived alone.

"I am Frances Sweet!" the old woman announced loudly. "That name used to mean something around here."

"I am sure it still does." Kit could not remember Aunt Freddy talking about a family named Sweet.

"Shows how much you know, young lady. Who are you, any-who?"

Warning bells went off in Kit's head. Even if this woman had information pertaining to the case, she would not be a reliable witness. The information itself might not be reliable. If she could not remember who Kit was a minute after introductions, what could she remember about the night in question?

"My name is Kathleen Shannon," Kit said patiently. "All I want to know is if you heard or saw anything unusual last Thursday night."

"Unusual?"

"Yes. Out of the ordinary."

"I know what unusual is! Don't be impertinent!"

"I'm sorry—"

"Some folks think we Bunker Hill people are above it all."

"I don't think—"

"We are! That's why we live here. Not down there with the rabble. If you want anything unusual, you go down there some-time. Where do you live, young woman?"

Kit cleared her throat. "Down there."

The old woman's eyes widened. "Are you being impertinent with me?"

"I assure you I'm not."

"What did you want to know, anywho?"

This would go nowhere. Kit could just see Frances Sweet in court on the witness stand, yelling at the judge that he was imper-tinent.

"Mrs. Sweet, I'm sorry to have bothered you," Kit said, stand-ing.

"Sit down!" the woman ordered. Her voice was so firm Kit complied immediately. "You want to know about the girl who was attacked, don't you?"

"Why, yes," said Kit, amazed.

A glint of friskiness flashed into the old woman's eyes. "Thought I forgot, didn't you?"

"I—"

"I know you did. Never mind. Folks always think that about me. I'm old, you know."

"I—"

"You don't need to say it! Doesn't mean my mind doesn't work still. I'm sharp as a razor, I hope to tell you."

"Mrs. Sweet—"

"Nothing gets by me. I see things. Look at this!" Frances Sweet picked up a sack that was lying on the floor near her feet. "Nothing gets by me."

Kit shook her head, confused.

The old woman stuck her hand in and pulled out a small, square tin. She held it up so Kit could read the red lettering: Heinzman's Freckle Salve.

"See that?" Mrs. Sweet said.

Kit nodded blankly.

"Empty," said Mrs. Sweet. "That tells me somebody with freckles has been walking around outside!"

The note of triumph in Mrs. Sweet's voice made Kit nod again, this time to humor her.

"And this!" The old woman reached into the sack and pulled out an old leaf. "What does that look like to you?"

"A leaf?" said Kit.

"Of course it's a leaf! But it's an *oak* leaf."

"I see."

"No, you don't!"

"I don't?"

"You don't see any oak trees outside my house, do you? No, there ain't an oak tree within a mile. Now, how did it get here?"

The wind? Kit wanted to suggest. But she was silent.

"I collect things, you see. Things I find on the ground. People think they can fool me, but they can't!"

"I am sure they cannot."

"And I see things. I have a window. I look out that window, and I see things."

"I am sure you do, Mrs. Sweet. Now, I don't want to take up more of your time—"

"You stay right where you are. I know why you came here, missy. The girl they found at Angels Flight was attacked by a Mexican. Right here! Almost outside my door!"

"Mrs. Sweet," Kit said, "did you see anyone that night? Out your window?"

"I always retire at precisely nine o'clock."

That would have been well before the attack took place. "Thank you, Mrs. Sweet," said Kit, getting to her feet once more.

"But I didn't that night," Mrs. Sweet added.

"You didn't—"

"Are you deaf? That was Thursday night. I had a visit from my ne'er-do-well son, asking me for money, as usual. Well, this time I wouldn't do it. No, sir. I told him he'd better get out and find work and quit his gambling. He's a gambler, I tell you."

"I see."

"I got very upset with him. He lost his father, you know. His father was a gambler, too. But I loved him." Frances Sweet sighed. "I couldn't sleep that night so I sat at my window—that's upstairs, you know—and I looked out of it for a long time."

"And what did you see?" Kit sank back into the chair, ears attuned.

Frances Sweet looked directly at her and shook her head. "Nothing, my dear. I did not see anything but Mr. Taylor on his way home."

The name jarred Kit. "Did you say Mr. Taylor?"

"Young woman, you *are* deaf. I distinctly said Mr. Taylor, Mr. Dayton Taylor. That awful man!"

"Where does he live?" Kit said.

"He is in the next house," Mrs. Sweet said, gesturing with her thumb. "I only wish he weren't. A more unpleasant neighbor I—"

"And you saw him from your window late on Thursday night?" Kit said excitedly.

"Don't you interrupt me, young woman!"

"I beg your pardon."

"That's better. Now you listen to me. I saw Mr. Taylor's carriage rattling along—it rattles, you know—and that bay horse of his that is the ugliest horse I ever did see."

Kit tried to be patient, but the news was almost overwhelming her. "Did you see Mr. Taylor in the carriage?"

"I didn't have to . . . what was your name again?"

"Kathleen."

"That's a pretty name."

"Thank you. Did you see—"

"I saw his carriage. That is all I saw. Did you say you were a lawyer?"

"Yes, ma'am. I—"

"Are you trying to stir up trouble?" Frances Sweet reached for a cane that was leaning against an end table. It had a large silver knob. She pounded the tip of the cane on the hardwood floor.

"Mrs. Sweet," Kit said, convinced now that the old woman's name was also her antithesis, "I only want the truth."

Now the woman was squinting at her, studying her. Then a light seemed to go off in the woman's head. "Are you defending that Mexican?"

Kit would not hide the truth. "Yes, Mrs. Sweet."

"Impertinent!" With the help of the cane, Frances Sweet stood up. "I don't want to talk to you any further!" She waggled the cane at Kit. "In my day they would have taken that Mexican to the nearest tree and strung him up! Why are you defending him?"

Kit tried to quell the anger within her. "Thank you for your time," she said.

"Did you hear me?" Mrs. Sweet demanded. "I asked you a question!"

Kit stopped and turned to the old woman. "Because he is a human being, Mrs. Sweet, just as you are."

The old woman's face reflected the shock of a lifetime. Suddenly she swung her cane at Kit, as if Kit were some vermin who had crawled out of a hole in the wall. Instinctively, Kit stepped backward as the cane swished in front of her. It whipped past and crashed into a vase on a table.

Shattered pieces exploded onto the floor. Frances Sweet, unbalanced from her attack, teetered and fell, hard.

"Mrs. Sweet!" Kit ran to the woman, who was moaning in obvious pain. Kit knelt by her side. "Are you hurt?"

Frances Sweet rolled onto her back, her face etched with distress. But she managed to open her mouth slightly and utter, "Impertinent."

"Don't try to move," Kit said. She reached for a pillow from the divan and placed it gently under Mrs. Sweet's head. The old woman did not protest.

"I know a doctor," Kit said. "I will have him come see you."

A slight change came into Mrs. Sweet's eyes, a softening. "Yes," she said. "A doctor."

"Have you a telephone?"

"By the staircase."

"Just lie still." Kit stood up and turned, taking one step before stopping cold.

Dayton Taylor stood in the doorway, a gun in his hand, the barrel pointed directly at Kit's chest.

Chapter 20

O'REILLY'S SALOON was a favorite watering hole for the policemen of Los Angeles. It was a particular favorite of Big Ed Hanratty, who made it almost a ritual to take his afternoon meal there—along with a hefty dose of beer—before going on duty. For him it was a place of good spirits and laughter before patrolling the netherworld.

Today, though, it was different. Hanratty was in a foul mood as he nursed a mug of beer at the end of the bar. He did not care to seek out companionship at the tables. He preferred to be alone.

He did not even look up when Harry Vaine took the stool next to him. And he only grunted when Vaine clapped him on the back and asked how he was.

"You look down in the mouth," Vaine said.

Hanratty didn't respond to the cop. He liked Vaine well enough. They had known each other for five years on the force. Harry Vaine was good for a story and a laugh. He was also highly educated, having graduated from a fancy eastern college.

"I know how you feel," Vaine said as he motioned for the bartender to bring him the same as Hanratty.

Now Big Ed looked at Vaine. "What do ya know, Harry?"

"About how you got worked over by a woman."

Hanratty knew how Vaine meant that. Jovially, with no offense
intended. But that was exactly what he was thinking about, and it
was not a jolly subject. Hanratty took a large portion of Vaine's
uniform in his meaty fist and pulled the cop toward him.

"So that's what ya think, is it?" Hanratty snarled.

"Hey, you lummox, let me go!"

"Then close your hole." Hanratty tossed Vaine backward like a
sack of potatoes.

"You don't have to be so unruly about it," Vaine said. "You're
acting positively barbaric."

"The harpy," Hanratty said, making the word come out in a
slow, dreadful incantation. "It ain't fitting for a woman to be allowed to ask questions of us on the witness stand! And just wait
until she bats them eyes of hers at the jury! They might let that
Mex go free, Harry!" Hanratty pounded his glass on the bar top,
spilling some of the suds.

"Easy there," said Vaine. "I am on your side, Big Ed."

"I'll have to go through the same thing in the trial! And then
she might bat them eyes at the judge. And then ya know what he
might do, Harry? Do ya know?"

"Do tell."

"He might throw that Mex's confession out of court!"

"No."

"Yeah! And then that little brownie might walk right out of
there a free man. I tell ya, I can't stand it."

Harry Vaine took a sip of the beer he had just been served.

"You know, that is a shame. It would be a crime against nature should that happen."

"Crime against what?"

Vaine slapped Hanratty on the back once more. "I'll explain it some other time, Big Ed. Right now we have to worry about a Mexican going free." Vaine paused and sipped his beer. "How would you like to kill the proverbial two birds with one stone?"

"Proverb . . ."

"Proverbial, you lummox. We can get the Mex and fix that woman's wagon at the same time."

Hanratty swiveled toward Vaine. "Meaning what?"

Vaine raised his eyebrows and spoke quietly. "Just suppose that Mex of hers were to bust out of jail?"

"Won't never happen," Hanratty said. "He's a scared rabbit."

"Rabbits run," said Vaine.

"I don't follow."

After a lingering drink, Vaine said, "We have not had good hunting around here for a long time."

Hanratty pondered this a moment, and then it dawned on him. A lowlife the world did not need would get what was coming to him. And the high and mighty Kit Shannon would get a lesson in the real meaning of justice.

Draining his glass, then wiping his mouth with the back of his immense hand, Big Ed Hanratty said, "Have another, Harry. On me."

———

Dayton Taylor's face was malevolent. For a long moment Kit wondered if he was actually intent on killing her.

Why would he be? And how long had he been standing there?

Mrs. Sweet groaned on the floor.

"I heard a noise, something crashing," Taylor said. He did not lower the gun.

"Mrs. Sweet is hurt," said Kit. "She needs a doctor."

"What are you doing here?" Taylor said.

"Put down that gun, sir."

"With what happened here the other night," Taylor explained, "you can't be too careful." He lingered with the gun for a moment, then slowly lowered it.

"I must use the telephone," Kit said. She rushed past Taylor, smelling his strong cologne, and found the telephone box on the wall. She lifted the earpiece and heard several clicks until the operator's voice queried her. Kit asked for Sisters Hospital and in a moment was connected. She got through to Jeffrey, who said he would come straight away.

As Kit turned from the telephone she saw Taylor, who said, "Now you'll tell me why you are here."

"Where are you?" Frances Sweet called from the sitting room. Kit ignored Taylor and returned to the fallen woman.

"I have a right to know," Taylor said, following.

Kit went to Mrs. Sweet.

"Is that Mr. Taylor?" the old woman asked.

"Yes," said Kit.

"Tell him to get his fanny out of my house."

Kit almost burst out laughing. But she composed herself and stood up. "Mrs. Sweet has asked that you please leave."

Taylor made no move to do so. "You're snooping around for that Mexican, aren't you?" He pointed at Frances Sweet. "What has she got to do with it?"

"I might ask you about your whereabouts last Thursday night."

Taylor's eyes burned. "You have the temerity to question me?"

"A young woman was attacked near your house, Mr. Taylor. Surely the police—"

"I don't have to tell you a thing!" Taylor said. "You are a blight on this community, all high and mighty! Why don't you get out?"

Kit became aware that Frances Sweet was pushing herself up into a sitting position. When Kit tried to help her, she waved her off and looked at Taylor.

"Dayton," Mrs. Sweet said, "*You* get out. Or I'll shoot you myself."

With a final glare Taylor said, "I won't forget this." He turned quickly and exited.

"Good riddance," Frances Sweet said. She reached out a bony hand and placed it gently on Kit's arm. "Will you stay with me?"

———

Kit thought Jeffrey Kenton must be the most wonderful doctor in the world. He was so gentle with Frances Sweet, even as she ordered him not to fuss about this or that, that he seemed to be handling precious china. He never stopped smiling or talking to the old woman in soft, calming tones.

Finally, Frances Sweet was comfortably set on the sofa, with pillows under her head and a blanket over her legs.

"Now, then," Kenton said, "you are not to do any dancing for at least a week."

A smile fought to appear on Mrs. Sweet's face. "You are an impertinent young man," she said. "But I like you. Don't know why, but I do."

"And I like you, Mrs. Sweet," Kenton said. "But not enough to live here. Who looks after you?"

"I can look after myself!"

"Of course you can."

"I have a woman who comes by most days," Mrs. Sweet admitted.

Kenton patted her hands. "That's fine. I'm going to send

around a nurse for the next day or two, just to check on you. All right?"

"I suppose," Mrs. Sweet said. She looked at Kit. "Will you come see me?"

"Do you really want me to?" Kit said.

"Such impertinence! Would not have asked otherwise."

Kit smiled. "All right, Mrs. Sweet."

Suddenly the old woman's eyes changed from hard crags to soft pools. "Thank you," she said.

After repeated reassurances from Frances Sweet that she would be perfectly fine, Kit and Dr. Kenton left. Dr. Kenton had a carriage waiting outside. He took Kit down Bunker Hill and back to her office on First Street.

"Thank you again for coming," Kit said.

"It was my pleasure," said Kenton. "You know, I never got to see your office the other day."

"It's nothing special," Kit said.

"I'll be the judge," Kenton said, jumping out of the carriage. He came around and helped Kit down. His grip was strong and sure. She felt she would feel confident under his care.

She gave him the grand tour of her office, which meant a wave of her hand at the four walls. She'd only recently begun her own collection of the California Reports, the appellate decisions that interpreted the laws of the state. Four paltry volumes lined a nearly empty bookshelf near the window.

"So this is what it looks like," Kenton said, nodding in approval.

"Then you approve?"

"More than approve, Kit."

She looked at him, wondering what he meant. As the sunlight streamed into the office he seemed more than a mere doctor. He was like some knight who went about answering the call of damsels in distress and healing the fallen with his touch.

Kit became a jumble of emotions in that moment, but she knew what she wanted. And as if she had sent out a message in clear, unambiguous words, Jeffrey Kenton crossed to her in three quick strides. She was suddenly in his arms, and as he lowered his face to hers, she felt herself falling into a dream. For a long, lingering moment in time she did not wish to wake up.

Chapter 21

Los Angeles Daily Times
Friday, April 1, 1904

A STUNNING CROSS-EXAMINATION
Defense Lawyer Darrow Exposes Weaknesses in
Prosecution's Star Witness. Sloate Conviction in Doubt

The courtroom of Judge David Lillick was the scene yesterday of a stunning cross-examination of Miss Elinor Wynn, chief witness against Heath Sloate in his felony trial. For two days the prosecution had labored over the foundation of its case and sought to complete the edifice with the testimony of Miss Wynn as its star witness. That structure may have come crashing to the ground, however, under the relentless hammer of the lawyer for the defense, Clarence Darrow.

Upon completion of direct examination by Deputy District Attorney C. C. McComas, Mr. Darrow rose to cross-examine. The Chicago lawyer is a lion of a man, whose voice and very presence command attention. It was no different on this occasion. The twelve veniremen in the jury box seemed to hold a collective breath.

Mr. Darrow began his questioning congenially, with all gentleness as befits the interrogation of the fair sex. Very early on, however, it became quite clear that the spider was gently prodding the fly into a web from which she could not escape.

At various points Miss Wynn seemed to become flustered, often contradicting in small detail her direct examination. Mr. McComas tried valiantly to help his witness by objecting to many of Mr. Darrow's questions, but Judge Lillick was not swayed. In fact, at one point he admonished McComas to keep his peace lest he hurt his voice with such frequent exercise.

From the gallery it appeared that the objections only served notice to the jury that Mr. Darrow was tearing a gaping hole in the tapestry of the prosecution's evidence. What emerged instead was the tattered picture of a once prominent but now confused young woman who was turning state's evidence in order to salvage what might be left of her ravaged reputation.

At the close of the nearly two-hour examination, it appeared to observers that the prospects of Heath Sloate's conviction had been dealt a mortal blow. So confident of this was Mr. Darrow that he announced the defense would call no witnesses, leaving it to the jury to decide if the prosecution's evidence met its burden of proving guilt beyond a reasonable doubt and to a moral certainty.

Closing arguments are scheduled for this morning at nine o'clock.

Kit put the paper down with a hollow feeling. That Heath Sloate might go free because a lawyer managed to confuse a single witness was despicable!

She sat at what had become her regular table at Garibaldi's Café on Spring Street. Here she would take her breakfast and scan the newspaper and prepare for her day. It was a regular place for some of the other lawyers in the city, too. A few of them had begun to greet her by name, as if she were a colleague and not a mere curiosity.

Earl Rogers came here regularly, and this morning was no different. He joined Kit by the window, holding his own copy of the *Times*.

"That Darrow," he said, "must surely be the second best lawyer in the entire world."

Kit made no attempt to hide her true feelings in a haze of small talk. "This is terrible news! You know what Sloate is."

Rogers motioned for one of the Garibaldi sons and ordered coffee. "Yes, but I also know Darrow. He is doing what he does best."

"Confusing witnesses?"

Rogers' blue eyes bore in on her. "Kit, you are a criminal defense lawyer. That is your job."

"No, Earl. My job is to seek the truth."

"No! That is not your job. Your job is to destroy the prosecution. In that way, you uphold the Constitution."

Kit closed her eyes a moment. "But I cannot bring myself to use my skills when I know it is contrary to the truth."

Rogers sighed heavily. "But the truth is for the jury to sort out, Kit. Every time you make the prosecution prove its case you protect others, those who might be railroaded because they did not have lawyers who cared to defend them."

Kit thought of Juan Chavez, perhaps guilty, but certainly not deserving of the treatment he was getting. Could she continue her defense of him even if she thought him guilty? When she had first come to Los Angeles, full of idealism about the law, justice seemed divided clearly into black and white. Now she knew there were shades of gray everywhere.

Oh God, she prayed in a way that had become familiar, *give me wisdom!*

As if sensing her struggle, Rogers reached out and patted her hand. "The truth is not something that falls in our laps, Kit. It has to be rooted out. Tell me, how is your defense of Juan Chavez coming along?"

"I have hit a wall," Kit said.

"There is a wall in every case, Kit. The lawyer's job is to find some dynamite."

"Where does one look?"

The waiter brought Earl Rogers his coffee, and the lawyer took a sip. "Have you been paid yet?"

"Next question, please."

"Have you interviewed the victim?"

"No. They have her holed up somewhere."

"Find her."

"How?"

"Detective."

Kit took a sip from her own cup of coffee. "I cannot afford to hire one," she said.

"Ah, Kit Shannon, will you ever learn? That is the reason you take the money up front, so you can pay to try the case! Filthy lucre is not a bad thing for the trial lawyer."

He was right, of course. She could not long afford to do this work for next to nothing. But that did not solve her immediate problem.

"It is a soft spot that I have in me heart for you, Miss Shannon," Rogers said in a theatrical Irish brogue. "There is a detective I know named Lassen. He owes me a favor. I will gladly allow you to cash in that favor. Call it a Christmas present."

"This is April, Earl."

"Never hurts to plan ahead. He is in the Bradbury Building.

Tell him I sent you and that if he finds the girl I'll send him a bottle of fine Irish whiskey."

Kit shook her head. "No whiskey, Earl. Send him some handkerchiefs instead."

"Done." The defense lawyer finished his coffee. "Want to come along?"

"Where?"

"To hear Darrow, of course. This chance does not come very often."

"I have already heard the great Earl Rogers," Kit said. "Why should I settle for less?"

His smile beamed light. "I knew there was a reason I liked you from the start. You are a woman of impeccable taste."

"Go," she said.

"I'm gone." He turned and walked out.

Kit finished her modest breakfast, then walked it off back to her office. As she approached it from the Broadway side, she noticed an older man standing on the sidewalk looking up at her building. When she was almost to him she was sure he was gazing into her window. She stopped, looked up, and saw a large, jagged hole in the glass. Where her name had once been, only shards stuck out like misshapen tusks.

Kit held her dress up, took the stairs two at a time, unlocked her office door, and burst in.

Bits of broken glass were strewn across the floor. In the middle of the spray was a brick, covered with paper tied up with a string.

Kit removed the paper and saw immediately it had a single line of typescript on it.

This is your last warning, Lawyer.

Kit was not surprised when the desk officer at police headquarters did not immediately respond to her request to see Detective McGinty. She asked a second time.

"He's busy," the officer said, gazing at his *Police Gazette* with a bored expression.

"Tell him it is Kathleen Shannon," she said.

"Who?"

The way he said it made Kit feel as if he knew who she was but did not feel it merited any attention.

"Officer," she said, "I am a citizen of Los Angeles with a formal criminal complaint. It is a complaint that Detective McGinty will be most interested in. If you get him now, I will not mention your obstinacy."

He frowned, then slammed the *Gazette* on his desk and glared at her. "Go on and find him yourself," he said, cocking his head toward the side door.

Kit did not hesitate. She entered the interior of police headquarters, finding herself in the smoky din of the city's law enforcement center.

She anticipated the hostile looks she received as she walked in, and for a moment she wondered if the genesis of the warning notes might be in this room. Why not? She knew from experience that many of the city's "finest" held a grudge against her. Some deeper than others.

And one who had a most compelling reason to hate her was walking toward her. Terrence O'Toole had been a chief witness in Ted's murder trial. Kit had raked him over hot coals in cross-examination, eliciting the fact that he had been drummed off the New York Police Department for taking protection money.

He stopped a few feet away from her and smirked. "Look what the breeze blew in," he said.

"Officer," Kit said curtly.

"Making the city safe for scum, are you?"

She did not care to be drawn into this conversation. She tried to look past him to see if McGinty was on the floor, but O'Toole moved to obscure her. "I asked you a question," he said.

"I am here to see Detective McGinty," Kit replied evenly. She was vaguely aware of others watching.

"I'll be seeing you again," O'Toole said. "And I'll be ready for you."

His malignant glare cut through her. It did not take much imagination for Kit to envision Terrence O'Toole on the other side of the law.

"All right, what's this?" McGinty's familiar gravelly voice boomed from the side.

O'Toole jerked his head at Kit. "Someone to see you," he said to McGinty. And with a final scowl at Kit, he walked away.

"You're getting to be a regular event around here," said McGinty. For once he did not have a cigar plugged in his mouth.

"Look at these," said Kit, producing the notes.

McGinty studied them a moment, then looked at Kit. "I warned you, didn't I? Didn't I say you were going to be hated in this town?"

"What do you intend to do about this?"

"Nothing."

"Nothing? Somebody has threatened me."

"It ain't a crime until somebody does something."

"Somebody did. Shattered my window. That's not only destruction of property, that's intimidation by force and threat. Someone wants to interfere with justice."

"Maybe somebody wants to see justice done."

"What do you mean by that, Detective?"

McGinty raised his eyebrows casually, as if this whole matter were a mere trifle. "The sooner your client gets what's coming to him, the better."

The silence in the room was like an echo of assent from everyone. Kit had the sudden feeling she was standing alone in a courtyard, surrounded by an enthusiastic firing squad.

"What about those notes?"

"We can't help you, Miss Shannon." He handed her the notes.

"You don't *want* to help," she said.

McGinty cleared his throat but said nothing.

"What kind of an officer of the law are you?"

"Now, hold on there—"

"You're a disgrace to the law!" And then, before turning her back on the room, she added, "That goes for the lot of you!"

Catcalls and insults followed her as she went for the door and burst out into the foyer. She did not give the desk officer so much as a glance. It suddenly seemed dark inside, and she longed to be in the sunshine.

She found it outside and paused a moment to catch her breath, feeling very alone. If the police would not help her in something like this, who would? If she was exempt from the protection of the law, who would protect her?

God.

The answer came into her head as sure as and clear as the bell of the trolley that passed by. She remembered what it said in the Book: *If God is for us, who can be against us?*

It was a promise held dear by all Christians down through the centuries.

And many, she suddenly thought, *who turned out to be martyrs.*

Chapter 22

JUAN CHAVEZ SHIVERED in his cell. The blanket they had given him was thin and did not keep off the cold. Juan loved the sun and the heat. He loved to spend lazy days in the Plaza when he could, sitting with his friends and talking about women.

He wanted a woman. To marry. To have his children. Never would he have done that terrible thing they said he had done! Why were they doing this to him?

He thought of his sister and her friend, the lawyer. Kit. She wanted to help him, he knew. But how could she? She was a woman, and the men were too strong. The policeman who beat him, how could she stand up to him?

How could she stand up to the crazy people calling for him to die?

He was not ready to die.

He was not as close to God as his sister was. Corazón visited him every day and prayed for him. She sometimes prayed without a rosary, which was strange. But she seemed to believe that God was listening to her, as if He were right there in the jail with them.

Someone in another cell screamed. Night was falling, and when that happened, it brought dark shadows inside the jail. At night there was no hope.

Juan closed his eyes and tried to talk to God the way his sister did. The words came slowly, and he felt a bit like a fool. But it was better than screaming.

Will there be justice for me? Juan asked. *Are you with such as us, mighty God?*

A creaking sound came from the end of the corridor, and a thin strip of light shot through the cells. Someone was coming.

Juan did not move from his cot. Whoever it was could not be interested in him.

Two sets of footfalls. Then they stopped in front of his cell. Two large, dark figures. Faceless.

"Get up, Chavez," said a familiar voice. It was the big policeman, the one who had beat him.

What was happening? There was jangling of keys. The other policeman unlocked the door to his cell.

"I said get up," the big one repeated.

Juan knew then he was going to die. They had come to kill him. Take him out and beat him until it was done.

O mighty God, where are you?

———

Kit could not sleep.

Something troubled her, but she could not give it a name. Perhaps it was merely her growing worry. Her immediate world was spinning rapidly, not merely with causes in the law but in matters of the heart.

Jeffrey Kenton was in her thoughts more insistently now. Here was a man who seemed almost too good to be true. He was handsome and thoughtful, gentle and sweet, and his kiss . . . well, his kiss was wonderful. The very memory of it sent a shiver of delight up Kit's spine. Yet something inside her held her back from freely letting go of her affections. *Fear,* she thought. This was uncharted territory for her, and she was alone.

But not fully alone. God was ever present. And that is why she rose from her bed, put on a robe and slippers, and took two books with her to the hotel parlor. It was comfortable there, with a good lamp for reading.

The embers of the evening's fire still glowed in the fireplace. They threw a dim reddish light into the immediate vicinity. Kit warmed herself for a moment, then lit the lamp before settling into a soft chair to read.

On her lap she had her father's Bible, a book she turned to daily and whenever the waters of her soul were troubled. The other book, the first volume of Blackstone's *Commentaries on the Laws of England,* was the foundation for her understanding of what she was doing in Los Angeles. She was practicing law, not as an enterprise of professional enrichment, but as part of God's eternal plan for bringing justice to the world.

She opened the lawbook first and read again a favorite passage:

> *Considering the creator only as a being of infinite power, he was unquestionably able to have prescribed whatever laws he pleased to his creature, man, however unjust or severe. But as he is also a being of infinite wisdom, he has laid down only such laws as were founded in those relations of justice that existed in the nature of things antecedent to any positive precept. These are the eternal, immutable laws of good and evil, to which the creator himself, in all his dispensations, conforms; and which he has enabled human reason to discover, so far as they are necessary for the conduct of human actions. Such among others are these prin-*

ciples: that we should live honestly, should hurt nobody, and should render to every one his due.

That is the meaning of justice, Kit thought. *Everyone his due.*

She closed her eyes and prayed. "Father, I thank you that you have chosen me to be a servant of yours. Strengthen me with the wisdom to see and the strength to persevere. Teach me what I must know to do the job you have called me to."

Help me, she added silently, *to serve Juan to the best of my abilities. Lead me to the answers, Father in heaven. Show me the way.*

Opening her most treasured possession on Earth, her father's Bible, she turned to the book of Psalms. Oh, how her father loved to read from that book! She could tell from his markings which Psalms were especially meaningful to him. As she turned the pages, her eyes fell on Psalm 27, which was well decorated with her father's scrawls.

> *The Lord is my light and my salvation; whom shall I fear? the Lord is the strength of my life; of whom shall I be afraid? When the wicked, even mine enemies and my foes, came upon me to eat up my flesh, they stumbled and fell. Though an host should encamp against me, my heart shall not fear: though war should rise against me, in this will I be confident.*

In the margin she read something her father had written: *Today my heart did not fear. 8/5/91.*

Tears came to Kit's eyes. "I won't fear, either, Papa," she whispered.

Kit was startled by a sound of running outside the parlor window. Getting louder. Coming up the steps and through the hotel doors.

Even before she saw Corazón, Kit sensed it was her. Indeed, Corazón flashed by the open parlor door, toward the stairs. Kit called to her. Corazón stopped, then rushed in, her face contorted in fear.

"What is it?" Kit said.

"Juan!" Corazón said, fighting for breath.

Kit stood and went to her. "Juan? What's happened?"

"No there . . ."

"At the jail?"

"Sí . . . I go to see him. They . . . no let me in. They say it is too late of night. I say I will no go but to see him . . . another say . . ." Corazón's voice trailed off.

"What did he say?"

"That Juan . . . he is gone! He is . . . how you say?"

"Escaped?"

"Sí!" Corazón began to cry.

Kit embraced her, wondering what to do. *Escaped? From the central jail? How could Juan have overpowered the jailers?* Something wasn't right.

"I've got to call the police," Kit said.

She sat Corazón in a chair and went to the hotel phone near the staircase.

"Police headquarters," Kit told the telephone operator, then interrupted herself. The thought struck her that the police were behind it. She had grown to distrust them as much as they distrusted her. "No. Connect me to Michael McGinty's residence. It's in the city directory."

"One moment," the operator said. Kit cast a quick glance at Corazón. Her shoulders were shaking.

"I will connect you now," the operator said.

There was a clicking and then the sound of muffled bell. Three rings later a tired voice said, "This bloody well better be important."

It was McGinty all right. For some reason, even though he was of little help to her, Kit felt there was a decency in him somewhere. She wanted to find it.

"Detective McGinty, it's Kit Shannon."

"Shannon! What are you rousting me—"

"Did you know Juan Chavez is gone?"

There was a slight pause on the line. "Spell this out for me, Miss Shannon," McGinty said.

"The story is he escaped, but I'm not buying that. Why haven't you been notified?"

"That's what you're doin', isn't it?"

"Detective McGinty, I think this is a setup."

"For what?"

"A killing."

When McGinty said nothing, Kit continued. "How else is it possible that he escaped? What if one or two of your men let him out so they could shoot him?"

"Do you know what you're saying?"

"I do. And I know that you do not doubt it may be true."

"You have done your best to hurt some of my men, Miss Shannon. Why—"

"We haven't got time to argue this. What are you going to do to help?"

Again there was a silence. Finally, McGinty said, "I'll look into it. I don't know what I can do, but I'll tell you one thing. If Chavez ends up dead, it will do us all a favor."

And with that the line went dead.

Kit held the earpiece in disbelief. Then she ran back to Corazón.

"They help?" Corazón asked.

"Maybe," Kit said.

"What do we do?"

Kit took Corazón's hands in hers. "We pray."

Chapter 23

ONE THING TOM PHELPS KNEW for certain—Kit Shannon was news. Everything she touched seemed to turn to printer's ink and headlines.

Now it was her notorious client escaping from jail! His fingers could not peck fast enough on the Remington to get the story done.

He had come into the office early after getting rousted by one of the police-beat boys. Tom knew the *Times* would be all over this, too, and he wanted to beat them to the street. He had half an hour to do it.

It took him twenty minutes. By nine A.M. the late-morning edition went out, and the story did just what Tom Phelps thought it would. It set Los Angeles on its ear. The word was that people couldn't buy the papers fast enough.

Kit Shannon was news all right, and at five minutes before twelve noon, the news herself stormed into the office.

"Tom," Kit said, "I can't believe you wrote this!" She waved a copy of the *Examiner* in the air like she was chasing away a bug.

"It's news, Kit." She was so pretty when she was angry.

"Can't you smell a rat?"

"I smell a story."

She took an angry step toward him. "This is a setup!"

Tom put his hands up. Through the smoky haze of the office Tom saw several reporters watching them. "Look, we can't talk here."

"Why not?" Kit said with heat in her voice. "This is supposed to be about the truth, isn't it? Or is it just about selling papers?"

"The truth sells papers."

"So does a lie."

"Kit, I know you are protective of your clients, but I have to—"

"You don't really care to know, do you?"

"Know what?"

"The whole truth—about how justice is handled in this city. You want a real story? I've got it."

Kit Shannon is news. . . .

"Let's hear it, then," Phelps said.

"Oh no. Not until I get a pledge from you."

"Pledge?"

"On your word of honor."

What was she driving at? It could all be a bluff. She could be clouded in her judgments. She was, after all, a little strong on the religious side. But then again, Phelps prided himself on a nose for a story. His nose was twitching now.

"What do you want from me?" he said.

"That when you find out the real story about Juan, about this case, you'll write it. You'll write it just the way it is. Even if it means—"

"My job?"

"Is your job worth turning away from what you know to be the facts?" Kit Shannon looked into his eyes with a gaze that pierced him to the marrow. He knew then that she had more integrity and character than he had.

"I'll agree," he said finally, "but only based on facts. If I find out you're imagining things, I'm going to write that, too. Agreed?"

"Agreed," Kit answered. "Now look at this."

She held out two pieces of paper to him. He took them and read.

```
You will not proceed further in the case of
the man Chavez. You are a meddler. I take
care of meddlers. I will take care of you
unless you back away. Believe me.

This is your last warning, Lawyer.
```

"How long has this been going on?" he asked.

"Since the start of the trial. Somebody wants me to just walk away."

"Any idea who?"

Kit shook her head. "I'm not exactly a favorite with the police. They won't lift a finger."

"You actually think it might be a cop?"

"I don't know. It could also be any of a number of people out there who would just as soon see Juan at the end of a rope than in a jail cell."

Tom studied the notes again. "Typewritten."

"To disguise handwriting, of course."

"Yes, but . . ." He looked around the room and spotted Ernie leaning over the desk of one of the city reporters. "Ernie!" He waved him over. The typewriter man shuffled over to them.

"Take a look at these notes," Tom said.

Ernie took them in his ink-stained fingers. He nodded a couple of times and sort of hummed to himself. "Looks like a Remington," he said.

"You can identify the machine?" Kit asked, sounding astonished.

"Sure," Ernie said proudly. "They each have their style. This here is from a front-stroke machine. The type has a little feathering. Your downstrokes don't leave that. Problem with a downstroke, though, is you have to lean over to see the line. This here could be from any one of the machines in this office."

Kit frowned at the news.

"But it ain't," Ernie said.

"Why not?" said Tom.

"Because I know every dang machine in this here building, ya lunkhead. Look at these notes again. See them raised caps? You think I'd let any one of 'em have a bad shift?"

"What does that mean?" Kit asked.

"In the '90s we had double keyboard machines." Ernie pointed to Tom's Remington. "Twice as many keys as that. One for your caps, one for your lower case. Too slow. We needed something so people could touch-type, you know, make with the flying fingers." Ernie wiggled his fingers in the air. "So to get caps, we came up with the shift key. See, one on each side? You hit that, the typebars go down, and the cap strikes."

Ernie slipped a sheet of blank paper in Tom's machine and demonstrated. He typed briefly, then showed the sheet to Kit and Tom.

Reporters are Lunkheads.

"Very amusing, Ernie," Tom said.

"But the caps is right where they're supposed to be. Perfect, because I love these machines like they were my own kids. I wouldn't send my kids out looking like this." Ernie slapped the threatening notes Kit had brought with her.

"But . . ." Kit looked at the notes again. "Some of the capital letters aren't raised. The C and B, for instance."

Ernie's eyes twinkled as he smiled. "Sharp cookie, you are. I was gonna tell you that myself. See, it is the left shift key that's the trouble. That's the one you depress for Y and I. But it's the right shift for B and C. See?"

"You're a poet, Ernie, but that still leaves us not knowing who typed these," Tom said.

"That much is true," said Ernie. "In the other note, it's the L that's raised. Same machine. And if you found me another piece of writing from that machine, I could tell."

"Then we will have to find it," Kit said.

"What are the chances of that?" Tom said.

"I have to believe they are good," Kit said, "with prayer and detective work. I will pray. You hire the detective."

"What!"

"You want the truth, don't you?"

"Listen . . ."

"And if I do find that machine, you will write the story as I tell it, won't you?"

Tom said, "All right."

"Lunkhead," said Ernie.

Just then a voice shouted from the hallway. It sounded like one of the copyboys. A kid named Sammy came bounding into the city room like he had just witnessed Lincoln's assassination.

"They got him!" he yelled. "They got Chavez!"

Every reporter on the floor, it seemed, shouted for the facts. Tom felt Kit put her hand on his arm, gripping it tightly.

"Yeah!" Sammy said. "They shot him!"

Kit's grip tightened like a vice as the noise of clamoring voices filled the room.

―――――――――

Frederica Fairbank pulled herself up to her full height of just over five feet. She was determined to hold her head high, though she knew disapproving eyes would be following her as she entered the Magnolia Room of the Beaudry Hotel for the Women's Club luncheon.

After Kit's outburst at Eulalie Pike's luncheon, Freddy had noticed a decrease in the volume of her social correspondence. Letters were fewer, invitations a mere trickle. Was it just her imagination, or had the sins of the niece been visited upon the aunt?

"Oh dear," she muttered to no one at all as she passed the potted palms of the hotel's lobby, barely glancing at the enormous elephant sculpture made entirely of walnuts. *Elephants never forget,* Freddy mused, *and neither does the social registry.*

The hostess of the luncheon, Mrs. Carolyn Goodall, seemed to raise her eyebrows a little higher than normal as Freddy walked into the Magnolia Room. "Good afternoon, Frederica," she said. "I see that you will be at table seven today."

Seven? Hadn't she always been at table one or two?

With a silent nod, Freddy strode further into the crucible of aristocratic reproach.

What was that over there? Freddy noticed, in a far corner, a small knot of women twittering behind their fans as they looked her way. It was the unmistakable look of gossip in progress.

And she, Frederica Stamper Fairbank, was the subject of it!

Needing to sit, Freddy went for her chair at table seven, which immediately halted the conversation among the other women seated there.

"Good afternoon, Freddy dear," Mrs. Jennifer Hawthorne said stiffly, as if it had to be dragged from her. The others merely nodded.

Courage, Freddy reminded herself, often came in the form of not looking stung. To appear so was social disaster, and she already had disaster enough on her hands.

"Good afternoon, everyone," Freddy said merrily. "Have you seen the latest French hats at the Broadway? Satin ribbons done up in rosettes? Simply charming!"

"Hmmph," Mrs. Hawthorne uttered. "I would have thought charm was something outside your immediate purview, Freddy."

The other ladies chirruped, bringing gloved hands to their mouths.

Freddy knew what they were thinking but kept her upper lip stiff. "Just what . . . are you talking about, Jenny?"

"Dear, of course it is that niece of yours. Her riotous behavior is an abasement. Why haven't you taught her the social graces?"

So this is what it had come to. Freddy had known, deep in her heart, that it had to happen. She had taken in her niece—with her wild Irish eyes and that flaming hair—knowing it was a risk. She wanted to make Kit in her own image, but instead Kit would not be tamed. She might as well have tried to turn a stormy Irish coast into a birdbath.

And now she was paying the social cost. But how should she respond? With sackcloth and ashes? Or should she try to salvage Kit's reputation somehow? One thing she would not do is turn her back on Kit, as she had almost done when Heath Sloate was turning her head with his lies. Yet she was not a social magician, either. Oh, what to do?

"Ah, Freddy." Eulalie Pike's voice cut the air like a surgeon's scalpel. "You made it after all."

After all? Freddy never had any intention of staying home. Freddy had always been one of the stalwarts of the Women's Club, there at the founding. Still Eulalie, as always, managed to direct her prod to the most vulnerable area of a person's spirit, regardless of their previous position.

"So nice to see you," Freddy said coolly.

"Oh, have I told you all the news?" Eulalie said, in the familiar tone of one who had, of course, not told anyone anything lest she forego the pleasure of having them beg to hear.

Which they all did, with the exception of Freddy.

"This will be of most interest to you, Freddy my dear," said Eulalie. "I have arranged the terms of a formal debate to be held at the Morosco Theater. Dr. Edward Lazarus has agreed to meet your niece, Freddy, in a public debate over the scholarly advances in theology. Isn't that just so exciting?"

All eyes were trained on Freddy as she felt her breath start to labor. "How . . ." Freddy could not think of a word.

"Oh, let's be grown up, shall we?" said Eulalie. "Your niece has been deserving of a public comeuppance for some time. This will be it. Believe me, Freddy, it will be the best thing for her, and for you. Perhaps after this debate we won't have to see her face on the front of the newspapers!"

So that was it. Eulalie Pike, and all of the other ladies here, were jealous of Kit. Jealous that she had garnered more attention in the last few months than any of them would in a lifetime. That, and the fact that she was strikingly pretty, was fuel for the public fire Eulalie wished to ignite. She would always seek to burn away all women who would not deign to bow before her in social obeisance.

Freddy's ire rose in a sudden burst. "I would not sell my niece short, Eulalie."

"But, my dear, Dr. Lazarus is a seasoned scholar. Your impulsive kin cannot hope to measure up."

"She has a way of surprising, even shocking, people." Oh, Freddy knew that all too well!

"Then it will be a lovely evening's entertainment," said Eulalie, sounding singularly unconcerned. "Glad to see you looking so well, Freddy dear."

More cheeps at the table. Freddy knew she did not look well at all. She wondered if she ever would again.

The gathering droned on, time seeming to drag endlessly through the afternoon. Freddy had always enjoyed her Women's Club meetings, but this time the arrangement held little joy.

As the speaker concluded a discussion on his recent visit to Sweden, Freddy had already decided to make her way home as quickly as possible. She felt light-headed and weary. Her heart was torn emotionally, and perhaps physically as well. Hadn't the doctor told her there were problems to consider? Well, it didn't matter.

She got to her feet and smiled at the women at her table. "This has been a positive delight," she said. "I've often considered traveling abroad to the Scandinavian countries. Perhaps now I shall."

The other women murmured their good-byes, as if unable to figure out quite how to take Freddy's apparent ease with the afternoon. Freddy felt a small victory in that at least. She nearly made it to the door when she found herself stopped by Delia Bryce.

"Mrs. Fairbank," the young woman called. "I'm so glad to have a moment to talk to you."

"I'm afraid," Freddy began, hoping to ward off a lengthy discourse with the girl, "I'm in a bit of a hurry."

Delia nodded and pressed something into Freddy's gloved hand. "I wonder if you would be so kind to pass this along to your niece. I had heard from Mother that she was no longer with you, but I thought perhaps she comes to visit."

"Yes, of course," Freddy replied, but in truth she'd seen very little of Kit.

"I hope you don't mind the imposition, but I wanted to get word to her as soon as possible."

"Word of what?" Freddy asked. It was really none of her business, but she had to know.

Delia looked embarrassed and turned her gaze to the floor. "Well, the truth is, Mother says that I may not make Kathleen my project, after all. I had hoped to have a party in her honor, but Mother said it would be best if we avoided confrontation."

Freddy raised her chin a degree. "I will do as you have asked."

Just then Delia's mother stepped up to join them. "Frederica, I hope you understand," Mrs. Bryce said, looking rather uncomfortable.

Freddy nodded. "Of course I understand. It takes times such as these to truly understand a great many things about life. Especially as to whom one's friends are."

Chapter 24

TED FOX TOOK A STEP BACK and looked at the skeleton. Beautiful. "She's looking like a real plane now, Gus," he said.

Indeed, the frame was finished. Crafted of spruce, held by crisscrossing brace wires, and capped by the rudder, all the monoplane needed was the final skin before she would be ready to fly.

Gus spit and nodded. "Looks is one thing," he said. "Flying's another."

The ocean winds swirled around them, kicking up sand and dirt. Ted waved his hand dismissively. "Flying's what this'll do."

"So you say."

"That's right. So I say."

"You need another test!" Gus erupted.

Ted looked at the skinny mechanic. In the back of Ted's mind a quiet but persistent voice acknowledged Gus's warning. But just as persistently, Ted ignored it. "We're going up as soon as it's fin-ished."

"I still say you're nuts. You're gonna break a leg or something, sure."

"Nonsense. I've taken spills before."

"And then there's all this work. We'll have to start from scratch."

"You afraid of work, Gus?" That was a low blow and he knew it. For a moment Gus's eyes showed real hurt, and Ted wished he could take the comment back. But it was too late.

The mechanic spit again. "If that's what you're thinkin', I'll take my business elsewhere."

"Forget about it, will you?" Ted said.

"I can't forget about it. I'm here every day with you, and all you been doin' is snapping all over the place. You won't slow down. You won't be careful."

"I haven't got time!" Ted said. "This is competition, Gus! Sur-vival of the fittest. The first to the line. The Wrights are going at it. And there's that Frenchie. He's working on a monoplane, too. You hesitate, you lose."

"Is that all that's going through your head?"

Ted narrowed his gaze. "What are you getting at?"

Gus pointed to his eyes. "You look at me, right in the lamps, and tell me you aren't doing this because of that Shannon woman."

The sound of her name was like salt on a wound. What Gus didn't know was that Ted read the newspapers every day to follow Kit. He cursed himself for doing it, but he did. And every day it was like opening the wound afresh.

Ted took two strides to Gus and grabbed him by his coveralls. "I am not doing anything because of her!" Ted said. "And I don't want to hear you say her name again. You got that?"

"Sure, sure," Gus said, gripping Ted's hands. He pushed the

younger man back a pace. "I sure am glad to see she ain't under your skin anymore!"

Ted glowered at him. "You ready to get back to work?"

"I guess that's the safest thing to do now, ain't it?"

Turning his back, Ted kicked at a scrub bush. A puff of sand flew off it. Ted kicked it again and again, until it was all but obliterated.

———

Kit was followed—actually followed!—by several newspapermen as she rode the trolley to the police station. Tom Phelps and some of his colleagues had grabbed their coats and hats even as she was rushing out of the newspaper building. She hopped on the trolley just before they spilled onto the street. So they followed on foot, running the four blocks like a crazy mob.

Along the way, they must have attracted the attention of reporters in the *Times* building. They would have seen this anxious rabble from the windows. And out they came, as well.

The journalistic mass was a minute or so behind her by the time Kit strode into the police station. She was not surprised to see several policemen standing near the front desk. It was almost as if they expected her.

"Where is Detective McGinty?" Kit said before anyone else could speak.

The gruff desk sergeant, whom she had encountered before, laughed from behind the small crowd. "I win, boys," he said.

A few of the cops laughed.

Kit felt every nerve in her body catch fire. "What is funny about this?"

"Oh, we just had a bet," the sergeant said, "about how long would it take for you to scurry your caboose down here. Looks like I was the closest."

Any trembling Kit might have felt was burned off by flames of righteous indignation. She walked purposefully toward the sergeant. The gang of police parted for her like the Red Sea. Kit saw only the face of the sergeant now, his sniggering expression fading as she came to his desk and leaned over it.

"So you think this is all a laughing matter, do you?" Kit said.

"Look, lady—"

"You think the law is something to trifle with?"

"Now you wait—"

"You are a disgrace!"

The sergeant stood up, his wooden chair pushing back and scratching the floor behind him. "Nobody talks that way to me!"

"I *am* talking that way to you!"

"Arrest her!" the sergeant ordered.

The other cops looked at each other, seemingly unsure what to do.

"I said—" Before he could finish, the doors of the station crashed open and the flock of reporters poured in. The lobby erupted in a cacophony of voices and footfalls.

Tom Phelps was in the lead. "What's the word?" he shouted.

A bevy of responses poured out. Police bellowing, reporters shouting. For a moment the chaos imitated an orchestra playing as loudly as it could, with each instrument on a different page.

"Quiet!"

The voice of Detective Michael McGinty brought everyone into silence. "This is a police station, not a bawdy house!" He glared at the desk sergeant. "What gives?"

Looking sheepish the sergeant said, "I . . . ordered her arrest." He pointed at Kit.

McGinty turned toward Kit and removed a fresh cigar from his coat. "I might have known." Then to the sergeant: "On what charge?"

The sergeant's forehead crinkled. His mouth opened slightly, then closed again. He shrugged his shoulders.

McGinty grunted. "All right, let's clear this room." He motioned for the cops to start ushering people out.

"Wait!" Kit said. "What has happened to Juan Chavez?"

"He's here," McGinty said.

"What is his condition?"

"Better than what's good for him."

"Was he shot?"

"Winged."

"I want to see him."

"Not now."

"I am his lawyer. I insist—"

"Nobody sees him until I say so. And I don't say so. Now clear out."

Kit did not move. She sensed something about McGinty that came to her all in a jumble, that deep down he was a fair man, but he was first and foremost a loyal policeman. He had to know something was not right about Juan's "escape," yet he could not say so to her now, with all of his colleagues gathered around. Perhaps if they were alone.

On the other hand, her history with the Los Angeles police was not a genial one. McGinty might very well toe the line with his brethren when push came to shove.

Kit decided to push. "I am not leaving until I see Juan," she said.

McGinty's eyes blazed. "I think you are, Miss Shannon."

"I have every right to be here."

"Not if I declare you a disturbance to our duties."

"Disturbance!"

"And that's what I'm declaring." He nodded to two policemen at his side. They immediately, and with broad smiles, grabbed Kit by the arms and began thrusting her toward the door.

"You can't . . ." Kit began, but she realized they not only could, they were. The reporters, delight on their faces, scribbled notes as she was dragged past them, through the doors, and out to the street.

As the cops let her go the reporters followed her out, shouting questions at her. And then the idea came to her. If the police were not going to listen, maybe the city itself would. Here were the men of the press, and here she was. . . .

"All right," she said loudly, silencing them. "I am going to give you a statement."

Their faces reflected a collective eagerness, with the exception of Tom Phelps, who said, "Kit, maybe you had better consider—"

"Shut yourself up, Tom!" another reporter said. "This ain't just your story!"

Others echoed the sentiment. Kit looked at Tom and almost took his advice. But now was an opportunity she might never have again. And Juan was sitting in jail without her.

"Here is my statement, gentlemen. My client, Juan Chavez, is being victimized by those who are sworn to protect him. I do not believe for a moment that he managed to escape on his own. I believe this was done to prejudice his trial, to make it impossible to choose a fair and impartial jury."

One of the reporters she didn't know said, "You got any facts to back that up, Miss Shannon?"

"Not yet. But if they exist, they will come to light. I promise you." She saw Tom Phelps looking at the ground. He wasn't taking notes.

"Are you claiming the cops set him up?" another reporter asked.

Kit felt herself falling deeper into a maelstrom. But there was no getting out now. "It is no secret that prejudice exists in this city against people who do not have white skin. You know that, gentlemen, yet you do not write about it. Now is your chance."

One of the reporters winked at her. "You know I will, Miss Shannon." The way he said it, however, gave her pause.

What had she just done? Was it merely her Irish impetuosity, or had she been filled with the Spirit of God?

She was not at all sure, and even less so when Tom Phelps shook his head at her and began walking away.

Chapter 25

TRY AS SHE MIGHT, Kit could not get rid of the thought that she had been unable to help Juan Chavez in his hour of most need.

How could she, with all the forces arrayed against her? Police, the wealthy, even her own aunt. Her only ally was Earl Rogers, but all he could offer her was advice. He was tied up in his own trial.

She sat disconsolate in her office, the sun setting outside the newly set glass of her window. Why was she even continuing this lone defense?

Because it was right, she told herself. Kit remembered Papa's voice, clear and strong, when she was a little girl. Many people in town liked their whiskey and didn't like her father telling them it was sinful to get drunk. When he said one night he was going out to talk about it, Kit told him there were too many.

"Now, don't you be worrying, daughter," he said in his resonant brogue. "One with God is a majority."

Kit remembered that now. Surely Papa would have told her that very thing had he been here in the office with her.

She slid her father's Bible in front of her and opened to a passage she had read many times in the last few months. The words of Jesus, quoting the prophet Isaiah as they applied to the Messiah: *The Spirit of the Lord is upon me, because he hath anointed me to preach the gospel to the poor; he hath sent me to heal the brokenhearted, to preach deliverance to the captives, and recovering of sight to the blind, to set at liberty them that are bruised, to preach the acceptable year of the Lord.*

"Deliverance to the captives," Kit said aloud. "To set at liberty them that are bruised."

She bowed her head and prayed that she would be a majority with God and set Juan free.

Then she threw herself into preparation for Juan's trial. She poured over the law, made notes, looked at cases in the California Reports. She began her trial brief—a combination of law and facts as known to her from the preliminary hearing. This was the essential base of all trials, as Earl Rogers had taught her. This, and knowing where the squirrel was.

She leaned back in her chair and remembered the story Earl had told her when they were preparing for Ted's trial.

Earl told of a fictional lawyer interviewing a group of boys for a job helping in his office. He told the boys: "A certain farmer was troubled with a red squirrel that got in through a hole in his barn and stole his seed corn. He resolved to kill that squirrel at the first opportunity. Seeing him go in at the hole one noon, he took his shotgun and fired away; the first shot set the barn on fire."

"Did the barn burn?" said one of the boys.

The lawyer, without answer, continued: "And seeing the barn on fire, the farmer seized a pail of water, and ran in to put it out."

"Did he put it out?" said another.

"As he passed inside, the door shut, and the barn was soon in full flames. Then the hired girl rushed out with more water."

"Did they all burn up?" said another boy.

The lawyer went on, without answering. "Finally the old lady came out, and all was noise and confusion, and everybody was trying to put out the fire."

"Did anyone burn up?" said another.

The lawyer, hardly able to restrain his laughter, said, "There, there, that will do. You have all shown great interest in the story." But observing one little bright-eyed fellow in deep silence, he said, "Now, my little man, what have you to say?"

The little fellow blushed, grew uneasy, and stammered out, "I want to know what became of that squirrel! That's what I want to know."

"You will do," said the lawyer. "You are my man; you have not been switched off by confusion and a barn's burning, and hired girls and water pails; you have kept your eye on the squirrel."

Then Earl had looked at Kit and said, "In every trial there is one squirrel to kill, and no more."

And so, she wondered, what would be the squirrel in Juan's case? The key issue? The singular fact that would be foremost in the minds of the jury?

When the answer came, it seemed as clear as the ocean air: identity. Right now the major obstacle in her path was Juan's "confession." But she was sure she could convince fair-minded men that it was not voluntary. More troubling would be the fact that Gloria Graham had identified Juan.

And where was Gloria? The detective, Lassen, still had not found her. The police were no doubt keeping her away until trial, not wishing to take any chances that she might talk to the papers or to counsel for the defense. Kit would not be able to look into her eyes until she confronted her in court.

She also faced the prospect of cross-examining Dr. Jeffrey Kenton. Her heart tensed. He would no doubt testify about Gloria's condition at the hospital and also about hearing her tell Hanratty it was Juan who did it. How could she possibly put his testimony under scrutiny? He was a decent, honest man . . . and she thought she might be falling in love with him.

Kit walked to the window, cupped her hands on the glass, and looked out over Broadway. The streetlamps barely lit a deeply darkened night. A few pedestrians moved along the sidewalks, but they were dark specters to her eyes. She saw a policeman on horseback and stepped back slightly. Had he looked up at her in the window?

She looked at the clock and saw that it was well past nine o'clock. She had been in her office, working, for over five hours. It was time to catch a Night Owl rig and get home to the Westminster.

Just one more task. If Earl was working late, as he often did, she wanted to ask him if she had found the right squirrel. She felt his advice on anything to do with a trial would be invaluable.

She gathered some papers and put them in her briefcase, doused her desk lamp, and locked the door behind her. The long hallway on the second floor was in shadows. The building's only electric light—nothing but a large naked bulb—glowed by the central staircase.

The wooden boards below her feet creaked as she walked the length of the hall toward the offices of Earl Rogers. No light shone from under any of the doors. Had she outlasted everyone tonight? Earl had once commented on her capacity for work, and she had replied that his own was amazing. What she did not add was that the only thing that kept him from doing more was his drinking. But she was heartened by his resolve of late to quit.

She tried the door to Earl's office. Locked. She knocked, but there was no response. Well, then, perhaps in the morning.

Something squeaked from somewhere near the stairs, and Kit cocked her head. Only silence. There had been some mice reported in the place. Indeed, numerous traps had been set and filled within the last few weeks. Could it have been the peep of vermin? Kit did not relish the thought of walking down dark stairs in the company of rodents.

She knocked on the door once more, feeling a certain anxiousness she could not quite explain. Was this tension a consequence of her office being violated by a brick through the window? In truth, she had to admit it was so. The person who had written her two warnings was still out there somewhere.

The thought came like a thunderbolt. Was he in here now?

She did not move from Rogers' door. Her breathing seemed loud enough to be part of a conversation.

Or was she just being a fool? Tired, anxious. She would go back to the hotel and take a hot bath. She would see Corazón and have a chat before bed.

Kit began walking toward the stairs. She heard the buzzing of the light bulb as she got closer, mesmerized for a moment by its light. Electricity was everywhere in the city now, and soon Los Angeles would be completely connected by wire. Edison's dream come true. A marvel of progress.

The light went out.

She was engulfed in darkness and silence. Why had it happened? These bulbs burned out often, she knew, but deep down she sensed that was not the reason.

Had someone switched it off? Someone who was in the building with her now? A building supervisor? Or someone waiting for her at the staircase? Someone she would not want to see.

Kit felt suspended between heartbeats.

Should she run? But where? The only way out was down those

stairs . . . unless she wanted to try the window at the end of the hall, which opened up to a fire escape.

But to get there she would have to pass the stairs.

Kit took a step backward, stopped.

Then she heard footsteps. Coming up the stairs. Slowly, purposefully.

This was no accident. It had to be him. The one who had warned her.

Corazón Chavez felt the urge to pray. She was alone in her simple quarters on the first floor of the Westminster, and the urge was strange to her. As a Catholic, she still said her rosary regularly. She prayed when told to by the priest. But Kit was helping her understand new things about prayer: Corazón prayed when she was afraid sometimes, and she always prayed for Juan.

But never had she felt something inside her, almost like a voice, urge her to pray. Kit had told her it happened that way sometimes. Kit's Christianity was so different from what Corazón knew of religion. Different, too, from what she had observed about most Protestants. They went to churches and lived in grand houses, but they did not seem to have lives that were very different from anybody else in the city. They often argued amongst themselves, but they were unified in one respect—they did not like Catholics.

Her father told her once this was because of Bishop Amat. As Protestants poured into the city in the 1870s, Bishop Amat forbade Catholics to cooperate with them. He forbade them to go to the public schools they built. His policies divided Protestant and Catholic in Los Angeles.

Now, even sixteen years after Amat's death, the Protestants still hated the Catholics. Corazón knew part of the reason was skin color. Most of the Catholics here were her people, the people who had been here long before the Anglos arrived. But Protestants were now the majority, in numbers and wealth and influence. And they intended to use that power to keep Catholics from ever regaining an equal footing.

Yet Kit was so different in her Protestant beliefs. God seemed so real to her, and she spoke of Jesus as someone she knew like a friend. Kit also told Corazón that the Holy Ghost was real, too, and that scared Corazón. At first.

But as Kit spent more time with her, reading to her from the Bible, Corazón had come to understand Kit's Christianity a little better. Kit said sometimes God would give you the urge to pray. All you had to do was follow it.

Kit told her to pray to God as if talking to a family member, not with words from memory, but from the heart.

But why did God want her to pray now? It was not just for Juan. It was for Kit.

Corazón crossed herself, slid to her knees by her bed, and began to talk to God.

Chapter 26

KIT WAS TRAPPED. Should she scream? Who would hear her?

The steps came without hesitation now.

Kit remembered the fire ax affixed on the wall near the stairs. The figure was almost to the top. She would have to act now.

She ran toward the stairs. It was like running in the middle of a twisting tunnel, with no light at either end. She would have to estimate where the ax was. She felt along the wall with her hands.

Nothing.

Where was it?

She saw something move in the darkness, a shadow, darker than the spectral dimness of the corridor. He was here.

Her hands moved wildly along the wall. Blindly she groped. Her breath came in fevered bursts.

The dark figure moved again. Toward her.

She found the handle of the ax, gripped it, but could not pull it from the hooks. The handle made a clumsy clattering sound against the metal braces.

And then two hands grabbed her by the arms.

"No!" she cried, struggling against the attacker, but he held her fast. Helpless, she could only mouth feeble protests and try to break free.

"You were warned," the attacker said. His voice was low and stank of liquor. Oddly, that gave her hope. If he was liquored up, perhaps she could find a weak spot.

The hope faded instantly as the hands shoved her backward. Her head hit the wall, jolting her, shards of pain shooting down her neck.

A calloused hand grabbed her throat and began to squeeze. Kit's mouth opened, fighting for air, unable to utter a sound now as the fingers dug into her flesh. *God . . . God . . .*

Kit flailed with her hands, but the blows did nothing. The man was large, muscled. And intent on killing her.

It couldn't be. Not now. Not with Juan needing her. It couldn't be. . . .

Suddenly the hand ripped from her throat. Kit fell to the floor, hearing her own awful, rasping sucking sound as she labored for air. She was only vaguely aware of another sound, like a man moaning.

Her attacker. For some reason, he was on the floor, too. Hurt.

Kit scrambled to her feet, sliding up the wall. Her head was aflame with pain, and the world spun around her.

And then she heard footsteps. This time, running down the stairs. Someone else!

She glanced down and saw the dark form of the man who moments before had wanted to kill her. The form was motionless.

Kit found the stairs. Still dizzy, she held the rail as she descended. The other person, the one whom she knew now had saved her life—where was he? *Who* was he?

Kit somehow found her way through the darkness to the front door of the building. It was wide open. She stumbled into the night.

———

Detective Michael McGinty said, "You are trouble, Miss Shannon."

Kit did not feel like arguing the point, but if she had she would have said it was trouble that seemed to be following her.

The two stood in the now-lit hallway of her office building. A uniformed policeman, one Kit did not know, stood close by. Kit rubbed her throat, which still throbbed from the attack.

"You all right?" McGinty said.

"I'll recover," said Kit.

"He won't." McGinty nodded at the body on the ground, a knife sticking out of his back.

"You want to tell me the story one more time?" McGinty said.

Kit recounted the attack, and the mysterious rescue.

"You expect me to believe," McGinty said around his cigar, "that somebody came in here and stabbed this guy, then just ran off?"

"I expect you to believe the truth," Kit said. "And that is the truth, as far as I know."

"It ain't too far, is it?" McGinty knelt by the body and began a search of the man's pockets. In the light, Kit could now see he was a huge man and rather shabbily dressed. But for his size he probably would not have stood out among the denizens of the mean parts of the city.

"Well, what have we here?" McGinty said. In his hand was a silver flask. He uncorked the top and smelled. "Whiskey," he said. "Pretty good brand."

Kit noticed the policeman eyeing her suspiciously. "Anything else?" Kit said to McGinty.

"Only some silver." McGinty stood up. "And you have no idea who this is?"

"None," Kit said.

"But he did say it was about those warning notes?"

"He said I had been warned, yes."

McGinty puffed studiously for a moment. "This ain't the guy who wrote them notes."

"No?"

"Look at him. He look like the kind of fellow who owns a typing machine?"

Kit shook her head.

"He look like the kind of fellow who drinks good whiskey out of a flask?"

Again, Kit indicated no.

"My guess is he's a rummy and somebody paid him to pay you a visit."

"That makes sense."

"Of course it makes sense. I don't flap my lips for no reason."

Kit felt hot under the collar. "Now will you take those notes seriously? Will you try to find out who wrote them?"

McGinty frowned. "That's what I'm doing. But that's not my only problem. I got a stiff on my hands, and you got no idea who did it."

"None."

"Maybe some avenging angel?"

Kit wondered who else it could have been.

"All right," McGinty said. "Come along. I'll see you home." He turned to the cop. "You stay here until I get back. And don't touch anything."

The cop nodded, giving Kit one last look of veiled contempt.

McGinty guided his carriage across town, which seemed for once in repose. "I suppose I owe you an apology," McGinty said.

Kit looked at him, surprised.

"I still think you're trouble," he said. "But somebody is really trying to scare you off." He paused, then added, "I wonder if it's a cop."

Kit was so stunned by the admission she could think of nothing to say.

"You and I both know you're not well liked by the boys," McGinty said. "I don't know if any of them would stoop to this, but if I find out one of 'em did, he'll have to deal with me. I promise you it won't be pretty."

"Thank you."

"Don't thank me yet. I still haven't cleared you."

"Me?"

"For all I know, you knifed that guy yourself."

Kit's face burned. "How could you even—"

"All I'm saying is I don't know what's going on and I'm not taking anything at face value. There's bad things going on in this city right now, and it's because of you."

"That is not at all fair!"

"Life ain't fair, Miss Shannon." He stopped the coach in front of the Westminster. "Now I advise you get inside, close your door, and don't come out until morning. I don't want any more stiffs tonight."

Kit suddenly felt very helpless and very alone as she opened the Westminster's front door. She was heartened to see Corazón waiting in the parlor. She ran to Kit and threw her arms around her. Kit held her dear friend close.

"I was so worried," Corazón said. "You were no here."

"Oh, Corazón." Kit kissed her cheek.

"There was bad for you, I think. I was praying, like you say."

"You were praying for me tonight?"

"Sí."

Perhaps, then, it *was* an angel who had saved her. Who knew, but God alone?

And who knew, but God, whether she would finally be able to defend Juan Chavez?

Part Two

Chapter 27

Los Angeles Daily Times
Monday, April 18, 1904

EDITORIAL
Is the Courtroom Any Place for a Woman?

The trial of Juan Chavez commences tomorrow. Perhaps this is an opportune moment for this city to pause in its understandable state of upset and consider a question that has too long been ignored. Is justice buttressed by having a woman serve as a criminal defense attorney?

We are mindful of the progress the fair sex has enjoyed in recent years. In many instances they have acquitted themselves admirably in emergency situations. That does not mean, however, that such activities are to be encouraged. Nature itself argues against it.

Nor is it likely that women, of their own free will, would to any appreciable extent assume the coarser vocations of men. The home instinct, if men will only give them the chance, is naturally implanted in the female breast; and most women would rather be a mother than a queen. Not that they are incapable of taking the place of men even on the battlefield, as witness the women of Carthage, of Limerick, of Saragossa, and the gallant defenders of the bailiff-assailed cabins of the Irish peasantry. But these are merely the exceptions that prove the rule.

Which brings us to the exceptional case of Kathleen Shannon, lawyer for the accused. Only two weeks ago it was Miss Shannon who intruded into the operations of the police and had to be physically ejected from the premises. This led to wild accusations about nefarious police activity, voiced in the street to assembled reporters, accusations that have thus far proved unfounded. We think that rules of evidence, wherein charges are not entertained absent reasonable grounds, would apply to public pronouncements indicting our law enforcement officials.

There are other long-standing and well-founded reasons that women ought not to engage in the manly art of legal battle. We note that since women may not serve on juries, ought we not exclude women from arguing to juries in courts of law? The trial of a case, especially a criminal case, is one that requires a strong and steady mind and a calm temperament, both of which Nature has bestowed chiefly upon the male of the species.

Perhaps the tragedy of the Juan Chavez case will serve a greater purpose: that of restoring a semblance of order in the courts by leaving the legal field to men.

"I came as soon as I saw this slander," Dr. Jeffrey Kenton said.

Kit fell into his arms. How had he known she needed him now? Her tears were barely dry on her cheeks and she had uttered his name longingly several times that morning.

Her office was a cold, dark cavern, where she was hiding from the world. She had read the *Times* editorial in open-mouthed disbelief. Her natural inclination to fight was nearly overcome by a wellspring of emotion, built up over the last two weeks. They had been the worst of her life.

Juan Chavez was seen by the general public as a monster, his guilt confirmed by his attempt to escape. Would she possibly be able to find twelve jurors who were not tainted by this feeling?

The man who had saved her life was still at large. The mystery of his identity tormented her, as did the unanswered question of who had sent the attacker. Whoever it was still remained unidentified, perhaps awaiting another opportunity.

On top of all that, the unthinkable had happened. Heath Sloate had been acquitted! Not guilty on all charges, due to the courtroom wizardry of Clarence Darrow. The thought of it still made her grind her teeth. The fact that he announced he was leaving Los Angeles for a long European sojourn was of absolutely no comfort to her. He was a man who deserved to be locked up, and now he wouldn't be. What would happen when he returned to Los Angeles?

And though she had not sought it, she was now the city's central public figure. The object of scorn in whispered conversations and now the subject of a vicious editorial, Kit found her only comfort in Jeffrey Kenton.

It had to be love. Had to be. She had reasoned it out, in an almost legal fashion. The evidence was so clear. Jeffrey was steady, affectionate, strong, and faithful. Faithful to her, but more importantly, faithful to God. And he was right here when she needed him.

She remained in his embrace for a long moment, then felt his hand gently tip her head upward. Lost in his kiss, Kit let her worries melt away.

Jeffrey shook the copy of the newspaper in his hand. "I don't want you to think of this again," he said. He put his arm around her and walked her to a chair, then sat opposite her. He gently took both of her hands in his.

"In fact," he said, "I want to take you away from all this."

Kit allowed herself a rueful smile. "If only it were that simple."

"Isn't it?" he said.

Kit felt his hands squeeze hers earnestly. "What do you mean, Jeffrey?"

"I have been wanting to talk to you about it, but I know you have been preoccupied with the trial. Now I cannot wait." He lifted her hands to his lips and kissed them softly. "I want you to marry me, Kit."

Kit felt a warmth she had rarely felt before wash over her. She pulled his hands to her face and rested them on her cheek. "This is awfully sudden." But even as she said the words, she knew she was glad he had announced his intentions.

"I find in my line of work that split-second decisions are what I do best. Saving or losing a life is often decided in the twinkling of an eye."

Kit smiled. "But those decisions are based on years of training and research."

"I don't need years of training and research to know how I feel about you. Some things are just evident to the heart. Even in medicine there are times when the choice I make is based more on a hunch and gut feeling than any surefire remedy spoken of in the annals of medicine. I know how I feel about you. I know it more clearly than I've ever known anything. I want to marry you. I want you to be my wife."

Kit's knees began to wobble. Her stomach did a flip as she dared to ask, "When, Jeffrey?"

His face lit up. "Today. We'll make it a scandal."

Her heart jumped in her chest. "Today?"

"Run off together. We'll just leave all this behind us. I expect to come into some money, and I've received an offer from a big hospital in Philadelphia. Let's go back there. You and I."

Kit's head seemed suddenly light. "But the trial . . ."

"You don't need that trouble, Kit. You've said yourself it looks nearly hopeless. Let another lawyer take over. The court will delay the proceedings until one can be found."

For a brief moment Kit considered blurting *yes*. Right now fleeing everything had a wonderful sound to it. "I can't leave Juan and Corazón," she said finally.

"I knew you would say that," Jeffrey said. "That's why I love you. When it is all over—will you marry me then?"

"And go away?"

"Would you consider it?"

There was no resistance in her. "I will, Jeffrey. I will go anywhere with you."

He kissed her again, softly and long. For one terrible second Ted's face flashed into Kit's head and sent a jolt of electricity to her heart. *No,* she told herself, *that is over.* Forever. Her tomorrows would be spent with Jeffrey Kenton.

Alfred Mungerley slapped Ted Fox on the back. A puff of dust flew from Ted's leather jacket.

"Magnificent," Mungerley said.

They were looking at the completed work—Ted's monoplane, stately in the barn on the bluff.

"Isn't she, though?" Ted said.

"And you are sure she will fly?"

"You will be a witness. The first."

"Capital, my lad. And capital is what you will get."

Ted smiled, and for the first time in weeks he felt free of the past—including women. Especially women. His last two experiences had been enough. First Elinor Wynn and her scheming ways. Then Kit Shannon and her beliefs. Why did she have to be so fanatical about them? Well, never mind. Women were not conducive to the furtherance of man in the air.

But Alfred Mungerley was. And his investment in Ted's fledgling venture was surely going to make them millions of dollars. What Henry Ford was doing for the automobile, the firm of Mungerley & Fox would do for the plane.

All it had to do was fly.

Ted stole a glance at Gus, who was wiping his hands on a rag at the far end of the barn. Gus had come around to the inevitable—Ted *would* be going up—but not without a considerable dose of grousing.

"I am glad to see," Mungerley said, "that your time away from the bank has been well spent. Frankly, I was not sure what I would find when I came out here."

"So you can see, sir," said Ted. "Friday is the day."

"I will be here," Mungerley said. He took a cigar from his vest pocket and snipped off the tip with a gold cutter. "Have you been following the adventures of Miss Shannon?" he asked.

Ted looked at the ground. "In the papers."

"She begins that unwinnable trial tomorrow. The whole city is talking about it."

"With one exception," Ted said, touching his chest with his thumb.

"Have to admire her backbone," Mungerley added, "if not her choice of profession."

Yes, Ted thought. *One thing Kit has is backbone.*

"But I would not want to be in her shoes," Mungerley added. "She will be an outcast after this, I'm afraid. Once you lose your social standing in this city, what is left for you, eh?"

Ted fought hard against the urge to go right then and see Kit.

To try to shake some sense into her. But why should she listen to him? She had Kenton now.

"Until Friday, then?" Mungerley said.

"Friday," Ted said.

"I am getting married, Aunt Freddy."

Kit watched as her aunt's face reflected a bevy of emotions, finally landing on tearful confusion. "Oh, my dear . . . that's wonderful news. Isn't it? Who is it?"

Kit laughed and hugged her. It was good to enjoy her embrace again, to be back in Aunt Freddy's mansion, which had once been a place of harmony. Back when Juan and Corazón were in good graces here.

"You don't have to worry, Aunt Freddy. He is socially perfect."

"Do tell!"

"Dr. Jeffrey Kenton."

"I know that name!" Freddy's face flushed with excitement. "Yes. The doctor! Oh, Kit, you have made me so . . ." She stepped back and looked at Kit with a frown. "You will not continue to practice law, will you?"

"Jeffrey has been offered a position at a hospital in Philadelphia."

"Philadelphia! Why can't you remain here?"

Kit forced a smile. "Scandal," she whispered.

"Oh, now you are making sport of your poor aunt."

Kit put her arms around Aunt Freddy. "No, dear. Never. But I believe God works in mysterious ways. I've wondered why I should have come to Los Angeles if not to practice law. Perhaps it was to meet Jeffrey. And to take what I learn with me here into some less volatile region."

"Now you are talking sense," Freddy said. "How I have waited for this moment!"

Clearing her throat, Kit said, "Just one thing, Aunt Freddy. I am committed to defending Juan."

A short *eep* escaped Freddy's throat.

"I do not believe he is guilty," Kit said. "I cannot leave him."

Freddy issued a long sigh. "No," she said, "I suppose you cannot."

Kit embraced her again. Did she really understand? Truly?

"But you will have your wedding here!" Aunt Freddy said. "In Los Angeles! I shall make it the event of the season."

"Just one request."

"Yes?"

"It's not to be officiated by Dr. Edward Lazarus."

Freddy put a hand on her throat. "Oh my, no!"

They laughed together and it felt good.

"We must celebrate!" Aunt Freddy said.

Kit beamed. "Yes! How shall we do it?"

Aunt Freddy's eyes sparkled as if she were young again. "I have just the idea," she said.

Chapter 28

AUNT FREDDY'S IDEA was dinner at the elegant California Club, as the guest of Alfred Mungerley.

It was actually a delight for Kit to get dressed up for the evening. She wore a Rouff creation that Aunt Freddy had ordered for her last Christmas. The gown of salmon-colored silk had been a gift that remained, at Aunt Freddy's insistence, in the closet until a full three months had passed.

"One simply does not slap new clothes on one's back the moment they arrive," Freddy had insisted. Kit thought it rather silly, given that when she'd come to stay with Aunt Freddy she'd been forced to accept a brand-new wardrobe in order to be socially fashionable. But she nevertheless abided by her aunt's wishes. She noted Freddy's approval tonight, however. Enough time had passed, and the Rouff gown was a marvelous success.

"Ladies, you look absolutely ravishing," Alfred Mungerley

stated as they joined him in the dining room. Getting to his feet, he gave them a slight bow.

And indeed, Kit thought, they were dressed as fine and socially acceptable as they could be. Aunt Freddy was resplendent in her brocaded silk gown of mauve, navy, and gold—although the high neck of the gown looked to be squeezing Freddy's throat uncomfortably. One would scarcely notice this, however, as her aunt's hat was such an overwhelming creation that attention was immediately diverted upward. Kit wondered how she kept the menagerie of bird feathers, ribbons, and other nesting material atop her head. The silly thing must have weighed a good ten pounds, but it was highly fashionable, and Freddy spoke of being the envy of her peerage because of this French handiwork.

Mungerley, dressed in a formal black cut-away coat and trousers, assisted the ladies with their chairs before seating himself. Kit marveled at the beauty of the artistically arranged table. Place settings of Limoges china with delicate gold trimming and scalloped edges glimmered atop the fine Irish-linen cloth. A crystal bowl of freshly cut white roses made a simple but stately centerpiece for their table.

"I am so glad I could entertain you and your lovely aunt tonight," said Alfred Mungerley when they were all settled.

"Thank you for having us," said Kit. She sensed some slight discomfort in Alfred Mungerley. After all, it was his employee who had allegedly been attacked by her client! But she also sensed that Alfred Mungerley had honed one of the most important of social skills—the ability to pick and choose which outrages to emphasize in friendly gatherings.

As if reading Kit's mind, Mungerley said, "Gives us some time to forget all the unpleasantness, eh?"

Even with effort, Kit knew she could not forget about it. Tomorrow Juan's trial would begin. There was no getting around that.

But for Aunt Freddy's sake, Kit was going to try to put it aside for at least an evening. "What a grand idea," Kit said halfheartedly.

"You know," Mungerley said, dropping his voice, "there is still time for you to withdraw from this trial."

Kit saw Mungerley cast a glance at Aunt Freddy. He continued, "Look around you, Kit." He swept his arm across the grand dining room, its five magnificent chandeliers illuminating the polished brass and mahogany of the interior. "Don't you realize you are at the summit here? That this can all be part of your life?"

Aunt Freddy nodded approvingly. "Listen to Alfred, dear."

"No one will think less of you," said Mungerley. "Quite the contrary, in fact. What brings respect these days is the insight to know what fights to pick. Someone who can do that is a very valuable addition to the community. Especially one about to take the prominent position as the wife of a respected doctor."

For a moment Kit saw a picture of herself, arm in arm with Jeffrey Kenton, entering this very room for a wedding reception. In her mind she heard the applause of the guests.

"Mr. Mungerley," said Kit, "I do appreciate your kind thoughts, but—"

"But you still insist on being high-minded," Mungerley said. "Well, that is what makes you such a potential asset to the community, Miss Shannon. Perhaps another might be more persuasive than I?"

Kit had no idea what Mungerley was referring to. He put a hand in the air and waved someone over. Kit looked in that direction and watched as a white-haired man with a white walrus mustache strode over to them. He seemed full of vigor and, behind steel-colored eyes, power.

"Kit," said Alfred Mungerley, "I should like to introduce General Harrison Gray Otis."

The man with the steel-colored eyes bowed. "So you are Miss Kathleen Shannon."

Kit cleared her throat and fought to keep from falling out of her chair. "General Otis."

"The general runs a little newspaper," Mungerley added with a lilt in his voice. "Perhaps you've heard of it?"

Oh, she had indeed. The sting from the editorial was still fresh. *What was going on here?* Kit wondered. Aunt Freddy and Alfred Mungerley did not appear surprised at his appearance. It seemed as if they had known Otis would "wander" by their table all along.

"I do indeed read the *Times*," said Kit. "I found this morning's edition particularly riveting."

"Ah," Otis said with a grin. "And what aspect of the paper was it that commanded your attention?"

Had he had a hand in the editorial? Did he have no idea what she was talking about, or was he merely playing dumb? Either way, what should she answer?

"The editorial page," Kit said.

Otis nodded. "The first page I read."

"And agree with?"

"Of course. This is my paper, after all. What did you think of this morning's editorial opinions?"

He was throwing out a challenge as surely as if he had slapped her with a glove. "I will say, General, that I found myself in disagreement."

Aunt Freddy peeped next to her. Mungerley shot Kit a disapproving, though knowing, look.

"May I join?" Otis said.

"But of course," said Mungerley.

Otis took the chair between Mungerley and Kit. "I am a frank man," he said. "So I shall be frank with you. I do not believe women should be practicing law. Especially where it concerns the criminal element."

"What recourse would this 'element' have if no one defended them?" Kit said.

The publisher did not sway. "Only their rightful place in the slammer, Miss Shannon. Despite what it says in our Declaration, not all men are created equal. Hard experience will teach you that."

Kit felt her face begin to heat up. "Hard experience has taught me the opposite," she said.

"Then you need more experience," said Otis. "I run a newspaper. The newspaper needs to be printed. I hire people to print the newspaper. The American way would be to allow them to advance based upon their initiative. That is not what they do, Miss Shannon. Shall I tell you what it is they do?"

Kit waited, knowing he would enlighten her anyway.

"They form unions, Miss Shannon, which are nothing but an association of like-minded slackers who seek more money for doing less work. Does that sound like equality to you?"

Kit did not wish to enter into a discussion of the labor movement. "But people, in dignity and worth, are equal."

"That is nonsense," said Otis. "A fairy tale for children."

It took every ounce of strength Kit had not to stand up and leave the table. But she stayed calm for Aunt Freddy's sake. Kit had caused enough scandal. Her aunt did not need one involving the publisher of the city's most influential newspaper.

General Otis was the one who stood up. "My guests have arrived," he said. Kit looked up and felt immediately besieged. Two large men walked up to Otis. One was the policeman Ed Hanratty. The other man she did not recognize.

"May I introduce Mr. Hanratty and Mr. Vaine?" Otis said. "Two of our city's fine policemen."

Kit held her tongue as Hanratty's eyes bore into her. "I've met Miss Shannon," the cop said.

The other one, Vaine, also looked at Kit as if she were a foreign object scraped off a shoe.

"Good evening, then," said Otis, leading his guests toward another room.

"Don't make an enemy of Otis," Mungerley said to Kit.

"Oh my, no," said Aunt Freddy.

"I wonder what he is doing entertaining policemen?" Kit said.

"He is our city's biggest booster," Mungerley said. "He supports the police wholeheartedly."

That, Kit thought, *may turn out to be a big problem.*

"Perhaps once you sleep on it," Mungerley added, "you'll change your mind."

Puzzled, Kit questioned him. "Change my mind about what?"

"Why, this whole Chavez ordeal, of course. Now that you know how everyone feels and, perhaps, better understand the full implications of such a matter, you can see for yourself how your decision to proceed with this case might risk your happiness in Los Angeles. After all, you are from a prominent family. One of the most prominent."

Aunt Freddy puffed up at this and nodded.

"No one would blame you for walking away," Mungerley added. "They would understand. They would say you have done the reasonable thing."

"I would blame myself," Kit replied.

"But think of the future—of your young man," Freddy said, unable to remain quiet. "Surely you don't wish to bring scandal and disrepute down on him."

Kit truly hadn't given this angle much consideration. "I believe Jeffrey understands why I must do this. He has said as much, and I believe him to speak the truth."

"But, my dear," Alfred Mungerley began in a fatherly tone, "he says those things because he's in love. What happens, however, when he finds his business in ruins because no one trusts his reputation any longer?"

"Why should they judge him based on what I do?" Kit said. "That hardly seems fair. Jeffrey Kenton is an excellent doctor. He's proven himself to this community."

"Be that as it may," Mungerley replied, "they will judge him. A man is expected to keep his household in proper order. If it's perceived that his betrothed is acting in a less-than-acceptable manner, many will begin to wonder if he's able to control his own actions."

"It's true," Freddy concurred. "We only tell you these things because you must learn and understand. Especially if you're to become a wife and take your place among the matrons of society."

Kit felt her cheeks grow hot as her temper flared. "Taking my place in society has never interested me."

"Ah, but it may well interest your husband," Mungerley said in a knowing manner. "Think of that. He realizes that you are the niece of Frederica Fairbank. He may very well be using that to his advantage."

Kit had endured enough of this conversation. "I will not believe that of Jeffrey. I choose to believe the best about a person until he proves himself otherwise. This also allows me to see the possibility for innocence in my clients. I trust God to guide me in those responsibilities. Even as I trust Him now to direct me to make the right decision regarding the future."

Mungerley smiled and nodded in acquiescence. "God is the proper choice for spiritual matters, Miss Shannon, but I've yet to see His name listed on the social register."

"Then perhaps it's about time."

They proceeded to dine on braised duck and candied carrots.

Mr. Mungerley insisted they have brandied cherries for dessert, but Kit found she had very little appetite. Her appetite for social talk was not hearty, either. She kept up as politely as possible but was relieved when the evening was over.

As the carriage took her home, passing the top of Angels Flight in the darkness, Kit could not shake the feeling that someone was watching her. Someone following the carriage, on foot perhaps. But she saw no one as she looked around.

She concluded she *was* being watched—not just by one person, but by an entire city. And tomorrow they would be watching in earnest.

The sooner she got to prayer and to bed, the better. She would need every ounce of strength and mental sharpness she could muster. The fate of Juan Chavez was about to be placed squarely in her hands.

Chapter 29

KIT AND CORAZÓN ENTERED the courthouse at precisely eight-thirty Tuesday morning. The predictable crowds were there, along with a legion of reporters. She had heard along the way that press men from as far away as New York were here to cover the story.

When she managed to fight her way into the courtroom—with the help of a large deputy sheriff—she found Tom Phelps waiting for her.

"Your judge is going to be Samuel Hollins Pardue," he said.

"How can that be?" Kit said. Pardue had presided over the preliminary hearing and was the one who allowed Juan's confession to be admitted as evidence. She had hoped that by arguing before another judge she would get another shot at having it thrown out.

"Judge Sullivan took sick, so they handed it back to Pardue," said Phelps.

That would mean she would have to convince twelve men, who

would have been hearing all about Juan in the papers and casual conversation, that the police had beaten the confession out of him.

Kit was even more upset when the deputy sheriff marched Juan into the courtroom. He wore the same dirty working clothes he had been arrested in.

"What is the meaning of this?" Kit said to the deputy.

He looked at her as if he didn't know what she was talking about, but she knew it was feigned ignorance.

"I brought a suit of clothes to the jail for him to wear," Kit said. "Why isn't he wearing them?"

"I don't know anything about that," the deputy said with defiance.

Kit knew there was nothing she could do. If the jailers had conspired to "lose" the suit, as was likely, she could not fight it. The jury would be looking at Juan dressed like an unkempt field hand.

Then, in the back rows of the gallery, a commotion broke out. Half a dozen or so young Mexican men—Kit assumed they were friends of Juan—were being told by another deputy sheriff they would have to leave.

Kit stormed down the aisle. "Deputy, you have no authority to ask these men to leave."

He looked at her incredulously. "I got other people who want these seats."

"These are people. They are sitting."

"But they're . . ." He did not finish, apparently becoming aware that reporters were listening.

"Courtrooms are open to the public by law," Kit said. "These men are members of the public. You have no right to exclude them. If you like, we will take it up with the judge."

The deputy backed up a step. "All right," he said, "but if there's any trouble, out they go."

"There won't be any trouble," Kit said. She smiled at the men, who looked as if they had walked right out of the fields and into the courtroom. She was glad they were here.

Finally, Judd Ashe appeared in the courtroom, looking fresh and ready for a fight. Earl had warned her about Ashe. *Do not underestimate him,* he said. *He fights to the death to win. He is a courtroom killer.*

Feeling more than a little like Daniel in the lion's den, Kit silently prayed for the same protection. The feeding was about to begin. She took out her father's Bible and touched the cover affectionately. " 'The Lord is my light and my salvation,' " she whispered. " 'Whom shall I fear?' " The words of the Psalmist comforted her. Let the lions come.

After Judge Pardue entered and called the case, the morning settled in to the selection of a jury.

Voir dire—French for "to speak the truth"—was that part of the trial where potential jurors were questioned for competence and possible bias. Kit felt her pulse quicken as the first twelve men filled the jury box. Earl had told her time and again that jury selection was the most important aspect of the trial, for even a winning case cannot get by a biased jury.

Which is exactly what Kit was facing now. As she studied the dour faces of the men taking their seats, she remembered something else Earl had told her. Voir dire was also the time to begin educating the jurors about the case they were about to hear. Through thoughtful questions, the skilled lawyer cannot only ascertain important information about bias; he can also instruct the jurors about the coming evidence and law. This would be essential, Kit knew, because of all the negative publicity surrounding the case.

Kit was heavily ruminating her questions when she heard the judge calling her name. "Miss Shannon?"

"Yes, Your Honor?"

"You may inquire."

Kit stood and walked slowly toward the jury box. She thought immediately about her suit, a woman's broadcloth ensemble of deep blue. Was it the proper attire for this moment? What might the men be thinking of her?

It was impossible to tell, for the eyes that stared back at her appeared hard and unconvinced. Save for the pair that belonged to a handsome man of about forty who sat at the end of the first row. His was the one sympathetic face in the bunch.

"Good morning," Kit began, a slight catch in her voice. "My name is Kathleen Shannon, and as you have no doubt heard, I am representing Mr. Juan Chavez in this case."

She paused to see if any of them would acknowledge her. Only the man on the end nodded.

What to say next? Earl had counseled her early that the one thing a trial lawyer must establish is trustworthiness. Be honest with the jury and they will be honest with you.

Kit swallowed. "While we are on the subject of myself, I would like to ask how many of you gentlemen read the editorial in the *Daily Times* yesterday?"

Several of the men looked at each other, and then gradually six or seven hands stuck up tentatively in the air.

"Thank you," she said. "And of those, how many of you agree with the opinion?"

A few more looks and the same hands went up.

Honesty, Kit thought. "I will not pretend that I am not disappointed," Kit said, "because I am. I have responded to the call to practice law because I believe I can speak for justice. And I do not believe the truth changes merely because it is spoken by a woman."

Judd Ashe said, "I must object, Your Honor. Miss Shannon is making a speech, not asking questions of the jurors."

Judge Pardue nodded. "How is this relevant, Miss Shannon?"

"It is highly relevant, Your Honor," Kit said, facing the judge full on. "If the jurors cannot accept a case as argued by a woman, it is prejudicial to my client."

The judge, almost impatiently, looked at the jurymen. "Gentlemen, I would like to see by a show of hands how many of you can lay aside any discomfort you have with a female lawyer and listen only to the evidence and the law."

All of the jurors put their hands in the air. Kit could barely contain her anger. Who was going to admit he couldn't be impartial?

"Move on," the judge ordered Kit.

To what? Kit thought.

The voir dire continued until the noon hour. Kit asked for several jurors to be excused, but the judge did not allow her to use any objections "for cause." That meant, despite the result of some of Kit's questions, he found none of the jurors to be so biased they could not hear the case. It also meant Kit's "peremptory challenges," which did not have to be justified at all, were used up quickly.

Judd Ashe seemed satisfied with the jury they finally selected. He had only used one of his peremptory challenges. He used it to dismiss the juror at the end of the first row.

"Gentlemen of the jury," Judd Ashe said as he began his opening statement, "the violation of a woman is among the most heinous of crimes. Those that commit such acts are unfit for civilized society. They are animals. Gentlemen, the prosecution will show you that such an animal sits in this courtroom, guilty of the crime of rape against an innocent young woman."

Ashe pointed directly at Juan. Kit could hear Corazón whispering the translation to him.

"There he sits, gentlemen, and you will hear the testimony of sworn witnesses that will prove, beyond a reasonable doubt, that Juan Chavez did savagely and maliciously violate Gloria Graham on the night of March the twenty-fourth."

He paused and walked to the front row in the spectator area. Gloria Graham, clothed in black, sat next to a policeman. Judd Ashe reached over the rail and placed his hand on her shoulder.

"You alone, gentlemen, can vindicate this young woman. You alone will judge the facts. At the conclusion of the case, the judge will instruct you on the law. I am confident that, when all of the information is given to you, you will do your duty and return a verdict of guilty." With a final nod, Ashe returned to his seat.

Kit stood for her statement. She paused a moment, then said, "Your Honor, the defense will waive its opening statement until the close of the prosecution's case. I would only ask the jury to remember the words Mr. Ashe just spoke—beyond a reasonable doubt. This case is full of tremendous doubt, gentlemen. I, too, believe you will do your duty."

As she took her seat, Judge Pardue said to Ashe, "Call your first witness."

Big Ed Hanratty took the stand. He was dressed in a tight, light brown suit and had his mustache freshly waxed. Under Ashe's questioning he recounted the same story he told in the preliminary hearing, embellishing it a little for the benefit of the jury. As Kit watched, she sensed the jurors forming a favorable opinion of Hanratty. To the men on the panel he was a man's man, doing his job, doing everything by the book.

Even beating a wild arrestee into submission with his fists. A few of the jurors were wranglers, men used to tough work based on physical strength. They would like Hanratty most of all. Kit studied their faces carefully as Hanratty told of Juan's alleged attempts to overpower him, resulting in the beating. According to

Hanratty, the beating took place after Juan's confession.

Then it was Kit's turn to cross-examine. She approached the witness, trying hard to look confident. If Hanratty were to sense any weakness in her, he would pounce on it.

Look for the side door, she reminded herself. Earl had told her one key to cross-examination was to keep the witness looking at the front door, while finding the right time to burst in through the side. To find the truth from a hostile witness, one had to know where the side doors were.

"Officer Hanratty," Kit said. "You have been a policeman for a long time, is that right?"

Hanratty pulled himself proudly up in his chair. "Near twenty years," he said.

"And before that, what was your work?"

The witness smiled. "A number of things. I was a stevedore in San Diego for a time, a wagoner in Arizona. Punched cattle some, too."

"Sounds like hard work."

"I never minded hard work, miss."

"Was it rough work?"

"Rough?"

"Did you sometimes run up against rough men who may have had, say, a disagreement with you?"

A broad smile broke out on Hanratty's face. "Oh, I get ya. Did I have to use me fists?"

"Yes, Officer Hanratty."

"From time to time I did, sure."

Kit glanced quickly at the jurors, some of whom were nodding. They were likely men who had known a few fights, too. It was part of being a man.

"Did anyone ever get the better of you?" Kit asked.

"In fisticuffs? Never."

"Never?"

"Well, when I was a kid, maybe. But once I got the beef on me, no man could best me." He stuck out his barrel chest.

"How many fights would you estimate you had in those days?"

Judd Ashe objected. "What relevance is this, Your Honor?"

"I will show the relevance," Kit said to the judge.

"I'll allow you only a few more questions along these lines," Judge Pardue said.

"You may answer the question," Kit said to Hanratty.

"I never kept count," Hanratty said. "But dozens. Had to be."

"Dozens of fights, and you never lost?"

"Never cried uncle once," Hanratty said, beaming at the jury.

"And as a police officer, you have had to subdue some pretty tough criminals, haven't you?"

Hanratty nodded. "Ya might say that."

"Ever get bested by one of them?"

"Never."

"Very impressive, Officer Hanratty. In fact, for the benefit of the jury, would you please step out here and stand next to me?"

"What is the meaning of this?" Judd Ashe said to the judge.

"Miss Shannon?" Judge Pardue said.

"Your Honor, I am almost finished," Kit said. "But Officer Hanratty's strength or weakness will be an issue here."

"Weakness!" Hanratty blurted. He did not wait for further directions. He stepped out of the witness box and stomped over to Kit.

He stood near her and faced the jury, pulling himself up to his full height. He stuck his chin out a little.

Kit turned quickly to Juan and motioned for him. "Come over here, Juan."

Juan, along with most everyone else within sight, looked confused. But with Corazón's prodding, he stood up. He took a few steps toward Kit, but when he looked at Hanratty, who was glaring back at him, he stopped.

"It's all right, Juan," Kit said. She held out her hand for him.

"What is the meaning of all this?" Judge Pardue said.

"Your Honor," said Kit, as Juan Chavez came to her side, "I am going to ask Officer Hanratty about his interrogation of my client." Kit stood between Hanratty and Juan, who was her height. The cop towered over both of them. "I wanted the jury to see the two men for themselves."

Then Kit stepped backward. The jury, and everyone else in the courtroom, looked at the nervous pair.

"That's enough," Judge Pardue said.

After Juan returned to his chair, and Hanratty to the stand, Kit jumped into her questions. She shot them fast and hard, determined not to give Hanratty any time to rest.

"Officer, you have testified the night of March twenty-fourth you beat my client, correct?"

"I had no other choice, I—"

"You can answer that question yes or no, Officer Hanratty."

"But—"

"Yes or no?"

"Yes."

"You testified that he attacked you."

"That's right."

"And you were frightened."

"Well, I—"

"Yes or no?"

Big Ed Hanratty's eyes began to dart between the jury and Kit Shannon. "I was sort of taken by surprise."

"Then you weren't really frightened—is that what you are telling us now?"

"Well, maybe a little."

"Which is it, Officer Hanratty?"

Judd Ashe said, "I object to this, Your Honor! Miss Shannon is badgering this witness."

Kit whirled at the prosecutor. "I'm sorry if my questions are too much for the manly Officer Hanratty."

Laughter filled the courtroom, and for the first time that day Kit felt like she had made a point.

Judge Pardue gaveled the courtroom to order. "Mr. Ashe, the questions Miss Shannon is asking are relevant. I will let Officer Hanratty answer as he sees fit."

Ashe paused a moment before resuming his seat.

Kit did not hesitate. "Were you frightened of my client or not?"

"I don't remember."

"So that is your third answer, is it? Now you don't remember?"

Hanratty shifted in his seat, his large chest seeming to sink. "All I know is I had to stop him."

"Stop him from what, Officer Hanratty?"

"Attacking me."

Kit faced the jury as she asked the next question. "So you would have this jury believe that you were so frightened or surprised or whatever it is you were, of Juan Chavez, that you had to beat him so severely that he was a bloody mess?"

Kit hoped the image of the massive Hanratty and the slight Juan, standing next to each other, would make any answer Hanratty gave seem the height of absurdity.

"I have told ya what happened," Hanratty said.

"I don't think you have, Officer," Kit said.

The policeman looked at her like a child caught stealing cookies. He quickly tried to hide the expression. Had the jury seen it the way she had?

"Isn't it true, Officer Hanratty, that you beat my client from the moment you had him alone?"

"Why, no!" Hanratty said.

"Isn't there another reason you beat him?"

"No!"

"Isn't it the fact, sir, that you beat him because you decided he was guilty?"

"No!"

Kit felt fury engulf her. "And a Mexican, too. You were going to be the judge, jury, and the executioner. Isn't that right, Officer Hanratty?"

"You can't prove that!" Hanratty blurted, and then immediately clamped his mouth shut.

"I see," Kit said slowly. "It may have happened just that way, but I can't prove it."

Hanratty paused, cleared his throat. "You are putting words in my mouth. Don't you put words in my mouth."

"Then give us the truth, Officer Hanratty!"

"I have done that."

"Juan Chavez never confessed, did he?"

"He did."

"You made that up, like you have made up this story about being frightened, the story you have now changed."

"No—"

"If you keep changing stories, Officer Hanratty, how can you expect the jury to believe anything you say?"

Hanratty looked at the jury and his lip trembled, as if he wanted to speak but couldn't come up with the words.

Kit did not allow him the opportunity. "I have no further use of this witness, Your Honor."

She returned to her seat, feeling both exhilarated and exhausted. This was only the first witness. Judd Ashe was just getting started.

Chapter 30

"DON'T TELL ME you ain't thinking about her," Gus said.

"I am telling you," Ted replied.

"You're a bad liar."

"You want a mouthful of knuckles?"

"Better that than you with a mouthful of propeller!"

Ted could not, would not, admit to Gus that he was thinking of Kit Shannon. But he was. Today was the first day of the trial of Juan Chavez. It seemed the only thing people in Los Angeles could talk about.

Today was also his test run. On Friday he would be flying for Mungerley and other potential backers. It had to be a success. Now he would take the plane up and try for a hundred yards. If he could get that, and land softly, then a hundred and fifty would be possible on Friday.

But even as the excitement of the run welled up within him, so too did the feeling that he should be in the courtroom. Why? Why should he feel that way when it was so clear he had no future with Kit Shannon?

He had heard the rumor about her engagement to Jeffrey Kenton. Why did he have such a bad feeling about that? Jealousy, of course. Hang it all! Would he never be free of that wild Irish rose?

Gus was right. If he didn't keep his mind on the business at hand he might stick the nose of the plane in the ground, or bust a wing, or do something else that would throw the whole project into jeopardy. If Mungerley and the others didn't see something good on Friday, it could set him back a year or more.

"All right," Ted said. "You made your point. Let's get back to work. I want to go up in an hour." Ted looked out at the bluff and the ocean beyond. The day was clear. He licked his index finger and held it up in the air. "The wind should be right then."

Gus grumbled. "If anything happens to this plane, by gum, I won't let you forget it."

"The plane? What about me?"

Gus spat in the sand. "I can always find another pilot." And then he broke into a gap-toothed grin.

"The prosecution calls Dayton Taylor."

Judd Ashe's words were barely out of his mouth when the courtroom doors opened and Taylor walked through.

Kit watched him strut down the aisle. When he glared at her she knew. This was as much about his dislike for her as it was for the truth. But she had no idea why he was here to testify.

After the oath, Judd Ashe asked, "You are a resident of Bunker Hill, is that correct?"

"Yes, sir," Taylor said.

"How long have you lived there, Mr. Taylor?"

"I have had a home on the hill for nearly seven years."

"Do you have a view of Angels Flight from your home?"

"I do, yes."

Kit leaned forward, studying Taylor's face. Whatever Ashe had up his sleeve, it was going to be important.

"On the night of March twenty-fourth, were you in your home?"

"Yes."

"And did you hear something?"

Kit said, "Objection, Your Honor. Mr. Ashe is leading the witness."

"Sustained," said the judge.

Looking annoyed, Ashe returned to the witness. "Can you tell us, sir, if anything out of the ordinary happened?"

"I heard what I thought was a woman screaming."

Ashe paused to let the effect sink in. Kit noticed the silence in the courtroom, as if everyone was listening with full attention.

"What time was it when you heard this scream, Mr. Taylor?"

"It was precisely twenty minutes after ten. I remember looking at my clock."

If Taylor was telling the truth, this was later than Kit expected. She watched his face carefully.

"What, if anything, happened next?" Ashe said.

"I immediately went to my front door and opened it."

"When you open your front door, Mr. Taylor, what is the view?"

"Straight down to Angels Flight, the platform."

"And how far away is the platform?"

"I would say one hundred yards."

"As you opened your door, what did you see?"

"A Mexican."

Kit tensed in her chair.

"A man?" Ashe said.

"Yes," said Taylor.

"How did you know he was a Mexican?"

Taylor shrugged. "I saw him clear as day."

"How could you seem him clearly?"

"The light from the house shined out and he was right on my front walk, only a few feet away from me."

"As far as I am from you?"

Taylor nodded. "A little closer even."

"What was he doing?"

"Running away."

"When you first saw him, he was running?"

"He stopped when I opened the door. He looked scared, like he had been caught or something. Then he took off."

"What did you do next?"

"I shouted after him, but he just kept on running."

"This man," Ashe said, pacing in front of the jury box. "Did you get a good look at him?"

"Like I said, he was very close."

"If you saw that man again, would you be able to identify him?"

"Oh yes."

"Mr. Taylor, do you see that man in the courtroom?"

Taylor turned his head toward Kit and Juan. "He is right over there, sitting next to Miss Shannon."

Ashe walked over to Kit's table and stood in front of Juan. "I would like the record to state that the witness, Mr. Taylor, has identified Juan Chavez as the man he saw on the night of March twenty-fourth."

Judge Pardue looked at the court reporter. "Put that in the record," he said.

"Your witness," Ashe said to Kit.

Kit looked at Juan. His face showed a mix of anger and confusion. Kit knew at that moment Taylor was lying.

She stood. Dayton Taylor looked at her defiantly.

"Mr. Taylor," Kit said. "What were you doing on the night of March twenty-fourth at twenty after ten at night?"

"Like I said, I heard a scream and I—"

"Excuse me, Mr. Taylor. I did not ask you what you heard. I asked what you were doing at the time?"

"Doing?"

"Yes, sir. Doing. Surely you were engaged in some activity other than standing by your front door waiting for someone to scream?"

A few of the audience members laughed. Taylor's face flushed slightly. "I was having a drink," he said.

"What sort of drink?"

"A drink. I don't recall."

"But you recall looking at your clock, don't you?"

"Yes, I—"

"And you recall the exact time, isn't that correct?"

"Yes . . ."

"Since you remember those details, don't you find it curious that you cannot remember what it is you had to drink?" Kit turned toward the jury.

Taylor's voice hardened with resolve. "I remember. It was brandy. I always have a brandy around ten o'clock at night."

Kit was once again sure he was lying, but now it was clear he would fight. He would be firm in his lies now. She could only pray the jurors would see through him. But how could she make sure?

She tried several questions about the details of the night, hoping Taylor would seem to be inventing his story as he went along. But he had an answer for everything. If she went on much longer like this it would only strengthen the crucial parts of his testimony.

Finally Kit said, "How is it that your memory of this night is so clear, Mr. Taylor?" As soon as she asked the question Kit was afraid she had made a mistake. Not only did her question seem petty, but it also opened the door for Taylor to say something that would further mark him as credible.

He leaned forward in the witness box. "I remember because it was something that shouldn't have happened on Bunker Hill."

There was a note in his answer, an attitude that made Kit curious. She wasn't sure what it was, but she sensed that she should encourage Taylor to continue.

"Why is that, Mr. Taylor?"

"Because Mexicans don't belong up there," he said.

He sat back in his chair, looking satisfied. *Mexicans don't belong up there.* Not on Bunker Hill. Not with the white people, the wealthy. It was a thought she was sure most, if not all, of the jurors would agree with. Most, if not all, of Los Angeles, too.

Kit turned to look at Juan, feeling the same hurt he must have felt as Corazón whispered Taylor's response to him. She looked out into the gallery where Juan's friends sat, wondering how much of Taylor's testimony they could understand.

She quickly turned to the judge. "Your Honor! May I request a recess until this afternoon?"

"Is this absolutely necessary, Miss Shannon?"

"I believe it is, yes."

"Does the prosecution object?"

Judd Ashe, looking serene, said, "No, Your Honor."

"All right," said the judge. "We will take our lunch hour early. Let us reconvene at one o'clock." He banged his gavel.

The deputy sheriff came and took Juan by the arm, leading him out the side. Kit pulled Corazón close to her. "I'm going to need your help," she said.

Ted Fox slipped his goggles on, the tint muting the bright sun. He stepped toward the plane and gave it a final look.

The plane was on its track, grooved wheels in place. Gus, looking sour, stood at the front with his hands on his hips.

"All set?" said Ted.

"I'm fine," said Gus. "And so's my plane. Just land her in one piece."

"*Your* plane?"

"Darn tootin'."

Ted shrugged and laughed. Gus was on his side, and he knew it. Gus wanted their baby to fly as much as he did. He had even donated a sock.

Gus's windsock barely flapped on the pole on top of the barn. Wind conditions were perfect. Ted put his leather gloves on. The sheepskin lining caressed his palms. He flexed his hands into fists a few times, and then stepped onto the ladder next to the plane.

"Then here we go," he said, as much to himself as to Gus.

Ted swung his legs into the cockpit. It felt perfect. Not only like it was made for him, but like he was made for *it*. This was his future, his destiny. What had Kit likened it to? The voice of God? In her mind, maybe. But looking at it from Darwin's point of view, it was simple nature. Ted had come to this moment in time through a long process of ascent. Call it fate, if you wanted. But now was the time.

Ted checked the rudder bar, pushing the pedals with his feet. The tail wagged. Now it was all up to the pistons Gus had so lovingly readied.

He looked at Gus. They were one thrust away from seeing if their grand plan was sound.

Gus had both his hands on one blade of the propeller. They had switched to the Phillips design—it looked like a propeller for a small ship—with a steep pitch near the hub. Ted knew the

Wrights were experimenting with a longer, thinner design. But he was sure, as Gus was, that the Phillips could support the weight.

Ted took one last look down the track toward his target—a large scrub with a red bandanna, over one hundred yards from the takeoff point. That's were he was headed.

If he took off. There was still the possibility that the plane would fare no better than the model. He might not even get off the ground.

Then the oddest thing happened. He wished Kit were here. He wished she could see him. He whacked himself on the side of the head. *Not now!*

"You going up or not?" Gus said.

Ted raised his hand. He saw Gus's eyes narrow, awaiting the signal. Ted whipped his hand down.

Gus lifted his leg, and then yanked the propeller down with one great thrust.

The engine popped and chugged to life. The prop spun, slowly at first. Then faster, faster, until it was blur. Ted felt the first pull of thrust and the tension cord holding fast from the rear.

Like a bird flying by, Gus rushed toward the tail. Ted watched until Gus got in place by the cord. The tail lifted slightly. The plane wanted to fly.

And so it was time. Ted lifted his hand once more, dropped it. Gus pulled the cord free.

The plane lurched forward.

The motion was faster than Ted had thought it would be. The image of a swan arising majestically from a lake had always been in his mind. This was more like being bumped from behind by a train.

The wheels grated against the wooden track, staying true. Wind whipped Ted's face. Every nerve inside him was alive. Forty feet of track to go.

Would the rudder hold? Ted vibrated in the cockpit seat, keeping the rudder straight with his feet. So far there was no pull from either side. The monoplane was balanced, the way it would have to be to fly.

Thirty feet. He started to feel lift as the cambered surface of the wings performed its work. The top curve stretched the air, thinning it; the underside slowed the flow, increasing pressure. The nose angled up.

Twenty feet. Was there enough power after all? That was the key. Ted got ready for the worst, just in case. If the plane didn't take off he would cut the engine and keep the plane steady as it slowed to a stop.

Ten feet.

And then the sound of the wheels stopped. The plane was off the ground.

"Whoooeeee!" Ted's voice cut the air like the wings of the plane. He was suddenly three, five, seven, ten feet up. He was flying.

The hum of the engine was like music. More than enough power! A hundred yards? He would make that easy.

Go for more, he thought. Then another voice hit his thoughts, and it sounded eerily like Gus's. *Set her down,* the voice said. *You have it made.*

In that split second, Ted felt intoxicated with joy. He had a choice. The plane was not in control, he was. A man was mastering the air. He was that man.

He glanced over the side. The dotted scrubs and sand mounds seemed to look up at him in awe. He gave them a friendly wave and did not feel foolish in the least.

The landing area he and Gus had smoothed out loomed ahead. Beyond that the bluff went on for several hundred more yards. He could try for more. What would be the harm? He could see the faces of his backers, mouths open in wonder.

Yes, he thought. *Just a little bit more.*

The scrub with the red bandanna passed under the plane. Ted thought he must be at least fifteen feet in the air.

Fifteen feet! Could he make twenty?

Suddenly the plane banked left. A gust from the ocean side. Ted pressed the rudder pedal and the plane responded. It came back right and caught the gust flush, lifting it sharply.

For a brief, exhilarating moment, Ted felt everything come together—flight, speed, control, height, and a certain connection to the air. It was more than physical. It was some primal force. He believed that man had evolved and, from his first conscious thoughts, wished to be like the birds.

Now he was, and once more he whooped.

Then another gust hit him from the side. A big one. Ted felt the plane bounce, as if something hit from under the left wing. And then he realized he was no longer in control.

He pressed the right rudder pedal hard. Then he heard a snap, heard a whipping sound under him. The rudder pedal went limp under his foot.

He was powerless to steer. The plane thrust sideways and forward at the same time. But it did not go down. It kept going upward, like a gull with its wings spread.

He had to cut the engine and bring it down. He flipped the switch and the engine quit. Now he was gliding, but without control.

And he was heading toward the ocean. The plane began to descend.

The bluff—it dropped off sharply just twenty yards ahead. For the first time Ted realized he could go over.

He could jump out. He was only ten feet or so in the air. The sand was soft.

But the plane. He couldn't let it go. No, he would make it. There was enough time.

Ted heard the shrill sound of Gus's voice. "Hey!" the mechanic screamed.

Ted quickly looked right and saw his assistant running like a gazelle toward him. He looked ahead. It would be close, but he would make it. The wheels would hit the sand. The plane would stop. The nose might hit the ground hard. Maybe the prop would crack. Couldn't be helped.

The wheels did hit the sand, and the plane did slow. But not quickly enough. Ted felt the nose dip down sharply. He had come to the edge of the bluff. He was going over.

No choice now. He had to jump.

He tried to push himself up from the cockpit seat. But he was held fast. Realizing his foot was tangled in the broken rudder wire, he pulled with all his strength, but to no avail.

Then the world started to spin crazily around him, becoming a chaos of sound and sight, of crunch and wind. He became a silly rag doll, unable to do anything but flail as he fell.

Chapter 31

FIRST VOICES. Then a blaze of pain. Finally, an awareness of light.

Ted Fox slowly struggled back to consciousness. His body felt like a crumpled wad of paper. The pain was so intense he wanted to give up to unconsciousness again. But no, that would be the easy way. And, he thought, he might never come back. Death was waiting for him with open arms.

What had happened? The plane . . . it had gone down.

"Ted." As if from some distant shore, Gus's voice cut through the stupor of Ted's mind. Ted felt his mouth open, his voice fight for words. A low, guttural sound came out.

The smell of salt air. He was by the sea. He was still on the ground. He tried to raise his head, but fresh pain shot from his neck to his chest. It felt like an explosion of liquid fire.

"Easy there," Gus said. "Easy." Ted felt hands on his shoulders, gentle and persuasive. "They're coming for you, son."

Who? The mortician?

"We'll get you to the hospital in short order. Don't you worry. Gus is here."

Ted fought for words. "Gus?"

"I'm here."

"The plane . . ."

"We'll build her again."

"It flew."

"You're right as rain, by golly. She sure did."

A thin, weak smile came to Ted's face. The knowledge of their success seemed to bring him strength. "Get me up," he said.

"No," Gus said. "You wait."

"I won't!" Ted was surprised at the vehemence in his own voice. He was going to fight through this pain, this accident. He was not going to be stopped.

He pushed himself up on one elbow. The pain was intense, but he was moving. At least he was moving.

Then Ted fell back, hitting his head on the ground. And between fresh bursts of pain he realized the truth—the terrible, frightening truth. He had no feeling in his legs.

———

"Clear that area!" Judge Pardue said.

Kit looked up from the knot of Juan's friends surrounding Juan at the rail. "If we may have just a moment, Your Honor?"

"Now, Miss Shannon!"

Kit nodded to the group. They began to shuffle back toward the rear of the courtroom.

"I am sorry, Your Honor," Kit said, "but this is a very emotional trial for many of—"

"I am not interested, Miss Shannon. May we proceed with the trial?"

"Of course. Again, I apologize."

The judge ignored her. "Mr. Taylor, please resume the stand. I will remind you that you are still under oath."

Taylor nodded as he took the witness chair. If anything, he looked more confident now. No doubt he had spent the recess talking with Judd Ashe, preparing for the final questions of Kit's cross-examination.

With a deep breath Kit approached the witness.

"Mr. Taylor," she said, "when we left off we were talking about your recollection of details that evening of March twenty-four."

Taylor smiled and nodded.

"I have only a few more questions," Kit said. "Do you wear eyeglasses, sir?"

"No," Taylor said proudly.

"Your eyesight is not questionable?"

"Not in the least."

Kit turned to the back of the courtroom. "Can you read that inscription, Mr. Taylor?" She pointed to the words carved in wood above the courtroom doors.

Taylor did not hesitate. "It says 'Equal Justice Under Law,' Miss Shannon."

"And so it does. I commend you."

Smugly, Taylor smiled.

"But on the night in question, Mr. Taylor, you were looking out into the darkness when you claim you saw the man outside."

"As I explained, the light coming from the house was bright."

"And it fell upon the man's face?"

"As I explained."

"Mr. Taylor, are you absolutely sure about what you saw outside your door?"

Leaning forward Taylor said, "As sure as I am sitting here, looking at you, Miss Shannon."

"Then would you, for the record, please identify who it is you saw that night outside your door?"

"I already did that, Miss Shannon. He's sitting right there at your table."

"I just want you to be sure, Mr. Taylor. Please look at him."

Taylor did, staring past Kit.

"Are you absolutely sure that is the man you saw?"

"Yes, it is, Miss Shannon. There is no mistake. I saw him outside my door that night. And, I might add, he looked like he had something to hide."

"Thank you, Mr. Taylor."

Kit turned from the witness and saw Judd Ashe staring at her. He seemed both incredulous and pleased. It was as if he believed Kit had just dug her own grave but was not quite ready to fill it with dirt.

Kit could not help the slight smile that came to her lips. She turned to the judge and said, "Your Honor, at this time I would ask Juan Chavez to please stand."

Judge Pardue, looking as perplexed as Ashe, shrugged his shoulders. He looked at the counsel table. "The defendant will stand," he said.

There was no movement from the counsel table. Pardue opened his mouth but suddenly stopped short.

Juan Chavez was walking forward from the back of the courtroom.

Then it was like a dam of noise burst. The reporters in the room began it, followed by the rest of the gallery. Judd Ashe was on his feet, shouting, "What is the meaning of this?"

Judge Pardue banged for order, even as he scowled at Kit. "Yes, Miss Shannon, what is the meaning of this?" But he knew. Kit was sure he and everyone else, including the jury, knew. Certainly Taylor did, as his face was suddenly a dangerous shade of red.

"Your Honor," Kit said, "the man at counsel table is Carlos Aruza, a friend of the Chavez family."

"Do you mean to tell me you planned this stunt?" said the judge.

"It is not a stunt, Your Honor, but the exposure of a witness not telling the truth."

"I object to that comment!" Ashe said.

"Order!" Pardue banged his gavel again. "Miss Shannon, I will see you in my chambers!"

Pardue was livid when Kit entered the office. "I have never seen such behavior in a courtroom!" he said.

Kit felt her knees trembling. She told herself to remain steady. She had anticipated this.

Judd Ashe closed the door behind him. "This is an outrage!" he said.

"I have the power to hold you in contempt," Pardue said, pacing in front of his desk. "Give me one good reason why I should not."

Kit exhaled slowly. "I will give you three, Your Honor."

Pardue stopped and stared.

"First," said Kit, "there is no basis for a contempt citation. The rules of procedure require a defendant to be present in court for trial. Juan Chavez was present in court. If you look at the rules, you will find no requirement that he be seated at counsel table."

Pardue flashed a look at Ashe. The prosecutor seemed confused. Neither one of them made a move toward the volume of procedure rules on the bookshelf.

"Second," said Kit, "the testimony of an eyewitness is subject to the highest degree of examination. The law holds that it is so powerful to a jury, it must be closely scrutinized."

Pardue remained silent.

"Finally, Your Honor, the search for truth is what guides your rulings as a judge."

"You presume to tell me my duty?" the judge said.

"No, Your Honor, only to explain my reasoning. In this search for truth, the rules of evidence have been formed over the centuries. And if there is one guiding principle that has emerged in all of that time, it is as Blackstone states: 'Juries are to be protected from biased or fraudulent testimony.' There was only one way for me to show the bias of the witness, Taylor, Your Honor. That is why I did it."

For a long moment Pardue seemed to churn everything in his mind. Judd Ashe broke the silence. "I am going to ask you to declare a mistrial, Your Honor. This jury cannot be fair now. We must start from scratch."

Kit wanted to say more but sensed she had said enough. It was all up to the judge.

Pardue heaved a heavy sigh. "I don't know why this always happens to me. Do you know that I had a lawyer pull a gun on another lawyer once? Right in front of the jury?"

Kit looked at Ashe, who seemed as perplexed as she was.

"Now it's women in the courtroom," Pardue said. "And circus stunts like what you just pulled."

"But, Your Honor—"

"Tut-tut, Miss Shannon. I am not going to pretend that I approve. But the state bar has, and I am not going to question their decision. What I am prepared to do, however, is report to them any improprieties that you visit upon my courtroom."

Kit was speechless. A report like that could put her entire career in jeopardy. But she had done nothing wrong. She was sure of it.

"That settles that," Ashe said. "A mistrial will be—"

"Hold on there," the judge said. "I did not say I would declare a mistrial."

"But—"

"No, I am going to allow the trial to continue."

"But, Your Honor!" said Ashe.

"I will let the jury consider what happened," Pardue said. "But I am also going to warn you, Miss Shannon." He pointed his finger at her. "Don't you ever pull something like that in my court again, unless you tell me you are going to do it. Is that understood?"

"Understood," Kit said.

"For your sake," said the judge, "I hope so. I am going to call a recess until tomorrow morning so you can think about that very thing, Miss Shannon."

Ted's first thoughts were of Kit Shannon. He wanted her here, in the hospital. With him. He was going to die.

No, it was just the pain that made him want to die. And it was the pain that made him long for Kit's comforting hand on his brow.

Yet that would never be. It was pure torture to think of it— worse than being housed in a broken body. But he could not stop thinking of her.

He was only vaguely aware of nurses scurrying outside the room. It was cold in here, dim. How did he get here? He must have passed out. The last thing he remembered was Gus talking to him near the beach. Where was Gus?

His legs. He still could not feel anything in them. A creeping fear took hold, constricting his breath.

What would he do without his legs? His dreams of aviation would be gone. He would be reduced to dependence on others. He would be weak. And in a Darwinian world, the weak did not survive.

He needed strength. He needed a miracle.

Miracle ... God was in the miracle business, but Ted did not believe in God. Not in Kit's God. But could he? For so long he had thought a deity was a crutch for people too weak to face the world.

But then, he thought bitterly, *I will need crutches for the rest of my life.*

A sense of hopelessness overtook him. He could do nothing to heal himself, and the God some called the Great Physician was not part of his reality. How he wanted Kit now, to convince him otherwise.

Dr. Jeffrey Kenton entered the room.

Ted's heart began beating wildly. Here was a man he could easily hate, but who now held his fate in his hands.

"How do you feel, Mr. Fox?" Kenton said.

"Like I must look," Ted said. "Worse."

"You're lucky to be alive."

"Am I?"

Kenton did not answer right away. Perhaps he had his own doubts.

"You could have, probably should have, broken your neck," said the doctor.

"Why can't I feel my legs?"

Kenton nodded. "You are very direct. I sense you would like me to be."

"I would."

"Your spinal cord was injured. It may be that you have what we call trauma—a shock affecting the nerve tracts. If that is so, there is a very good chance you will recover the use of your legs."

"And if that isn't so?"

Kenton looked at the floor. "Then you likely would not."

Ted's body shivered.

"There is one more thing," Dr. Kenton said.

Ted waited.

"The bone of your left leg was shattered."

"Maybe it's good I can't feel it then."

Kenton allowed himself a smile. Ted studied his face. The smile looked pained.

"It is so, perhaps," Kenton said. "Shall I continue to be direct?"

"Yes."

"It may be necessary to amputate."

The word hovered in the room like a vulture. "When will you know?"

"Soon," said Dr. Kenton. "I'm sorry."

Ted believed he was. "No need to be sorry, Doc. Those are the cards."

"I'll be back soon to check on you," Kenton said and turned.

"Doc?"

Kenton faced Ted.

"Be good to Kit."

Kenton nodded. Then he left the room.

———

"It was good what you did?" Corazón questioned Kit once they were back at the hotel.

"I showed that Taylor was lying," Kit replied. "So that much was good. But I drew negative attention to myself from the judge, and that was not so good."

"But that man he no see Juan," Corazón replied. "That is good."

Kit sighed. There was no way to fully explain to Corazón that this was only a minor victory. She wouldn't know for some time whether it had planted any reasonable doubt in the minds of the jurors.

"We need to continue praying," Kit finally said. "This entire matter is in God's hands. He alone can allow for the truth to be revealed."

Later that night, after Corazón had gone to her own room, Kit lay awake thinking about the day. Eventually her thoughts turned to Jeffrey. She would eventually have to deal with him in court, but more importantly, she needed to think about her marriage plans.

"Oh, God, am I doing the right thing? Jeffrey loves you, and he seems so completely devoted to me. How could I ever want for anything more?" She sighed and looked up at the shadows on the ceiling.

"I can't deny that my feelings for Ted are still buried deep inside. It hurts to know that he so completely dismisses his need for you. I care about him, Lord. I care that he finds his way to you. I care that he comes to know you for himself. Please make yourself real to him, God. Even if we're not meant to be together, I want him to know the peace of having you as the Lord of his life."

Kit drifted off, the prayer still on her lips as veiled and curious shapes came to mind in the form of dreams. Eventually the forms came clear and she found herself surrounded by the faces of the people she loved and cared about—much like the artistic rendering in the newspaper. One by one they began reaching out to take hold of her, pulling her in one direction and then another. The grips became tighter, more painful. Kit pleaded with them to stop, but the images took on ghostly, grotesque forms and only laughed at her efforts.

She fought against them, but they were tearing her apart. With a start, Kit sat straight up in bed, panting from the battle. Realizing it was only a dream, she steadied her breathing and rubbed her arms, as if to ward off imaginary pain.

"Only a nightmare," she whispered. "Nothing more. It can't hurt me." But tomorrow the nightmare might very well be real. And that nightmare could hurt her—and Juan—a great deal.

Chapter 32

THE NEXT MORNING Judd Ashe called Jeffrey Kenton to the stand.

Kit's heart pounded like the judge's gavel. She knew Jeffrey was going to be called, but now that the moment was here she wondered how she was going to face him. How do you cross-examine someone you love?

Jeffrey took the oath and sat in the witness chair. For a brief moment his eyes met Kit's. She looked down at her notes.

"You are a medical doctor, is that correct?" said Judd Ashe.

"Correct."

"And you are on the staff at Sisters Hospital?"

"I am."

"Were you on duty during the night of March twenty-fourth and early morning hours of the twenty-fifth?"

"I was."

"And was an emergency case brought into the hospital that night?"

"Yes."

"Please describe for the court and the jury the details of that case."

Hands folded serenely on his lap, Jeffrey said, "A police officer, Ed Hanratty, brought in a young woman. She had been badly beaten. She had blood and bruises on her face and, I determined, on other parts of her body."

"Was this young woman conscious?"

"Yes, but terribly distraught."

"Is that young woman in the courtroom?"

"Yes," said Dr. Jeffrey Kenton. He pointed to Gloria Graham, sitting in a chair just behind the prosecutor's table.

"For the record," said Ashe, "Dr. Kenton has identified Gloria Graham."

"So noted," said the judge.

"How long did you attend to Miss Graham?"

"I would say forty-five minutes or so."

"Was anyone with you during this time?"

"Only Officer Hanratty."

"Any nurses?"

"The attending nurse left the room shortly after Miss Graham was brought in."

Kit frowned and quickly scribbled a note.

"Now," Ashe said, "did Miss Graham say anything to you?"

"Yes." Jeffrey shifted in the chair.

"What did she say?"

"Objection," Kit said. "That calls for hearsay."

"Overruled," said Judge Pardue.

"You may answer," said Ashe.

"She told me . . ." Jeffrey hesitated. ". . . that she had been violated."

"Sexually?"

"Yes."

"And did you determine if that was true?"

"I did. And it was."

Judd Ashe paused, then said, "Did you hear the victim, Gloria Graham, identify the man who attacked her?"

"I object!" Kit said. "That is hearsay once again."

"I did not ask her for the name," Ashe said. "I only asked if he heard her give an identification."

"I will overrule the objection," said Judge Pardue.

"I did hear her make an identification," Jeffrey said.

"Take the witness," Ashe said to Kit.

Take him where? She had questions, but how could she ask them? Kit thought for a moment of simply letting him go. But his testimony had hurt Juan by painting a picture of a savagely beaten and violated woman. If she did nothing to blunt that testimony, she would not be serving her client. The skirmish in her soul kept her in her seat.

"Do you wish to question this witness?" Judge Pardue said.

Kit still did not know the answer. She looked at Juan and Corazón. Their eyes pleaded with her for help.

"I will inquire," Kit said. She stood and took a moment to compose herself. Jeffrey looked at her with eyes as warm as a summer's day. *Only a few questions,* she told herself, *and then let him go.*

"Good afternoon, Dr. Kenton."

"Good afternoon, Miss Shannon." He smiled. Kit felt her pulse quicken. Could the jury see what was between them? She was sure they were blind if they could not!

"You stated that the victim was badly beaten," Kit began. "Is it possible that her condition could have been caused in some other way?"

"I am not sure I understand your question."

"For example, in a fall or some other accident?"

"No, Miss Shannon."

"Is that your opinion, or are you saying there is no possibility?"

Jeffrey's brow pinched. "Certainly there is a remote possibility that it could have happened some other way."

"Thank you, Doctor." Should she stop now? No, it was too soon. Juan was her client. In a court of law, that had to trump even love.

Kit remembered the note she had written to herself when Jeffrey was testifying. She retrieved it from her table, read it quickly, and then asked, "You testified that a nurse was on duty when Gloria Graham was brought in."

"Yes."

"And that she left the room?"

"Yes."

"Why did she leave?"

Jeffrey cocked his head. "I assume she had other duties," he said.

"Did you ask her to leave?"

Slowly, Jeffrey shook his head. "I don't believe so."

Despite her feelings for Jeffrey, Kit felt the heat of battle intensify in her. There was something about his answer that did not sit right. "Wouldn't that be odd, for a nurse to leave you when you had an emergency?"

"No, Miss Shannon," Jeffrey said somewhat sharply. "The night nurses at Sisters must attend to many matters."

"You did not ask her to leave?"

"Why would I do that, Miss Shannon?"

Suddenly he seemed angry. And why not? She was questioning his integrity.

"I have no further questions," Kit said. Her eyes lingered on Jeffrey for a moment, asking for forgiveness. Then she turned and walked quickly to her seat.

Judge Pardue excused Jeffrey. With a final look at Kit, he left the courtroom.

———————

"It was horrible!" Kit said.

Jeffrey put his arms around her and pulled her close. "For me, as well," he said.

They rode in Jeffrey's enclosed carriage—Jeffrey had hired a driver for the lunch hour—leisurely taking in the groves of gum trees and stretches of orchards in Vernon, a beautiful horticultural suburb of Los Angeles. To the left Kit could see the Los Angeles River winding between its leveed banks, under numerous bridges, and through the city in a tortuous course toward the ocean.

"I don't ever want to go through that again with you," Kit said.

"Never again, sweetheart."

"Say that again, Jeffrey."

"Sweetheart."

She lifted her face to him, and he kissed her gently. Longing stirred within her. A longing to be free of all the muck she had felt in the last days, weeks, months. Yes, even since she had arrived here.

What did God want from her now? Why had He brought her here?

To save Juan? To meet Jeffrey? To go through the valley of the shadow, for reasons only He knew? But what of the future?

It was sitting next to her. Doctor Jeffrey Kenton—who was holding her safe in his arms—was her future.

"When shall we go?" she said.

Jeffrey pulled back so he could look at her. "Do you mean it?"

"How soon?"

"I can start to make the arrangements today."

"Grand," she said.

"What is it, dear?"

"Hmm?"

"You sounded troubled just then."

Kit gazed out the window at a cascade of pepper trees lining the street. They seemed, for the moment, like a row of inquisitors. "It's Juan," she said.

"I know, I know." Jeffrey pulled her close again. "I think you have performed your duties magnificently."

"Do you really?"

"I do. Your client could not have a better advocate."

"Do you think the jury . . ."

"The jury will do what is right, Kit."

She nodded. "Jeffrey, there is something else that bothers me."

"What is it, dear?"

"I never got to ask you, but when you examined Gloria Graham, could you tell if she had been drinking liquor?"

The heavy clapping of horse hooves vibrated the cab. Jeffrey removed his arms from Kit so he could look at her fully. "Kit, my interrogation is over."

"I know that. I just . . . it has been eating at me. Something isn't right in what we've been told."

"You know I can't—"

"Jeffrey, I must know."

"Kit, I am a doctor. You know as well as I that the relationship I have with my patients is confidential."

Yes, she knew. Just as it was with her and her clients. She was wrong to ask.

"Oh, Jeffrey," she said, falling onto his chest. "Let us never have secrets between us. Let us love each other always."

His lips brushed her forehead. "Always, my love. Always."

Chapter 33

JUDD ASHE STATED, "The prosecution calls Gloria Graham."

A collective murmur rippled across the room. Kit was well aware this was the most important witness of all. She had no idea what the jury thought of the previous witnesses. But what they thought of Gloria Graham could send Juan to prison—or set him free.

Gloria Graham looked scared. Her eyes darted around like mice in a maze. Her hands—fingers entwining and releasing—moved up and down on her lap.

Kit studied her closely. Was she merely nervous? That would be understandable. But there could be other reasons. Kit remembered another lesson Earl Rogers had taught her. Many lawyers try to take careful notes about what a witness says before they cross-examine. Rogers never did. Instead, he watched their face and hands.

Often they would signal by gesture or look that they were unsure about something or, worse, lying.

Judd Ashe handled Gloria with care. "Now, don't be nervous, Miss Graham. I know this is very difficult for you."

The witness nodded.

"But you understand how important it is for you to be as clear as possible for us, don't you?"

Again, Gloria nodded. Judge Pardue leaned over and said, "Miss Graham, for the benefit of the record, please answer out loud. That man over there, the court reporter, is taking down what you say." He seemed like a father instructing a nervous daughter.

"I am so sorry," Gloria said.

"Continue," Pardue said to Ashe.

"How are you employed, Miss Graham?"

"I'm a maid for Mr. Alfred Mungerley."

"Of Angeleno Heights?"

"Yes, sir."

"How long have you worked for Mr. Mungerley?"

"Nigh on four years, sir."

"Now, Miss Graham, during the time you worked for Mr. Mungerley, did you come to be acquainted with the defendant, Juan Chavez?"

Her darting eyes looked at Juan quickly, then back at Ashe. "Yes, sir."

"Would you please tell the jury how you came to know the defendant?"

"He works for Mrs. Fairbank, at the place next to Mr. Mungerly's. Works in the garden mostly."

"Did you ever talk to him?"

Gloria shook her head.

Kit felt Juan's arm on hers and turned to him. "*No es verdad,*" he whispered. *It is not true.* Kit patted his hand.

"You never had an occasion to talk to the defendant?" Ashe said.

"No, never."

"Why not, Miss Graham?"

She looked surprised at the question. "Well, because, he was a . . ." She hesitated, looked confused for a moment, and then said, "Because he was just a hired hand, an outside worker."

"Did the defendant, Juan Chavez, ever attempt to talk to you?"

Gloria looked down at her hands. "He tried."

Kit felt Juan's hand again, but this time she did not turn to him. She put up her own hand to signal him to be quiet.

"How did he try, Miss Graham?"

"Well . . . one day when I was bringing the laundry back to Mr. Mungerley's, I went up the back way, not up the front way like usual." Gloria looked up from her hands for a moment, then back down. "He was in Mrs. Fairbank's yard, and he . . ."

"He what, Miss Graham?"

"He had his shirt off."

There was a gasp from a woman sitting in the front row, loud enough for all to hear.

"Did he try to speak to you?" Ashe said.

"Yes."

"What did he say?"

"He . . ."

"Don't be nervous, Miss Graham. We are only interested in the truth. You are in court now. There is nothing he can do to you."

Kit said, "I object to that comment, Your Honor."

"Sustained as to the last comment," said the judge. "Members of the jury, you will disregard the district attorney's last statement."

You can't unring the bell, Kit thought bitterly. Ashe knew exactly what he was doing. The question was, did he know she was lying?

"What did the defendant say to you, Miss Graham?"

"He looked at me and said, 'Come to me tonight.'"

Juan, listening to Corazón, tensed palpably next to Kit.

"Were those his exact words?"

"Yes, sir."

"How long ago was this?"

"Only just a short while ago."

"A matter of months?"

"Yes, sir."

Kit looked at the jury. Every one of them seemed attentive to Gloria's testimony. Most of them looked to be on the edge of outrage.

"Turning to the night of March twenty-fourth," Ashe said, "can you tell us where you were in the early hours of that evening?"

Gloria cleared her throat. "I had gone downtown to window shop. I can't afford fancy clothes, but I like to look, you see. I walked to Angels Flight and took it to the top. I was returning home to Mr. Mungerley's."

"Let me stop you there, Miss Graham," Ashe said. "When you got in the car at Angels Flight, were you alone?"

"Yes, sir."

"And the fare for the ride is collected at the top, isn't that right?"

"Yes, sir."

"Now, as you rode to the top, did you notice anything unusual?"

"Yes, sir. I saw someone running up the stairs."

"Running?"

"Following the car, sir."

"And were you able to recognize who it was?"

"Yes, sir. It was Juan Chavez."

More gasps from the audience. Kit looked at the gallery and

saw the intense interest there. Ashe had prepared Gloria well. The story was making great theater.

"Were you frightened?" Ashe said.

"A little. He must have been following me all night."

"Did you think about asking for help—from the wheel man, perhaps?"

"Yes, I did, but I thought I could talk to him. I never thought he would try to . . . to . . ."

"Rape you, Miss Graham?"

She nodded.

"Answer aloud, please," said Judge Pardue.

"Yes," Gloria said.

Judd Ashe allowed the weight of the answer to have its full effect. He paced in front of the jurors, saying nothing for a long moment.

"To spare you any more of this, Miss Graham," Ashe said finally, "I will remind the jury of Dr. Kenton's description of your injuries. I have only one more question to ask you. Is the man who raped and beat you the defendant, Juan Chavez?"

Gloria looked at Juan. "Yes," she said.

"Your witness," Ashe said.

Kit took a deep breath. She would have to be careful, very careful. Gloria clearly had the sympathy of the jury. A direct attack on her credibility would do more harm than good. But Kit had no choice but to go directly to the heart of it—Gloria Graham was lying. But why?

"Miss Graham," Kit said, "I believe you testified that you work for Mr. Alfred Mungerley."

Gloria's eyes were no more steady with Kit than they had been with Ashe. She did not meet Kit's gaze directly. "Yes."

"But you are not currently so employed, are you?"

Now Gloria looked at Kit quizzically. "I don't understand."

"Well, you have not been working at his house since the night you were injured, have you?"

"No, miss."

"In fact, you have not been living there, have you?"

"No . . ."

"Where are you living now, Miss Graham?"

"Objection," said Ashe. "Irrelevant and immaterial. Miss Graham's location is confidential, to keep her from possible harm."

"Sustained," said the judge.

Kit looked at the judge. "But, Your Honor—"

"I said sustained, Miss Shannon. Move on."

"Then I will ask Miss Graham what money she is living on, wherever she is staying."

Before Gloria could answer Ashe spoke. "We will inform the court that our office is making provision for her during the course of this trial."

"Very well," said Judge Pardue. "Now move on."

Kit had the distinct impression the judge wanted to protect the witness. That was unfair under the rules of evidence. A judge was to be impartial. But this was not the time to argue the point.

"Miss Graham," said Kit, "when Mr. Ashe asked you whether you had ever talked to my client, and to your answer of 'No,' he asked 'why not?', you hesitated at first. Do you recall that?"

"Objection," Ashe said. "That misstates the evidence."

"Your Honor," said Kit, "I would like the court reporter to read Miss Graham's answer."

Judge Pardue scowled. The court reporter, a dapper man taking shorthand notes on long, green paper, suddenly found himself the center of attention. "Is this absolutely necessary?" the judge said.

"It is," said Kit. "Please read the exchange when Mr. Ashe asked the witness about talking to Mr. Chavez."

The reporter flipped through the last few pages of his notes.

Then, in a virtual monotone, read the exchange.

> *Question: You never had an occasion to talk to the defendant?*
> *Answer: No, never.*
> *Question: Why not, Miss Graham?*
> *Answer: Well, because, he was a, because he was just a hired hand, an outside worker.*

"Thank you," Kit said. "Miss Graham, were you about to say because he was a Mexican?"

"Objection!" Ashe shouted. "Incompetent, irrelevant, and immaterial!"

"Sustained!" Pardue said. "Miss Shannon, I am warning you."

Kit stole a glance at the jury. It was not good to be warned by the judge. Jurors, Rogers had told her, think of the judge as one rung under God.

"I beg the court's pardon," Kit said, "but I should like to examine the witness on this question. My client is of Mexican descent. I would like to know from the witness if that has at all affected her testimony."

Kit could almost feel the outrage emanating from virtually everyone in the courtroom. To make such a suggestion was an affront, especially in a case of rape. To question the honesty of a white woman against a brown man! It just wasn't done.

"No, Miss Shannon," said the judge. "I have sustained the objection. Move on."

She was beginning to feel like a steer being prodded to move along to the slaughterhouse.

"You testified that Juan said, 'Come to me tonight.' Were those his exact words?"

"Yes," Gloria said.

"But Mr. Chavez does not speak English."

There was only a momentary pause before Gloria said, "I understand Spanish, Miss Shannon. Enough to get by. Enough to know what he said."

Kit decided not to press the point. Gloria no doubt had some understanding of Spanish from her years as a domestic, working with hired hands and the like. This part of her story would be hard to crack.

"Miss Graham," Kit said, "you testified that you were downtown just before this incident took place, is that right?"

"Yes," Gloria said.

"Window shopping?"

"Yes."

"At night?"

Gloria hesitated. "Yes."

"How long did you shop the windows, Miss Graham?"

"I don't remember a time."

"How long must you have been looking into windows, then? Hours?"

"I told you I can't remember."

"What about your best estimate, Miss Graham?"

"Your Honor," said Ashe, "the witness has testified she cannot remember. We are not interested in estimations."

"But we are interested in the truth," Kit said, "and in why witnesses can remember some things but not others."

"Enough," said Pardue. In a gentler voice he said, "Miss Graham, is it possible for you to estimate the amount of time you spent in window shopping?"

"I don't think so," Gloria said.

"Thank you," said Pardue. "Move on, Miss Shannon."

Sighing, Kit said, "What else did you do while you were downtown, Miss Graham?"

"What else?"

"Did you have something to eat?"

"Yes, I believe I did."

"Did you have something to drink?"

Gloria looked surprised. "What do you mean?"

Kit perceived the scent of a fresh trail. "Liquor, Miss Graham. Did you have any liquor?"

As Gloria's eyes widened, Ashe objected again. Kit hoped the jury would see it as an attempt to interrupt a promising turn in the cross-examination.

Judge Pardue said, "I will allow the witness to answer this one question. Miss Graham, take your time to answer this. Did you have any liquor to drink on the night you were attacked?"

Gloria seemed to recover her balance. "No," she said firmly. "I never drink liquor of any kind."

The change in the witness was suspiciously sudden. Now Kit had a decision to make. Could she trust the jury to see what she saw? Had she injected just enough doubt to make a conviction unlikely? If she kept going, there was a chance Gloria, emboldened, would become a stronger witness. She was certainly being helped by the judge.

What to do? Cross-examination was not good for "fishing trips." Yet Gloria Graham was vulnerable. Somehow, somewhere, Kit was certain she was hiding something. But how to find it?

"I have no more questions," Kit said.

Even before she got back to her chair, Kit heard Ashe say, "Your Honor, the prosecution rests."

Chapter 34

EARL ROGERS TAPPED HIS FINGERS together. "Don't put him on the stand," he said.

Kit was afraid he would say that. They were in his office, and as the sun set outside his window, Kit felt the prospects of a favorable verdict for Juan setting with it.

"But I have no other witnesses," Kit said.

"Your client can't speak the language. A jury should not hold that against him, but it will. That's hard experience, Kit."

"Then what do I do?"

Rogers looked at her steadily. "You stand up and tell the court that the defense also rests. You say that the prosecution has failed to prove its case. Then you ask the judge to dismiss the charges."

Kit's mouth dropped open. "Really?"

"He will deny the motion, of course."

Confused, Kit shook her head.

"Then you go to closing arguments. And you argue the Great

Rule. You tell that jury that ever since man became aware of justice, those accused of a crime are presumed innocent. Innocent! Yes, completely innocent until proven guilty beyond a reasonable doubt. And then you show them how this case is riddled with reasonable doubt."

Kit nodded. She agreed with the Great Rule. It was the essence of justice. Without it, the poor and weak would be helpless to stand up to the awesome power of the state.

"Any other advice?" she asked.

Rogers smiled. "You believe in God. I suggest you pray to Him. Hard."

There was no better advice. As Kit left Rogers' office and walked the hallway toward her own, she began to pray earnestly for strength and guidance, but most of all for the ability to communicate—to remind the jurors about the Great Rule that protected all of them.

She entered her office and closed the door. An orange glow from the setting sun illuminated her office. She went to her window and looked out.

Something moved on the street below.

A man. She was sure she had seen a man looking up at her window. But he had moved quickly out of sight.

Was it just her imagination? McGinty had not solved the mystery of the man who had attacked her or the one who had saved her.

She tried not to think of it. She felt very alone. Jeffrey was not with her. She wanted him. But that was not to be, not tonight. Tonight she would have to pray and work. Tomorrow she would plead for Juan's freedom.

———

"She flew," said Gus. "By gum, she flew."

Ted smiled and it felt wonderful. Even though the pain was still with him, he had at least accepted it—like an unwelcome guest who has an engraved invitation.

But Gus was more than welcome. "How far?" Ted asked. "Did you measure?"

" 'Course I did. You think I'm gonna let you bust up my ship and not get a measure?"

"*Your* ship?"

"I'm the one nursin' her back to health while you lie around on your rudder all day!"

A laugh worked its way out of Ted's throat, followed by a sharp jolt of pain. "Just wait till I get out of here. They're gonna have to nurse you."

"Hundred and fifty," Gus said.

Ted looked at him, astonished. "A hundred and fifty yards?"

"Easy. And if you knew what you were doin', it could have been two hundred, maybe two-fifty."

Unexpectedly, tears crept into Ted's eyes, stinging them. "We did it."

"Yeah, but we still . . . what's the matter?"

"I'm just . . . thanks, Gus. Thanks for everything."

"Hey, now, you make it sound like you and me are quits or something. No, sir. Even though you busted up my ship, as soon as you can get yourself out of here we'll—"

"Gus."

"—take 'er up again, soon as we fix—"

"Gus!"

"What?"

Ted reached up from his bed and grabbed Gus's shirt, pulling him closer. "Listen. You build it again. And find another pilot."

"Find another . . . You losin' your nerve?"

"No, Gus, my leg."

The mechanic's face turned pale. "No."

Ted nodded. "Some other hero will have to conquer the skies."

"Can't be. No, it—"

"Face it, Gus! And don't say any more about it. You got that?"

"Sure, Ted. Sure."

The eerie silence was broken by a pretty nurse. She held a stack of newspapers in her arms. "I'm sorry," she said when she saw Ted had a guest.

"No," Ted said. "Come in. This is Gus. Stay away from him. He's trouble."

Gus scowled at the nurse, who seemed suddenly confused. "I have those papers you requested," she said.

"Just put them on the table," Ted said. As she did, Ted looked at Gus. "Thanks for coming. You don't have to come again."

"Try and stop me," Gus said, putting his hat on with a defiant tug. He turned and walked out without another word.

The pretty nurse came to Ted's bedside. "Are you feeling better?" she said.

"Now I am," he said.

She blushed.

"What's your name?" Ted asked.

"Martha," she said.

"You're very young to be a nurse."

"I am training, sir." She pulled a fresh blanket over him.

"Practicing on me, eh?"

"Oh, sir." Martha had a charming laugh, too.

"You like it here?"

"It has been very exciting."

"My presence?"

Martha smiled. "We have been very busy with the emergency cases. You're one."

"Of a number?"

"Oh yes! It started with Miss Gra . . ." She stopped herself.

"Were you going to say Miss Graham?"

Martha shook her head. "I've said too much."

She had indeed. She had been about to say Gloria Graham, and that meant it was about Kit and her case. Ted could not stop himself. He reached for Martha's hand. "Tell me, were you on duty when Gloria Graham was brought in?" Ted had followed the case in the newspapers. The reporters said it looked bad for Kit. He wanted to know why.

"I'm not supposed to talk about it," Martha said.

Ted did not let go of her arm. "Look at me, my dear. Do I look like a threat to anyone? I ask because I have been following the case, and any news would be welcome for me. I might even forget my bones are rattling inside my skin."

The nurse hesitated. Then her eyes softened. "All right. But promise you won't tell on me."

"I promise, Martha."

She told him, in whispered tones, about the night Gloria was brought in. The big policeman. The tension she felt from Dr. Kenton. And how badly Gloria was hurt. She was sure that was why Dr. Kenton had conferred with another doctor, who had obviously been taken from his bed.

A distant voice sounded in Ted's head. "Doctor? What doctor?"

"I do not know, sir," she said somewhat shyly.

Suddenly Ted forgot about the pain in his body. "Where did you see this doctor?"

"Only from a distance. He was talking with Dr. Kenton and the policeman."

"Where?"

"I only . . ." She paused. "I should not say anything more."

"Martha."

"I have said too much. Dr. Kenton said this was a matter for the police and I was not to speak of it. Please, sir."

Ted patted her hand. "All right. But now you must do me a favor."

"Sir?"

"It's very important. Will you?"

"I will try."

Chapter 35

"GENTLEMEN OF THE JURY," Kit said. "This is the last chance I will have to talk to you."

The twelve stone faces looked back at her. They hid their emotions well. Kit had no idea what was in their hearts. Nor in the hearts of the gallery that was packed to standing room. Earl Rogers was there with Clarence Darrow next to him. Reporters from every paper in California, and some from New York, anxiously awaited the outcome. Aunt Freddy had made it, brought by Alfred Mungerley. Even Frances Sweet, the witness she had interviewed, was in the courtroom. She had even smiled and winked at Kit before the session began.

But it did not matter in the slightest what the audience thought. It did not matter that this story would spread across a nation, and perhaps an ocean or two. No, the only thing that mattered was what these twelve jurors thought of this final plea by Kit Shannon.

She had not slept the night before. But her fatigue left her body, which was energized for the closing argument. Judd Ashe had made his closing argument and would get a final rebuttal after she was finished. She had only this moment with the jury.

"In a criminal trial," Kit continued, "the prosecution gets the last word with the jury. This is the only chance for Juan Chavez to plead his innocence. He, and I, thank you in advance for your attention."

She paused and looked at Juan. His face was strangely serene. Corazón told Kit that they had prayed together last night, and a sense of peace had come over them. They had placed all of their faith in God—and in Kit Shannon.

Kit turned back to the jury. "Under our system of justice, any defendant is presumed by law to be innocent of any crime, innocent until every essential element of a crime is established beyond a reasonable doubt."

Remembering what Earl Rogers had told her, that a judge was considered a near deity, Kit motioned toward Judge Pardue. "The judge will instruct on the law, gentlemen. He is going to tell you that it is incumbent upon the prosecution to prove every material element of the offense beyond a reasonable doubt. *Every* material element. And if you have such reasonable doubt on any one essential, it is your sworn duty to acquit Juan Chavez."

The words were coming straight from her heart now. "The judge will also tell you that you are not bound to anything any witness says if they do not produce a conviction beyond a reasonable doubt in your minds that what they say is in accord with other facts, or with common sense. Yes, gentlemen, even in courts of law, common sense is still considered worthy of respect."

There was a chuckle from the gallery, and at least one juror smiled. One juror! That was all she would need to keep Juan from conviction. But that would only be a mistrial, and another trial would follow shortly after that. No, she did not want just one juror. She wanted them all. She wanted an acquittal.

She went through the testimony of the witnesses, pointing out inconsistencies, reviewing their demeanor. Everyone saw and heard the same witnesses, but had the jurors seen and heard what she had? Would they be reasonable men?

That was the crucial question. For passion could overcome reason, and that was the danger here.

"I am almost finished, gentlemen," Kit said. She had been arguing for almost two hours. "But I must speak to you of one more matter. Mr. Ashe told you in his argument that this case was not about skin color or prejudice. If he believes that, gentlemen, I believe he is naïve."

Ashe jumped to his feet. "I must object, Your Honor!"

"Sit down, Mr. Ashe." Judge Pardue's tone was sharp. "Miss Shannon is addressing an issue that you yourself brought up. You may address the jury on rebuttal."

With an audible huff, Ashe plopped back in his chair.

"Yes, gentlemen," Kit said, a burst of vigor coursing through her, "at this time, in this city, we must be brave enough to look into our own hearts and root out what prejudice is there. Will you do it? Will you twelve men, whose faces are white, look inward and not let the fact that my client's face is brown affect your decision?"

Kit felt her hands trembling. She had crossed a threshold. There was no going back.

"As a people, we in Los Angeles are a bundle of prejudices. We are prejudiced against other people's color. Prejudiced against other people's religion. Prejudiced against other people's politics. Prejudiced against people's looks. Prejudiced about the way they dress."

She glanced into the audience and saw Mrs. Eulalie Pike, who wouldn't have dreamed of missing this event, fanning her face. The court was completely silent, seemingly suspended on her every word.

"All I ask, gentlemen, is this: That you are strong enough, honest enough, and decent enough to lay aside prejudice in this case and decide it as you ought to. I believe that you are. Because I believe each one of you, when you swore your oath, did so in the sight of God."

She was standing now in the middle of the courtroom and felt all eyes on her. "The book of Proverbs says, 'To do justice and judgment is more acceptable to the Lord than sacrifice.' That is the more acceptable thing. I now leave in your hands the doing of full justice. And if you do that, gentlemen, you can sleep well because God will be awake."

Spent, Kit returned to her chair and sat down. Juan put his hand on her arm. Judd Ashe's rebuttal was filled with thinly veiled outrage. Kit felt helpless as she listened, wondering if he was making any headway with the jury. At least he was brief.

Then Judge Pardue instructed the jurors on the law and dismissed them to the jury room to deliberate. Juan was removed to a holding cell to await the verdict.

Corazón embraced Kit. "God will do this justice," she whispered. "Thank you, my great friend."

Kit squeezed her. "I love you, Corazón." Kit felt gentle sobs in her shoulder.

Then it was as if a mob circled her. Reporters were shouting questions. People she did not know appeared, wanting to get close to her. She felt pressed back against her counsel table.

"I will have nothing to say until after the verdict," Kit announced, though her statement did not stop the reporters. Questions flew at her like buckshot. "Please!" she said.

Finally, a deputy sheriff began shooing the crowd back, shout-

ing a few choice words in the process. His size and manner, however, won the battle.

As the crowd thinned, Kit saw Earl Rogers at the rail, smiling.
Darrow was next to him. She went to Rogers and extended her
hand.

"Thank you for being here, Earl," she said.

"I wouldn't have missed it," said Rogers. "I am proud of you,
Kit."

"Miss Shannon," Darrow said in his deep, sonorous voice. "I
have been in many courtrooms and heard many fine speeches. In
fact, I've given a few of my own. But I must say never have I heard
one more eloquent, more heartfelt, or more honorable. Well done."

Kit's tongue got tied up in her mouth. She finally managed to
say, "Thank you."

"You will be a formidable opponent," Darrow added.

"Opponent?"

"When we have our debate about the Bible."

Kit had forgotten all about that. She swallowed. "Of course."

She knew then she would need her Bible tonight. The only
thing she had left to do was wait for the jury. It might be a matter
of hours or days. She could not possibly stand the pressure without
the comfort of God's Word.

———

There was also the comfort of Corazón, who brought Kit to
her family's home for the evening meal. In the Chavez family's
dimly lit hovel, Kit felt welcomed and warm. A crucifix hanging
on the wall above the table reminded Kit that Christ was a part of
this family. The loving kindness of Señor and Señora Chavez made
it clear that the Spirit of God had been made welcome. Señora
Chavez sat Kit between her two youngest children—eight-year-old
Rosa and six-year-old Pablo—and said, "We pray."

Kit watched as the family crossed themselves in unison and bowed their heads. Kit closed her eyes and listened to the sonorous language of prayer. Though she didn't understand every word Señor Chavez spoke, she caught phrases that suggested thankfulness for Kit's part in their lives and requests for God to care for their son and to see justice served.

When the prayer concluded, Señora Chavez spoke to Corazón in Spanish, all the while smiling at Kit. Señor Chavez seemed content to merely smile and nod at Kit all the time, as if constantly giving his approval.

"Mama gives you food in thanks," Corazón interpreted. "She is sad Juan should be in jail and much sad she no have money to pay you."

Kit returned Señora Chavez's smile and shook her head. "Please tell her I am glad to have been a help and that I did not take Juan's case for the sake of the money. I took it because I wanted to see Juan treated fairly."

Corazón relayed the message even as Kit labored with her doubts. Could she have done more? In a town well known for hiding its true face from the world, Kit couldn't help but feel she had been duped by the entire city.

Corazón passed a baking dish to Kit. "This is *muy delicioso*. Mama, she make it special for you."

Kit breathed in the aroma. "What is it? It smells heavenly."

Corazón smiled and began to serve Kit from the platter. *"Pollo Polenta*. It is the mush and the chicken baked together. Mama puts spices and sweet peppers in with *queso* . . . cheese. It is my favorite."

Kit knew if the aroma was any indication, it would be one of her favorites as well. After serving the polenta, Corazón passed a bowl of pinto beans and then a plate of tortillas. It was simple fare, but Kit felt as though it were a feast for a queen. And by the looks on the faces of Corazón's sisters and brothers—Dorotea, twelve, and Jorge, thirteen, rounded out the family—they felt the same.

Kit thought back to her dinner with Alfred Mungerley. Nothing served to her on that fine china had tasted half so good. Perhaps it was because she knew both Aunt Freddy and Mr. Mungerley disapproved of her vigorous defense of Juan, but in this home she was perceived as a friend. She couldn't help but remember a verse from Proverbs: *"Better is a dinner of herbs where love is, than a stalled ox and hatred therewith."*

Kit was filled with more than good food. A special fondness enveloped her. The chattering of the children, the quick-flying Spanish, the smiles and laughter—it was not what one would find in the finer social clubs. The fare was simple, the surroundings dirt poor. But there was more love here than in any home she had visited in Los Angeles.

After dinner, Kit bid the Chavez family farewell. She saw the veiled hope in their eyes and prayed that God would honor their faith. *Help them through this,* she prayed silently as Corazón kissed her parents good-bye.

Kit hired a hack to take them back to the hotel. Settling back against the well-worn leather seat, Kit tried to keep hold of the warmth of the family meal. But she couldn't help feeling that she'd left too many stones unturned in Juan's case.

"I wish I could have done more," she said without thinking.

"You do everything," Corazón said, reaching out to grip Kit's hand.

Kit hadn't meant to speak the words aloud. "I'm sorry," she said, giving Corazón's fingers a squeeze. "I just wonder if there isn't something I should have seen or understood."

"Kit, you are my good friend, and you do more for my brother than anyone. God, He tell you how to do your job. You told me this. You trust Him, and I know He is good."

"Yes, Corazón. God is good and worthy of our trust. We must trust that justice will be served and that truth will win out."

Chapter 36

AT TEN-FORTY the next morning, Judge Pardue called for the jury. Slowly, like wooden soldiers moved by a patient hand, they filed back into the jury box. Kit could not bear to study them. She could not bear to look away. It was impossible to read their faces.

Once again Judge Pardue's courtroom was so packed there was hardly air to breathe. Juan and Corazón seemed frozen with fear. Kit was sure that the beating of her heart was so loud that everyone in the courtroom might think a Salvation Army bass drum was just outside on Temple Street.

Her only comfort was Jeffrey, who sat in the first row. He had brought her to court. In fact, he had spent all morning with her in her office as she waited for the notice that the jury had reached a verdict. That it had come after a total of four hours of deliberation—two hours the day before, two hours today—was no indication of its content.

"But it must be good," Jeffrey had counseled as they rode toward the courthouse. "If the verdict was guilty, it would have come quickly."

Kit wanted to believe that.

"And it may even be possible that they have reached an impasse."

Which would mean a hung jury. But after only four hours? It was not impossible. Men had a way of determining intentions and drawing lines quickly.

"Either way," Jeffrey said, "it can only be good news, I think."

"You are a love," Kit said. "I shall be happy to have your sweet little fibs for the rest of my life."

As Jeffrey smiled at her in the courtroom, Kit felt a peace enter her. Her husband-to-be told her with his look what he had said out loud earlier. She had done all she could. Now it was up to God.

Kit put her hand on Juan's arm. His deep brown eyes swirled with alarm. But as she tried to comfort him with her touch, he began to reflect calm. And trust. That she had earned his trust was a great reward.

She was startled to attention by Pardue's voice. "Gentlemen of the jury," he said. "Have you reached a verdict?"

An older man with a drooping white mustache—juror number six—stood up. "Yes, we have, Your Honor."

Judge Pardue turned and looked at Juan. "The defendant will rise," he said.

Kit stood up first. Juan tried, but his legs gave way and he fell back into his chair. A slight murmur arose from the gallery. Kit and Corazón each took one of Juan's arms and lifted him gently.

The judge waited until Juan was steady on his feet. Kit kept hold of his arm.

"To the charge of rape," the judge said, "how does the jury find?"

Kit heard the words as if they were spoken from some deep cavern. They echoed off the cold walls, falling with forbidding solemnity on the ground beneath her feet.

The juror with the white mustache turned his head, slowly—agonizingly slow—until his eyes met Kit's, went through Kit's, all the way through her head to Juan.

"We find the defendant guilty," he said.

In the next moment Kit felt an eternity of emotion, and Juan's body tensing, first as if he did not understand the words that had been uttered, then collapsing with recognition of his fate. He fell straight down in Kit's grasp, missing the chair, hitting the floor like a discarded sack of refuse.

Noise broke out around her—chairs scraping on the floor as reporters leaped to their feet, voices cheering approval, a lonely wail from the back of the courtroom where Juan's friends and family were—and it seemed like the noise would take her with it to a hellish place where there would be no peace or quiet again.

———————

When she lost her mother at thirteen, Kit never had anyone to take her place. Certainly the sisters at St. Catherine's were not the mothering sort. Especially Sister Gertrude, who was the very opposite.

Nor was there anyone to fill that hole in Kit's heart in all the time she spent in New York. Not even her beloved law teacher, Melle Stanleyetta Titus, could do it. From her, Kit had learned the law and to have confidence, as a woman, to perform the function of a lawyer.

But there was no one to whom she could run for comfort, who would hold her like only a mother could, stroke her hair, and tell her everything would be all right. Now, as if God had provided a drop of relief into the chasm of her despair, Aunt Freddy was there for her.

It was Aunt Freddy who had insisted on bringing her home after the verdict. Home to Angeleno Heights. And it was Aunt Freddy who held her now as Kit sobbed into her ample bosom.

"There, now," Aunt Freddy said. "There. You did all you could."

Kit did not believe it. And she did not want to cry. Not in front of Mr. Mungerley, who had provided the carriage that brought them all here. But she could not stop the flow.

"Yes," Alfred Mungerley said gently, like a father. "You performed brilliantly, Miss Shannon. You have every reason to be proud."

"Do you hear that?" Aunt Freddy said. "Alfred knows."

No, Kit could not believe it. If she had performed brilliantly, Juan would be free now. Oh, she would write an appeal, of course. But she knew in her heart how little chance there was of a verdict being overturned.

"Now you listen, child," Aunt Freddy said. "We are all proud of you. Even though you know it has been a bit of struggle for me to have a niece in lawyer's garb"—Freddy cleared her throat—"I have grown rather to enjoy it. Anything that gives Eulalie Pike a pain in her . . . neck is a pleasure for your old auntie."

Kit forgot her sadness for the moment and managed to laugh. It felt like when she was a little girl, and her mother could get her to laugh when she was melancholy.

"And now a little surprise," Aunt Freddy said.

Kit sat up, wiped her sore eyes with the kerchief Aunt Freddy had given her, and listened.

"Alfred and I have decided to host the biggest wedding this city has ever seen."

Kit blinked. "You mean . . ."

"Yes, you silly goose. For you and Dr. Jeffrey Kenton!"

The news thrilled her but gave her pause. It was so sudden. Yet it would bring such joy to Aunt Freddy.

"Yes," Kit said. "That would be grand."

"It will be!" Alfred Mungerley agreed. "As our great president would say, 'Bully!'"

Jerrold, the butler, appeared in the doorway of the study. "Someone is at the door, madam."

"Has he a card?" Aunt Freddy said.

"He has no card, madam. And may I say..."

"Continue."

"He looks rather... common."

"What on earth?"

Alfred Mungerley said, "I will go and see to—"

"See to nothin'," a voice said. The common man had walked right into the room.

"What is the meaning of this?" Aunt Freddy said.

Kit recognized him. "Aren't you—"

"Gus is the name, Gus Willingham," he said. "Sorry to interrupt yer party."

"The impertinence!" Aunt Freddy said.

"Young man, I must ask you to leave," Mungerley said.

"No, wait," said Kit. She knew he was here to talk to her. "What is it you want, Gus?"

"Well," he said, "I didn't know if I should, but then I thought I should, so I am."

Kit shook her head. Aunt Freddy looked dazed.

"I know how things were once," Gus said, shuffling his feet, "and they ain't that way no more, and I'm glad they ain't, I don't mind saying..."

"Is he daft?" Aunt Freddy asked.

"What is it, Gus?" Kit said.

The mechanic ran his fingers through his hair. "It's Ted."

Kit's heart seemed suspended in air. "What about Ted?"

"He's hurt. Bad hurt. Down at Sisters right now."

The news pulled Kit to her feet. "When did this happen?"

"Couple days ago."

Couple of days? Why hadn't she heard? Why hadn't . . . Jeffrey! Why hadn't Jeffrey told her?

"I must go see him," Kit said. "Now."

Chapter 37

KIT WAS MET AT THE DESK by a forbidding-looking nurse. "Whom do you wish to see?" the nurse said coldly.

"Ted Fox."

"I am sorry, but Mr. Fox is going to be in surgery."

The news chilled her. "Dr. Kenton, then."

"Dr. Kenton will be performing the surgery. If you would like to come back—"

"Where is Mr. Fox now?"

"Room 200, but no one can—"

Kit charged for the stairs. Behind her the nurse bellowed, "Wait!"

But Kit did not wait. She practically flew up to the second floor and past a bewildered nurse to the first room, marked *200* on the door. She pushed it open.

What she saw took her breath away. Ted lay on a bed, his face pale and gaunt. His eyes, only half open, seemed almost lifeless.

"Ted?" Kit said softly, afraid she might startle him into shock. He turned his head slowly toward her. His eyes opened a little more.

"Kit . . ." His voice was thick, slow.

"Yes, Ted."

"I . . ." The effort to speak seemed to tax him, and his eyes closed again.

Sedated, Kit thought.

Ted raised his arm, weakly. Even his hand seemed to have lost mass. It frightened her. She took his hand.

"Need to tell . . ." Ted said.

"Don't speak," said Kit.

"Yes . . . listen . . ." He swallowed with great effort. "Been reading . . . the trial . . ."

Her body tensed. "What about the trial?"

"Kenton . . ."

At the sound of the name Kit felt an impact like a fist. She squeezed Ted's hand, willing him to talk.

Ted spoke between labored breaths. "He said . . . no one there . . . no one there when the cop . . . heard her . . ."

The blanks filled in Kit's mind. "You mean when Gloria Graham was questioned?"

Ted blinked his eyes once. "Yes . . . somebody else . . . a nurse . . ."

"A nurse was in the room?"

Ted grimaced. "No . . . nurse saw somebody . . ."

Kit's stomach twisted. Behind her, the sound of someone coming in.

"What is this?" Jeffrey said.

Kit saw his anger. "Jeffrey, I—"

"This man is about to go into surgery!"

"Kit . . ." Ted's voice was weak but imploring.

"How dare you barge in here without consulting me!" Jeffrey's rage was terrifying.

"Please, Jeffrey, this is—"

"Leave, Kit. Leave now. I will speak to you later."

Yes, he was right. She had been impulsive, disrespectful to him. He was the doctor, after all.

Then she looked at Ted's face. Her heart burst. He had such a look of fear and resignation she could not bear to walk out. She had to find out what was happening.

"I want to talk to you now, Jeffrey."

Jeffrey's voice held a seething anger. "I told you we would speak of it later."

"No, I must insist." Kit was aware this was the man she was going to marry. More, that what she was saying to him now might cost her that future. But too much was on the table now.

"Outside," Jeffrey ordered. "Now."

Kit walked from the room. Jeffrey followed close behind, took her arm, and marched her to the end of the hallway.

"You are acting like a madwoman," he said through his teeth.

"Jeffrey, why didn't you tell me Ted was here? I thought we pledged no secrets between us."

"Dearest," he said, "I did it to spare you."

"Spare me?"

"May I remind you that you were in the middle of a trial? I did not want your mind to be torn. I know what Ted Fox meant to you once."

Yes, she thought, trying to keep that in the past tense. It made sense, what he said. But if so, why did she have a nagging doubt welling up inside her?

"What is wrong with Ted?" she asked. "What are you going to do?"

Jeffrey looked at his hands. "His left leg has to be amputated."

Life seemed to flow out of Kit in one horrible gasp. "No . . ."

"If I don't do it, the infection will kill him."

Kit closed her eyes, then opened them when she felt his hands on her shoulders. "Kit, you were wrong to come here," Jeffrey said. "Wrong to see him now. You realize that, don't you?"

Kit looked into his eyes and saw a man she loved yet did not fully know. "Yes, Jeffrey. But my motives were not wrong. Ted said something about the night Gloria Graham was brought in—"

"Must you go on? The trial is over, Kit."

"He said someone else was here." The words were out.

It took a painfully long time for Jeffrey to answer. "Are you questioning me?"

She was. She did not want to. "I must know, Jeffrey."

His eyes darted then, looking to see if anyone was listening. She studied his face, as she would any witness. She couldn't help it.

"Listen to me, Kit. Listen very carefully. There are some things it is better that you don't know. Do you understand me?"

"When is it better not to know the truth, Jeffrey?"

"Now," he said. "You must trust me."

As she looked into his face, she realized she did not trust him. And that realization hurt her more than he could ever know.

She took a step away from him. "You committed perjury."

"You do not understand."

"I think I do."

"There are interests here."

A horrible thought entered her mind. The thought of Ted on an operating table, his leg being cut off, something going wrong . . . *I could not save him.*

The last words were in Jeffrey's voice.

No, dear heavenly Father, it was too terrible. It couldn't be. But he had lied. Jeffrey had lied to her on the witness stand, and he had lied now.

"You are not going to operate on Ted Fox," she said.

His look could not have been more shocked. "You *are* mad."

"I am a lawyer," she said. "And I represent Ted Fox. Before I let you near him, I am going to call in another physician."

A cold silence fell between them. Finally, Jeffrey nodded slowly. "So that is how it is, eh? Very well. And after he is dead, you shall have to live on, knowing what you did."

Hurt overwhelmed her growing anger. "How can you have done this, Jeffrey? You lied to the court, lied to me. I thought your ethics came from God."

"Put away childish things, Kit. I've seen too much of life to rely on the ethics of God."

"But all your talk of Christianity—what it meant to you."

"To please you, my dear. Was that so entirely wrong? To win the heart, sweet lies are a time-honored weapon."

No," Kit said, taking a step back. "Nothing is sweet in lying about God. For that you will have a higher authority to answer to."

Jeffrey shook his head. "It didn't have to be this way."

Kit's mind hummed crazily. She had to put away her pain—focus on the truth. "Who was the man, Jeffrey? Who was the man who was here that night?" *Could that man have been the guilty one? But if he was here with the policeman, it had to be someone with money and power. Someone who could buy protection. It had to be someone like . . .*

"Taylor," she said. She watched Jeffrey's eyes. They were silent and cold.

"If you so much as breathe his name . . ." Jeffrey said. "He is a dangerous man."

"How can I not? How can *you* not?"

"This is real life, Kit. And life is dangerous. Take Fox if you want him. I won't stop you. But our conversation never took place."

But it did. She had the awful truth. But how could she possibly prove it without Jeffrey's help?

"I hope you know what you have done here today," Jeffrey said. "I loved you, Kit. I was going to make you my wife."

Kit felt a jolt of pain in her heart. She looked away from him. Then, in her mind's eye, she saw the face of Juan Chavez. She could not look away from that face.

"Good-bye, Jeffrey," she said. Fighting back tears, she went to make arrangements for Ted to be moved.

———

Kit knelt at the tiny altar, clasped her hands together, and began to pray. She needed God more than ever. So did Ted Fox.

The tiny chapel was located on the lower floor of City Hospital. She was thankful they had one.

City Hospital was not nearly as well-appointed as Sisters. Within a stone's throw of the train depot, it was a plain brick building that operated on city funding.

Here, at least, Ted was away from Jeffrey Kenton. She still could hardly believe what had happened.

Kit's emotions had almost torn her apart on the ride over. Ted looked pained, yet relieved to be with her. When she had told him what she was doing he assented, even through his sedation. But Kit could not help but worry. Was he truly in danger of dying? Would his leg have to come off?

O God, she prayed in the carriage, *save his life. All of it.*

The doctor who received Ted, Dr. Atwater, was an older man. He looked like a kindly grandfather. Kit was immediately relieved. She told him everything she knew, and he took charge of Ted immediately.

He was with him half an hour before coming out to confer with Kit.

"Your friend indeed has an infection," Dr. Atwater said. "But I may be able to stave it. We won't know for a day or so. If I can't, then I will have to amputate."

Kit nodded. She felt she could trust him.

"Are you a praying woman?" he asked.

"Yes."

"Then I suggest you do it. We have a chapel here. . . ."

And so Kit prayed. It seemed like hours, and the hours seemed like days. But she stayed, pleading for Ted's life and limb.

Chapter 38

JUDD ASHE DID NOT FEEL the triumph he should have. Even though the district attorney, John Davenport, insisted on offering him a drink of fine brandy. At the California Club, no less.

"You did a wonderful job, Judd," Davenport said, raising his snifter.

"Thank you," said Ashe.

"Saved us a lot of trouble around here."

"Sure."

"And put a pin into that Shannon woman."

Ashe said nothing.

"What's wrong, Judd? You don't look like a man ready to celebrate."

"I can still drink." Ashe took a sip of brandy. It burned down to his stomach.

"Anything else?" said Davenport.

"I just advise we don't sell Miss Shannon short. She did a tremendous job."

Davenport looked incredulous.

"Oh yes," said Ashe. "Outstanding. She's good. Very good. If she sticks around, we are going to have our hands full."

"I don't know what the world is coming to."

"Sir?"

"Eh?"

"I need to tell you something about the trial."

Davenport nodded. "Fire away."

"Something is troubling me about it."

"Not the verdict, I hope?"

"No, I think we have the right man. I am just troubled by how we got him."

"Be specific."

Ashe took a long sip of brandy. He considered his next words carefully. "Our witnesses. Hanratty. Taylor. The girl herself. I was not comfortable with their testimony."

"These kinds of cases are not comfortable. You know that."

"Especially Taylor. He doesn't smell right to me."

Davenport huffed. "Listen, Dayton Taylor is one of the most powerful men in the city. He can smell however he likes."

"Well, it shouldn't stink up a court of law." Ashe was amazing even himself. Why should he feel this way? He had built his career on winning tough cases. He just won another one. But this victory didn't taste like the other ones. Was it something about this Kathleen Shannon? Her passion for her client, for justice?

Davenport leaned over and patted Ashe on the arm. "Come on, now. The water is over the dam. Go on to the next case. You'll feel better if you do."

"I don't like being made a fool of."

"You weren't made a fool! You are a city hero."

"I prefer my heroics be earned."

"Let me give you some advice," said Davenport. "Forget it. Forget all about it. Even if Taylor embellished his story—even if he lied!—it doesn't matter. What matters is the conviction. What matters is we put away a bad man. What matters is the city is at peace. And what matters is that this office did it, Judd. We all owe you a great debt."

Ashe finished his brandy in one hot gulp. "I think I need another drink. Maybe a few."

"I'll join you. This is a night for celebration."

Judd Ashe said nothing. He looked into the fireplace and watched the flames dance.

———

She was being followed.

Kit knew it, though she could not see it. Someone was out there, watching her. Waiting.

Or was it just her overworked imagination?

Even now, in the bright morning sun, walking along crowded streets, she felt it. Was this the way it would be from now on? Around every corner, someone waiting to do her harm?

As she entered her office, she half expected someone to be inside, lurking there.

It could very well be her mind. It was taxed. Even though she had prayed a long time this morning with Corazón, Kit did not feel peace. Her world was falling apart.

The man she had expected to marry had lied to her, in court and out. A man she had once loved now lay in a hospital, his life in the balance. And a man who had trusted her to find justice for him sat in a jail cell, awaiting his official sentence.

That is what she had to concentrate on now. In two days Judge Pardue would announce the sentence. It could be anywhere from five to twenty years in state prison. Kit's job would be to present mitigating circumstances—anything that might convince the judge to show mercy to Juan.

She would work on a brief today and file it with the court in the late afternoon. And then she would begin the appeal.

But as she began to write her thoughts, she felt a despair take hold of her. The chances of Juan's conviction being reversed were non-existent. Judd Ashe had presented a tight, carefully crafted case. And Judge Pardue had not done anything so inappropriate that an appeals court would find reversal necessary.

She had to face it. The only way to free Juan would be if new evidence came out. And that would mean a witness changing his story.

Her mind closed in on Dayton Taylor. What was he doing at the hospital that night? Why had Jeffrey sought to hide the fact?

It was not likely that Taylor or Jeffrey—or the cop, Hanratty, for that matter—would ever come forward with the truth.

She did her best to concentrate on Juan's case.

About an hour later she heard a knock on the door. It startled her. She was jumpy, all right. She went to the door and, without opening it, asked who it was.

"Lassen," the voice said.

She let Sean Lassen in. The private detective was dressed in a dapper suit and wore a bowler on his head. He could have been an Eastern dandy. But Kit knew, from what Earl Rogers had told her, that he was one tough customer.

"I have news," Lassen said.

Kit had almost forgotten about him. "Is it good news?" That's what she needed today.

"Lassen keeps at it until the news is good, ma'am. I found her."

"Gloria Graham?"

"The very same."

That was the answer she was looking for. If anyone could break this case open again, it would be the victim. But would she?

"Can you take me to her?" Kit said.

"It would be a pleasure," the detective said.

He took Kit to a rooming house in Holly Wood. The inn had a saloon on the first floor and rooms on the second. It had the look of the Wild West about it, a remnant of a world America was fast leaving behind.

Lassen pulled his carriage to a stop well down the road from the inn. "Best if you walk the rest of it," he said. "Her room is on the other side, upstairs, in the corner. There's outside stairs. I suggest you take them."

"You're not coming with me?"

"Better if I stay right here. If I see someone coming, I'll get you."

Kit felt a small measure of comfort. She trusted him, but he was still only one man.

The road was dusty as Kit approached. She walked around the back of the inn, with its weather-weary exterior, to the west side. Indeed, a stairway was there. She took it.

She found the corner room and knocked. At first, she heard nothing. Was anyone inside? She knocked once more.

The door opened and Gloria Graham stared out. Her face was shocking. Her eyes were set in dark circles and she seemed to have aged ten years.

Her expression was equally shocked. "How did you—"

"Gloria, I must talk with you."

"How . . ." Gloria began to close the door. Kit stopped it with her hand.

"Gloria, please—"

"I don't have to talk to you!"

"No, you don't. But I—"

"Get away from me! Get away before I scream!"

"I can help you."

She looked at Kit suspiciously. "That's a laugh! You help me?"

"If you'll let me."

"The way you helped me in court? The way you questioned me? All high and mighty. What gives you the right?"

"I am only searching for the truth." Kit kept her hand on the door. At least Gloria wasn't still trying to close it.

"What truth?" Gloria said. "Yours? What about my truth?"

"The truth doesn't change."

"Oh yes, it does! It's different if you live down here than if you live up there! They can be like God, up top of Angels Flight. We're nothin' but their garbage down here."

"Gloria, I know who did this to you."

She looked at Kit wide-eyed. "You know nothin'."

"You. Here. This place. Who is paying the bills?"

Gloria was silent. Her tired eyes scanned Kit's face.

"I know who it is, Gloria, and there's an innocent man in jail because of him."

"He's guilty!"

"You and I know that's not true."

"I don't care."

"Yes, you do. Because he's from down here, too. He's part of the garbage. And they are just going to throw him away if they can."

Gloria stared at Kit for a long time. When she spoke again, her voice was tired. "Just go away, Miss Shannon. You can't help him no more. You can't help me. Just go."

"Help me get him."

"Who?"

"Taylor."

Gloria's eyes widened. "Go away!"

"I need you, Gloria."

"I'll die! They'll kill me!"

"No—"

"Go away!" She pushed Kit hard with one hand. Kit stumbled backward as the door slammed.

Chapter 39

WHEN HE WAS TWELVE, Ted Fox was almost killed by a horse. It had been in Pittsburgh, where his mother's family lived. He had wandered out from a stuffy party where the adults kept talking about someone named Elizabeth Cady Stanton, and whether she was an affront to women.

Ted could not have cared less about women, affronts, or parties. He wanted to find a good tree to climb. The best one appeared right across the street from the home he was visiting, and he took off to conquer it. He did not hear the hoofbeats of the fast-approaching horse—until it was too late.

Horse collided with boy, and Ted was out cold for what turned out to be hours. When he finally came to, his mother sitting at his bedside, he thought he was dead and in heaven. And then the pain began.

He knew he was not in heaven, and that the world was a scary place. Even with his mother there.

I could die at any time, he had realized. It had almost happened once. It could happen again.

A certain fear took hold of him for a time, until Ted made a decision. He could walk through life afraid of what might happen to him, or he could look life in the teeth and jump at it.

He decided to jump. In fact, he jumped off roofs. He jumped out of trees. He jumped on horses and anything mechanical. Even while his father was grooming him for a career in finance, Ted would be thinking about jumping into the air—about flying.

And he never feared death again.

Until now.

Lying helpless in a hospital bed, his leg bound with more linen than a laundry, Ted Fox realized he did not want to die. Even if it meant losing the use of his legs.

Last night he had felt a tingling in his toes. He had thrown off the covers and looked to his feet, to see if he could wiggle them. A horrified nurse rushed in to cover him up. Ted told her to get away, but she was undeterred. She called for Dr. Atwater.

He calmed Ted down and told him he may have been experiencing ghost feelings—the same phenomenon of the brain where amputees still "feel" something where their lost limb would have been.

Or it could be a sign of healing.

He then told Ted that the decision about whether to amputate his leg would be made today.

So Ted waited and reflected on why he had suddenly come to fear death. It was not a failure of nerve. He knew he had plenty of that. No, it was something else. A sense of things unfinished. Not just his flying. It was something more. Unfinished business with Kit Shannon, for one thing. And maybe, just maybe, with her God.

When he was healthy and strong, God did not enter his thoughts. He entered his speech occasionally, in an epithet. But now Ted had the incredible thought that it was possible God had spared his life.

He should have died in the crash. He had come very close to doing so. That he was alive at all might be God's doing. And warning. Could it be that God's eternal judgments were real? That decisions made on earth would have consequences forever? Was that the reason God had given him another chance?

Ted looked up at the ceiling in his hospital room and whispered. "God, if you are there, give me a sign. Show me."

In the back of his mind he knew what he believed the sign should be. A healing. A restoration. Life.

He waited for a flash of light or a voice from heaven. What he got was the stubborn nurse again, telling him it was time to have a sponge bath. He had sounded like a god of wrath as he told her to get out and leave him alone. For once, the nurse appeared cowed.

Presently he fell asleep and dreamed of birds. He saw them floating majestically on air currents by the white cliffs of Dover, which he had seen as a boy. And then, off in the distance, a man-made bird. A monoplane. Equally majestic, it skimmed the waters easily and powerfully. In the cockpit he saw himself.

He was awakened by Dr. Atwater. "How you feeling, son?"

"Hiya, Doc," Ted said groggily. "All right, I guess."

"Good, good. If it's any comfort to you, your color is better."

"It must be the wonderful food."

"In spite of it, I think." The doctor looked at the floor a moment, as if he saw an unsightly stain. "My boy, I am going to operate on you."

"Operate?"

"Your leg, son. I can't save it. We have to amputate below the knee."

The dream of birds vanished in Ted's mind, replaced by icy darkness.

———

As a lawyer in Los Angeles, especially as a protégée of the great, but often besotted, Earl Rogers, Kit had learned where many important people liked to drink. Detective Michael McGinty, unlike most of the beat cops who frequented O'Reilly's Saloon, favored a place on Fourth and Hill. When informed that McGinty was off duty, that is where Kit went immediately.

She had to find him. Time was of the essence. The longer things dragged out, the longer Juan would be held unjustly. And the harder it would be to get Taylor.

Entering the dark saloon from the sunny street, Kit could not immediately see faces in detail. She sensed, though, that all the faces were male. And all were looking at her. *A stranger in a strange land,* she thought. *Like Moses.*

No one spoke to her. As her eyes became acclimated to the gloom of the place, she saw a bartender shaped like a barrel staring at her. Unfazed, she went to him.

"I'm looking for McGinty," she said.

The bartender, whose face was round and rough, said, "So?"

She was thinking about an answer when she heard McGinty's voice, as if from a fog. "Over here, Miss Shannon."

The bartender said, "You want me to remove her, Mike?"

"No," McGinty said. "She'd be on you like red on a rooster."

Kit followed the voice to a wooden booth. McGinty sat there, nursing a mug of beer.

"Buy you a drink?" he said winsomely.

Kit sat down. "No, thank you."

"You track me down to my bar and won't drink with me?"

"This is business."

"You may not have noticed, but I'm off duty." He took a long sip of his drink.

"This can't wait," Kit said.

McGinty looked less than impressed. "Well?"

"I want you to conduct a search."

"Oh, is that all? And where do you want me to search? The White House, maybe? Mr. Teddy Roosevelt's drawers?"

"The home of Dayton Taylor."

Over the rim of his glass, McGinty's eyes narrowed. He finished another sip and wiped his mouth with the back of his hand. "You *are* daft."

"What if I tell you I have information that the man who has been writing me threatening notes, the man who sent someone to attack me, is none other than Dayton Taylor?"

"If you told me that," said McGinty, "I'd tell you that you'd better watch what you say."

Kit did not hesitate. "Taylor was at the hospital the night Gloria was brought in, even though Dr. Kenton denied anyone else was there."

"Hanratty was there."

"I am not talking about Hanratty. Besides, he would deny anyone was there, too."

"Why don't we just ask him, then?"

"No."

"Why not?"

"Gloria is frightened."

"You are a regular fount of information. How do you know that?"

"I spoke with her. She's being put up in a rooming house outside the city. If you confront Hanratty, the word may get out before we have the proof we need."

"Don't start talking about we, Miss Shannon. And what proof?

All you have given me is a cock-and-bull story based on nothing I can see."

"You've seen the notes."

"How do you know Taylor wrote them?"

"There has to be a connection between the man at the hospital and those notes."

"Why? It could just as easily be anyone else who wants to see you put in your place—which, by the way, is about half this city!"

Kit had no ready answer for that. She only had a strong hunch. But search warrants could not be supported by hunches.

"Whoever sent that man to attack me had to have money," Kit said.

"Lots of people have money."

"And a motive to lie."

"Lie?"

"Taylor lied on the stand."

McGinty waved his hand. "The jury didn't think so."

"The jury didn't want to think so."

"What is your angle, Miss Shannon?"

"I think Dayton Taylor raped Gloria Graham."

The silence in the barroom seemed eerily still. It was almost as if they were the only two in the room. McGinty looked around before speaking in a low but adamant tone. "You can't make wild charges like that! Taylor is a respected man in this community!"

"It wouldn't take much to find out if he is involved," Kit said.

"What are you suggesting, Miss Shannon?"

"Search his house."

"For what?"

"A typewriter."

McGinty looked at her like she belonged in an asylum.

"Please. Juan Chavez is innocent, and I think you know it."

"I don't know any such thing."

"You believe it, though."

"My job isn't to believe or not. It is to deal in facts and evidence. You are as crazy as a loon."

"Why won't you help me?"

"Why should I help you?"

"Because you know I wouldn't ask if I wasn't convinced."

McGinty sighed. "That is rich. I go to a judge to ask for a search warrant, and he asks me why, and I say, because Miss Kit Shannon is convinced. I'd be laughed out of his chamber."

He was right, of course. Her speculations were not probable cause. The Constitution forbade search warrants that were not supported by a sworn affidavit to that effect.

"Consent," said Kit suddenly.

"Eh?"

"You can ask Taylor for consent to search his home."

"Now I know you are crazy."

"You can ask him."

"He doesn't have to give me consent to search his house. He can slam the door in my face."

"And if he does, you will have good reason to investigate him further."

McGinty paused, as if granting her the point.

"He is the type of man who cannot hide what he is thinking," Kit said. "And he has pride. My guess is that he will ask you in to show you he has nothing to hide."

"This is just insanity, Miss Shannon. I'd like to help but—"

"Would you really? Or are you just saying that so I won't be on you like red on a rooster?"

McGinty did not speak for several minutes. He turned on the bench and looked out into the murk of the barroom, silently drinking his beer. Kit sensed she had gone far enough and waited.

"Why do you do it, Miss Shannon? All this? Why? I can't understand it. You're a fair-looking woman. Why all this trouble?"

He sounded sincere and deserved an answer. "It is what the Lord requires of me—to do justly, to love mercy, and to walk humbly with Him."

"Is that the Bible?"

"That is the Bible."

McGinty nodded. "All right. But I know a little of the Scriptures. Doesn't it say in there that everything is vanity and a chasing after the wind?"

"The book of Ecclesiastes," she said.

"Well, if I find out this is just chasing after the wind, there will be hell to pay. And I'll be the one collecting."

Kit tried to swallow, but her throat was dry. "Shall we go?" she said.

Chapter 40

THEY TOOK ANGELS FLIGHT up to Bunker Hill.

The seats seemed harder to Kit this time, the ride shakier. McGinty's stone silence did not help. Every grinding sound, every squeal of cable, reminded Kit of iron shackles. She had forged them herself by getting McGinty to come with her. She might be wearing them soon if things did not go as she hoped.

It was nearly four o'clock now. She wondered how Ted was doing. She would go to see him soon. In the rickety car she prayed silently for him. *Keep him in your care, dear God. Stay close to him.*

The car came to a jolting stop. McGinty, still silent, led the way to Dayton Taylor's home.

Kit's heart beat savagely as they approached the door. Everything seemed to come down to this moment. If things did not go well, it could be a setback she would never overcome.

McGinty pounded the brass knocker. It seemed an eternity before the great front door opened.

A young domestic—looking eerily like Gloria Graham—answered. Her eyes were opened wide.

"Is Mr. Taylor at home?" McGinty asked.

The maid's lower lip trembled. "Whom shall I say. . . ?"

"Detective Michael McGinty, please."

She opened the door and allowed them to enter the foyer. It was of mosaic tile and paneled wainscotting—richly appointed. The maid bowed quickly and scurried off.

"Doesn't look like we're expected," McGinty said.

Kit breathed in deeply and caught the scent of cleaning oil, the sort used on a firearm.

She heard angry steps coming toward them. When Dayton Taylor appeared, and saw who was in his house, his face seemed to expand.

"What is she . . . what are you . . ." He fought for words.

"Mr. Taylor, I'm Detective—"

"I know who you are. Answer my question."

McGinty cleared his throat. He seemed awed by Taylor. Not a good sign, Kit thought.

"I've come on an official matter," McGinty said.

"Police business?"

"Yes."

Taylor turned his gaze to Kit, but spoke to McGinty. "Has this anything to do with the trial?"

"Maybe," said McGinty.

"Then I have nothing to say. I testified in open court."

Kit felt angry fires in her chest. *You lied in open court,* she wanted to say. She held her tongue.

"I know that, Mr. Taylor, but—"

"You talk to Ashe if it concerns the trial, not me. He is my lawyer."

"He is the people's lawyer," Kit said.

Taylor's eyes bore into her. "What impudence! When I want you to speak to me, I shall address you!"

Kit fought hard not to say the words charging into her mind.

"All right," McGinty said, "let's all hold our horses. This doesn't have to be unpleasant."

"It is already unpleasant," said Taylor. "State your business and get out."

Kit thought she saw a flicker of concern in McGinty's eyes.

"Do you own a typing machine, Mr. Taylor?" McGinty asked.

Taylor looked incredulous. "Typing machine?"

"Yes, you know—tap, tap, tap."

Taylor looked back and forth between Kit and McGinty, like a cornered animal facing two hunters. His face was not hard to read. He seemed ready to strike at them both.

"No," he said firmly. "I do not own any such machine."

McGinty scowled at Kit. "No machine?"

"As I told you! What is the meaning of all this? I have a right to know!"

McGinty scratched his head. "You mind if we take a look around?"

"I most certainly do!"

"Because I can go and get a search warrant if I have to."

Taylor's eyes were violent. He seemed too angry for words.

"But if you'll cooperate," said McGinty, "we can get this over with now."

"This is not going to be forgotten," said Taylor.

"Where do you have your office?" McGinty said. "For correspondence and the like?"

"My study."

"May I see it?"

Taylor turned without a word. McGinty and Kit followed him. Taylor led them to his study, rich in wood and beams. The head of a gazelle was mounted over a fireplace. At the far end of the study sat a desk with neatly stacked papers on it.

Taylor walked to the desk and pointed at it. "There. Satisfied?"

McGinty, with Kit close behind, examined the desk. Kit saw that some of the papers had ink jottings on them. No sign of typescript. And no sign of a typewriter anywhere in the room. There was not even a rolltop desk or cabinet where such a machine might be.

With a sigh, McGinty said, "Sorry to have troubled you, Mr. Taylor."

Kit's entire body tensed like a fist. She wanted to protest, but McGinty's look told her not to.

"You have troubled me," Taylor said. "And I won't forget it. No, I won't forget it from either one of you. I believe you know the way out, Detective."

The walk to the front door was one of the longest of Kit's life. She could feel the anger pouring out of McGinty. He did not unleash it until they were on the street.

"I never should have listened to you!" he said.

"Taylor is lying!" Kit said.

"And how do you know that, Miss Shannon? Another of your hunches?"

She didn't know how she knew. She just did.

"I'll thank you not to bring me any more police work," McGinty said. He shoved a fresh cigar into his mouth but did not bother to light it. "Now, if you'll excuse me, I have some real work to do." He walked toward Angels Flight. He did not invite Kit to join him.

She stood there and watched him go. It seemed like all hope for Juan Chavez was going with him. How could she possibly get Taylor now?

She became vaguely aware of a tapping sound. It was some distance away, but persistent, like an ambitious woodpecker. The sound was insistent enough to pull Kit from her thoughts and make her turn toward it.

At first she saw nothing. But the tapping got louder, and Kit looked up and saw, in an upper window, the widow Frances Sweet motioning at Kit with her cane.

"I saw you going into that man Taylor's house," Frances Sweet said. "Nothing gets by me, I hope to tell you."

Kit was in the same room where Taylor had once raised a gun to her—and where Frances Sweet had once tried to hit her with a cane! Things happened in this room. Kit sensed that now would be no different.

"I would not presume to think anything could get by you, Mrs. Sweet."

"That's right, young lady. I know what's up. You are trying to get at Mr. Taylor."

Kit shook her head. "I had an idea about that, but now I don't know."

"That awful man!"

"Being an awful man is not against the law."

"Well, it should be!" Frances Sweet pounded her cane on the floor.

"Why did you wish to see me?"

The old woman looked at her slyly. "I want to help you get him."

Kit did not want to dismiss Frances Sweet, but this was all a fool's errand. They could not plot to "get" Dayton Taylor. This was an eccentric widow ranting away because she disliked her neighbor. This was not the stuff of law.

"Mrs. Sweet," said Kit, "I appreciate your wanting to help me. But the police and—"

"Hang the police!"

"Sometimes I wish I could. But they deal with evidence, and there is no evidence against Mr. Taylor."

"Isn't there?"

The way Frances Sweet said it made Kit sit up in her chair. "What are you saying?"

"I have evidence."

"What sort of evidence?"

"Are you interested now?"

"Very."

"I thought you would be. Nothing gets by me, I tell you." She reached next to her chair and came up with a linen sack. She placed it on her lap and patted it like it was a Christmas package. Then slowly, she reached into the sack and pulled out a handful of papers. Specks of black flew around from them, like mosquitoes. The edges of several of the pages were burned.

"Got these from the back of Mr. Taylor's," said Frances Sweet. "Two nights ago. He was burning things. I always get curious when people burn things."

Kit tried to comprehend. "You took Mr. Taylor's private papers from a fire?"

"Of course not! The fire was out."

"But you took them—"

"That's what I did. There's letters here, and notes of one kind and another. Now I am giving them to you." Frances Sweet placed the singed pile on Kit's lap.

"You stole his mail?"

"He was burning it, child!"

What difference that made, Kit did not know. What she did know was that she could not resist Taylor's personal mail. She looked at the pile.

And what she saw on the top took her breath away.

Chapter 41

SO THIS WAS THE SIGN, Ted thought bitterly. This was God's answer to his prayer.

He was a man with one leg now. A cripple. An object to be pointed at by small children. A man forever dependent on others to open doors and pull out chairs while they tried not to look embarrassed.

He embraced the bitterness. It kept away thoughts of the future—a future that did not include aeroplanes or adventure.

The fact that he had regained feeling in his right leg was of no consolation. He was like a baby now. A nurse had to dress him and lay him on the bed.

Ted had hardly noticed the darkness falling outside his window. For him, all of life had become dark. Night, with the prospect of sleep, was the only thing he had to look forward to.

Dr. Atwater came in. Ted couldn't hate him, though he wanted to.

"Young man," Atwater said, "you are going to recover."

"Recover to what?" Ted said.

"A full life."

Ted laughed mockingly.

"I know you don't believe it now," said Atwater. "That's quite common. In time you will—"

"Thank you very much, Doctor. When can I leave?"

"I thought a stay of a week would be advisable. That way—"

"A day," said Ted.

"No, that is completely out of the question."

"I can't drink in this hospital, can I?"

"Of course not."

"Then I am going to get out of here tomorrow."

"Fox, listen to me," the doctor said. "You may feel you are unique, but you are not. Our Union and Confederate men, our boys in Cuba—many have sustained much worse. And many still walk among us, and find their way."

"I've see them begging on the streets, too."

"Nothing is written in stone. What matters is what you have up here." Atwater tapped the side of his head. "I want us to start there," Dr. Atwater said. "That's why I think you should see your visitor."

"I have a visitor?"

"Indeed. A pretty one."

Kit was here. "No, thank you," said Ted.

"But, Fox—"

"Tell her to go away."

"Tell me yourself," said Kit. She stood in the open doorway.

"I'll return later," said Atwater. He closed the door as he left.

Ted felt his heart being ripped apart. "Please go."

"I wanted to see you." She made no move toward him. Or away.

"You've seen me. Now go."

"I want to stay."

"Do I have a say in this?" He felt his voice tense, like a fist.

"Of course," Kit said.

"Then do what I ask. Go away. Don't come back."

"When shall I see you, then?"

"Never."

She looked at him for a long time.

"I've decided to go away," Ted said.

"Where?"

"Anywhere but here. Maybe Europe for a while. I hear cripples can do all right in France."

"Ted—"

"Spare me your pity, Kit."

"I offer none."

"Then why are you here?"

"Concern. For someone I care about."

Ted felt pulled in all directions at once. His heart burned for Kit. He wanted her to fall into his arms now and never go. But he could never let that happen, ever. He could never share her life, her beliefs. And if he could not have all of Kit, he wanted none of her. Nor could he ever offer himself to her. He was half a man now. He wanted her gone forever.

"I want you to go now," he said. "No more talk."

"Please let me stay."

"No."

"Ted, look at me."

He did. Reluctantly.

"I will do as you ask, if you look at me and tell me. If I believe this is what you truly want."

Looking at her then was harder than anything Ted had done in his life. He willed his eyes to stay locked on hers. "That is what I want," he said finally. "I wish you well. Don't come back."

She took a small step toward him. For a moment he thought she would come to him. But she stopped and quickly turned away. With her back to him she said, "Good-bye, Ted," and walked to the door.

Ted stifled a call to her, and that moment was like a death. He thought then that death was preferable to life. He wished they had not taken his leg, for it was killing him. It would have been better had it finished the job.

———

Corazón spoke to her brother in Spanish, through the bars of his jail cell. "You must not give up, Juan," she said.

Juan's face had already given up. So had his eyes, his spirit. Corazón could tell. Her brother had been the happy one. No longer.

"Why should I not give up, sister? This is not our land. We are slaves now."

"Yes, but that is what I am trying to say. Kit has said—"

"Kit! She tried to help but she could not. They will never let her win if a Mexican is charged. Leave me alone."

"No," said Corazón. "We must pray to God."

"God does not look at the *pueblo* of Los Angeles."

"He does! This is what I have learned from the Bible. God's own people were slaves once, but He rescued them. Now Jesus rescues God's people."

"Where is He, eh? Where is Jesus for our people?"

"He is with us when we ask Him to be."

"I asked God to help me, and now I am going to prison."

"Not yet. Kit says the judge will listen to her."

"That is stupid. He is one of them."

"Do not say that, Juan. Do you remember how Mama would tell us the stories of the saints?"

"Yes. Pretty stories."

"How they would perform miracles?"

"So?"

"God still performs miracles, and we do not have to be a saint. Kit says that we can pray to God for a miracle."

"And if I go to prison, what then?" Juan asked.

"Always pray."

"You pray for me, sister. Then visit me in prison."

Corazón put her hand through the bars. Immediately a loud whack on the bars made her pull back. A jail guard glared at her.

"Hands on this side," he growled.

Corazón wondered when she might get to touch her brother again.

Chapter 42

PRESS ON, Kit told herself. *For Juan.*

She was a lawyer. Her client was not guilty. She owed him her best efforts. Even if she had to work through the pain in her heart.

She tried to push thoughts of Ted out of her mind. It was time for sentencing—her last chance with Judge Pardue. If he did not respond to what she was going to present, all would be left to the Court of Appeal. A long shot.

The courtroom was full again this morning. The reporters were here for the final curtain, the end of the drama. She had heard a few of them betting on the sentence Juan would receive. Most of their money was on twenty years.

What hurt more than that was Juan's face. It was resigned to the worst. And he would not look at her.

Judge Pardue entered the courtroom and called it to order. "In the matter of the People of the State of California versus Juan

Chavez, does the defendant have anything to say before sentence is pronounced?"

Kit stood up. She had rehearsed what she was about to say for hours. "Your Honor, you are empowered by the Penal Code to consider any evidence that may tend to mitigate the severity of the sentence you are considering. According to the code, this evidence may include evidence pertaining to the circumstances of the crime itself."

She paused and saw Judd Ashe looking at her with a mixture of disbelief and awe. So much so he did not say a word.

"Miss Shannon," Judge Pardue said. "Are you telling me that you intend to offer evidence concerning the terrible crime for which your client was convicted? Excuse me if I am at a loss to see how that could help you in any way."

"If Your Honor pleases," Kit said, "the code speaks of evidence 'pertaining to' the circumstances of the crime itself. I wish to present such evidence to the court."

At this point Kit expected an objection from Ashe. As the prosecutor, he would be entitled to protest the introduction of new evidence. But he remained strangely silent.

As did the judge, for a long time. This was the first hurdle. If he did not receive the evidence she had, there would be nothing left but the pronouncement of sentence.

"This court," Pardue finally said, "wishes to bring this matter to a quick resolution. Miss Shannon, how long will it take you to present this evidence?"

"I have only one witness," she said.

"Is there an objection?" Pardue said. It was a virtual invitation. But Ashe said, "No, Your Honor."

"None?" said Pardue.

"It is the duty of the People to seek justice," Ashe said. "We would like to hear Miss Shannon's evidence."

Kit could not believe what she had just heard. She wanted to stop there and tell Judd Ashe what courage he had just shown. But she couldn't, for the judge said, "Present your witness, then, but be quick about it."

Heartened, Kit turned to the gallery and said, "I wish to call Earnest Parks."

Her witness was sitting next to Tom Phelps. She knew Tom could not resist a scoop, and she had told him that he'd better show up with Ernie if he wanted one. Here they were. The rest was up to her—and the judge.

Ernie came forward and was sworn in.

"Mr. Parks," Kit began, "would you tell the court how you are employed?"

"People hire me," he said. The spectators laughed. The judge looked sour.

"I mean where are you employed now?" Kit said.

"Oh. I work for Mr. William Randolph Hearst at the *Examiner*."

"And what sort of work do you do?"

"The best," he said, creating more laughter.

"I understand that," said Kit. "But what are your duties?"

"I fix machines," Ernie replied. "Linotype, typograph, slug casters, rolling press, typewriters. You name it."

"I would like to focus on the typewriters. You are an expert?"

Ernie sat up a little. "Mr. Hearst wouldn't hire a nincompoop."

"No," said Kit, "I suppose not. But please tell this court how you have come to be an expert in typewriters."

Ernie turned to the judge and told him about his work with Remington and his many years servicing typewriters. The judge actually looked interested. At one point, he asked Ernie a question for clarification. To Kit, this was a good sign.

When Ernie finished his background, Kit turned to Pardue.

"Your Honor, I would now like to introduce into the record three typewritten notes. The purpose is to have Mr. Parks identify the origin of these writings, according to the characteristics of the type."

"But that would just be his opinion, wouldn't it?" said the judge. "Opinions are not evidence."

"But they may be," said Kit. "According to section 1870, subsection nine of the evidence rules, evidence may be taken that is the 'opinion of a witness respecting the identity or handwriting of a person' or on a 'question of science, art, or trade, when he is skilled therein.' Your Honor, I am asking you to deem Mr. Parks skilled in the trade of typewritten communication, which is now a modern, technical form of handwriting."

Judge Pardue looked at Kit and slowly shook his head. "Miss Shannon," he said, "I must say your knowledge of the rules of evidence is just this side of astounding. You may question the witness."

A wave of relief washed over Kit. She went to her briefcase and retrieved three pieces of paper. She put the first one in front of Ernie.

"Mr. Parks," she said. "Would you please read this message to the court?"

Ernie picked up the paper and held it in front of his face. " 'You will not proceed further in the case of the man Chavez. You are a meddler. I take care of meddlers. I will take care of you unless you back away. Believe me.' "

"Please hand the note to the judge."

Ernie did. Judge Pardue took it with keen interest.

Kit handed the second note to Ernie, who read it aloud: " 'This is your last warning, Lawyer.' "

Kit had Ernie give the judge the note. "Now please tell the

court," she instructed, "whether you believe these notes were written on the same typewriter."

"I don't believe," Ernie said. "I know."

"How do you know?"

Ernie explained the matter of the shift keys to Judge Pardue, and how the capitals controlled by the left shift were slightly raised.

"I now show you the third writing," said Kit. "For the record, this is a single sheet of slightly yellow paper, with some signs of burning around two edges. Please examine it, Mr. Parks."

Ernie took it and scanned the page. A few moments later he looked up. "Same machine," he said.

"It is your opinion," Kit said, "that this third letter came from the same typewriter that produced the first two notes?"

"That's a fancy way of saying what I just told you," said Ernie. "It's got the same raised caps, controlled by the left shift. Same height—about a point. Same machine."

"Your Honor," said Kit, "with your permission, I would like to read this into the record."

"Proceed," said the judge.

Kit took the letter from Ernie and read: " 'We must hold firm to what Mr. Joseph Pomery Widney has shown. It is the Anglo people who are destined by divine providence to rule in Southern California. Los Angeles is to become the Aryan city of the sun. Only the Anglo people have the intelligence and vigor to rule here. It is the Anglo people who understand the production and handling of money. It is the Law of Survival of the Fittest. We may pity the weak; indeed, Christian charity demands that we must. But we cannot change the Law.' "

Kit paused. The entire courtroom was still. She gave the letter to the judge.

Pardue put the three writings side by side and looked between them. "For the record: They do appear to be from the same typewriter, as the witness has said. It appears to be a letter, but there is no signature. The bottom of the page is charred, perhaps obscuring the signature line. What do you make of all this, Miss Shannon?"

Kit said, "The threatening notes, Your Honor, were intended to obstruct justice by intimidating an officer of the court. That is a felony. It is a reasonable inference that the man who physically attacked me was doing so at the behest of the one who wrote these notes."

"Physically attacked?" Judge Pardue said.

"Yes, Your Honor. I will provide the court with a written account. What I am asking for now is a stay of sentence until this evidence can be further investigated."

The judge thought carefully. "To what end, Miss Shannon? We have no way of knowing who wrote these, do we?"

"May we approach the bench?" Kit said.

"Yes," said the judge.

Kit waited for Ashe to join her at the judge's bench, so she could speak without the rest of the court hearing.

"I know where the third letter came from," said Kit.

"Where?"

"I would withhold the location for the moment, Your Honor."

"But why?"

"Because to make this evidence hold, I will need the help of the district attorney."

Ashe looked surprised. "Me?"

"Yes, Mr. Ashe. If you help me, I think we can find the real perpetrator of the crime against Miss Graham."

"But Mr. Chavez has been convicted," Ashe said.

"Do you really believe he is guilty?"

Ashe thought a moment. "What is it you have in mind, Miss Shannon?"

Chapter 43

THE LIGHTS of the California Club lit up the night atop Bunker Hill. To Kit, the illuminated windows looked like the eyes of a jack-o'-lantern—multiple eyes watching the dark city below.

Michael McGinty said, "I have a bad feeling about this."

"I will take the responsibility," said Judd Ashe.

"But it's Miss Shannon's idea," McGinty replied. "And her ideas have ways of exploding in your face."

A tall man in an elaborate blue coat with gold braids came out of the Club's front doors and approached them. "The gentleman you have summoned will be here momentarily," he said stiffly. "May I add that he is none too pleased."

"Noted," said Ashe. "Thank you."

The attendant bowed and turned like a soldier, then marched back inside. The door did not close. Dayton Taylor burst through it.

"What is the meaning of this?" he sputtered.

"Mr. Taylor," said Ashe, "if you wouldn't mind stepping over here just a moment?"

"I was having my dinner! There are several important people in there. . . ."

"If you please," said Ashe, as if it were an order.

Taylor heaved a sigh and followed Ashe down the walk and toward the side of the Club, a more private venue. They were lit faintly by light from a second-story window.

"Ashe, what the devil are you up to?" Taylor said. "What are you doing with *her*?" He pointed a stubby finger at Kit. "And you, Detective! I thought you had learned not to disturb ordinary citizens!"

"Don't bluster, Mr. Taylor," Ashe warned. "It won't work. We have reason to believe you know more about this Chavez case than you have admitted."

Taylor's jaw went slack.

"Miss Shannon will explain," Ashe said.

Kit stepped closer to Ashe and held up the notes. "I hold two typewritten notes, Mr. Taylor. Two of them are threats to me. The third is a portion of a letter. It was written on the same typewriter as the threatening notes."

Taylor looked flustered, glancing at his three questioners.

"Mr. Taylor," said Kit, "this letter was found in a bin outside your home, in a batch of burned papers."

A stiff breeze blew past them, ruffling the papers Kit held in her hand.

"How did you get that?" Taylor said, his voice subdued.

"That is not important, Mr. Taylor. What is important is what this letter tells us."

"All right," he said impatiently. "I do own a typewriter! But I never use it. My secretary handles all that."

McGinty said, "Why'd you lie to us, Taylor?"

"Because I resented your intrusion," he said. "You are not entitled to question me in my own home!"

"That don't give you any right to lie to the police!" said McGinty. He looked at Ashe. "So he owns the typewriter. He threatened Miss Shannon. He sent the man who attacked her. I'll take him in."

"No," said Kit. She saw Taylor's face changing expressions with every word.

"What do you mean?" said McGinty.

"Mr. Taylor did not write this letter," said Kit. "This letter was written *to* him."

McGinty now looked as confused as Taylor.

"Let me read it," said Kit. " 'We must hold firm to what Mr. Joseph Pomery Widney has shown. It is the Anglo people who are destined by divine providence to rule in Southern California. Los Angeles is to become the Aryan city of the sun.' "

She paused and studied Taylor's face. A faint recognition was creeping into it. Kit went on. " 'Only the Anglo people have the intelligence and vigor to rule here. It is the Anglo people who understand the production and handling of money. It is the Law of Survival of the Fittest. We may pity the weak; indeed, Christian charity demands that we must. But we cannot change the Law.' "

Kit put the letter down and looked into Taylor's eyes. "Mr. Taylor, you know who wrote this letter. I believe I know, too."

Taylor rubbed his face with one beefy hand. "I . . . I . . ."

"Out with it," said Ashe. "If you don't tell us who it is, you could be a party to obstruction of justice, maybe worse. But if you do, I can promise you that you won't be prosecuted."

The breeze picked up, making an eerie sound like a distant, ghostly voice.

"Who was it?" McGinty snapped.

Taylor seemed frozen. "I . . ."

"Tell them, Dayton." The familiar voice came from behind Kit. She whirled around and saw Alfred Mungerley's face emerging from the shadows.

Taylor's eyes widened. "Alfred, they . . ."

"Never mind," said Mungerley. He took two steps into the light. That's when Kit saw the gun in his hand.

"Mungerley!" said McGinty.

"Now, let us all reason together," he said. "We are all on the same side of the fence, shall we say?"

"Put the gun away," said Ashe.

"Not yet," said Mungerley. "Not until we agree on a few things. You cannot seriously entertain the notion that I should be held responsible for any of this, do you?"

"You threatened Miss Shannon."

"Unfortunate, but necessary. I am actually quite fond of Miss Shannon, as she knows."

Kit shook her head. "Fond enough to send someone to kill me?"

"Reason with you," said Mungerley, "albeit in a stern fashion."

"You are crazy," said McGinty.

"You know so little, Detective," Mungerley said, shaking his head. "How can any of you even entertain the idea that my life would be of less value than a Mexican's?"

"You raped Gloria Graham," said Kit. "And you would let an innocent man go to prison for it."

Now Mungerley's face tightened. "She is not one of us, either! She is from down there." He waved the gun toward the city below. "She is barely above the rank of Mexican. We can't let this get out of hand."

"Put the gun away and come peacefully," said McGinty.

"That cannot be," he said.

"Do you plan to shoot all of us?"

"Don't be a fool, Alfred," said Taylor.

"Shut up," said Mungerley. His eyes had a wild look to them now, especially when he looked at Kit. "You," he said to her. "You just had to stay in this, didn't you?"

He aimed the pistol at her chest.

Ashe raised his hand. "Mungerley!"

Alfred Mungerley did not lower the gun. And then, suddenly, he stiffened. His eyes looked upward, then rolled into his head.

His arm fell, his body followed, and Mungerley crumpled to the ground. That's when Kit saw the knife sticking out of his back.

"There!" McGinty shouted. He pointed to the darkness behind Mungerley. Kit looked and saw a shadow moving. Someone running.

"Stop him!" McGinty said. He took off after the suspect.

"Get a doctor," Ashe said to Dayton Taylor.

———

"The truth! Now!" Judd Ashe said.

Gloria Graham quivered in her chair. *And well she should,* Kit thought. Gloria's former allies—Ashe and Detective McGinty—were facing her with their arms folded. They were not going to move from her room until she told them what she knew.

Tears came into her eyes. "He said he would take care of me," she said.

"Who did?" said Ashe, the prosecutor.

"Mr. Mungerley." Gloria folded and unfolded her hands.

"When did he say it?"

"At the hospital that night."

"Miss Graham," said Ashe. "Was it Alfred Mungerley who raped you?"

Slowly, as if with great effort, Gloria Graham nodded her head.

Kit went to Gloria and put a hand on her arm. "Tell us how it happened," Kit said. "It is very important that we know."

"Must I?" she said.

"You must," said Ashe. "You have committed perjury, Miss Graham. You have placed an innocent man in jail. Unless we hear the absolute truth from you, you will be punished for that. If you tell us now, and I mean the whole truth, I will see to it you are not prosecuted."

"But I am afraid of him," she said.

"No need," said McGinty. "He's going to recover from his wound, but if you tell us what happened, we'll make sure he never hurts anyone else again."

Gloria paused a long while before answering. "I was making merry that night. I had too much to drink—I know I shouldn't have. I'm not a bad girl, honest."

She looked for confirmation from her questioners. Kit patted Gloria's arm. "Go ahead," she urged.

"I came to Angels Flight. It was closed for the night. I had to climb the stairs. I was going to walk back home to Mr. Mungerley's. But I was dizzy. I didn't know where I was going. I walked down a street. It was dark. I don't know how long I walked around and around. But then a horse almost ran me over. I stumbled and fell out of the way. That's when I saw it was Mr. Mungerley's carriage."

"What was he doing there?" McGinty asked.

"The California Club," said Kit. "It's just up the road from Angels Flight. He was probably on his way home."

"He was angry with me," said Gloria. "He raised his voice. He sounded odd."

"In what way?" said Ashe.

"Like he was crazy almost. He had liquor on his breath. But that's allowed for him. Not for me. I thought sure he would let me go from his employ. But he put me in his carriage. And then he closed the top."

Silence. Then Gloria spoke in almost a whisper. "He started to . . . he tore my clothes. I screamed once and he hit me. He hit me . . ." She stopped for a moment. "And then he was . . . he had his way with me." She was fighting soft sobs to continue. "I passed out. When I woke up I was hurt all over. I didn't know where I was. The cop found me."

"Hanratty," McGinty muttered.

"I was in the hospital with the doctor and the cop when Mr. Mungerley came. He talked to them. Then he talked to me. I was scared. He told me what I had to do."

She took a deep breath. "I had told Mr. Mungerley that Juan made advances to me. It wasn't true. But then he said I must claim that Juan did this to me. He said he would give me money if I did what he said. And if I didn't, he would see to it I never had anything."

Kit felt a chill. That Alfred Mungerley could present one face so easily to the world, while hiding another so cold and calculating, apparently believing it was his right as one of the privileged few, was frightening. And his ability to convince others—like a bigoted police officer and an esteemed doctor—to go along with him, was equally frightening.

Her musings reminded Kit of a conversation she'd had with Jeffrey. She looked at McGinty. "Dr. Kenton said he expected to come into some money. It must have been from Mungerley."

"I plan to talk to him," said Ashe ominously.

"I hope that you do," said Kit.

Chapter 44

OUTSIDE THE DISTRICT ATTORNEY'S office, McGinty asked to walk Kit to her office. "I suppose I owe you an apology, Miss Shannon," he said. "You were on the right track all the time."

"Thank you, Detective."

"But you know, being on the right track isn't always going to get you where you want to go. There's folks don't like where that track leads."

"I know that well."

McGinty plugged his mouth with a fresh cigar. "I know there's some answering the police force will have to do."

Kit was stunned but gratified. "Will it?"

"I'm not the Chief."

"But you can talk to him, can't you?"

"Don't know. But I can keep on eye on the cops in my charge."

"That would be a good thing."

"For you, too."

"What do you mean?" Kit questioned.

"I know what our boys think of you and the way you tear at them in court."

"Tell them to tell the truth."

"If it were that simple. Just keep your wits about you and if you need anything, call me."

Stunned again, Kit said, "Thank you, Detective."

McGinty took out his unlit cigar and looked at it. "Don't thank me yet, Miss Shannon. Your toughest days may be ahead of you."

She did not like the sound of that. But it had the ring of hard truth. They walked on in silence, finally arriving in front of Kit's office. McGinty shook her hand. "You make this an interesting town, Miss Shannon."

Kit wondered if this was a compliment, coming from a police officer.

"And this case isn't over," said McGinty.

"What do you mean?"

"Who put that knife in Mungerley's back?"

Who indeed? Kit could offer no answer.

"Just one favor," McGinty said. "If you ever find out, you let me know."

"You will be the first to know," said Kit.

McGinty looked down First Street, teeming with well-dressed pedestrians going about their business. "I don't understand why they do it, Miss Shannon. Men like Mungerley and Kenton, men with power and position—with everything. You have a theory about that, Counselor?"

Kit nodded. " 'The heart is deceitful above all things, and desperately wicked. Who can know it?' "

"Bible?"

"Bible."

The crowd in Judge Pardue's courtroom no doubt thought the sentencing of Juan Chavez would proceed without further incident. The only one who seemed uncertain was Tom Phelps. He cornered Kit at the rail before the judge entered.

"What is up your sleeve?" he said.

"Why, Tom, are you fishing for a scoop?" said Kit.

"Please, Kit."

"You remember our bargain?"

"Bargain?"

"You said you would tell this story, the right way, when the facts became known. I am going to hold you to it."

Sheepishly, Tom said, "I'll do anything for that scoop."

"Then I will give you an exclusive."

Tom's eyes beamed. He readied his pencil.

"After the proceeding," said Kit.

"Aw, come on!"

Kit walked to her counsel table.

Judge Pardue took to the bench and called the case. Judd Ashe stood up immediately. "Your Honor," he said, "at this time the People move to vacate the conviction of Juan Chavez and suspend all further action against him."

An explosion in granite could not have rocked the courtroom more. Cries of outrage mixed with gasps of confusion. A reporter fell off his chair, crashing to the floor with his pad.

Judge Pardue pounded for order and waited patiently for the red-faced reporter to regain his seat. Then he cleared his throat. "Based on what the prosecutor has offered, this court is going to grant the motion. The conviction of Juan Chavez in this matter is vacated and the defendant hereby released."

The pandemonium that ensued was nothing the judge could

control. He walked off the bench, leaving it to the deputies to restore order.

Juan embraced Kit, sobbing, whispering, "Gracias! Gracias!" Corazón did the same. Kit offered thanks in her own mind to God. Then she felt surrounded by a throng, a gaggle of voices.

She saw Tom Phelps break through the crowd. "I'll write it!"

"I'll tell it," she said.

And two hours later, she did.

———

Los Angeles Examiner

A MOST REMARKABLE CASE
by Tom Phelps

It is the highest duty of the criminal defense lawyer to protect the innocent. It is the glory of the law when that duty also protects society and makes the world a better place in which to live. Here in Los Angeles, we have recently been witness to both of these occurrences through the honorable work of a most remarkable lawyer named Kathleen "Kit" Shannon.

The trial of a young Mexican laborer, Juan Chavez, on a charge as base and loathsome as can be imagined, exposed a part of ourselves that needs a thorough examination. For if we are to progress as a city and as a nation, the dignity of every person before the law must be preserved, regardless of color or creed.

This remarkable story begins when Kit Shannon first learned that Juan Chavez had been charged with the crime....

———

Kit sighed as she lowered the paper. Tom had come through, and perhaps that was the reason she had gone through this trial. Her story—which was really Juan's and all others who lived "below" Angels Flight—had been told to thousands. She hoped one of those thousands was General Harrison Gray Otis.

Two other items, however, gave her pause. One was the announcement of the planning stages for the debate she was to have with Edward Lazarus and Clarence Darrow. It was being billed in the paper as a three-way "disputation" concerning the Bible—Darrow for the atheists, Lazarus for the progressives, and Kit for the "old-fashioned way." She saw Eulalie Pike's hands all over that characterization.

God, it seemed, had done it again. Placed her in a situation for which only He could provide the strength. She was actually starting to look forward to seeing how God would work.

But the other item burst her heart. On the social page, in small type, she read: *Mr. Theodore Fox leaves the city today for parts unknown. The erstwhile aviator, who suffered the loss of his leg in a flying accident, says only he will be heading east. We wish him well.*

A soft knock on her office door snapped Kit's attention from the paper. "Enter please," she said.

The door slowly opened and a pretty Chinese woman entered on her tiny feet.

"Wong Shi!" Kit stood to greet her.

Wong Shi bowed. "I pay in full," she said.

Kit laughed and patted her shoulder. "Oh, Wong Shi, that is quite all right. You don't have to—"

"No, no!" Wong Shi cried. "You give me my life! I pay in full!"

"But . . ." Before Kit could finish, Wong Shi was at her door motioning for someone to come in. A young Chinese man, wearing a bright blue bandanna on his head, which set off a red scar running down his right cheek, stepped in. His eyes were dark and forbidding, until he smiled at Kit. Though missing several teeth, his grin was warm and friendly.

"Him Chow Lin," said Wong Shi. "Him Hop Sing."

Kit took a moment to understand. The man's *name* was Chow Lin, and he was of the Hop Sing tong, the same tong Wong Shi's fiancé had belonged to.

And then the realization hit Kit like a flash from dark clouds. "You mean he is the one who . . ."

Wong Shi was beaming as she nodded her head. "He save you two time. Last time man with gun!"

Kit almost lost her balance.

"So I pay in full, is right?" Wong Shi said.

"Oh . . . yes," Kit stammered.

"No chickens!"

It took several moments for Kit to come back to a semblance of reality. "Now, Wong Shi, and Chow Lin, we must talk to a detective about this, a man named Michael McGinty. We must tell him what happened."

"Chow Lin in trouble?" Wong Shi said.

"No. No trouble. He saved my life twice. It's just that the police like to know about these things. Detective McGinty will be very happy to have cleared this up."

"Me happy, too," said Wong Shi.

Chapter 45

A WHIFF OF COAL DUST kicked up from the tracks in a breezy swirl. To Ted it smelled a little like dying, mixed with only the faintest scent of purpose.

He was dying to the old life, once and for all. The train would soon take him to parts unknown, and frankly, he didn't care where he ended up. Officially, his fare would take him only as far as St. Louis. He would make further plans when he got there, if indeed he made plans at all.

Ted shifted on his crutches. He was still not used to them. They seemed more like unwanted growths under his arms than functional aids for his mobility. And he had needed help with his satchel. He would always need help. He grimaced at the thought.

Gus came back with Ted's ticket but didn't immediately hand it to him. "I still say yer runnin' out on me."

"No more on that, Gus. Just hand me the ticket."

"I ought to go with you, make sure you don't get into trouble."

"The ticket."

"Even though I'm daft to be thinkin' it."

Ted snatched the ticket from Gus's hand. But the motion dislodged the crutch under his left arm. Ted fell backward, hopping on his right leg. He hit a bench and fell, hard, into a sitting position. The stump of his left leg stuck out from the bench, a harsh reminder of his clumsiness.

"Now see what you did?" said Gus. He picked up Ted's crutch and handed it to him.

"Go on, Gus," Ted said. "Get out of here."

The mechanic hesitated, rubbing his palms on his dirty overalls.

The train whistle blew. It had a harsher sound than Ted had ever heard before.

"It's time," Ted said. He struggled to a standing position again. He held out his hand. Gus did not take it.

"The devil take you," Gus said.

Ted looked hard at his friend. "It wouldn't sit well with me if that's the last thing you said."

"Ain't there anything that can make you stay?" Gus said.

Ted thought on it. He took one last look at the station, at the long platform with all the waiting passengers and well-wishers—women kissing their husbands good-bye, children laughing in anticipation of a grand train ride.

Could anything make him stay?

Only one thing, and he saw it in his mind's eye. It would be a woman with auburn hair, walking toward him from the far end of the platform. She would be in a white spring dress, and her gait would be confident yet the essence of feminine beauty. She would have Irish in her eyes and passion in her voice—passion for justice and the will of her God.

Only that one thing, and yet not even that. For what could the vision say that would sway him? He did not even want to hear. Ted Fox tried to shake the vision from his mind, lest it torment him forever.

But the vision did not shake. Strangely, it grew stronger. Ted blinked his eyes and realized that it was no vision at all.

Kit Shannon was at far end of the platform, and she had her gaze fixed on him as she walked his way with a purposeful, unstoppable stride.

One part of him wanted to turn and run. Run for the train. But he could not run. Not anymore.

Another part of him wanted to meet her halfway, to take her in his arms. But he knew if he did, that he would never let go.

Torn, he stood there like a statue, waiting.

When she got to him she did not hesitate. "You are not going anywhere," she said.

Ted reeled on his crutches and for a moment thought he might fall. Steam hissed from the train in the Los Angeles depot. A conductor shouted, "All aboard!"

"I have to go, Kit," said Ted. That was what came out, from the deepest part of him.

"You're running away," Kit replied firmly.

Ted glanced at Gus, who looked at the ground and sauntered away, allowing the meeting to take place in private.

"Kit," Ted said, "I have my ticket."

Kit put out her hand. "Give it to me."

Ted shook his head. "I can't stay."

"Why not?"

"Because . . ." His voice trailed off. "Why are you hounding me, Kit?"

"God is not through with you," she said.

"I am half a man," Ted said. "What can God do with half a man?"

"Why don't we try to find out?"

"We?"

"That's what I said."

Ted felt his chest tighten. "There is no we, Kit. You made that plain."

"Perhaps it isn't so plain."

"And you want me to stay just so you can find out?"

Kit nodded.

He looked into her green eyes and knew if she said much more he would stay. He made his next words blunt. "Sorry. Not interested."

"I don't believe you."

She was arguing now, like the lawyer she was. But he could not do this to her. He could not make himself a project, a ruined man relying always on the sympathy of a woman because of her good heart.

"Believe what you want," Ted said, "I'm getting on the train. Good-bye, Kit." He surprised himself with how quickly he turned. He moved toward the tracks.

"Ted . . ."

He did not look back. If he did, it would be over. He would not have the will to leave. *Get on, get on,* he told himself. Kit Shannon needed a future free of Ted Fox. She needed her work, and she needed a man who shared her faith and who would not be a millstone, like he would be.

She did not call his name again. Gus joined him at the train, threw Ted's satchel on board, and offered his hand. "Take care of yerself," he said.

Ted shook Gus's hand but had no words. As he got on the train—struggling with the crutches but refusing to be helped—he felt he was leaving more than part of his body in Los Angeles. In a way, he was leaving the better part of himself.

Kit stood on the platform until the train was out of sight. As the crowd around her gradually began to dissipate, Kit remained motionless until she was the only one left at the tracks.

"God is not through with you," she had said. And she believed that. Even though he did not stay. Even though she had lost her plea.

"Lord God," she whispered, "may your hand be with him. Protect him always. Open his soul, and shine your light so brightly that he cannot but see you. And if it be your will, God, bring him back to Los Angeles. Back to me."

She saw a final plume of smoke on the horizon and heard the train whistle in the distance. It sounded like the plaintive cry of a bird flying out to sea.

Then she turned and started back toward the city.

Don't Miss *Angel of Mercy,*
Book 3 in the SHANNON SAGA,
Coming in Summer 2002!

When an old enemy of Kit Shannon is arrested on suspicion of murder, he insists Kit is the only one who can represent him. She refuses at first, but moved by his desperation and the plea of his wife, Kit agrees to assist him through the prelimary hearing. His possible guilt tests Kit's resolve to represent only the innocent. But step-by-step, Kit discovers there is more to this case than meets the eye. Much more.

Even as Kit and her trusted friend, Corazón, seek the truth, Kit's personal life is in turmoil. Will Ted Fox return? Will her great-aunt Freddy ever trust in Jesus and turn from the spiritualism so rampant in the city?

In the hot Los Angeles summer of 1904, Kit will have to use every ounce of intellect and faith she has to find the truth and save those she cares about most.

Their Only Hope Was a Miracle

Can God Turn Tears Into Laughter?

From the acclaimed author of *Eve's Daughters*, comes the story of Eliza Wyatt, a widowed mother of three, who's asked God for an angel to help keep her family alive. She is desperately struggling to run the family orchard as the country around her plunges into the Depression. But when a stranger in need and a crazy widow are the only answers she receives, Eliza thinks God may not be listening.

Hidden Places by Lynn Austin

Page-turning Fiction From Kristen Heitzmann!

Driven by hope and vengeance, Carina Maria DeGratia sets out for a new life, but soon finds that the town called "the diamond of the Rockies" is anything but luxurious. Realizing she can no longer depend on her family's reputation, she must instead learn to rely on others to help her. Two men vie for her trust, but both hide a secret. Will Carina learn the truth—and confront the secrets hidden in her heart—in time to prevent tragedy?

The Rose Legacy by Kristen Heitzmann